HEATHERSLEIGH HOMECOMING

MICHAEL PHILLIPS

BETHANY HOUSE PUBLISHERS
MINNEAPOLIS, MINNESOTA 55438

Heathersleigh Homecoming
Copyright © 1999
Michael Phillips

Cover illustration © by Erin Dertner, exclusive represented by Applejack Licensing.
Cover design by Dan Thornberg

Published by Bethany House Publishers
A Ministry of Bethany Fellowship International
11400 Hampshire Avenue South
Minneapolis, Minnesota 55438
www.bethanyhouse.com

Printed in the United States of America by
Bethany Press International, Minneapolis, Minnesota 55438

Library of Congress Cataloging-in-Publication Data

Phillips, Michael R., 1946–
    Heathersleigh homecoming / by Michael Phillips.
        p.   cm. — (Secrets of Heathersleigh Hall)
    ISBN 0–7642–2237–6
    ISBN 0–7642–2045–4 (pbk.)
    1. World War, 1914–1918—England—Devon Fiction. I. Title. II. Series:
Phillips, Michael R., 1946- Secrets of Heathersleigh Hall ; 3.
PS3566.H492H46   1999
813'.54—dc21   99–6750
                                                                          CIP

To the sisters of
The Mother of Good Counsel Home
St. Louis, Missouri
and to the sisters of
Christusträger Schwestern
Hergershof, Germany

MICHAEL PHILLIPS is one of the premier fiction authors publishing in the Christian marketplace. He has authored more than fifty books, with total sales exceeding five million copies. He is also well known as the editor of the popular George MacDonald Classics series.

Phillips owns and operates a Christian bookstore on the West Coast. He and his wife, Judy, have three grown sons and make their home in Eureka, California.

Contents

❖❖❖

Part III: England, 1915

Part IV: Shock and Grief, 1915

Part V: Heathersleigh Homecoming, 1915

Jungfrau/ Interlaken Region, Switzerland

Eiger   Mönch   Jungfrau

Lauberhorn

Männlichen

Wengen

Grindelwald

Lauterbrunnen

Brienzersee   Interlaken   Thunersee

EUROPE, 1914-1915

ORKNEY ISLANDS   Scapa Flow   NORWAY
SCOTLAND   North Sea   Stockholm
                              SWEDEN
                    DENMARK
                              Baltic Sea
GREAT BRITAIN   Hawsker
AND IRELAND   Head
                                   Danzig
                         Berlin   RUSSIAN EMPIRE
              London   Antwerp   Warsaw
Plymouth   Brussels   GERMAN EMPIRE
ENGLISH CHANNEL   Portsmouth   BELGIUM
              Calais
         Cherbourg   Paris   Munich   Prague
                    Basel   Vienna
         FRANCE   Luzern   Budapest   AUSTRO-HUNGARIAN
              Interlaken Innsbruck   EMPIRE
              Milan   Trieste
                    ITALY   ROMANIA
                         Belgrade   Bucharest
                         SERBIA

After he had spent everything, there was a severe famine in that whole country, and he began to be in need. . . . When he came to his senses, he said . . . "I will set out and go back to my father and say to him: Father, I have sinned against heaven and against you. I am no longer worthy to be called your son; make me like one of your hired men." So he got up and went to his father.

Introduction
The Universal Parable

———— ♦♦♦ ————

*C*he remarkable thing about the Bible is that its stories are timeless and universal, and also very, very intimate. From Genesis onward, the insightful reader sees both the great, sweeping, majestic human condition, and his *own*, mirrored in the men and women of the scriptural account.

In compiling the Holy Book, though using fallible men to do so, the Holy Spirit has woven a miraculously *personal* tapestry of human life. Only the most unseeing individual can progress far in the Bible without eventually standing back to gaze with wonder at that tapestry, realizing that the emerging portrait being woven into the fabric ... alongside the face of the Lord ... is his or her own countenance and spiritual character. Nowhere do we find this personal tapestry more clearly than in the Gospels.

The Gospels paint a picture of *you* and *me* beside that of the Man whose life story they tell.

Though on the surface the Gospels appear to be a biographical account of Jesus Christ, at a more profound level they are intended to prompt a far deeper response than a typical biography. The Gospels tell two stories. They illuminate both the character of Jesus *and* that of his listener.

At every point this dual story is active. Response to Jesus is everything—whether it be the response of James and John, Peter and Andrew, the crowd, the rich young ruler, the Pharisees, children, blind men, prostitutes, tax collectors, kings, prophets, wise men, or shepherds.

Jesus continually looks into the eyes of his listener and says, "This story, this teaching, this principle, this parable, this truth is about *you* as much as it is about me. What will you do? You must in some way acknowledge what I say, who I am, and my Father's claim upon you. In short ... you must follow me or turn your back and walk away. Neutrality is not possible. You *must* respond."

I intentionally use the word "listener" in the singular. Jesus always gazes into one set of eyes at a time. Jesus spoke to crowds, to groups of Pharisees, to the twelve, to the seventy. But he always addressed each *individual* as if he or she were the only one present. That is why I say the scriptural account is a tapestry of the Lord's face and *mine* and *yours* . . . as if we are the only persons in the universe. It is the story of *my* personal response—as I become that *listener*—to the Lord's teachings, to his challenges, and to his claim upon me.

As I read of him walking beside the Sea of Galilee and approaching the sons of Zebedee, it is not primarily to them he speaks at that moment. The words "Follow me," in that timeless and universally intimate eternal now, are intended for only *me*. James and John have already made their decision. Now it is my turn. Will I leave *my* nets and follow him? That is the eternally significant question.

No abstractions clutter the Gospels. The four books penned by Matthew, Mark, Luke, and John are, of course, important literary and historical documents—probably the most significant historical documents ever written. But they are not *primarily* historical. Their first purpose is not to record history but to elicit response. At the core they are *personal* documents.

I repeat—response is everything. Jesus lived, Jesus taught, Jesus died . . . to be *responded* to. If I read the words "Follow me" as spoken only to James and John or Peter and Andrew or the rich young ruler, as detached historical encounters having little immediate bearing upon me, the life of Jesus itself loses its power in my life altogether. It is either my story, my response . . . or it is nothing.

Where do I take *my* place in the gospel drama?

Am I one of the seventy? Do I stand watching and listening among the crowd? Am I a silent and unresponsive observer of the miracles who walks away thinking to myself, "Hmm . . . interesting," but who never appropriates that miracle of new life for myself? Am I an angry Pharisee? Am I a Thomas full of questions, a Nicodemus who comes by night, a Martha who fusses, or perhaps the rich young ruler, who, when confronted eye to eye with the challenge of following, sadly turns and walks away?

Where do you find *yourself* in the gospel drama?

Within the Gospels this principle of personal response is no more vivid than in how we relate to the parables. Do we see our own faces in those seemingly simple stories? If not, we have missed their life-changing import. We have not beheld the gospel tapestry in its full yet very subtle and weakness-exposing glory. Its colors and textures shift and change in the light, and must be turned just so for the images being fashioned by the divine hand to be seen for what they are. It is a tapestry-portrait of intricate colors and blends, whose figures and representations often do not reveal themselves at first glance. As Jesus tells each and every parable, he holds up a mirror in which I am intended to see my *own* face. That is the subtlety of the tapestry-in-progress.

We are all well familiar with the parable we call "the prodigal son," found in Luke 15:11–31. I call it the universal parable. I am convinced that it represents a microscopic view of the entire human drama on earth. We have a good, prosperous, and benevolent Father, from whose loving presence we have strayed. It happened in the garden with Adam and Eve. It happens with every man and woman who has ever lived. We leave our Father's home. We leave the garden life he intended for us, wandering from his embrace, abandoning our trust in his goodness, disobeying his commands, squandering our inheritance as his sons and daughters. Call it *sin*—which it is. Call it *disobedience*—which it is. Call it *rebellion*—which it is. Or say simply that we have turned away from the loving care of our Creator-Father. All these descriptions of our condition are appropriate and true. We are a prodigal humanity.

In actual human lives such as yours or mine, not every individual is a wicked and visibly rebellious person. There are axe murderers and prostitutes and good churchmen and -women. Yet whatever the individual characteristics of the far countries to which we each go, we are all prodigals together. Our universal straying, therefore, takes many forms—from outright rebellion and disobedience against God, to casual independence and unintentional drift. We want our inheritance, which is life, but we want it apart from him. We do not want to live out that life in our Father's house. We are just like the prodigal son. The underlying prodigal-mistake to which all succumb is a universal one: We think it is possible to create a satisfying life apart from the God who created us, or if we do include him in our calculations we do so on our own terms, keeping his expectations and demands at a minimum. In the end this lethal assumption is always revealed for the fallacy it is. All must eventually do what the prodigal did—arise and return to our Father.

We must go home.

And what do we find when we return? That our Father's goodness and love and grace and forgiveness are boundless in open-armed embrace. He has been waiting for us all along! Indeed, he has been watching for us—believing we would return. He is waiting to run out and greet us with rejoicing even before we are all the way back. That is the kind of Father we have. Nowhere do we see God himself so succinctly and wonderfully characterized as in the father of the prodigal in Luke fifteen.

The prodigal parable is universal for another reason. Most men and women, especially in today's world, find themselves living out one or another aspect of this story within their own family relationships. When I say, as I did earlier, that we all find ourselves in the Gospels, I think we also all find ourselves within this one parable—as a father, a mother, an elder brother, as one of the servants, possibly as a neighbor or cousin or uncle or aunt, as one of the prodigal's friends in the far country to which he sojourned and where he gradually squandered his inheritance . . . or as the prodigal himself.

Do you know anyone at this moment who is estranged from mother or father? Then you are living out, right now, a role within this parable. And it may be that you will be called upon to take an active part in the unfolding drama before it reaches its conclusion.

Never has the story been so heartbreakingly applicable within Christian families as it seems to be during these times in which we live. The assault upon the institution of the family has rarely been so unrelenting and severe. That assault is coming precisely at the point where young people are the most vulnerable—in the transitional stage between childhood and adulthood. They are encouraged and goaded by every element of society to become antagonistic toward, lose their trust in, and often break off their relationship with their parents completely. Scarcely does a family exist without scars from the battle.

To understand the complexities of that battle, and to be encouraged and energized to give God thanks in the midst of it, I think we profit enormously by reading afresh the parable of the prodigal, with the gospel mirror held up to our own souls. In some cases this prompts the conviction of the son to arise and return. In others it allows the parental heartbreak to accomplish its divine purpose. To others it gives great hope.

Often the complexities and prayerful struggles within the parable are not apprehended at first glance. It takes time, and often personal experience, to delve beneath the surface to gain some of the deeper insights and ask some of the more difficult questions prompted by the story. What, for example, was the role of the prodigal's mother during the time her son was away? How did her mother-heart bear up under the season of waiting? And how long was the prodigal away—a year . . . ten years? Was there contact with him during that time? Did he write home and ask for more money once his inheritance ran out? Did his mother ever send him a care package? Was there communication between father and son prior to that tearful meeting on the road?

I find these questions not only fascinating, but also of huge practical consequence for those suffering through painful and fragmented relationships. In attempting to apply the truths of Luke fifteen, prodigalized families face a wide range of questions not specifically addressed in the biblical account. What ought to be a father's or mother's response if the homecoming is not accompanied by true repentance? What does a parent do if the visit is not for the purpose of reconciliation at all but is self motivated and ends with the question, "Dad, I need some money." What if the angry prodigal comes home simply because there is no place else to go?

When does one kill the fatted calf and rejoice at the homecoming? What might be the adverse effect of celebrating prematurely? What is the nature of the inheritance? Is it always financial? Are there other "inheritances" which today's prodigals squander?

What about "prodigals" who never actually leave home, whose rebellion is lived out right under the parental roof? How do parents in such circumstances carry themselves? What about those whose rebellion against parental authority is obscured by an immature, self-righteous form of seeming spirituality which looks down on their parents rather than holding them in honor and esteem? Many prodigals go through life and never see their own face in the mirror when they read Luke fifteen, and thus never recognize themselves as prodigals at all.

What about interfering relatives, grandparents, siblings, and friends who justify the actions of the prodigal and subtly blame the parents for family division, preventing the "husks of the swine" to accomplish their chastening and redeeming work? What about those who hide behind the curtain of neutrality, not wanting to "take sides" in a family dispute? These are they who never recognize that when Jesus told the parable there was a true right and a true wrong, and that while *forgiveness* was called for from the parental heart, it was the prodigal from whom *repentance* was required.

What about those "Job's counselors" who sow seeds of dissatisfaction, discontent, and brooding accusation, those who call themselves the prodigal's friends, but who are in fact purveyors of the modern psychology of guilt-free nonaccountability? They want to be accepting, noncritical. These are they who dismiss any need on the prodigal's part to face with tearful remorse what is genuine wrongdoing and sin. These so-called friends can be the most damaging of all, excusing rather than confronting, shifting blame, justifying, speaking subtle and character-damaging lies into the prodigal's receptive ear: "They don't understand . . . it was right for you to do what you did . . . you have to shed your youth and be who you are . . . it is right and normal to stand up for your individuality and independence . . . you have to be yourself, not what they expect you to be . . . they were controlling and you were right to break free. . . ." Such fleshly evasions prevent rather than exhort toward wholeness.

Homecoming is impossible as long as the Self rules, as it surely does in these blame-shifting and self-justifying excuses which are in the very societal air we breathe. And as long as homecoming is delayed, for just that long is mature character likewise prevented.

At root I find intriguing the simple question *why*? Why did the one son go and the one stay home? Why do young people raised in the same environment respond to their circumstances so differently? Why do young people raised in loving and caring environments find it necessary to rebel against them?

These and a host of other extremely difficult questions are faced every day by the families of prodigals—questions that test the limits of their faith and endurance. In this age when personal accountability is such an odious concept in the world's eyes, and when intolerance, anger, and blame toward parents are the *last* things young people are encouraged to face and repent of—even by Christian peers, pastors, youth leaders, mentors, and friends—it is becoming sadly more and more rare that full reconciliation occurs in most families. All too few Christian teachers, pastors, and counselors are calling upon young people to *repent* for their prodigal hearts.

Our society expects us to "live with our differences" rather than seek biblical solutions for broken relationships. The prodigal story, therefore, as familiar as it is to most of us, is being lived out to its reconciliatory and healing climax less and less with each passing year.

We ought not underestimate each of our own vital roles in the ongoing drama of this parable. There are prodigals around us at every moment. They are in every crowd, every Bible study, every prayer group, every school class, walking beside us on the sidewalk, standing in line with us at the bank or market. Every congregation every Sunday is filled with them.

But the prodigals among us—and you may be one of them, as may be your pastor, your teacher, your brother or sister or best friend—are not always dressed in rags and eating with pigs. Prodigals can be respectably clothed and comport themselves as anything but what they are. Church activities and spiritual groups and cliques can be well-disguised far more easily than one might think. Many prodigals are well-groomed behind smiling facades of self-sufficiency and independence.

Yet there they are in our midst. And too few of us are urging them toward the most important business of their lives—home-going.

Here is an enormous truth: The door into knowing the Father's heart, the door into intimacy with God our Creator, often opens first toward one's earthly parents. Your opportunity is to be a true friend to the prodigals you encounter—not one who justifies and excuses them in their quiet pride and self-reliant alienation. You who understand the import of this parable, *you* can be the best friend it is possible for a prodigal to have. You can help turn their hearts toward home.

There is an order to be observed. God gave us parents so that we would learn to love, honor, obey, and trust *him*. Such is the underlying lesson in the classroom of that earthly relationship. It is a school which cannot be bypassed. Where a wrong attitude exists toward a parent, that same attitude will inevitably lie as an unresolved irritant and inhibition to growth in one's relationship with God. It is simple cause and effect in the spiritual realm. Secretly harbored anger, bitterness, resentment, and unforgiveness—no matter how far shoved into the subconscious—will forever prevent the deepest intimacy with God . . . until they are held up to the light and relinquished.

Be a friend to the prodigal.

Hold up the mirror of accountability.

Be the Lord's ally and partner for the reconciliation of the world, by urging, exhorting, and encouraging toward homecoming.

Such is among the reasons for this series—to explore some of these complex but vitally timely issues and challenges in more depth than usual. Especially is it my hope to prompt reflection and prayer in two areas, one on each side of the generational fence:

First, to explore the grief and suffering of the father and mother during what must surely be one of the greatest trials of life. I hope this will enable us to come more personally to grips with the opportunity they have to learn to thankfully partake of that waiting, prayerful, hopeful, tearful, agonizing aspect of the divine Fatherhood.

And second, to explore what it means to "go home," and how to do so fully and completely, so that the heart of the prodigal is truly made whole. I find myself intrigued by this process, wherever and in whatever circumstances a prodigal finds himself—and sometimes it is a long process which must come in slow stages and by infinitesimal degrees— of awakening to the necessity of at last saying, "I will arise and go to my Father."

Therefore, as interesting, even compelling, as may be many of the other personalities in this saga, especially those of Charles and Jocelyn Rutherford, this will always in a foundational way be Amanda's story.

Real-life circumstances, however, are unpredictable. It is a wise man or woman who when confronted by some duty or necessity fulfills it quickly. Delay can be costly. Healing can occur within a single heart, and God will use such to fulfill his purposes. But in terms of earthly relationships, reconciliation is often sought too late. A lifetime of grief must then be borne which might have been prevented had the promptings toward awakening been heeded earlier.

Homecoming ought never be put off.

One final personal note concerning the location of the fictional Chalet of Hope. The high mountain air in that region is just as described—at least I found it so. I have never forgotten the overpowering sense of wondrous *quiet* when standing at Männlichen overlooking the awe-inspiring drop of more than 4,700 feet straight down into the valley of Lauterbrunnen. Since that moment I have always wanted to set a story there.

It was to those same high Alps that George MacDonald traveled in 1865. I like to imagine him standing at that very spot and feeling similar sensations. Very soon thereafter he used the region as a backdrop to recount the quickening of spiritual consciousness in one of his most memorable characters, Robert Falconer. It was also very near this setting where Hannah Hurnard received the inspiration for and wrote *Hinds' Feet on High Places.*

It seemed fitting somehow that Amanda likewise be given an opportunity to breathe that cleansing air, to see what it might be able to accomplish toward her dawning awakening.

Prologue

Jungle Mission

♦♦♦

1897

♦♦♦

The cluster of small buildings—primitive by London standards, but luxurious alongside the huts of sticks, straw, and mud found in the nearby jungle—had seen many happy times since the mission sent the young couple here.

But on this day the memory of singing and laughter would turn to weeping.

The season when hymns of joyful praise echoed from the mouths of the native Maoris was over.

The witch doctor had declared it. None dared question his pronouncement. In the superstitious minds of the tribe, his power was greater than that of the young French missionary and his English wife, whose pregnancy the native women had watched progress with eager curiosity and anticipation.

It was now ten minutes past the toll of the chapel bell.

Husband and wife sat silent and waiting in the small church they had completed with the help of the villagers six months earlier. Both knew something was wrong.

Fifteen, eighteen, even twenty worshipers should have been here by now. There were always between fifteen and thirty on hand, a good many of the village men among them. There had even been talk that the chief was showing interest in hearing the stories firsthand, rather than from his people, and might make an appearance.

But it was becoming more obvious with every passing second

that such a singularly important event would not happen today.

"Where is everyone?" finally asked the young mother-to-be. Her voice did not exactly contain fear, yet betrayed the concern that had been building in her mind.

"I don't know," sighed her husband, trying to sound calm. In truth, he was more worried than he let on. As he had lain awake last night, his wife of two and a half years breathing softly and peacefully beside him, he had heard disconcerting sounds far off through the Wanganui jungle. He did not want to wake her then, nor did he want to alarm her now. But he had a bad feeling.

For another five minutes husband and wife sat in silence. Both were praying in mounting anxiety.

The missionary slowly reached over and took his wife's hand. She clutched it too eagerly. He knew the instant he felt her clammy perspiration that she was scared.

It was time to get her to a safe place. It was obvious there would be no service on this day. He started to rise.

Suddenly a dull, thudding *thwack* echoed through the chapel.

The missionary wife leapt out of her seat.

"What was that!" she exclaimed.

Her husband knew well enough exactly what it was. Some of the native men had taught him the use of bow and arrow, with which every man in the jungle was deadly accurate.

He was on his feet in an instant, pulling his wife's hand with sudden urgency.

"Come . . . come quickly!" he said, moving toward the door.

"What—"

"Just come!"

In moments they were out of the chapel and flying across the ground to the small adjacent structure of their home. He half dragged her behind him as fast as she could manage.

A quick glance over their shoulders revealed that the first fiery arrow had been joined by a half dozen more. Within minutes the chapel was ablaze.

"*Schnell . . . geh unter . . . in dem Keller!*" implored the Swissman, in panic abandoning his English as he threw back the faded, threadbare scrap of rug and yanked up the hinged door.

It had been one of the instructions he had argued against when they sent him here. How could he earn the trust of the natives if he kept secrets from them? But he had built the secret room below the floor of their home at the insistence of the board's director. Now he was glad for the mission's foresight.

He fairly dove into the dark opening himself, then quickly helped his wife down the steep ladder, a precarious operation given her advanced condition. He fumbled about, lit a candle, settled her onto a cot, then turned.

"Where are you going!" she said. She no longer tried to hide her terror.

"To talk to them," he replied. He turned back briefly to face her.

"No, please . . . stay with me."

"If they don't see me, they will search until they find us."

"Klaus . . . please!"

"I have to talk to them and show them I am not afraid."

"But I am afraid!"

He paused, drew his face close to hers, gazed into her eyes, and kissed her.

"So am I," he said softly. "But the Lord is our protector. He sent us to these people. We must not flinch at the devil trying to undo our work. We knew there would eventually be resistance. We have to weather this with courage and faith, even if it means starting over."

"Please, Klaus—"

"Just pray, my love. He is with us."

"But—"

"Blow out the candle when I am gone," he said. "Here are the matches in case you need them. I will be back before you know it."

He squeezed her hand, kissed her again, then turned and hastily ascended the ladder.

Tears filled her eyes even as she felt the baby kick inside her womb.

Why did men insist on being brave and courageous and spiritually-minded at times like this?

Before she could think further, she heard the secret door above close tightly down upon the floor. A scraping sound followed. Klaus must have moved something on top of it.

She leaned over and blew out the candle, and was left alone and trembling in the darkness.

PART I

♦♦♦

On the Run
1914

1

Whisperings

✦✦✦

*H*igh on a mountain path, where the air was thin, clean, and invigorating, a woman in her late forties—bundled up with several sweaters, mittens, and hat—walked alone, her heart full of prayer for one whose name she did not know.

As is not unusual for men and women of prayer, both her object and purpose were vague and undefined, yet such did not deter her from the vitality of this day's supplications. What had prompted her up and out at this early hour, only the Spirit of God knew. She had ceased inquiring into whys, wherefores, times, and seasons years before. She had begun to learn that most elemental yet difficult of life's needful lessons—to *trust*.

It had not been an easy lesson.

She had studied in the various classrooms of tragedy, heartbreak, and disappointment. And Romans five had done its work. Suffering had indeed produced perseverance, character, and hope within her. Nor had that hope disappointed, for God had poured out his love into her heart.

As the Comforter had carried out that maturing operation within her, she had come to cherish the healing power of hope, and thanked God for developing within her an expectant heart.

Though her memory bore its share of deep personal scars, her eyes glowed with peace and with the wisdom that came from walking at her Master's side in that hope, listening to his voice rather than trying to make sense of life's unanswerables.

She knew her heavenly Father. She knew him to be both sovereign and good, and infinitely so. In that truth she rested, because she knew she could trust him. As she prayed on this morning, therefore, she knew that all would be well.

Last night's was the first snowfall of the season, a mere dusting of half an inch. Autumn had scarcely begun, but she could feel the change in the air. Colder temperatures would come, and snow would descend upon them by the yard rather than the inch. Yet she always relished in the first fresh fall of every new winter. It never failed to remind her of the gentle, quiet ways in which God often answered her prayers differently than he had Peter's from the Joppa housetop, not with giant white sheets, but rather with tiny crystalline flecks of joy. How many times, it seemed, did the snow come quietly and at night—like a million silent invisible answers to prayer—to cover the landscape with peace.

And with the powdery whiteness had come again, as so many times before, the sense of preparation for a new opportunity to care in some way for one of God's dear ones.

When he first began sending people, she had been full of questions. As years had passed, however, and her comrade sisters had joined her, and as people had come and gone, she had learned that when the prompting came, she must simply pray for a quieting of her heart, that the Spirit's needful whisperings might be heard.

Who was coming and what might be the need were specifics rarely revealed beforehand. She and her sisters must merely be ready, and pray for the human soil into which they would be given opportunity to plant the seeds of their compassion, prayer, and tender ministration.

Twenty minutes ago before coming out, she had given instructions to Sister Agatha to begin getting a room ready.

2

Out of Vienna

On a train increasing its speed as it bore south out of the great Austrian capital of Vienna, Amanda Rutherford Halifax sat back in her seat with eyes closed, trying to steady her nerves, calm herself . . . and think.

Her heart was pounding like a hammer on an anvil.

The image and voice of her husband of less than a month, Ramsay Halifax, still rang in her ears crying after her in angry defeat as the train pulled out of the station.

"Amanda . . . Amanda!"

The echo of his shouts reverberated in her brain. She had never seen such a side of him before that moment. The look of wrath in his eyes pierced through her as if he was glaring at her even now, as in truth he was, though all he could see was the back of the last car of the train.

She could never go back to him, thought Amanda, not ever again. Not after what she had learned. Not after realizing what he was, and how she had been used.

The sickness gathering in her stomach right now was not about politics. It had nothing to do with conflict between nations. At this moment she was not thinking of the fact that the world was at war. Her personal anguish concerned no ideologies.

It was about another woman. Amanda felt dirty.

How could she have been so foolish as to marry Ramsay!

She thought she knew him. But she hadn't known him at all. She had only seen the surface, what he had wanted her to see—the suave, confident journalist, so dashing and charming and worldly-wise. She had never paused to look beneath the smiling veneer, to ask herself what Ramsay might be like inside.

Now she was far from home. Reminders of the war were all around her—the propaganda posters lining the station walls, soldiers everywhere en route to the nearby battlefields in Belgium and France. She was trapped in a foreign country that was fighting against her homeland, alone behind enemy lines.

Tears gradually filled Amanda's eyes.

They were not quite yet the tears of contrition, but rather tears of mortification at having been so blind. But at least she had awoken from the stupor that had landed her in this fix. Therefore, the tears were beginning to wash the cobwebs from her brain. Her heart would come in for its share of that same cleansing in time. When it did, full healing repentance would not be far behind.

But right now Amanda's thoughts were on the present.

How was she ever going to get back to England!

If the little money she had stolen at her mother-in-law's house in Vienna didn't run out, surely someone would hear her accent and get suspicious.

If she could just get across the border into neutral Italy, and then maybe into France.

But how!

Oh, God, she moaned silently, *help me!*

Even as Amanda sat frantic and afraid, though temporarily out of reach of her husband in the southbound train out of Vienna, Ramsay Halifax stood on platform nine of the Südbanhof, peering into the distance where the train had disappeared from sight seconds earlier. He could still faintly make out the dim clacking of its iron wheels receding along the tracks.

Within seconds his mother hurried up, followed a moment or two later by their white-haired colleague Hartwell Barclay. Though puffing, his face showed no sign of red. He was, in fact, boiling over in a white wrath. Mrs. Halifax's eyes, too, glowed with a fire into whose origins it would be best not to inquire. Their collective fury at that moment might have been enough to cause any but the most stouthearted angel to tremble.

Neither of the two older members of the triumvirate was accustomed to being outwitted, especially, as they judged her, by such a lightweight as Amanda. She had been so easily manipulated and brainwashed in the beginning. It never occurred to either that she would actually summon the gumption to resist them, much less make a run for it. They had turned her to their cause with so little effort, they had never considered the possibility of her defection. They had also underestimated the faculty her father had honed in her for vigorous *thinking*. Indeed, even Amanda was unaware of it. But in time the mental vigor that Sir Charles Rutherford had trained into all three of his children would find its muscle, and enable this wayward child to discover her way.

Now she was gone. All three who stood on the empty station platform knew that if Amanda was allowed to get to the West, she could seriously threaten their subversive spy network.

Barclay turned to Ramsay.

"You fool!" he seethed. "Why didn't you see this coming?"

"Look, Barclay, don't play your power games with me!" young Halifax shot back. "It won't work. You don't intimidate me."

"How could the two of you let her out of your sight!"

"I told you before," rejoined Ramsay, "the two of *us* happened to be gone at the time."

"You should never both have left!" persisted the elder statesman of the three. Though an Englishman, he had cast his lot with the German and Austrian cause. He knew perhaps better than either of the others how much they stood to lose if Amanda divulged what she knew to the right people in London.

"Be that as it may," Ramsay shot back, "you were the only one home when she bolted. Why didn't *you* stop her?"

"Please, please!" interrupted Ramsay's mother. "This is no time for argument. We still have to stop her."

It fell briefly silent. Barclay calmed.

"Who do we know in Trieste?" he said at length.

"I believe we do have some people there," replied Mrs. Halifax.

"Wasn't Carneades planning to stop over there for a few days on his way back to Rome?" said Ramsay.

"That's right!" exclaimed his mother.

"We need to send a telegram," said Barclay. "There's no time to lose!"

He turned quickly and led the way across the platform.

"Ramsay," said Mrs. Halifax as they hurried back into the station, "run ahead and check on the next train south. If we make contact and Carneades is able to intercept the train, you will have to go after her yourself and bring her back. If not, we'll get in touch with Matteos."

Ramsay nodded, then broke into a run toward the platform tunnel.

3

Chalet of Hope

In a large, geometrically laid-out, and nicely trimmed garden, more than half empty now and with most of its remaining contents turning brown, two warmly dressed women, by appearances in their mid-thirties, quietly cultivated the rich black dirt with hoe and rake. They paused now and then to remove the dead leaves and vines from the spent plants. Between the women a wicker bushel basket collected refuse for the compost pile.

The morning was crisp. The elevation was not so very high in this protected meadow of the Swiss Alps, only some 4,100 to 4,200 feet—

higher, it is true, than all but Britain's loftiest peaks in the Highlands of Scotland. The fact that their efforts of this morning, however, had begun by scraping snow off the rows indicated plainly enough that the few hardy autumn vegetables remaining had less than another month before the entire garden would be put to rest for its season of winter dormancy.

"Sister Hope says we are expecting a guest," said one, a Dutch woman by the name of Anika.

"Do you know the details?" asked her friend, German-born Luane.

"None are known. As always . . . we know not the day nor the hour."

"Who do you think it will be this time—a mother with young children, a family escaping the war. . . ?"

"Perhaps another solitary young woman to join us. I remember how lost I was when I arrived."

They continued to talk quietly as they raked and cleaned the ground. In front of them rose the Jungfrau and her accompanying sister sentinels, dazzling white now from last night's snowfall. This high sweep of peaks retained spots of white most of the summer, but now the entire range was freshly blanketed.

Anika and Luane were so accustomed to their surroundings and the spectacular scenery that they now scarcely gave thought to what a picturesque vista their home, the mountains, and even they themselves in the garden would have presented to the eye of an artist. The peaceful panorama of which they were part was enhanced all the more by Sister Galiana with a yoke over her shoulders, from which dangled two milk pails as she walked from barn to house, Marjolaine returning from the chicken coop with a basket of the morning's eggs, Regina sitting on the porch churning yesterday's milk to butter, and Clariss behind the house hanging linens on the line for what promised to be a fine bright day in spite of the chill. From the house could faintly be heard the singing of Sister Agatha's voice through the open window of the guest room, which she was airing out and making ready with clean sheets and down comforters.

On the opposite side behind the two garden workers stood the chalet which was home to the nine members of their small Alpine community. It sat at the edge of a small wood some four hundred yards down the slope from the village of Wengen. A stream ran from the wood near the house into a small pond, which was frozen over through the winter months, but around which during the summer bloomed more than two dozen varieties of Alpine wild flowers.

It was not a particularly remote locale for the Swiss Alps. Villages, hamlets, and farms were scattered about the landscape everywhere, both high and low. But the city-dwellers in the European metropolises from which most of the sisters had come would have considered it remote indeed. The nearest city of significant size was Bern, thirty-five miles to the northwest. In the opposite direction to the northeast, beautiful Luzern lay some forty miles distant. And five miles straight down to the mouth of the valley, situated between the two lakes Thunersee and Brienzersee, sat the fabled resort town of Interlaken. The entire region was known as the Bernese Oberland.

The village of Wengen itself sat perched on a delightfully isolated grassy and lightly wooded plateau almost straight above the long, narrow valley of Lauterbrunnen, at a height some fifteen hundred feet up rocky and forested slopes. The way up and down wound along a wagon trail of multiple switchbacks, which became increasingly difficult to navigate as winter advanced. Most of the villagers brought in supplies by mule and cart, in sufficient quantity to sustain them most of the winter, though a few treks were made as weather permitted during the winter months as well. Train service ran from Lauterbrunnen into Interlaken, and was being planned one day to traverse the slopes onto the mountain plateaus. For the present, however, it was a journey which must be made by foot, cart, or wagon.

Above Wengen, sheer cliffs rose more than three thousand feet to the plateau of Männlichen and the ridge of the Lauberhorn. Wengen was thus situated approximately a third of the way up a breathtaking rise of nearly a mile straight above the valley floor from Lauterbrunnen to the Lauberhorn. It was indeed one of the most startlingly beautiful places of geographic glory to be found anywhere. And wherever one stood, from Lauterbrunnen up to Wengen, thence up to Männlichen, and all the way across the upper plateau and down the slope to Grindelwald, whether on valley floor or high on the edge of sheer drop-off of glacial granite, always the three grand guardians of the region, the Eiger, the Mönch, and the Jungfrau herself, stared down in their snowy, solemn, and majestic silence.

It was an unusual group dwelling together at the Chalet of Hope, these nine sisters who had committed to one another their hands, their hearts, their futures, and their common vision of friendship and service.

They had been set apart to singleness and to ministry, and had been brought together by mutual love of their Lord to share and encourage one another toward these two high callings. Had they been Catholic, they would no doubt be members of some convent. As most were Lutheran, however, with two or three evangelicals and one Catholic among them, their order was an unofficial one, neither sanctioned nor supported by church or denomination.

They took no vows, except in their own hearts. Many others came and went. Yet the core of the five who had been together now for nearly fifteen years had dedicated themselves to this place and its ministry.

Their future was here. They sought no other life but to do what God gave them to do each day, and to keep their hearts open to receiving the next visitor, or visitors, he would bring.

He continued to send them people in need—usually women, though not always. And now, with Europe at war, the difficulties, anxieties, and personal crises of those crossing this out-of-the-way path would surely increase.

The chalet itself had once been a hunting lodge built by a French financier from Annecy. It possessed enough rooms to comfortably house more than thirty, and an imposing kitchen with pantries and cellars and storage facilities capable of maintaining a small army. One end of the kitchen opened into an equally spacious dining and sitting room, with a massive stone fireplace set into the opposite wall. This central room could easily seat a hundred. Indeed, the place might well have been a resort or hotel rather than a hunting lodge.

At present it was neither lodge nor hotel, but served as home to the simple needs of the sisters, though its facilities were always available should the Lord require them. A large wood table where the sisters took their meals and did much of their work sat roughly a third of the way between kitchen and fireplace. Throughout what they called the great room, couches and chairs were spread about, along with potted plants, bookshelves, sideboards, and cabinets, so as to create several separate areas within the whole. The favorite sitting area, where they gathered most evenings, sat directly in front of the fireplace. Rough wooden beams spanned the whole above, supporting a second floor up to which a wide stairway of thick sawn planks led from the front entrance hall.

Light must surely have been a passion of the Zurich architect hired by the Frenchman. For despite the coldness of the winters, and belying the normal custom of the time, numerous windows everywhere had been built into the walls. Every room throughout the chalet, therefore, was bright and cheery, though occasionally such cold resulted from the lack of insulation that no amount of wood in the several fireplaces could succeed in overcoming it. But light was better than darkness, especially for such as these, and clothes, extra socks, mittens, and thick blankets were plentiful. Where light reigned, cold could not long dampen the spirit.

In addition to the expansive ground floor salon, there were any number of parlors and sitting rooms scattered elsewhere about the two floors, and no fewer than twelve bedrooms, allowing each sister to have private accommodations.

And of course there was a library, not large but well stocked with the right kind of books. The sisters were fond of literature, especially the classics, and gathered two evenings a week to read aloud.

Several outbuildings—including a barn for their cattle and goats and donkeys, which had to be kept in all winter, a workshop, an equipment shed, and a chicken coop—were scattered irregularly about the chalet grounds.

The house and buildings were kept up by Sister Gretchen, away at present for a few days to visit a sister in Milan. A native of Bavaria in southern Germany, Gretchen was second in age only to Sister Hope, and was considered a mechanical genius in the eyes of the other women. Indeed, she was gifted with uncanny dexterity and unusual physical strength for a woman of rather typical feminine physique. However, she was not above occasionally employing one or two of the village men to assist her in maintaining the chalet and small farm to impeccable Swiss standards of tidiness.

In the Frenchman's later years the Wengen chalet had become his home. After his own and then his wife's death, it passed into the hands of the woman the others all simply called Sister Hope. The name had been well chosen, not only by her parents but by the Lord. The other sisters honored her as deeply as they loved her, which was a great deal to say on both counts.

Of doctrines they held few. Their theology was simple: to seek to do the Lord's will, and to serve whomever he saw fit to send up the path from the valley to their doorstep.

They interpreted that will—in the absence of any direct leading—as laboring diligently at what was set before them. They did not fret over receiving a new daily revelation of God's will. Instead they went about in a continual attitude of *Lord, what would you have me do?* while simultaneously applying their hands cheerfully to the thing in front of them.

They worked hard tending their two gardens, caring for their three cows, seven goats, two donkeys, and two dozen chickens, and keeping up the chalet, the farm, and the grounds. They ate well, were nearly always provided an abundance, and were happier than any of them had ever dreamed they would be.

The villagers considered the sisters somewhat a strange lot. But the fact that one of their own local Swiss was among them helped the people of the hill country accept the unusual community.

Though the Swiss spoke an intriguing mixture of Italian, French, and German, the natives who dwelt in the shadow of the Alps considered themselves neither Italian, French, nor German. They were feisty, proud of their *own* race, and not eager to open their hearts to outsiders.

That the Swiss of this region had done so with the inhabitants of the chalet said more about the sisters than it did about the people of Wengen.

4

Trieste

$\mathscr{A}$manda jerked upright in her seat.

The train was slowing. How long had she dozed off?

She glanced outside. Night had fallen. They were coming into a city. She looked at her watch. Nine-fifty-two.

It must be Trieste. She had slept for half the trip.

Amanda shook herself awake, trying in vain to work the kink out of what she suddenly realized was a very stiff neck.

They continued to slow, and finally pulled into the station. As Amanda gazed absently and still a little sleepily out the window, she noticed a partially balding and stocky man waiting at the platform. Unconsciously she pulled back from the window with an involuntary shudder.

Why did he seem familiar? The way he eyed the train made her instantly uncomfortable.

Was it the expression on his face? Yes, something about the look in his eyes as they roved about . . . it made her shiver. He was obviously looking for something . . . or someone. His expression reminded her—

That was it!

That penetrating, probing expression of evil intent reminded her of Mr. Barclay!

Amanda's heart began to pound. Almost the same moment it struck her that the man was looking for *her*!

But she was not acquainted with a soul here. No one knew she was coming.

Cautiously Amanda turned and peeked outside again, inching one eye out from the edge of the window, taking care not to be seen. He was still there, walking slowly back and forth across the platform, scanning the rows of train windows—

Suddenly she remembered!

She *did* recognize more than just the expression in his eyes! She had seen this same man once in Vienna—and not long ago—at the house on Ebendorfer Strasse. He had been talking with Mr. Barclay.

He was one of them!

She jerked back from the window. She would have to get off the train without him spotting her. How, she wasn't sure—mingle closely with other passengers, she supposed, or work her way forward to get out from one of the cars not so close.

If she could just get past him and into the station! Then she would check for the first train into Italy.

She had heard another passenger say that the border was only twenty-three miles away.

If there were no trains into Italy later tonight, she would have to find someplace nearby to stay.

Ramsay Halifax sat silent and fuming as the southbound train bore him along the same route through the Austrian countryside that Amanda had taken earlier.

He hated to leave Adriane so abruptly just when she had arrived in Vienna. And he had had about all of Barclay's abuse he could tolerate. Unfortunately Amanda had put them all in a pickle. The little minx!

He leaned back and closed his eyes. The overnight train was not an express. He would not arrive until morning. He might as well make the best of it and try to get some sleep.

It was a minute or two after seven o'clock when Ramsay stepped off the train onto the station platform of the Austrian-held seaport of Trieste. His disposition had nowise improved from the sleepless, jerky, interminable ride to the northern Adriatic coast.

He was surprised to see Carneades waiting for him . . . alone.

Their Greek colleague spoke first in answer to the look of question on Ramsay's face.

"Your mother's second telegram reached me in the middle of the night," he explained. "She said you would be on the morning train."

"Where's the girl?"

"I don't know. I never saw her."

"What—didn't you get our message to intercept her?"

"Yes, of course. I was right here, on this very platform, when last night's train arrived."

"And?"

"And nothing. She wasn't there."

"You imbecile! How could you let her slip through your fingers?"

"Watch what you call me, Halifax. She wasn't on the train, I tell you. She must have gotten off between Vienna and here."

Ramsay paused and tried to think, not an easy task given the shape his brain was in at the moment. He had seen Amanda with his own two eyes as her train pulled out of Vienna. The only stops scheduled between there and here were at Graz, Klagenfurt, and Ljubljana. She would not have gotten off in any of those cities. It didn't make sense.

"She *must* have slipped past you," he said at length.

"I tell you, Halifax—"

"Look," interrupted Ramsay, "she *has* to be bound for Italy. There's no other explanation. So she had to have come through here."

"And I tell you, I saw nothing."

"She's making for the border as sure as anything," Ramsay went on, ignoring him. "We'll check when the next train departs for Italy.— Which way's the ticket office?"

5

Liaison to the Admiralty

The British battle cruiser HMS *Dauntless* steamed out of Plymouth in the grey light of dawn. Its course would take it westward through the English Channel, then north through the Irish Sea, and around the west and north of Scotland to the sheltered waters of Scapa Flow in the Orkney Islands. Much of the crew was still relatively raw, and it was no time to risk encountering a German U-boat in the Channel or the North Sea, where the whole fleet command was in terror of the German submarines. It was the first time in its history that Great Britain's sea barrier of safety had been breached. Throughout the United Kingdom people feared the U-boats entering their very harbors undetected. The news was full of it. Never had the British people felt so exposed and vulnerable.

The crew of the *Dauntless* would complete its training en route and in the Orkneys, then join the Mediterannean fleet later in the year.

Belowdecks in his private cabin, Commander Charles Rutherford—his commission in His Majesty's Navy newly activated—special assistant to the captain and personal liaison to the First Lord of the Admiralty Winston Churchill, stood at his porthole gazing at the passing landscape of the Devonshire and Cornwall coast.

The emotions stirring within him were many and conflicting. The feel of the sea beneath his feet reminded him fondly of his youthful service in the navy. Those had been happy times, and were associated with his meeting and then falling in love with Jocelyn, and their first contented years together at Heathersleigh Hall.

But watching the coastline pass reminded him also of the present, and the wife he was leaving behind. Times were different now. Today's was a dangerous world. He had seen the anxiety in her eyes of what this parting might mean when they said good-bye two days ago.

———————◆◆◆———————

But, Charles," Jocelyn's voice had pled, "I still don't see why you have to go. I've almost reconciled losing a son to the war . . . but a husband as well!"

"You are not *losing* us, Jocie," replied Charles. "We'll be back before you know it," he added, trying to sound cheery and optimistic. "Don't you know what all the papers are saying, that the war will be over by Christmas?"

Despite his words, neither of them believed the reports.

Charles had had too many frank discussions with the First Lord of the Admiralty not to realize the gravity of the situation, and the personal risk to which he was exposing himself by answering Churchill's summons to the war effort.

"Come, Jocie," said Charles after a brief pause, "let's have one more time of prayer together in the heather garden."

Husband and wife left the house and walked slowly across the lawn toward the wood. In front of them spread the heather garden, which had become such a special place of prayer as they had developed and expanded it through the years.

No one in the family knew when the first species of the wiry shrub had been planted at Heathersleigh Hall. But following Charles' and Jocelyn's own spiritual awakening, and encouraged by their friend, London pastor Timothy Diggorsfeld, to use it as a prayer garden on behalf of their daughter Amanda after her painful departure from Heathersleigh, Jocelyn and Charles had cultivated and widened it to its present state.

The heather garden had now become a complex maze of twisting paths through more than a hundred plants of heather of probably three dozen varieties. It was most spectacularly colorful during the two prominent blooming seasons, between July and September for summer varietals, and from Christmas to February for winter species. However, on hand also were more unusual forms of the shrub, such that *something* was always in flower—in either white, pink, or purple, and dozens of intricate blends and variations of each.

Jocelyn's thoughts on this day, however, were not on the beauties of the garden. They sat down on their favorite bench in a secluded alcove amongst several dwarf pines.

It was silent for five or ten minutes as they sat hand in hand. Silence when they were together did not bother them. Their spirits were equally communicative with or without words.

At last Charles began to pray.

"Lord," he said softly, *"as long as we have been trying to obey you and listen to your voice, it sometimes seems you are so silent. It is difficult to know what you want us to do. We desire to do your will. But what is that will. . . ? It is hard at times to know."*

He paused. Silence settled again for a few moments. Then he continued.

"As we now embark on this new phase of life, we pray that you would keep us in your will. I ask that you would comfort my family in my absence—my dear Jocelyn and Catharine. Encourage them during this time, which we pray will be brief. Protect our whole family as the separations increase. Watch over George and me. May we grow closer together as father and son through this experience.

"And we pray for our Amanda, wherever she is at this moment. Though such seems impossible to my limited sight, and though she tells us she is now married, I ask again, as I have so many times before, that you would bring her home and restore her here once more as part of our family. As terrible as war is . . . use it, Lord, in all our lives for the perfecting of your purpose for us. We pray especially that in Amanda's life, these times would work toward the healing of her confused and wayward heart. Reconcile her to us, and restore her to yourself. Place within her being the desire to be your humble and obedient daughter."

Charles' voice fell silent. He exhaled a long sigh. Jocelyn was softly weeping.

For another twenty or thirty minutes they remained together in the garden, quietly talking over many things. That evening they spent in the library with their daughter Catharine. George had already been gone for a month. It was a quiet and peaceful family time together, though tears flowed several times from the eyes of the two women.

Early the next morning, Sir Charles Rutherford left Heathersleigh for Plymouth.

◆ ◆ ◆

Charles' thoughts came once more to the present. Still the coastline passed outside his porthole as the *Dauntless* gradually increased in speed. When would he see his beloved Heathersleigh again? he wondered. He had tried to reassure Jocelyn and Catharine that his duties would not keep him away for long, but in truth he knew how very dangerous this mission was. British naval losses in these opening months of hostilities had been greater than anyone had expected. So far six British steamers had been captured by the Germans and four battle cruisers sunk by German submarines. On land the German advance into France had been halted at the Seine, the Marne, and the Meuse. The Germans had begun a slow retreat, but the prospects of this conflict being a long and arduous one were grim indeed.

Shaking such concerns from his head, his thoughts and prayers returned to Amanda.

Where was *she* at this moment? What would she do now that Europe was at war? The thought brought a lump to his throat and his eyes briefly filled. He could not help wondering if he would ever see her again. He loved her so much. He and she were so much alike. He smiled as he remembered her spunk, laughter, and sense of humor.

The thoughts were too painful to bear. He blinked quickly several times and drew in two or three deep breaths.

At least, thought Charles, he would soon be reunited with his son, Amanda's older brother George, who had preceded him to the Orkneys. If there was any consolation in all this, that was probably it. Churchill had assured him, as part of Charles' resuming his commission in this capacity as his special liaison, that they would be assigned duty on the same ship. George's orders would transfer him to the HMS *Dauntless* once Charles arrived at the Scapa Flow battle station.

He turned back into his cabin, sat down on his bunk, and read again the communiqué from Churchill that had been delivered upon his arrival by a young lieutenant by the name of Langham, the First Lord of the Admiralty's assistant.

My dear Charles, it read.

Words cannot express the respect I have for you, and my personal sense of gratitude for the sacrifice you are willing to make for your nation at this perilous hour. I told you before the war that I needed people I could trust. You are such a man, and my load is lightened knowing that you are on my leadership and advisory team. We both realize that the fight before us will not be as easy as some newspapers try to tell the citizenry. Everything de-

pends on the fleet, and in these opening months the British fleet is disquieted about the very foundations of its being. We have our mighty ships, and every man from stoker to admiral is ready to die in carrying out his duty. And yet it cannot be denied that the U-boats have caused the Grand Fleet to be uneasy. Our ships have no resting place except at sea. Conceive it, Charles— I scarcely can do so even as I write the words—the ne plus ultra, the one ultimate sanction of our existence, the supreme engine which no one has ever dared to brave, whose authority encircles the globe—the British fleet . . . is no longer sure of itself. The notion is so astonishing as to seem incredible. Yet it is true. The idea has infiltrated everywhere that the German submarines are coming after us into our very harbours.

On the South Coast no one would mind, for we can take our vessels inside the Portland breakwater and literally shut the door. But on the East Coast no such sealed harbour exists. We had hoped that Scapa, where you will be bound even as you read this, could remain protected from the submarines by its currents. And yet, Charles, just days ago submarines have been spotted in Scapa Flow. At least such is the report. I am not sure whether I believe it, but it has certainly had the effect of increasing the trepidation of the fleet. The mere apprehension of submarines attacking the sleeping ships on which all else reposes would be sufficient to destroy that sense of security which every fleet demands when in its own harbours.

In any event, it is into this tense and uneasy atmosphere that I am sending you. I hope wise and level heads such as yours will be able to exercise a calming effect on the men. Only so will the Grand Fleet be able to regain the courage and confidence so vital to our success. This, then, is your first assignment—work to instill courage and confidence. Assure the men that we shall prevail.

I hope and—though I hesitate to say it to such a devout man as yourself for fear you will think I do so employing a mere figure of speech, but I assure you I mean it most deeply—I also pray that this separation will not prove unbearably difficult for your wife, who must love you very much. I wish you the best in this endeavour, my friend, and a speedy homecoming, and give you again my hearty thanks.

Yours,
Winston S. Churchill*

---

*Parts adapted from Winston Churchill's own words, found in Chapter 17 of *The World Crisis*, vol. 1, 413–414.

6

Close Encounter

♦♦♦

$\mathscr{A}$manda darted nervously from the train across the platform area while the stocky man was glancing the other way. She kept close to the opposite side of a large woman with three children, trying to look as if she were with them. Quickly, when the coast was clear, she ran into the Trieste station.

The next scheduled train into Italy did not depart until 7:13 A.M.

Standing with bag in hand in front of the schedule board, she thought a moment.

The man would come this way looking for her any minute.

She turned and hurried outside into the darkness. The night air was warm and fragrant. On the slight breeze she could faintly smell the Adriatic Sea less than a mile away.

She began walking in search of a hotel but quickly tired of it. There was nothing nearby and the night was getting late. She did not particularly like the looks that came her way from the few people who were about, especially the men.

Exhausted, and much too warm in her heavy winter coat, Amanda finally crept back toward the station. Watching the entryway carefully, she made her way inside, then hurried to one side of the room into the corner shadows. The man appeared nowhere in sight.

She sat down on a nearby bench and tried to make herself comfortable. Slowly, one sleepless minute went by, then another. The night hours dragged on. She was afraid to close her eyes lest the man might still be about, yet was unable to keep her head from drooping in sheer exhaustion.

Somehow the dreary, miserable night passed. As light finally began to dawn Amanda was more weary than ever. Her eyelids sagged yet more heavily. Before long she was sound asleep.

Suddenly she came to herself.

She jolted upright and her eyes shot open in a fright. It was bright and light. Morning had come!

She glanced quickly at her watch. It was 6:55. She had nearly missed her train!

Hastily she jumped up, grabbed her bag, and ran to the ticket window.

With ticket in hand a few minutes later, her money now nearly three-quarters gone, she looked hurriedly around for the platform she needed.

She had just located the way to track three when suddenly Amanda's feet froze. For an instant she stood motionless, like a terrified frog suddenly caught in the death stare of a snake whose mouth was three times its size.

How could it be!

There was Ramsay walking into the station!

He had just entered from another platform with the same man she had seen last night!

Summoning every ounce of willpower she possessed, Amanda forced her legs into activity. She turned in the direction of platform three.

Resisting the impulse within her to break into a run, she began walking toward the train, which was scheduled to depart in just four minutes. Deliberately but with measured step, she made her way toward the tunnel as quickly as she dared. Any second she expected to hear a voice behind suddenly call out her name. Surely he would see and recognize the back of her coat and the hat with her brown hair coming out from under it! Every step was an agony of steady determination.

She rounded a corner out of sight of the station hall and ticketing area. Instantly Amanda broke into a frantic dash for the track.

Two minutes later she seated herself on board, as far from a window as she could get.

7

Across the Border

$\mathcal{A}$s Carneades led him into the Trieste station Ramsay hurriedly glanced about.

The place was filled with the general buzz of conversation, bustle, and noise as the morning crowd of travelers moved about in all directions at once. Ramsay looked to his right and left, scanned the area, then located the schedule board. He ran toward it.

It revealed a 7:13 departure for Milan.

"That's it," cried Ramsay. "Seven-thirteen. Where's platform three? It might not be too late!"

"This way," answered Carneades, lumbering into a run.

Ramsay broke into a sprint, quickly passed him, and now ran through the tunnel almost in Amanda's very footsteps of only a few short minutes earlier.

Unfortunately, the engineer of the Milan express, a crusty Italian who had worked for the railroad since he was fifteen, kept rigorously to the schedule and sent steam to wheels at the precise instant the second hand of his watch rounded the apex of 7:13 on the dot.

When the two men hurried up to the platform, therefore, it was only in time to see the last coach of the westbound train departing the station about fifty yards down the track.

A great imprecation exploded from Ramsay's lips. He saw nobody at the windows this time. But an inner conviction assured him that Amanda was on that train.

"Do you have a car?" he said to the Greek.

"A friend's," replied Carneades. "It's outside."

"Let's go, then!" cried Ramsay. "The train will stop at the border. If we fly, we just might be able to make it. We'll catch her there!"

Forty minutes later Amanda stepped out of the coach and followed the other passengers toward the border inspection station.

Though Italy was the third member of the Triple Alliance and on friendly terms with Germany and Austria-Hungary, she had become angered by the Austrian ultimatum to Serbia in August and had declared her neutrality. She was presently engaged in a shrewd diplomatic game between the two sides in the war. Amanda knew she would be reasonably safe once inside Italy. The delay while passports were checked would not be long. Yet with a war on, security even at a friendly border such as this had been tightened.

Amanda stood in line pulling out Gertrut Oswald's passport. *Hurry, hurry*, she thought. *Can't you move any faster!*

The minutes dragged by. One by one each of the passengers was cleared through the gate, then returned on the Italian side back to the waiting train. Impatiently Amanda shuffled and glanced nervously about.

The roar of an automobile engine broke through the faint hissing coming from the stopped train. Amanda turned toward the sound. A black sedan was racing toward the scene. It screeched to a stop on the other side of the tracks about a hundred yards away. Two men jumped out from each side.

Amanda's heart suddenly leapt into her throat.

No . . . not again! How *could* he have followed her here!

Almost at the same moment the lady in front of her walked through the gate.

"Pass," said the guard.

Amanda shoved the stolen passport into his hand, glancing nervously back and forth between the guard and her pursuer.

Ramsay was running toward the inspection booth! His footsteps echoed on the pavement stones.

"That man," she said frantically to the guard. "He is—"

A shout sounded.

"Stop that young woman!"

Amanda glanced fearfully behind her.

"Don't worry, Fraulein," replied the guard, gesturing Amanda through as he handed back her passport. "We will take care of him."

Amanda dashed through the gate and toward the train.

Ramsay ran up to the small guardhouse.

"You've got to detain that woman," he said, flashing his passport as if to run straight through. "She is—"

"You're the one we will detain," interrupted the guard. He stepped forward to block Ramsay's way.

"What are you doing, you fool!" exploded Ramsay. "She's English, and a spy. She's trying to get—"

A shrill whistle drowned out whatever else he might have been planning to say. Within seconds Ramsay found himself in the grip of two Austrian soldiers clutching both his arms.

"You're making a mistake," he cried. "I'm not—"

"None of your impertinence," rejoined the guard. "You're the one who made a mistake trying to accost that young lady."

"You won't get away from us, Amanda!" Ramsay shouted through the gate. "I'll follow you wherever you go. You are my wife now. You cannot escape me!"

Trying desperately to shut out his voice behind her, Amanda stumbled into the train.

She found her seat and looked out the window. They were leading Ramsay away. He was struggling and straining, but to no avail. The first soldiers had now been joined by two others.

The passport line contained ten or twelve more people. If only the train would get moving before he managed to convince them that he was telling the truth.

Ten minutes later, seeing no further action outside involving Ramsay, Amanda felt the train jerk again into motion.

8

Dreariness

The ride to Milan was anything but pleasant.

As the minutes dragged by, Amanda's spirits slowly began to sink. Despite her success thus far, she had not managed to lose Ramsay. He knew right where she was. And she knew he would never give up.

Maybe Ramsay was right. She could never hope to escape.

What was the point of trying?

They would never let her into France anyway. Ramsay would find her eventually and take her back to Austria. What was the use? She would never get back to England.

And with what she knew, they would probably kill her. Murder did not seem to bother them. They had killed the archduke. She would likely be next.

The chilling words she had overheard from Mr. Barclay's mouth several nights ago came back to Amanda's memory: *"Find some means to eliminate her."*

The words rang over and over in her brain . . . *eliminate her . . . eliminate her.*

Gradually despair stole over her. She could almost feel Mr. Barclay's eyes probing, staring, searching. As she imagined his gaze upon her, the former drowsiness of will slowly settled over her consciousness.

It was hopeless. Why didn't she just give in? Where was the hope in anything? What did she have left to live for?

A young lady several seats forward in the coach turned to speak to a companion. Something about the shape and expression of her face reminded Amanda momentarily of Catharine. The thought of her younger sister only saddened Amanda all the more. Catharine had always seemed so young and small that Amanda had taken her for granted. She had been shocked during her brief visit to Heathersleigh to realize what a striking woman she had become. Suddenly Amanda missed her very much. How comforting it would be to have a sister with her right now.

But she didn't. She had sacrificed that relationship along with everything else when she left Heathersleigh. She had thrown away her past back then. Now she had thrown away her future as well.

And for what? For a man who had never really loved her at all.

Nausea swept over her at the thought of what she had allowed herself to become involved in.

It was a dreary, drizzly, disheartening day in England as well as Italy. A great cloud had descended upon the whole continent, with the five Rutherfords of Devon, spread out now across Europe, under the very middle of it. Even George, training in the Orkneys, was feeling more alone and downcast than usual. Only Catharine, the youngest of the three young people, had not been affected by the grey, dismal atmosphere.

The mood at Heathersleigh was subdued and quiet. Charles had now been gone for two days.

As she walked up to the second floor of Heathersleigh Hall, Jocelyn tried to buoy her spirits by imagining where her husband might be at this moment. He was to have set to sea at daybreak this morning, she thought. It was now midmorning. That should put them somewhere probably just off Land's End. They would soon be turning to head north.

She entered the library, where she knew Catharine had gone to read. Her younger daughter was dressed in a cheery yellow dress. Jocelyn smiled. How like Catharine to defy the weather!

"Hello, dear," she said. "How would you like to join me for some tea? Sarah will be up with it shortly."

"Yes, thank you, Mother—that sounds good," replied Catharine.

"I thought I might come up and sit with you," added Jocelyn, taking a chair opposite her daughter. "I need to lose myself in a book to get my mind off your father's being gone. Any suggestions?"

"I told you how much I am enjoying *Ben Hur*. I'm almost finished. Why don't you read it next?"

"I think I need something more along the lines of an old-fashioned romance and mystery. I don't want to have to think. It makes me too sad."

"Because Father's gone?"

"And George . . . and Amanda."

"*I'm* still here, Mother," teased Catharine with a cheerful smile.

"I know, dear," replied Jocelyn. "And you can't know how thankful I am for it! Your being with me is the one thing that makes me able to keep my head up at all."

"Mother!"

"I mean it, dear. But at the same time, it is so incomplete when our whole family isn't together. Don't you feel it?"

Catharine nodded. "Of course. George is my best friend," she said. "Well, except for *you*, I mean. But they'll be back, Mother. We just have to keep believing and praying for that day when we are all together again."

"When you say that, do you include your sister?"

"Of course," replied Catharine. "I pray every day that Amanda will come home."

"I suppose I need to take a lesson from you," said Jocelyn with a thin smile. "But I have to admit, praying with faith gets more and more difficult the longer she is gone. I know I have to keep hoping, but—"

The tears—always nearby—suddenly arrived on the scene again without warning.

The next instant Catharine was on her feet and at her mother's side. She knelt down beside her mother's chair and put her arms around her. Jocelyn wept freely for a few moments on the great strong shoulder of her youngest daughter, who had become a very compassionate young woman.

Gradually the two women eased back. Jocelyn dabbed at her eyes, then kissed Catharine affectionately.

"Thank you, dear," she said. "I hadn't had my cry yet today." She tried to laugh. "It always makes me feel better to get it over with."

She drew in a deep breath, then rose.

"But I still think I need that mystery," she said. "Perhaps I shall peruse the shelves a bit.—That is, after tea," she added. "I think I hear Sarah coming with the tray."

After two stops and the passage of about four hours, Amanda's train arrived in Milan. It was early in the afternoon.

A three-hour layover was scheduled before the next train for France. Ramsay was sure to catch up with her now, Amanda thought hopelessly. He might even have called ahead to notify the authorities to hold her until he arrived.

The train stopped and the doors opened. Half expecting to be arrested on the spot, tentatively she picked up her carpetbag and crept out. She stepped onto the platform. No uniformed guards were waiting. But Ramsay would probably appear any moment. Her brain was in such a fog she did not think that it would have been impossible for him to arrive ahead of her.

With three dozen other passengers Amanda walked into the station, found a vacant seat, and sat down. Feeling hungry and more forlorn than she had ever been in her life, Amanda was too despondent even to find something to eat. She was beginning to feel weak. She had not eaten since sometime yesterday.

Tears of hopelessness began to fill her eyes.

Hardly realizing what she was doing, she began silently to pray. *"God, I was so stupid for not listening. I never thought I needed anyone, but now I realize I do need your help. Please, God . . . help me."*

Amanda glanced up.

Across the station a lady was eying her strangely.

9

Clandestine Beacon

*E*ven as Charles Rutherford was bound north by sea, on England's opposite coast, Irishman Doyle McCrogher and Charles' friend and former parliamentary colleague Chalmondley Beauchamp sat high in a lighthouse situated on a coastal plateau on North Hawsker Head east of the Yorkshire moors. These were times which made of men both heroes and traitors, and Beauchamp had chosen for his personal destiny the latter.

McCrogher was at the light's controls. Beauchamp was studying the code book he had managed to pinch from the Admiralty before defecting from London. It gave the disposition of many of the fleet's ships as well as depth charts for all its harbors, along with the secret codes for passing on the information.

The mist on England's east coast had lifted, and they had climbed the whitewashed column of the slender lighthouse about thirty minutes before. At present they were the only two inhabitants of the red-roofed house which sat below. It would be the scene, however, of many comings and goings in the months ahead—activity which they would do their best to keep out of the London *Times*. With England at war, the sorts of people who would be coming here would definitely not want their presence known.

Built to keep vessels from disaster on the shoals and reefs of the Yorkshire coastline at night and during storms upon the North Sea, it might have seemed peculiar that the unlikely pair were so busy shortly after noon on a calm day with the sun high in the sky. It was indeed an odd time for a lighthouse to be about its business. But the objective of this particular lighthouse was not to warn ships off the rocks, but to guide German U-boats toward their destinations, and signal instructions to be relayed to their counterparts in Germany and Austria.

A few minutes after McCrogher's initial message, a series of return lights flashed back in code.

"They say they've got a bloke what's needin' t' come ashore," said McCrogher.

"Do they say who?" asked the Englishman.

"One o' their spy blokes that's wantin' t' fetch that book o' yours there."

"Anything else—is anyone coming ashore to stay?"

"Don't know, Mr. Bee'ch'm."

"Right. Well, I suppose we'll find out soon enough. Signal them back, then get down to the dinghy and go out for him."

10

Milan Station

♦♦♦

*A*manda did her best not to look at the lady she had noticed a few moments ago. But she could not prevent her eyes from periodically wandering in that direction. Whenever she glanced toward her, the lady seemed to be watching her.

At length the brown-haired woman rose. She was of medium height but somewhat stocky build, with round face and tall forehead. She approached Amanda where she sat.

Ramsay Halifax sat on the express out of Verona. He had been lucky to get on another westbound so quickly. He was only a couple hours behind Amanda now, which this particular express should make up half of by the time he reached Milan.

Just wait till I get my hands on that vixen, he thought to himself.

His hand unconsciously tightened into a fist. Had Amanda seen him now, she would not have recognized him from the dashing man who had so charmed her back in England three years before.

If Ramsay had been angry before, he was enjoying one of Mr. Barclay's white furies now. He had been detained for questioning at the border more than an hour before the imbecile guards finally realized he was telling the truth.

The fools! he thought. *The absolute idiots!*

He nearly had his hands on her. If they had just let him through to begin with, by now he would be almost back to Vienna with her. Was he going to have to chase her all the way to France before this was over!

The idea roused his passion to yet greater heights. When he did get his hands on her, he would make her pay for this ridiculous escapade!

Amanda glanced away as the woman approached. Should she get up and run away? But before she could think *what* to do, it was too late.

"Young lady," said the woman in a kindly voice, "you look lost . . . do you need some help?" she said.

"Why . . . what do you mean?" replied Amanda. Her tone was uncertain.

"Only that you look like you need a friend."

The statement took Amanda off guard, as did the woman's English.

"But . . . are you British?" she asked.

"No, but I speak English and German. Something told me English was right in your case."

"Is it that obvious?" replied Amanda in a nervous half laugh. "I have been trying to pass myself off as an Austrian."

"Perhaps not," smiled the lady. "I just had a feeling. My name is Gretchen Reinhardt, dear," she added, sitting down beside Amanda. "What's yours?"

"Uh . . . it's Amanda. Actually, you're right—I do need help. I've got to get to France."

"Why France?"

"I need to get back to England. A man is chasing me. I am in dreadful trouble."

"What kind of trouble? Should we alert the authorities?"

Amanda's face fell. "I am afraid that would hardly help. He is Austrian, and actually . . . he is my . . . I can hardly say it . . . I should never—"

She broke down in tears and glanced away.

A moment later Amanda felt the woman's hand on her own.

"If you can trust me, Amanda dear," she said tenderly, "I think perhaps I may be able to help you. Would you come with me?"

"I don't understand," Amanda said, sniffling and looking back up toward her. "Come where?"

"I am leaving on a train north in a few minutes. I was waiting for it just now when I saw you. We will get you a ticket. If you can trust me, I would like to take you with me."

"You mean . . . *north*—out of Italy?"

"Yes, Amanda dear."

Could she believe her ears! It sounded too good to be true. Yet . . . who *was* this woman? She couldn't just leave with a total stranger.

Or could she? Something in the lady's tone and expression, mostly her eyes, told Amanda she could indeed trust her.

"But . . . but where are you going?" she asked.

"I live in Switzerland," the lady called Gretchen replied. "Switzerland is neutral, you know. Once there you will be safe. Then you can decide what to do next. But first it might be wise to get you out of your immediate situation."

"Will they let me across the border?" asked Amanda.

"The Swiss authorities are very understanding," answered Gretchen. "I am certain they will."

She had not proved herself a very good judge of character up till now, Amanda thought to herself. Perhaps it was finally time she began looking inside people for the right kinds of things. And if she did intend to begin now—

For an instant she was almost reminded of her mother. Again tears tried to rise in Amanda's eyes. If ever she wanted her mother, it was now. Just to feel her arms around her, to be safe again, sitting on her bed, listening to her soothing voice.

She had never felt so lonely and sad in her life. How could she have let herself stay away from her mother for so long? All she wanted at this moment was to be a little girl again, safe and secure in her mother's arms.

She looked up through her tears . . . yes, she had the distinct sense that this lady was trustworthy and good, and would let no harm come to her.

Amanda tried to smile, then nodded.

"Yes . . . yes, I will go with you," she said.

"Good," said Gretchen, rising. "Here, let me take your bag.—Have you had any lunch?"

"I'm afraid I haven't eaten all day," said Amanda, standing wearily to follow her.

"You must be famished! We must take care of that too. I have some sandwiches. We shall eat them together once we're on the train."

"But I still don't understand why you would do this," said Amanda as they walked to the ticket window. "You don't even know me. Why would you help me like this?"

Gretchen smiled.

"We have been expecting you, dear," she said.

"We?"

"Myself and my friends. The moment I saw you I instantly asked the Lord if you were the one. He told me you were."

Her statement met only a look of yet deeper perplexity on Amanda's face.

"Don't worry," said Gretchen cheerily. "You will understand in time."

Amanda *didn't* understand yet. But if she had decided to trust this woman, she would do so immediately.

Ramsay ran into the waiting area of the Milan station.

A quick glance about revealed no sign of Amanda. He ran to the ticket window.

"I just arrived from Verona," he said. "When was the last departure west?"

"The westbound to Turin has not left yet," the man answered. "The two trains join here in Milan."

"When does it leave?"

"Not for another thirty minutes—on platform four."

Already Ramsay was making for the train. Within minutes he had talked the conductor into allowing him on board.

A thorough search of every coach, however, did not turn up Amanda anywhere. He descended back onto the platform, now more confused than angry. What could have happened to her?

He would keep watch, he thought. She must be hiding somewhere, waiting for the last moment to board.

Behind him on an adjacent track, the northbound train for Switzerland ground into motion and began to pull out. Absently Ramsay turned and glanced toward it. For a fleeting moment the horrifying idea struck him that maybe he was mistaken about Amanda's destination.

Just as quickly he dismissed the thought. He turned around again, wondering if he should search the Turin express again.

In one of the windows of the northbound behind him sat a certain Swiss woman on her way home from a visit to her sister in Milan. Had she observed the young man stewing about on the platform trying to decide what to do, she would have had no idea that he was searching for the very one she was now doing her best to make comfortable beside her.

Spread out on the seat between them were a few simple sandwiches, which looked to Amanda like the very bread of heaven. For once in these last two days Amanda's attention was not drawn outside. Neither of them ever knew, in those few fateful moments, how close to each other they had been.

Seconds later the northbound was gone.

Ramsay Halifax, meanwhile, stood alone in Milan on platform four more mystified than ever.

By the time he began walking back into the station, however, the temporary detour of his mood into perplexity was well on its way back toward rage once again.

PART II

Refuge

1914–1915

11

Messrs. Crumholtz, Sutclyff, Stonehaugh, & Crumholtz

*T*he morning's light drizzle had gradually turned into something heavier.

As Bradbury Crumholtz walked along the cobbled avenue under his black umbrella back toward his office, the gentle rain falling on the cloth-domed roof above him made him pensive, as it often did. Solicitors dealt in facts, of course. His profession had forced him to be more pragmatist than philosopher. Yet his was a far more reflective nature than either father or uncle, from whose combined shares he had inherited sixty-three percent of the firm that twice bore his name, appearing as bookends on the sign painted in black and gold on the window looking out upon the heart of Exeter's business district.

The will he had just read—to the silent stares and sniffles of a small room of black-clad mourning nephews and cousins and aunts and one very aged great-great-grandmother—had put him in an even more somber mood than usual. He did not know the family, longtime residents of the city. Yet the mere setting unnerved him.

He did not like reading wills. It was an aspect of his duty he would just as soon do without. Probably not unlike officiating funeral services for those of the clerical profession, he mused. He wondered if ministers and vicars and priests enjoyed their death-business any better than he did his. He ought to ask one sometime.

The two ideas—the will executed by his firm, and curiosity concerning thoughts of ecclesiastics at funerals—gradually merged in his mind as he turned onto High Street. How exactly the progression of ideas followed one upon the other he could not have said. But before long he found himself thinking about the old woman from the country who had visited him several days ago with her strange business.

He had drawn up a will for her too, although he yet had a little more research to do into the legalities of the terms specified on the deed, to see whether she indeed possessed legal right of bequeathal in the peculiar affair. He had thought of her on and off ever since and had not been quite able to get her out of his mind.

Why did memory of her visit strike a clerical chord of recognition in his brain? Something had been gnawing at him, something he seemed to be forgetting out of the distant past . . . something important.

The old deed with its peculiar terms . . . yes, there was a bishop involved. That must be the connection between clerics and wills that set him off on today's rainy, philosophical ramble.

Clerics and wills . . . hmm . . .

No, something else was pricking at his brain, from farther back in memory. The fellow's name from the woman's deed . . . what was it . . . somehow it rang a faint bell . . . but from where? Clerics and wills . . . what was the connection?

Crumholtz reached the front door to his office when suddenly a flash of mental light stopped him in his tracks.

Crompton!

Of course! It was the name on that envelope from years ago that his uncle had been given, to be opened on some occasion or another. He remembered his uncle's instructions when he told him about it. An altogether peculiar business.

He stepped under the awning, lowered his umbrella, and hurried past his secretary and into his office, his curiosity now aroused. He went straight to the safe containing such unique documents for which the firm was responsible and proceeded to open it.

Five minutes later he sat with the three documents in his hands, the will he had been asked to draw up, and the two sealed letters. He had been puzzling over them for several minutes. Strange that after all this time, suddenly into his office would walk the very heir that the instructions concerning the old document from 1856 had apparently foretold. Whatever contents this sealed envelope held, he remained legally bound, as had been his uncle and father before him, not to open it until the prescribed conditions were fulfilled, if such a time ever came at all. That it now seemed to be approaching with that very woman's advancing years, he was all but certain.

Did she have a premonition of what was in the envelope? he wondered. Did she even know the document existed at all? She had made no mention of it. His uncle had said not a living soul knew of it save the representatives of Crumholtz, Sutclyff, Stonehaugh, and Crumholtz.

What could it all be about? Why had this letter been separate all these years from the deed?

A mysterious case, he thought . . . one which he hoped he might live long enough to see through to its conclusion. This will he had recently executed was one whose reading he was not eager to see necessitated by the passing of one so pleasant as his recent visitor—and the old woman seemed in the most robust of health and vigorous of mind—but at whose reading he would certainly not mind being present. In fact, he was now curious to see how the business with the old cleric and her will turned out.

A minute or two longer he sat, then rose and replaced the two new documents with the older one in his safe, together now until such time as they were needed.

12

Alpine Waking

Amanda awoke to bright sunlight streaming through the window. Outside she heard birds chirping and someone singing in the distance.

She lay for a long time warm and contented, not eager to creep out from the depths of the heavy feather bed. The cold on her face told her that to rise meant leaving this pleasant warmth for an icebox. And inside the bed, it could not have been cozier. How long was it since she had felt such a sense of comfort and safety?

At last she rose, quickly put on the thick robe and slippers from the stool beside the bed, and walked to the window. The sight that greeted her eyes was something no amount of preparation or foresight could have led her to expect. Spread out and sloping nearly straight up before her stood the most spectacular peaks of grandeur imaginable, dazzled with the purest white and reflecting the morning's sun here and there with blinding shafts of brilliance. She stood awestruck for several long moments.

She had known they were going to Switzerland. In some vague way she supposed there would be mountains. But she had been too exhausted to conjecture about the matter further.

She had, of course, heard of the Swiss Alps all her life. She knew they were rugged and topped with snow. She had even seen photographs. But nothing could have readied her for the fantastic reality of seeing them so quiet, so white, so solemn, so powerful—and so *close* she could almost reach out and touch them!

Two or three women were outside working and walking about. Amanda watched for several minutes, beginning to wonder what kind of place she had landed in.

Slowly she dressed with the clothes that had been given her the night before and put on a shawl, a deepening sense of wonder stealing over her, reflecting back on last evening's arrival. Dusk had descended as they rode by wagon the last thirty minutes up a steep, winding road. If the mountains had been visible as they went, she had not noticed them. After their arrival she met several women whose names she had already forgotten. It quickly became a blur . . . the light meal, the kindly reception, the hot bath, the fresh warmed nightgown, and finally losing herself in the depths of the wonderful bed.

Not sure what to expect, she left the room and timidly went downstairs.

"Good morning, Amanda!" sounded Gretchen Reinhardt's voice.

Amanda turned to see her new friend from yesterday approaching from the large fireplace.

"Did you sleep well?"

"Yes . . . yes, actually I slept very well," replied Amanda. "I feel like I slept through half the morning."

"Not quite," laughed Gretchen. "It is only a little after eight. Are you ready for some breakfast?"

"That sounds good—thank you."

The woman who had befriended her in Milan led her across the expansive room into the adjoining kitchen area where heat from the cookstove turned the kitchen into an oasis of warmth in the middle of the chilly morning. Another woman was working at the bread counter kneading a large batch of dark brown dough.

"You remember Sister Hope," said Gretchen.

"Oh . . . yes—hello," said Amanda.

"Good morning, Amanda," replied the other, turning to face them. "We are delighted to have you with us. Let me welcome you again. You looked so tired last night, I doubt you remember much of what was said."

The friendly woman cast Amanda a warm smile that seemed to come from her very heart. She was an inch or two taller than Gretchen and several years older. Her thick black hair, tending somewhat to disorder simply from its mass and quantity, was now about half grey and fell loosely from her head almost to the shoulders. The somewhat long face framed by it was accented by pronounced high cheekbones and a solid, angular chin. Overall it was a look of strength, though the eyes of dark grey hinted at reservoirs of sadness which might be capable of overflowing in tears. The smile, however, dominated the rest of the face's features, radiating the joy that comes from having encountered life's hardships and emerged a victor in the contest. One able to perceive beauty in age might have called her look graceful, perhaps even stately, though not brought about by earthly circumstance. A few wrinkles graced the edges of eyes and mouth, adding a luster of maturity to the overall countenance. Her frame, though not bulging, was solid, even rugged, and was clearly acquainted with hard work.

She approached. "Excuse my hands—I'll try not to get flour on you." She embraced Amanda in a warm hug, energetic yet gentle.

"Sit down, Amanda," said Gretchen. "Would you like some tea?"

"Yes, please . . . thank you."

Several minutes later the two who called each other Sister Gretchen and Sister Hope sat down with Amanda at the large table. In their midst had been set several platters containing all the thick brown bread any of them could possibly eat, fresh butter and cream, cheeses and jams, some crackers, a variety of sliced meats, a large bowl of yogurt, with a steaming pot of tea and soft-boiled eggs on their way.

Amanda ate more than she would have thought possible and drank three cups of tea. It was so relaxing and the food so simple and wholesome that she found her appetite greater than she realized. Conversation flowed freely, and Amanda found herself quickly at ease with the two women.

"Sister Gretchen has told me a little of your story," said the older of the two, whom Amanda had by now begun to assume was in charge of this place, whatever it was. "She said you were trying to get out of

Italy so that you might return to England."

Amanda nodded as she set down her cup of tea.

"I am embarrassed to say," she replied, "that I got myself involved with some people I shouldn't have. They called themselves the Fountain of Light, but it took me some time to realize that light was the last word I would use to describe their influence on me."

"There are many who use words such as light and truth," remarked Sister Hope thoughtfully, "but not nearly so many who live by their principles."

"I came to the Continent this past spring," Amanda went on, "having no idea what was going to happen. I thought I was just going on holiday, accompanying an older lady as her companion. As it turned out, I did not go back to England with her as I had planned. I really wasn't thinking very clearly, because these people, I learned only recently, turned out to be a spy network. Unfortunately, by then—"

Amanda stopped abruptly and glanced away. She wasn't ready to go so far with personal honesty and self-exposure yet as to tell them about Ramsay. She didn't want to talk about him. She didn't even want to think about him.

"Let me just say," she continued after taking a deep breath, "that when I finally woke up to what I had allowed myself to become involved in, Europe was at war and I was in Austria. I realized I was in danger and suddenly was very afraid. So I looked for an opportunity, and when it came I ran away from the house where these people had their headquarters, or so I assume, and took the first train out of Vienna that wasn't going to Germany."

Amanda fell silent. It seemed like such a long time had passed. In fact, she had only escaped from the house on Ebendorfer Strasse three days ago.

"Where did you go?" asked Sister Hope after a moment. "Vienna is some distance from Milan."

"Trieste," replied Amanda. "From there I managed to get into Italy. That's also where I realized I had been followed, and I was terrified all over again. I don't know what I would have done if Gretchen hadn't befriended me," she added, glancing toward her savior of the day before with an uneasy smile.

Why was she being so talkative all of a sudden? Amanda wondered to herself. And with almost total strangers? Yet there was such a difference here from the house in Vienna. She had felt it immediately last night, though they had arrived after dark. Everything about the place seemed to exude openness and acceptance.

And, strange to say, *light*.

The house on Ebendorfer Strasse, where they *talked* about light, was so filled with darkness. Even as she thought back to Vienna now, the house itself, with its long interior corridors and pulled drapes and hushed conversations and unfriendly looks, was chilly and foreboding.

The moment the sun came up this morning, blazing into her window off the snowy mountains, she knew she had come to a place of light indeed.

She hadn't been able to define it back then. But the moment she and Mrs. Thorndike had arrived in Vienna she felt like a stranger in the midst of strangers. It was a peculiar, dark, ominous place. Ramsay's mother had told her to think of it as her home. How could she have been so foolish and blind? What in the world had she been thinking? Or had she been thinking at all! After being gone from Ebendorfer Strasse only a few days, the whole bleak experience was already beginning to fade into a fuzzy blur of nonreality.

She felt more at home here after less than twelve hours than she had ever felt there. Or than she had felt during her three years with the Pankhursts in London, for that matter. Emmeline Pankhurst and her daughters had warmly welcomed Amanda into their home, but Amanda had eventually realized that their kindness had far more to do with her value to them in promoting their cause of women's suffrage than in what she meant to them personally. Disillusioned by the women's movement, and feeling used and betrayed by the Pankhursts, she had left their home two years ago and had had no contact with them since. Somehow this quiet place in the Alps was different. She knew she could trust these women. She knew she was among friends. She felt more at home here than anywhere but—

Again she stopped herself. That was another avenue of thought she was not anxious to explore at present. Sister Hope's voice interrupted Amanda's thoughts.

"Well, my dear, you are welcome to stay with us as long as you like," she said. "Many people have discovered themselves refreshed and invigorated for life's battles here among the Alps. I pray it will be such a time for you. Some stay for a day, others for a week, still others a year. However we can be of help and encouragement, it will be our privilege to do so. When the time comes that you feel you should continue on, we will do all we are able to help you get back to England. Our one desire and prayer is to serve you."

"I . . . thank you," replied Amanda, taken aback by the forthright statement. "I don't know what to say. Nobody has ever said anything quite like that to me before."

Sister Hope smiled. "Perhaps not," she said.

"What do you mean . . . *serve me*. Serve me . . . how?"

"We all have needs that the Lord wants to attend to within us. To the meeting of that need—and whatever ministry of service it involves—we are dedicated."

"But . . . what a remarkable thing," said Amanda slowly, in almost a bewildered tone. In truth, she was barely able to make much sense out of the words.

"Such is the purpose of the chalet," added Sister Hope.

"Is . . . is there a cost for my staying?" said Amanda. "Is this . . . some kind of hotel or guesthouse? I'm afraid I have very little money."

Both women laughed with delight. It was a laugh of pure pleasure with which Amanda took not the slightest offense. How could she? The laughter was so merry and gay that after a second or two she found herself joining in at her own unintentional joke.

"No, my dear Amanda," replied Sister Hope after a moment. "This is just our home, isn't it, Sister Gretchen?"

"Are you really all sisters?"

Again laughter filled the kitchen.

"Only in the Lord," replied Sister Hope. "Every one of us came here originally without the slightest thought of making it our home. Now we are pleased to be able to offer our hospitality to all who come, even as many of us arrived originally, as strangers. Our guests are truly our guests. There is no cost."

"But how do you . . ."

"How do we afford to open our home in this way?"

Amanda nodded.

"The Lord makes provision."

"Do you have . . . jobs?"

"We make things. We sell cheese. And as I say, the Lord makes provision."

Amanda reflected for a moment.

"I still don't know what to say," she said at length, "other than *thank you*. You are very kind and generous."

13

The Sisters of the Chalet

$\mathscr{T}$hree days had passed since Amanda's arrival.

All nine of the sisters kept busy at their various duties about the place. Amanda was provided for, waited on, served meals, her bed made up, her room cleaned, her clothes washed, her every need attended to. It was like having nine servants waiting on her.

All was done with happy cheeriness, without expectation or obligation. Each one went out of her way to make sure Amanda knew that the sister *enjoyed* doing whatever she could for her. More than a mere guest, Amanda was treated as an honored guest.

It was obvious that these ladies relished in the deeds of ministration. Every word to Amanda was spoken with the utmost graciousness, courtesy, and respect. She felt like a princess, and as if they were her loyal and devoted subjects. Yet a great change had come upon her since her childhood. Now she did not expect it, or even feel deserving of such treatment.

Circumstances had humbled her, with the result that Amanda now received all that was done for her with the simplicity of a grateful heart. She was appreciative of the smallest kindness. Her eyes were being opened to many things, not the least of which was that she had not always been particularly nice to those around her. The realization somehow elevated the simple kindnesses of others to a new level of importance in her eyes.

She could hardly believe the sisters treated everyone who came in such a manner. And yet why not? She was no more special than anyone else, cast adrift by the fortunes of war, caught in difficult circumstances away from home, with no money and nowhere to turn. She represented nothing more to them than anyone they might meet, unlike with the Pankhursts, who regarded Amanda as a societal trophy to gain for their cause.

Had each of the sisters come in some similar circumstance, Amanda wondered, been welcomed as she, and found it so homey and wonder-ful that they simply decided to stay? Had they learned to be kind from the kindness they had each received during their *own* time of need?

Amanda found herself wondering about each of the women—whose ages ranged from about twenty-five to fifty. What were the circumstances that originally brought each one here to this out-of-the-way place?

In an environment of kindness and selflessness, it could hardly be helped that eventually Amanda would begin to look for ways to join in with the activities around her. Such was only natural. Gradually she observed the routine of one, now another of the women, and began to offer her assistance, following them about, taking a basket of clothes into the house, or a bucket of milk from the barn to the pantry.

Before a week was out, she was making up her own bed and helping to set the table or wash the dishes in the kitchen. No better way exists to learn ministration than by observation and practice. What Amanda had been incapable of seeing through the eyes of her childhood, she now began to apprehend through the eyes of her emerging adulthood. And her soul responded accordingly. The remarkable change that slowly stole over her was so gradual that Amanda herself scarcely saw it.

Accompanying this subtle shift in outlook—from *being* served to wanting *to* serve—two things began to happen.

Hands of service always bring lightness to the step and a song to the heart. Amanda found unexpected bursts of joy springing up within her heart. She had, of course, had moments of what she might have called happiness in her life. But not like this. These were sensations she had never felt before. Never had she truly desired to do for others above what she wanted for herself. Without realizing it, such was exactly the effect of the sisters' kindness. The greatest transformation of human life was occurring within her—the transition out of the dungeon of *self* into the sunlight of *selflessness*. It simply made Amanda happy to help, to smile, to lend a hand. Work itself became enjoyable. It filled her with a fatiguing kind of pleasure to have hands and muscles busy, even with chores she once might have looked upon as a drudgery.

At the same time, she found now one, now another memory arising out of her past. Yet they did not bring with them a flood of confusing emotions such as had stirred within her for the last five or six years, but rather were tinged by the quiet glow of nostalgic fondness. As her past gradually came to life again within Amanda's memory, its re-minders were sadly pleasant, rousing no anger as before, but instead calling forth vague longings she could not define.

The first morning she joined Sister Marjolaine in the chicken shed gathering eggs, she happened to glance up after a minute or two. Marjolaine was watching her curiously.

Amanda smiled in puzzlement.

"You've collected eggs before," said Marjolaine in answer to Amanda's wrinkled expression. "You handle them like an expert."

"Why do you say that?" laughed Amanda.

"I've been watching you," replied the small woman in her characteristic high voice. "You pick each one up gently, then brush or blow away the loose dirt, and then set them gently onto the straw in your basket. And you're careful they don't roll into one another. You look like one who has gathered eggs all your life. Where did you learn it?"

Amanda returned her question with a curious expression of her own spreading over her face.

"I . . . I don't know. I don't think I've ever . . ."

Slowly a memory dawned from years before.

She paused, an egg still clutched between her thumb and two fingers. Amanda's mind drifted back.

The image of a child filled her mind. The little girl was eagerly tromping out to a chicken hut alongside a stout woman dressed in a blue-and-white frock.

"Can I get the eggs? Let me get the eggs, Sarah!" the little girl was saying in an importune voice that rang out in that debatable region between question and command.

"Eggs are easily broken, Miss Amanda," replied Sarah Minsterly.

"I've watched—I can do it."

"Then I shall show you again," said the lady as they entered the hut. "If you are careful, you may place the eggs in the basket. Now watch very closely, Miss Amanda. You must pick them up one at a time, with very gentle fingers," Sarah went on, taking out a single brown egg, carefully brushing it off and blowing upon it. "When it is clean, lay it gently inside the basket.—There, you see. Just like that. Each one . . . very slowly. Now it is your turn, Miss Amanda."

Amanda smiled and glanced again at Sister Marjolaine, who was so tiny that beside Amanda she almost appeared as a child herself.

"Yes . . . now that you remind me," she said, "I *have* done this before. But it was many years ago, when I was a girl."

"I was sure of it. I could tell," replied Marjolaine, laughing sweetly.

Amanda placed the egg in the basket, remembering Sarah Minster-ly's words clearly now. They continued on until all the eggs had been gathered, then returned to the house together.

The following afternoon, Amanda approached as Sister Clariss was hanging out the day's laundry. She picked out a few items from the basket and began pinning them to the line. The activity, the clothespins in her hand, the smell of fresh linens, and the gentle breeze on her face gradually put Amanda in a quiet mood. Her subconscious was being pricked, though again she did not realize it at first.

A minute or two went by as both young women worked side by side. It was Sister Clariss who spoke first.

"What is that tune you're humming?" she asked.

Amanda stopped abruptly. "I . . . I don't know," she replied. "I didn't realize I was humming. I suppose I was daydreaming."

"It sounded like a pretty song," said Clariss. "I haven't heard it before."

They returned to their work. Again Amanda began to hum, conscious of it now. As the tune found its way through the ridges of her brain, she began to think of a day several years before—she was probably fourteen. She and her mother and Sarah were outside at Heathersleigh hanging out linens and towels.

Her mother was singing. In the ear of her memory Amanda could hear her voice so clearly now:

"Ride a cock-horse to Banbury Cross
To see an old lady upon a white horse. . . ."

Catharine was bustling about trying to help but was hardly tall enough to reach the line. The sun was shining, it was a pleasant day, and everyone was happy.

Everyone but Amanda. Her own attitude was far from cheerful. She was irritated at being made to help. A sour disposition clouded her entire countenance, and she made certain the towel she was pinning to the line took long enough that the basket would be empty before she was done with it. She might have to be out here, but she didn't have to enjoy it. She was determined to make sure her mother knew she hated it, and equally determined to do as little as she could get away with.

Her mother continued to sing and chat with Sarah, then paused to teach the rhyme to Catharine. After the brief explanation, her mother began singing again.

"Rings on her fingers, and bells on her toes,

She shall have music wherever she goes."

All the while Amanda stewed silently. Even the memory made her stomach churn—not, however, from irritation at her mother, but from the uncomfortable feeling of remembering what an irritable child she had been. How had her mother put up with it!

She shook away the memory. This one was far from happy. It was too painful to look back on the incident with the new eyes of her awakening conscience.

What could account for the change? she thought. Today she was doing the very same thing and enjoying it as she had rarely enjoyed anything in years. What was the difference? Why was this work here actually fun?

Was it something about this place . . . or had she really changed so much?

14

Reflections on Their Guest

$\mathcal{S}$ ister Hope sat at her desk with several papers in front of her. The afternoon was unusually warm for fall, and her window was open.

The snow everywhere but on the mountains was gone. It felt as though summer had returned for a brief visit. From outside she now heard a voice singing a bright melody.

She rose and went to the window.

It was thus that Sister Gretchen found her a short time later as she entered Hope's small office. Hope turned, her eyes full of tears.

"What is it, Hope?" Gretchen asked with concern.

Sister Hope smiled. "I was just so overcome with gratitude," she replied. "How the Lord manages to use this chalet in lives is so wonderful. Even after all these years I find myself amazed by it, and thankful anew."

"To what do you owe this day's outbreak of gratitude?"

Hope motioned her closer, pointing outside. Gretchen smiled and nodded. She had noticed the change in their guest too.

"I heard our dear Amanda singing as she was gathering a few flowers for the table," said Sister Hope.

"The transformation is indeed remarkable," returned Sister Gretchen. "When I saw her in the station at Milan, never had I seen such despondency on a girl's face."

"Obviously it is nothing we have done," rejoined Sister Hope. "It is never anything *we* do. Yet once again we are privileged to behold one of God's flowers beginning to unfold. All it takes is a little warm human sunshine, and it is astonishing how the human plant blossoms of itself."

"The Lord is good to allow us to watch him fill people with hope."

"My thankfulness to him never ceases."

"Such was your vision in the beginning, Hope. I can only imagine how gratifying it must be for you."

"I could not carry out this work without all of you, and you especially, Gretchen. I am so glad you brought Amanda to us. Although I do not think she is meant to remain long."

"Nor do I," rejoined Sister Gretchen. "I sense that the Lord has another destiny awaiting her."

"My thought exactly. Somehow she will become a significant woman in his plan. I do not see what it is, but the Lord has a wonderful future of service marked out for her."

"Has she spoken more to you about herself? Do you know anything about her?"

Sister Hope shook her head. "Nothing," she said. "Her background is not important for now. If the Lord desires for us to know more, Amanda will tell us in her own way and at the proper time."

"Though she appeared as forlorn as a waif, almost from the moment I saw her," said Sister Gretchen, "I had the impression that she was a young lady of breeding and culture. The way she expresses things, her mannerisms, how she carries herself, they all speak of parental care and training."

"I have noticed it too."

"It would not surprise me to discover that she is a young lady from an important family."

"The moment I heard her name I immediately thought of the seventeenth-century Scottish covenanter Samuel Rutherford."

"Do you suppose there is some relation?"

"I have no way to tell. Whoever she is, it is clear the Lord brought her to the chalet for a higher purpose than we are able to see at present."

Meanwhile outside, having no idea she was the object of such a discussion, Amanda was walking with Sister Galiana in the direction of the barn. They were chatting freely as they went.

15

Jilted Farmer's Daughter

*A*manda entered the cool dark of the quiet barn. Sister Galiana immediately set about cleaning the stalls of the three cows who were outside enjoying a few final days of fresh grass before winter's cold set in for good. As they talked, Amanda unconsciously slipped on a pair of boots from near the door, then picked up a pitchfork and began to help.

A few minutes went by. Sister Galiana gradually began to stare, as had Sister Marjolaine a day or two earlier, at her new assistant.

"You handle that fork like you know how to use it," she said.

"Do I?" laughed Amanda. "I didn't think about it."

"You have done this before."

Again the words caught Amanda off guard.

"I just picked it up," she said slowly, "and . . ."

Once more the years fell away. Suddenly she was a girl of nine again. Instead of a barn in the Swiss Alps, in her mind's eye she was now standing in the small familiar barn beside the cottage in the woods between Heathersleigh and Milverscombe.

A faint image came to mind of her attempt to gather courage to let the cow whose domain she had entered scoop a few oats out of her hand with its long, wet bovine tongue. Then the scene shifted to another day in that same barn. Gradually the memory came into clearer definition. She had taken it into her young head to help clean out the stall.

"Careful there, Miss Amanda," she heard Bobby McFee's voice caution in his melodic Irish tongue. "A fork's a tool, not a toy. Let me show ye how to use it proper."

A brief lesson followed in where to place her hands on the handle.

"First we clean out the old mucky stuff," said the wizened old man.

"'Tis not the pleasantest of work about a barn, but necessary. Fork it up onto the cart ... that's it. Careful that it doesn't splat on ye and make a mess. Then I'll wheel it outside to the pile. After the stall's clean, we'll break out a new fresh bale."

Several minutes later the stall was empty of refuse and a new bale in place. Bobby sliced off a chunk with the tips of his fork and shook it loosely into the bin.

"Just like that, and Flora'll have a nice wee bed of straw to sleep in tonight," he said.

Following his example Amanda attempted herself to wield a forkful of new straw. But instead of scattering nicely as Bobby's had done, it fell in a clump. A few deft strokes of the older man's fork remedied that quickly enough.

"Good work, Miss Amanda," said Bobby. "I'll be makin' a lady farmer out o' ye in no time."

Amanda smiled at the memory. She would like to see Bobby and Maggie again, she thought. It had been too long.

While her mind had drifted off, Sister Galiana continued to scoop and clean. Amanda now rejoined her, and again they fell to talking.

None of the sisters intentionally set out to open their personal histories to a guest. But as hesitant as they were to direct attention onto themselves, they yet recognized the truth that every man's or woman's story is uniquely capable of helping another whose experience may cross it at some serendipitous moment of intersection. The relaxed atmosphere, as well as a very natural curiosity, often prompted dialog with their guests in such a way that the tale of each of their pasts spoke in its own way now to one, now to another who came. So while they did not press, neither were they reluctant to share when the opportunity arose. They knew that the Lord used human circumstances to speak to hearts. They were always willing and happy for him to use their own.

"I notice you often working in the barn," said Amanda. "You are out here every day, even though most of you change chores from day to day."

"You are right," replied Sister Galiana. "I love barns and cows ... anything to do with animals. I come in here to work or be with my animal friends whether it is my day for it or not."

"Why?"

"I was raised on a farm in Germany," replied Sister Galiana. She was several inches shorter than Amanda, not tiny like Sister Marjolaine but rather of stocky build, with round face and blond hair woven in a single braid down in back to the middle of her shoulder blades. "I was engaged to a young farmer lad from the next village," she went on. "We had been sweethearts for three years. The wedding was planned and was to be such a gay time. Everyone in the village intended to come, with music and dancing. I was so happy."

Sister Galiana paused. A look of pain came over her face.

"I am sure you have guessed," she went on, "that the happy day did not turn out as I had hoped. Because obviously here I am, and I am not married."

"What happened?" asked Amanda.

"Two weeks before the wedding, my young man suddenly disappeared. He was gone a week. No one heard from him. I became dreadfully afraid, thinking something terrible had happened. Then just as suddenly I received a brief letter in the post, telling me that he was sorry, that he wished me well, but that he could not be my husband."

"But why?" asked Amanda.

"He told me that too," replied Sister Galiana, then paused and glanced away briefly. "It was because he had just married another young lady," she said after a moment, "from a neighboring village. He had not had the heart to tell me to my face. He knew it would hurt me. So he wrote me a letter instead."

She paused again and let out a long sigh. Telling the story never made it easier. There was always pain with the remembrance.

"I can hardly believe he would do such a thing!" said Amanda with rising emotion. "The thought of it makes me furious."

"It made me angry too," rejoined Sister Galiana.

"What a cowardly thing, not even to tell you himself. I think I would have hit him!"

"I thought of that too," laughed Sister Galiana. "Unfortunately, since I could not hit him in the face, I took my anger out on God. It was a silly thing to do. But I was young and immature. All I could think was, 'God, how could you let this happen to me!' I didn't say it humbly, as a prayerful question, but angrily. I blamed God that it had happened. After a while I became as mad at God as I was at the young man. Once I started being angry with God, I became bitter toward everybody and everything. I'm afraid I wasn't a very nice person for a while."

"I can hardly imagine it of you," said Amanda.

"I was much different than today. I was irritable, grumpy, critical, sarcastic. I was so angry inside that I hated everything. Being here has changed me completely."

"How did you come here?" asked Amanda.

"I was on holiday with some friends," replied Sister Galiana. "We came to the Alps to ski. I fear I was a little reckless. Anger can make a person behave very foolishly. During that time I call the angry phase of my life, I tried to pretend I didn't believe in God at all. I was reckless about many things. I think perhaps I was trying to mask the hurt I still felt inside with an impetuous attitude. I drank three glasses of wine for lunch, despite the protests of my friends, then went up onto the mountain to ski like the stupid girl I was. I promptly fell down a steep slope and broke my leg."

Amanda could not help laughing. "I'm sorry," she said, "but you said it so humorously."

"It is funny to think about it now," said Sister Galiana, laughing along with her. "Funny because of how foolish one can be when young. But, as I was soon to learn, God does not turn his back on angry and foolish girls even when they do their best to turn their backs on him. He was caring for me all along, though it took me some time to realize it."

"How did he care for you with a broken leg in the snow?"

"Because who should find me lying there in the snow in an agonizing tangle with my skis, moaning and crying out for help, but dear Sister Agatha on her way back to the chalet from visiting her mother."

"Sister Agatha lives nearby?"

"Oh yes, just over the ridge."

"What did she do?"

"She made me as comfortable as she could, then hurried for help. They brought me here, where Sister Gretchen and Sister Hope set my leg."

"Did your friends discover where you had disappeared to?" asked Amanda.

"Not until the next day. They were worried sick. But Sister Hope went down to the hotel where we were staying in Lauterbrunnen and eventually found them."

"I take it you didn't return to Germany?"

"I remained here at the chalet until my leg was healed. By then I had done a good deal of changing inside. I knew I wanted to make this my home."

"I can see why," remarked Amanda, thinking how much at home

she already felt after only a few days here. She no longer sensed an urgency to return to England.

"But even that part of the process wasn't altogether easy."

"Why do you say that?" asked Amanda.

"Sister Hope can be very blunt when she needs to be," smiled Sister Galiana.

"In what way?"

"She is not afraid to be painfully honest," replied Sister Galiana. "If she sees something that needs attending to, she will tell you."

"Attending to," repeated Amanda. "I'm not sure I understand. Do you mean if someone isn't doing their work?"

Sister Galiana laughed. "No, nothing like that," she replied. "We do our work because we enjoy it. No one has to make us. I was speaking of things that need attending to in the heart, things of character and attitude."

"That sounds, I don't know—like it ought not to be any of her business."

"If it is God's business, then Sister Hope considers it her business. And when one comes to the chalet, that makes it her business too."

"Why, is the chalet hers?"

"She would say it belongs to God, which of course it does. But it is hers too."

"She doesn't still do that to you, does she," asked Amanda, "—tell you when you're doing something wrong?"

"If I need it, of course she does. I want her to," replied Sister Galiana. "But it isn't merely telling us when we do something wrong. It goes deeper than that. She prays for us, for our growth and maturity in the Lord. She is our best friend. She is helping us become the daughters of God we each want to be. She does nothing more than we would all do for ourselves, if we had the wisdom, selflessness, and courage to look deep within our hearts for those attitudes that are not pleasing to him. She has eyes to see what we do not. So I *want* her to tell me what she sees in me—when I'm being selfish, and when I'm holding some portion of myself back from the Lord."

"Does she . . ." Amanda began. Her voice trailed off.

"Are you wondering about Sister Hope herself?" smiled Sister Galiana. "Are you thinking that perhaps it does not sound fair, wondering who tells Sister Hope when her *own* attitudes are not what they should be?"

"I confess, that *is* what I was thinking," admitted Amanda.

"Many newcomers struggle with that," replied Sister Galiana. "But such questions, and I mean no offense, Amanda dear . . . but such questions arise out of an immature outlook. Wisdom does not ask such questions but seeks only the truth. When you have been here some time, such concerns fall away completely. One quickly realizes that Sister Hope possesses the wisdom she does because for many years she has been applying far more strenuous standards to herself and the condition of her *own* heart than she would ever dare with another. What she might bring to *my* attention usually involves the most elementary principles of maturity. In her own heart I know that she wrestles with much higher things of personal dedication and relinquishment of self. I have seen her fall on her knees weeping for what most would consider the most momentary lapse."

"Such as what?"

"A brief sharp word, a seemingly inconsequential rousing of wrong-spirited anger within her."

"But you are right—those are tiny. Everyone gets angry now and then."

"That is true. Things that you and I would excuse within ourselves drive Sister Hope to confession and renewed prayer for a yet more broken self on God's altar."

"Isn't that rather extreme?" suggested Amanda. "How can someone live like that? Everybody has faults. Nobody's perfect."

"She lives like that because she takes the Lord's words seriously," replied Sister Galiana. "She expects herself to heed the Master's commands and live by them. Even the tiniest. When she does not, she considers it not just an accident that she excuses but disobedience. It makes her angry with herself to see that she has not obeyed."

A brief silence followed.

"It is that dedication to be the Lord's daughter in all ways large and small," added Sister Galiana, "that gives her the right, if that is the word to use, to say whatever she feels led to say to the rest of us. She expects less than a tenth the same standard for us as she does herself. The more deeply one knows Sister Hope, the more one treasures, even yearns for the insight of her spiritual eyes, painful though her revelations may be. She knows people because she knows herself. As I said, I *want* to know what she sees in me—painful or not—because I completely trust her instincts and insights."

"That is a remarkable thing to say about anyone," said Amanda, hardly able to take in the idea of such a radical basis for relationship.

"Sister Hope is a remarkable lady," said Sister Galiana.

Amanda was quiet for several long minutes, contemplating the unusual perspective.

"Most people would resist such a thing coming from someone else," she said at length.

"Only those who do not understand the ways of the Spirit," replied Sister Galiana. "I do not say I did not resist at first too. I argued and complained against what I considered her presumption. She made me confront my selfish attitudes. In the frame of mind I was in when I came here, her words angered me. I did not like them at all. Yet at the same time I was surrounded with such love that I found I could not take the one without the other."

"What eventually changed for you?" asked Amanda.

"When Sister Hope confronted me about my anger toward God, I fussed and complained. But down inside ... I knew it was all true. Everything she said was right. It was as if she had known me all my life. I marveled that she could know me so well. She knew me better than I knew myself. But I have seen it time and again with those the Lord sends us. Sister Hope always knows. As I said, she knows people."

"So what happened?"

"Eventually I submitted."

"I'm not sure I understand what you mean."

"I allowed God to begin remaking me according to his plan rather than my own. Once that transition was made, Sister Hope needed to say little more. Once I gave my heart entirely to the Lord, then *he* took over what she had begun."

Again Amanda was pensive.

"Anger against God is always just a way we hide our anger with ourselves," concluded Sister Galiana. "And my experience has also taught me that the seeming pain of the present really does often lead to something better in the end than what we could have imagined. Had I not gone through what I did, I would not now be here."

"You had two kinds of pain to teach you that," said Amanda.

"You're right," laughed Sister Galiana, "—a broken heart and a broken leg! But how thankful I am that the Lord prevented my being married. It was the best thing he could have done for me."

"Why do you say that?"

"Oh, because I was about to marry a young man with such character flaws as I never dreamed were there. What kind of person would do what he did! I did not know him at all. The Lord protected me from what would surely have been a life of misery."

The words stung Amanda. But she did not let herself dwell on them. "Do you ever think about being married?" she asked.

"Occasionally. But I am happier than you can imagine. If the Lord has marriage in my future someday, I will rejoice. But I do not seek it or hope for it or even think about it. I am content. I will be completely content to remain as I am all my days."

16

Churning Butter

◆◆◆

The following morning at breakfast, Sister Gretchen announced, "I will be churning butter this morning. I need a volunteer."

Groans sounded from several of the others.

"I thought you all loved everything you do," laughed Amanda.

"Churning is such hard work," said Sister Marjolaine. "I am not so strong as Sister Gretchen."

"But Sister Gretchen loves it," added Sister Agatha. "Her arms are more muscular than all the rest of us put together."

"That is because I *make* them strong with good hard work . . . like churning," she replied. "Besides, what would Malcolm think to hear you talk like this?"

"Who is Malcolm?" asked Amanda.

"The hero in the book we've been reading. You remember, from a few nights ago."

"Oh yes, I didn't know you were talking about him."

"You'll encounter him again tomorrow evening."

"Only briefly," put in Sister Galiana. "We should be through with the book next time."

"Well, perhaps I shall have to read it all for myself," replied Amanda. "In the meantime, I would like to learn how to churn butter," she added. "I didn't know it was hard work."

"I will work the other churn," said Sister Luane.

An hour later Amanda sat with Gretchen and Luane on the front porch. Gretchen was explaining the process. Sister Anika had just deposited two large cans of yesterday's cream in front of them.

"When we plan to make butter," Gretchen explained, "we collect one morning's milk and let it sit the rest of the day. Late in the afternoon the cream is poured off. Then the following morning we churn."

"So this is yesterday's cream?" Amanda asked.

Sister Gretchen nodded.

"It's not so difficult for the first hour," said Luane as Gretchen lifted one of the cans and poured the contents into the churn. She did likewise with the other into the second churn. She and Luane attached the two lids over the paddles, set the empty milk cans aside, then sat down and slowly began to lift the round handle up to the top, then push it back down. They continued the process in a slow, steady motion.

"What happens after an hour?" asked Amanda.

"The cream gradually begins to thicken," replied Gretchen.

"The thicker it gets, the more wearisome the work," added Luane. "The paddles inside turn differently when you're pulling up or pushing down. As it thickens and the paddles begin to coat up, it becomes very hard to move them up and down. And then, all at once, the thickened cream turns to butter and buttermilk and separates."

"But your muscles will thank you for the exercise," Gretchen added. "Here, Amanda, try it while it is yet easy."

They traded places and Amanda began to slowly pump the churn. She and Luane worked together for some time in silence.

It was another characteristic of the chalet that while all the sisters were ready and willing to talk when they had something to say, none felt awkward for seasons of silence when they did not. As she pumped, Amanda gazed around and drew in a deep breath of fresh air.

"Why is everything so clean here?" she exclaimed after a few minutes, "so fresh, so alive? Why do I feel as though I am thinking more clearly than I ever have in my life?"

"Do I not recall your uttering almost those same words after you had been here a week or two, Sister Luane?" said Gretchen.

"I was recalling that very thing when Amanda was speaking," Luane replied. "I remember wondering if the clarity of the air could result in such mental focus."

"Clarity—that is the precise word to define it," rejoined Amanda. "I feel as though I'm getting little bursts of brightness every once in a while—I don't know, as if an invisible arrow of light had suddenly shot into my brain. I know it sounds funny, but that's what it seems like. I'm remembering things I haven't thought of in years. And with such clearness they could have happened yesterday."

"It happens with nearly everyone who comes here," answered Gretchen.

"Do you mean remembering things, or the mental focus?"

"Both. It is different for everyone, of course, yet similar at the same time."

"Why is that?" Amanda asked.

"I have come to the conclusion," replied Gretchen, "that there is indeed some wonderful quality in the air itself. It is the only thing I have been able to imagine to account for the fact that so many who come to the chalet find their senses coming zestfully keen and alive, and their mental and spiritual acuity so sharpened. It is air one almost feels could be eaten, full not of noise and bustle, but of the vibrant hush of *life* itself. Sometimes when I am out walking, I feel as though I am going to burst for joy . . . just in the fullness of the *silence!*"

Again, as if there could be no other fit response to her words, a deep and contented quiet fell among the three women. Amanda gradually began to recall another day long before.

This was not the first time she had churned fresh cream after all!

How could she have forgotten? She was sitting with Bobby McFee—it all came back so clearly now. He had tried to explain the process too, using some of the same words as Gretchen and Luane. But instead of sitting patiently, she had squirmed and tried to get at the stick before Bobby was ready to yield it. And then, her patience spent, the moment the work became difficult she quickly got up and left Bobby to finish alone.

Where were these things coming from? Why were so many incidents like this popping out of her memory all of a sudden?

Somehow the memories were different here.

Now that her recollections were coming under the influence of this invigorating Alpine air, she wondered how Bobby and Maggie had ever put up with her!

As her thoughts drifted back to the present, at length Amanda realized her movements were slowing down.

"I can feel my arms beginning to ache," she laughed.

"Let me have a go at it," said Sister Gretchen. "I am used to it."

"No, please, I would like to finish it out to the end," said Amanda. "I don't think it's hardening yet. I'm only tired from the motion. But I quit the last time I held a churning stick in my hand. I don't want to quit a second time, even if it means I can't lift my arms when I am done."

"I'll be ready if you change your mind."

"How did you come here, Sister Luane?" Amanda asked as she continued to churn.

"I served as a nurse in the Balkan states during the recent conflicts," she began. "I was there for five years. But when hostilities intensified a couple of years ago, the mission I worked for took us out. It was no longer safe. But there was no secure hospital where they wanted to relocate me immediately. I had heard about the chalet here and wrote asking if I might come for a visit. Sister Hope invited me to stay as long as I liked. I have been here ever since, and am enjoying it very much."

"Do you plan to return to nursing?" Amanda asked.

"I do," nodded Luane.

"When?" asked Amanda.

"I don't know exactly—when a protected situation somewhere opens up. I would like to care for the wounded. I have always felt my calling to be near the field of battle. Christ's love is so desperately needed there. But because of the war, being relocated is proving difficult. I expect to be contacted by the mission anytime. Yet I am in no great hurry. Coming here has been not only a respite for me but eye-opening as well. As a result of my time here, I think I will be a much more compassionate nurse in the future."

"It seems it would be frightening to be close to the war," said Amanda.

"Sometimes, yet with it there was such an opportunity to be of help."

Each one of them, Amanda thought, had such an interesting story to tell. Sister Luane was here for reasons that could not be more different than Sister Galiana's skiing accident. More and more she found herself curious to know every one of their stories.

"Are your arms tired yet?" asked Gretchen.

"Yes!" groaned Amanda. "I can hardly keep moving the churn."

"Let me feel it."

Sister Gretchen took the handle. Amanda's arms drooped nearly to the floor.

"No wonder!" she exclaimed, opening the lid and peering inside.

"Just as I thought—butter on the paddles, and buttermilk at the bottom of the churn! You did it, Amanda, from start to finish!"

17

Vienna Storm Clouds

*S*ince his return to Vienna six days ago, the life of Ramsay Halifax had been as unpleasant as any week in his life.

His mother treated him with lofty silence and mostly avoided him. Mr. Barclay continued sarcastic and peevish, losing no opportunity to dish out deriding remarks, just as he had the moment Ramsay set foot back in the house after his unsuccessful sojourn into Italy.

"How could you let her get away!" Barclay exploded before Ramsay had spoken a word.

"Look, Barclay," Ramsay shot back, "I've been nearly to France looking for her. I'm tired and hungry. Can't you give me a chance to sit down before starting in on me?"

"I have bigger concerns than your comfort," rejoined Barclay cynically.

"Why didn't you go yourself if you think I'm such an incompetent?"

"I should have! Then she'd be back in our grasp by now."

"Don't be so sure of yourself, Barclay!" rejoined Ramsay testily. In truth, he was angry with himself too. He had been so close several times. He still couldn't believe she had slipped through his fingers. It only heightened his fury toward Amanda. If he ever did get his hands on her, she would regret what she had done.

"What about Carneades?"

"He's less than useless," replied Ramsay. "I have the feeling Amanda walked out of the Trieste station right under his nose.—Where's Adriane?" he asked, turning toward his mother.

"She's gone—on her way back to Paris."

An oath exploded from Ramsay's mouth. He turned, left the room irritably, and went upstairs.

Hartwell Barclay wasted no time in returning to the subject of

Amanda at the earliest possible opportunity, which turned out to be that same evening at dinner.

"Look, Ramsay," he said, "you and I may occasionally have our differences. But we mustn't lose sight of the fact that on the loose as she is, that English wife of yours poses a grave threat to our success. We have to get our hands on her."

By now both Barclay and Ramsay had cooled sufficiently to discuss the situation practically. Ramsay had had a nap and a bath and was, if not exactly in better spirits, at least feeling more comfortable and glad to be back in Vienna.

"I cannot imagine she is dangerous to anyone," he replied, taking a sip of a decent German red wine. "You're exaggerating the problem."

"She was here too long," Barclay went on. "I have an uneasy feeling she may know more than you think."

"She knows nothing. She was a feeble-witted simpleton."

"We can't take any chances. I suspect she may have stolen some documents relating to our operation."

"What do you suggest, then?"

"We must continue the search."

"I tell you, she vanished in Italy without a trace," said Ramsay. "She is probably back in England by now."

"Nevertheless, we must cover every possibility. We have people in our network throughout the region. Italy will soon be joining the war effort. I want to go over your movements in detail and set a probe in motion. If she purchased a ticket anywhere, or crossed one of the borders, there will be records. Something will lead us to her."

"If I couldn't find her," said Ramsay, "—and I know Amanda—no one else is going to pick up her steps after all this time. Certainly not Carneades. Especially if she managed to get into France."

"We have people in France as well," replied Barclay. "We will check the border records. I am hopeful she may still be in Italy. A young single woman traveling alone leaves footprints. I will contact our man Matteos."

"I hope he is not the fool Carneades turned out to be."

"He will not disappoint us. We *will* find her."

18

A Walk to Grindelwald

*W*ould you like to go with me over the hills today, Amanda?" asked Sister Hope at breakfast. "I must see a man in Grindelwald about the possible purchase of a plot of land bordering the chalet property. The day appears perfectly suited for just such a walk."

"Oh do, Amanda," chimed in Sisters Anika and Regina at once.

"It is a spectacular climb," added Sister Agatha.

"Climb!" laughed Amanda. "I'm not so sure I like the sound of that!"

"I should have said a spectacular *walk*!"

"How far is it?" asked Amanda.

"Four or five miles over, and the same back," replied Hope. "I will be gone most of the day."

"It sounds like an adventure. I would love it."

"It will be a *long* day."

"My arms are aching so badly from yesterday's churning, I don't think I could do a thing with them—"

Everyone laughed.

"—so maybe today I ought to use only my legs."

"You'll use them all right!" said Gretchen. "By this evening they will be in the same condition as your arms."

"You will not deter me!" said Amanda. "However exhausting, I think it sounds like fun. Tonight I will relax in front of the blazing fire and listen while Sister Anika reads."

Amanda and Sister Hope set off about an hour later, making their way first along a well-worn path that led up steep slopes and through wooded terrain. After a walk of about ninety minutes and breathing heavily from the climb, they came out upon the plateau of Itramenberg. There they paused to catch their breath.

It was a different vista than Amanda had yet seen, offering a whole new panorama of the region. She stood turning her head slowly about and gazing with wonder in every direction. They were so high up it almost seemed she might float off the top of the mountain. The sensation made her feel carefree and happy, like a child again. Amanda did not know it, but they had ascended to heights where lessening oxygen began to affect the lungs. For the rest of the day she found herself breathing more rapidly than usual.

As she stood beholding the sight, to the south the ridge of Alps, of which the Jungfrau was a part, was visible almost in its entirety, with more peaks rising behind it in the distance. A vast, high, sloping plateau stretched from where they stood toward the cliffy feet of the peaks some two or three miles distant, then sloped down in the direction their walk would take them. The plateau was green with mountain grasses even at this time of year.

Amanda skipped about, looking for a flower to pick. As she did, the distant memory of walking with her mother came back to mind, when she and George had raced to pluck the first daisy of spring. The memory calmed her spirit. She walked slowly back to where Sister Hope stood waiting for her.

"The air is so still and clean," she said softly. "It is just *so* beautiful. I feel like I'm on top of the world."

"Our chalet is down there," said Hope, pointing in the direction of Wengen.

"Now I know how it looks to a bird," said Amanda. "We are so high above it!"

"Further over the ridge beyond Wengen," she went on, with her back to the wide, high plateau, "you can see the valley of Lauterbrunnen. And away off there to the right you can just make out Interlaken and the edge of Thunersee."

Amanda followed her pointing hand and eventually took in an entire 360-degree circle with her gaze.

They turned away from the steep ledge and set off in the opposite direction on the trail that led down the gradually sloping plateau toward Grindelwald, an easier walk now. As they went they began to talk casually. It had become obvious to Amanda long before now, both from Hope's accent and much that she said, as well as from occasional references to London, that like her, Sister Hope was English.

"You are from England, aren't you?" asked Amanda at length.

Sister Hope nodded and smiled.

"How did you ever wind up here?"

The question prompted the older woman to grow reflective. A faraway look came into her eye as they walked. She could almost hear again, across the miles, the sound of the famous preacher who had so moved her youthful heart in the big tent. That was the night when she answered the call. It was a moment that changed the direction of her life forever.

"It all began for me," she answered slowly after several long seconds, "with a preacher by the name of Charles Spurgeon. Have you heard of him?"

"I think so," replied Amanda.

"I was a city girl, you see," Hope continued, "raised in London and Birmingham. When I was nineteen I attended a special youth meeting the tabernacle was holding near where I lived."

"The tabernacle?"

"Mr. Spurgeon's church in London—the Metropolitan Baptist Tabernacle. Mr. Spurgeon himself came from the city to preach at the Birmingham meetings. He is dead now, which makes the memory all the more dear. I was eager and enthusiastic. I went forward, dedicated my life to the Lord, and immediately wanted to become a missionary and go to the mission field."

"Did you?" asked Amanda.

Another smile came in reply.

"Eventually," replied Sister Hope. "But not for several years after my conversion."

$$\bullet\ \bullet\ \bullet$$

Come, you who are homeless and burdened with the cares of the world, you who have no place to call home. He will be for you what you have always longed for—a place of refuge, a haven of rest, a home for your soul. . . ."

The preacher's words went straight to the girl's heart.

"Did he not say," the man went on, "'*Come unto me all you that labor and are heavy-laden, and I will give you rest*'? Take him at his word, then. He knows the ache of loneliness in your heart. Take him at his word, for he can heal it, for he said, '*In me you will find rest for your soul.*' "

Was ever one more truly in need of just such a home, a refuge, as she herself? thought the young woman as she sat listening.

She looked up into the aging bearded face, searching even

from her seat so far back among the sea of people. He must be looking straight toward her! He must have chosen those words because he knew.

Home . . . a home for her soul!

The words were too wonderful to believe. Could it possibly be true? Could such actually exist . . . for her?

Again Rev. Spurgeon was speaking.

"And now, youths and maidens, one word to which I hope you will pay special heed. Perhaps you think that religion is not for you. How long, young man, will you say it? Till you are twenty-one? Are you sure that you will live till then? Let me tell you one thing. Men do not get better if left alone. It is with them as with a garden. If you let it alone and permit weeds to grow, you will not expect to find it better in six months—but worse. Men talk as if they could repent when they like. Some say, 'I shall turn to God later.' But such thoughts are a folly. Now—the present moment—is all the time we have, all the time any man or woman ever has. . . ."*

Before many more minutes were past, Hope was on her feet walking down the aisle to answer the minister's invitation.

The next days were a blur of happiness. For the first time in her life she truly felt that she had a family who loved her and cared for her. All the people from the meeting showed such kindness.

And never would she forget the stirring message of the final evening under the tent.

"It is not enough, dear brothers and sisters," Rev. Spurgeon said, "that we commit our own hearts to the Lord Jesus. Once we do, a yet greater call rests upon us. Our Master commands us to take the gospel of his redeeming love unto all the earth. He calls us one and all as preachers and missionaries to the lost souls of the world."

As nineteen-year-old Hope sat listening, peculiar sensations began to pulse within her, stirrings she could not explain. Again it seemed the preacher was speaking to no one but her.

"And upon some," he went on, "that call is greater yet. To these few he calls to leave all, to leave even the comfort of homeland, to serve him in the faraway fields of mission, so ripe with

---

*The first portion of this paragraph adapted from Charles H. Spurgeon's sermon entitled "Heaven and Hell," originally preached on September 4, 1855, in a field beside King Edward's Road in Hackney.

the harvest. If you are such a one, brother, sister—listen to his voice at this hour. If the call to foreign missions is upon you, then I urge you to come again and make public that commitment."

By now Hope was trembling, her heart beating within her. Never had such feelings come over her. She knew his words were meant for her.

"Let not your exertions end in tears," Spurgeon continued. "Mere weeping will do nothing without action. Get you on your feet, you that have voices and might, go forth and preach the gospel, preach it in every street and land of this city. You that have wealth, go forth and spend it for the poor and sick and needy and dying. You that have time, go forth and spend it in deeds and goodness. You that have power in prayer, go forth and pray. You that can handle the pen, go forth and write—every one to his post in this day of battle. Let us go forth unto all the world, each to his own place where God . . ."*

Again she found herself on her feet, heedless of the turning of heads around her.

She had heard the call, and she would answer!

Even as she made her way down to the pulpit where Rev. Spurgeon stood, visions rose within her mind's eye of serving her new Lord in distant foreign lands. She could imagine no higher ambition.

After the service, she sought the minister. He was clustered about with people, but she waited patiently until at last she stood facing him.

"What do I do?" she asked a little nervously. "I am ready. How do I go to the mission field?"

"The Lord will indeed honor your commitment, dear sister," Spurgeon replied. "I will give you the address of our mission board in London. Write to them, and they will help determine your qualifications and what missionary service you will be suited for."

He handed her a card with the address.

She took it, a little crestfallen it is true. She was ready to leave for distant lands *now*, this very night! There was nothing to keep her here. The idea of writing a letter did not satisfy the yearning

---

*This paragraph adapted from Charles H. Spurgeon's sermon entitled "India's Ills and England's Sorrows," originally preached on September 6, 1857, in a service on a day set aside as a national day of humiliation.

she felt as she had listened to his preaching.

Writing a letter would take so long. But if she demonstrated her willingness and enthusiasm by going to the mission ready for anything, they would see that she was in earnest. Surely they would send her out immediately.

As much as thought of returning to the city made her shudder, she gathered together all the money she had and what few worldly possessions she owned, then set out on the train from Birmingham to London within a few days.

She arrived in London and walked straight from the station to the address on the card, a considerable distance and taking her more than an hour, carrying a heavy suitcase in each hand.

At last she stood in front of the Baptist Missionary Society. She walked in, face flushed from the walk and full of eager hope.

"I am here to be a missionary," said Hope to the lady at the desk inside.

The receptionist looked up with something of a blank stare, though a kindly one. "You say you've come to be a missionary?" she said.

"Yes, the preacher at the meeting in Birmingham gave me your card when I answered the call. His name was Mr. Spurgeon. He said you would tell me what I am qualified for and send me to the mission field."

"And what training have you had?"

"I haven't had any training. That's why I am here."

"Hmm, yes . . . I see," said the lady. "Unfortunately Rev. Spurgeon did not have time to explain everything to you."

"Everything . . . like what?"

"My dear, being a missionary requires training . . . and support."

"Support—I don't understand. What kind of support?"

"Financial support."

"I don't understand. I thought . . ."

Young Hope's voice trailed off. This was not going the way she had anticipated. Fatigue was setting in from the days of meetings, then the train ride, and now the long walk through London's streets.

"You have to raise a portion of your own support," the woman went on, "or have a church willing to sponsor you. We receive donations, of course, but it is not enough to pay all of our missionaries' expenses. We mostly pay for materials and building supplies. If you qualify—"

"*Qualify* . . . I thought anyone . . ."

"If you do, as I said, we will make what effort we can to help you raise support. But the missionaries themselves have to raise enough to cover a good deal of their own expenses."

"But why . . . why can't I just go?"

"It takes time for all this to be arranged. Sometimes these preparations require years."

"Surely I could be of help to somebody." Her eyes began to fill. "Why should it take so long when all I want to do is help people?"

"I am sorry, dear—you are young and inexperienced. You need training as well as financial support. I am afraid there is nothing I can do for you at this point. I suggest you talk to your pastor."

Hope could still recall the great preacher's words—"*He calls us one and all as missionaries to the lost souls of the world.*"

And now this lady said she couldn't go, that she needed training and money, that she had to *qualify*. She thought all she needed was a willing heart.

She had no money! If she had to have money to go to the mission field, how would she ever be able to go!

"But the preacher said we were to go into all the world. He said nothing about all this."

"The board has regulations, my dear. If you receive some training, and if your church agrees to help support you, perhaps in time you could—"

"I don't have a church. I don't have a pastor. I don't have anything. And I used every penny I had just to get here. Now I have no place to go."

The woman seemed genuinely moved by Hope's plight.

"My dear, my name is Lanore Weldon," she said, doing her best to sound cheerful. "We do have an opening in our office right here. It is a paying job—not very glamorous, I will admit. But at least it is working for the mission board, which is a *little* like being a missionary, don't you think?"

London! thought Hope. She hated the city. She hated the very thought of staying here, even if it meant serving the Lord.

How could she ever be a missionary . . . in London!

Slowly she turned and left the office. Once back on the dreary sidewalk and walking away, in no direction and with no destination, tears of disappointment and loneliness at last began to fall in earnest from her eyes.

———◆◆◆———

Before Hope could complete her tale, she and Amanda arrived in Grindelwald. When her business was done, they enjoyed tea and a light snack together at one of several cafes, and then began the return walk to Wengen. Amanda's legs were tired, as much from the altitude as the exercise. Yet she felt such a sense of exhilaration that she was eager to begin again.

19

Raw Trainees

———◆◆◆———

*F*rom an obscure vantage point upon board the HMS *Dauntless*, Commander Charles Rutherford watched as the vessel's newest midshipmen and cadets finished their morning drills. They had been at it since before daybreak.

"You are the sorriest set of trainees I've ever laid eyes on!" shouted the lieutenant in charge to the line of recruits as they stood before him stoically at attention.

"Such a fat collection of milksops and weaklings I have never seen . . ."

Charles chuckled to himself at the words.

". . . couldn't fight your way across the street, much less across a continent . . ."

Every recruit for generations had endured the same insults and had been put through the same grind, thought Charles.

"We put to sea in two days. How do you expect us to win this war with such . . ."

Charles turned his gaze away from the drill deck and surveyed the other ships lined up along the shoreline of the Scapa Flow. Many had already put to sea. Two steamed out just this morning. The naval effort was gearing up quickly to combat the German fleet, which had already sunk several ships. All the United Kingdom trembled in dread of possible invasion. Fortunately, there had been no submarines in Scapa Flow as earlier reported, or anywhere else for that matter. But the orders were still to get out onto the high sea as quickly as possible and thus reduce the risk.

As Charles' eyes took in the scene, he could not shut out the barking commands of the lieutenant behind him. He smiled again. How well he remembered his own days as a new trainee, and the lieutenant just like the one now putting these new cadets and midshipmen through their paces. He had to endure the same rigorous hours and odious duty, the same insults. It was Royal Navy tradition.

Poor George, he thought. He was having a rougher time of it than the rest. There must be no hint of taking it easy on him because of his father's presence on board. So the lieutenant was bending over backward in the opposite direction.

Charles did not watch the drills often, and tried to stay out of sight when he did. His father-heart would have rescued George from it had he been able, or taken the abuse himself. But this was the Royal Navy, not Heathersleigh. To interfere would be the worse thing he could do. There was no reason to interfere anyway. George was handling himself well under the adversity.

"You there, Midshipman Rutherford!" barked the lieutenant. "Stand forward."

Charles again peered down to the deck below as George took three strides in front of the line of cadets, then locked his legs again in place, his eyes staring straight ahead.

The lieutenant came forward and brought his face straight into George's with a menacing glare. A long, tense silence followed.

"Did you shave this morning, Rutherford!" he shouted in George's face.

"Yes, sir."

"Get some help next time! Perhaps one of the others will show you how it is done."

"Yes, sir."

"And your uniform—what excuse do you have?"

"Sir?"

"Your uniform is dirty, Rutherford! What do you have to say for yourself?"

"That these are fresh trousers this morning, sir."

"Silence! I will be the judge of whether they are fresh or not."

George continued to stand stoically at attention while the lieutenant now scrutinized him from head to toe, then took a step back.

"On your knees, Midshipman Rutherford."

George hesitated momentarily.

"On your knees! I want you to scrub this deck.—Petty Officer Blankenship," he cried out, "bucket and brush, front and center."

George slowly bent to the deck. The bucket of water arrived, full to within half an inch of the brim. The lieutenant deliberately took the end of the mop handed him by the petty officer, then shoved the bucket toward George, making sure the water sloshed over and onto him. As he did, he stepped back to avoid any backsplash on himself.

"Scrub, Rutherford!"

George dipped his hand into the bucket, found the brush, and began to scrub the deck. The other cadets watched in silence, staring ahead, each hoping he would not be next.

For about a minute nothing was heard but sloshing water and the scrubbing of the brush.

"At ease, Rutherford," said the lieutenant.

George stopped.

"On your belly, Rutherford."

Again a moment's hesitation.

"You seem to have trouble obeying orders.—On your belly!"

George now flattened himself on the wet deck he had just scrubbed.

"Twenty push-ups in double-time!"

Still the cadets stood watching without expression as George complied.

"On your feet, Rutherford!" now barked the lieutenant.

George stopped the exercise, lay for the merest second, then stood back to his feet, breathing heavily.

"I see that the knees of your trousers and your shirt are wet and soiled, Rutherford," the lieutenant shouted. "What do you have to say for yourself?"

George was silent.

"Rutherford, I am speaking to you!"

"Yes, sir."

"I think you are a mummy's boy, Rutherford. What do you have to say?"

"Nothing, sir, that you are right, sir—my uniform is dirty, sir."

"That is better. You will find that it goes easier when you obey the first time. Is that understood, Rutherford?"

"Yes, sir."

"About face, Rutherford. You will be confined to quarters this evening for sloppy dress. Let that be a lesson to the rest of you.—Left face!"

The line instantly snapped ninety degrees to its left.

"Gunnery drill to aft, flagmen, fore, radiomen first deck, engine room detail to third deck—dismissed to your posts. Forward . . ."

Charles turned and made his way down the ladder to the main deck. The line of midshipmen marched by in single file past him as they separated for their assignments. Charles saluted and held his hand to his hat as they passed.

George approached a third of the way through the line. He gave no sign of recognition toward his father other than a brief flickering glance of his eye, then returned to the back of the head in front of him. Charles likewise gave no hint that they were even acquainted. At the end of the column the lieutenant returned Charles' salute, then continued past.

That evening Charles popped briefly into George's barracks at a time he knew he would find him alone. They saluted.

"Not such a pleasant day, eh, George?" he said, easing himself into a bunk opposite George's.

"I've had better," replied George with a groan. "Actually, it was better before you came.—Sorry, Father."

"I'm not surprised to hear it," laughed Charles. "All part of the game."

"Some game!"

"You're holding up well, George, my boy," said Charles. "I'm proud of you."

"I was so angry this morning!" said George. "It was all I could do not to lose my temper."

Again Charles laughed.

"I know exactly how you feel," he said. "I went through it too. It's all part of the regimen. Lieutenant Forbes is a good man. He bears you no ill will."

"I do not like to disagree with you, Father, but he has it out for me. Can't you tell?"

"I know it looks that way, son. But actually, he's showing you favoritism."

"What! With that kind of treatment?"

"Why do you think he picked *you* to put through that ridiculous exercise?"

"I thought because he doesn't like me."

"Don't you think Lieutenant Forbes knows it's all nonsense as well as everyone else?"

"I don't suppose I thought about that. I just thought he was being unreasonable."

"Not at all, George, my boy. He put you through all that just because he knew you *wouldn't* lose your temper, and would obey whatever he said. He chose you because he knew he could depend on you. He chose you because he wanted to show the other cadets how a true navy man obeys orders under stress. And you came through with flying colors."

"If you say so!" laughed George, already starting to feel better about the incident. "I was still pretty mad."

"But you controlled it. Those cadets may face enemy fire and torpedoes before long. They will need to trust Lieutenant Forbes enough to obey his every command, no matter what he orders them. To do so may save their lives. Your obedience today, and not giving way to your temper, was part of that valuable lesson. And he did you another favor besides."

"What's that?"

"Your peers will respect you for weathering such treatment. What would they think of you if Lieutenant Forbes made it easy on you because I am here?"

"I don't suppose they would like it much."

"You see . . . Lieutenant Forbes is actually helping you out."

"You put an interesting interpretation on it!" said George.

"Mark my words, once we set sail and before we return to England, Lieutenant Forbes will be one of your best friends on this ship. He will depend on you, and you will trust him. The others will see it, and will respect you both more highly as a result."

"How do you know that, Father?"

"It is always the cadets they're hardest on who are the ones to watch. They are pushing to see who has leadership qualities and who doesn't. If a young man can't take the pressure, he's not going to be fit to lead. Command means pressure and stress. They've got to find out who can hold up and keep his head under it."

"I see what you mean. I still don't like it," laughed George.

"No one does. But stress is what fashions leaders.—Well, I had better get out of here," added Charles, rising. "You're supposed to be confined. We don't want anyone thinking I'm breaking the rules."

"You don't have anything to worry about," George said. "You outrank Lieutenant Forbes."

"Perhaps. But you'll never catch me using that fact unfairly, or my credibility and yours would both be undercut. Lieutenant Forbes has to have my support too. Everything through channels, you know."

"Thanks for coming by, Father. I needed the dose of encouragement."

Again father and son saluted. Then Charles left George alone again and returned to his own cabin.

20
The Will of God

◆◆◆

*A*s Amanda and Sister Hope made their way back over the hills, they talked casually about many things. Again the subject of the chalet's ministry came up. Amanda was more curious than she realized about the spiritual aspect of the sisters' activities. She found questions popping out of her mouth she had not planned. Eventually her questions led down a path she would not have anticipated.

"But what is it you want people to do when they come here?" she asked. "What do you tell them?"

"We encourage people to do only one thing," replied Sister Hope.

"What is that?" asked Amanda.

"The will of God."

Amanda took in the words as if there was nothing so unusual about them. She did not notice how accustomed she had already become to the spiritual outlook of those around her.

"But that is so general," she said. "What exactly do you tell each person?"

"That she must discover for herself," replied Hope. "God's specific will for every person isn't necessarily the same. There is an individual will which God speaks into every hungry heart."

"How does someone know what it is for them?"

"'Lord, what do you want me to do?' is the prayer we pray at the chalet," Hope explained. "We encourage all who come likewise to pray those words. More than merely pray them—to live by them. If we had a creed, which we do not, it would be summarized by those eight words."

Amanda took in the statement thoughtfully. It sounded just like something her father would say.

"Some of the sisters arrived much like you—lost and alone," Hope went on. "They found that God's will for them was to remain with us so that they might pass on the ministry which they received."

"What do you think God's will is for me?" asked Amanda.

"You will have to find that out by asking him, Amanda, and by searching your own heart."

"But . . . but that is not something I know how to do."

"It is something we all must learn."

Amanda paused briefly. Then, without having planned it, said, "My father and mother tried to teach me. You're a lot like my mother, actually. I don't suppose I was particularly receptive to their efforts."

"Many young people would say the same," rejoined Sister Hope.

"For some reason it doesn't sound so bad coming from you."

"Another statement many young people would agree with."

"Why?"

"They find words of instruction not nearly so odious coming from another as from their own parent."

Amanda nodded. "Now that you mention it," she said, "I probably would have become angry with my mother for talking about the will of God."

"Two different people can say the exact same words, but from one the response will be reflection and soul-searching, while the very same words from a parent might rouse annoyance and irritation. It has always seemed illogical and silly to me, but then I am not in a position to under—"

Hope stopped abruptly. That part of her story, she decided, would be best left until later.

"Another reason it does not seem so bad to you now," she went on after a moment, "is because you are beginning to *want* to know what to do more than before. Hunger makes a world of difference. Probably there was a time, if as you say you were not altogether receptive, when you were less than enthusiastic about the spiritual training they were trying to give you. Am I right?"

"Less than enthusiastic would be putting it mildly," replied Amanda.

"But if your father and mother tried to teach you," Hope ventured cautiously, "it may be from them, even now, that you could most effectively learn about the will of God as we were talking about earlier."

"Why do you say that?"

"Because such is God's way. It is the best method for learning. Many are not fortunate enough to have parents who train them in God's principles. They must learn of God's will elsewhere. But those whose parents do attempt to teach the things of God should learn from that primary source of training before they go elsewhere for spiritual counsel. Your own mother and father no doubt planted many seeds within you and prayed for you—"

The words made Amanda bristle momentarily. Even now, she did not like the thought of her parents praying for her.

Sister Hope saw the reaction and stopped. She had no desire to press it. A brief silence followed.

"Did you learn of God's will from *your* parents?" Amanda asked, trying to divert the conversation into other channels.

Hope smiled. Amanda thought it was a sad, though not discontented, smile.

"No, my dear," she answered at length. "I am afraid it was by other means that it was necessary for me to learn it."

"Yet you say I ought to learn it from my parents?"

"It is always the best way, my dear. There are other means to learn God's will, of course. God uses a variety of means to teach us the intricacies of seeking his will in our lives. As young people grow, God brings them many teachers and counselors and friends in addition. This is a healthy part of the maturing process. But if one has the opportunity, there is no *greater* way than learning of one's heavenly Father from one's earthly father and mother. Many do not have that opportunity. Those who do ought not to squander it."

Amanda was quiet. Certain places within her were growing uncomfortable. It was time to talk about something else.

Suddenly she realized she had not yet heard the rest of Sister Hope's story.

"But how could I have forgotten!" Amanda said. "I wanted to hear what happened to you in London after you left the mission board."

Sister Hope laughed. "It is a long story," she said. "Perhaps we ought to postpone it until another time. We're almost home."

"You won't forget?"

"From the sound of your voice, I doubt you will let me!"

21

Reading Night

When they arrived back at the chalet, the sun was setting. The moment they walked in, the long day suddenly caught up with Amanda. She flopped into a chair in front of the fireplace. When supper was called, she found herself nearly too exhausted to pull herself to her feet and shuffle to the table.

"How are your legs?" asked Sister Gretchen.

"Worn out!" moaned Amanda. "I am not used to such exercise."

The warm meal with the sisters, however, revived her spirits considerably. It was reading night, and though she could hardly keep her eyes open, she would not miss it for anything. She had looked forward to it all day.

After cleaning up the dishes, they adjourned into the sitting room, where Gretchen had a fire blazing nicely in the hearth. They gathered around in chairs and couches. Sister Hope brought in a tray with two teapots, then returned for a tray of cups. Ten minutes later everyone was settled and cozy, warm cups in their hands, and ready for the evening's literary adventure.

They were just finishing up a book written in 1875 by the Scotsman who was one of Amanda's father's favorite authors, though she did not at present make the connection.

Sister Anika, who had been reading this particular volume to the others, picked it up, found her place, and continued where she had last left off. She read for perhaps an hour, then concluded with the following words:

That same night Mrs. Catanach also disappeared.

A week after, what was left of Lord Lossie was buried. Malcolm followed the hearse with the household. Miss Horn walked immediately behind him on the arm of the schoolmaster.

Lady Florimel wept incessantly for three days; on the fourth she looked out on the sea and thought it very dreary; on the fifth she found a certain gratification in hearing herself called the marchioness; on the sixth she tried on her mourning dress and was pleased; on the seventh she went with the funeral and wept again; on the eighth came Lady Bellair, who on the ninth carried her away.

To Malcolm she had not once spoken.

Mr. Graham left Portlossie.

Miss Horn took to her bed for a week.

Mr. Crathie removed his office in the House, took upon himself the function of steward as well as factor, had the staterooms dismantled, and was master of the place.

Malcolm helped Stoat with the horses, and did odd jobs for Mr. Crathie. From his likeness to the old marquis, as he was still called, the factor had a favour for him, firmly believing the said marquis to be his father, and Mrs. Stewart his mother. Hence he allowed him a key to the library, of which Malcolm made good use.

The story of Malcolm's plans, and what came of them, requires another book.

The chalet fell silent for a few moments.

Suddenly everyone was aware again of the blackness of the night outside the windows, and that the evening had advanced. A few heads began to look about, expecting Sister Anika to go on.

Slowly it began to dawn on one, then another, that she was *not* going on.

"What—that's not the end!" cried Sister Regina.

"That is it," said Anika, who now closed the book with a flourish of finality.

"But I want more!"

"It is as he says," rejoined Anika, "the rest of the story requires another book."

"Then let's start it immediately!" Regina insisted. "That ending was too abrupt."

"I thought we were going to read something older next, from the eighteenth century," said Sister Marjolaine.

"Hadn't someone suggested *Robinson Crusoe*?" Hope asked.

"But we can't leave off Malcolm's story now," pled Regina. "Please, we *have* to read the next one!"

"Do we have it in the library?" asked Agatha.

"I believe so," Anika replied.

"I don't think we had better continue with *anything* else just now," Hope said, "or we shall lose our dear Amanda."

"I am still awake!" Amanda objected drowsily from her chair.

"Yes, but I've been watching those heavy eyelids of yours!"

"Well then, we shall have time to think about the books that have been suggested before next time," Marjolaine laughed. "And I am ready to make acquaintance with my bed too, along with Amanda!"

22

Telegram

$\mathcal{T}$he communiqué which arrived at Nr. 42 Ebendorfer Strasse in Vienna contained unexpected news.

"I was certain Matteos would find out something," said Hartwell Barclay enthusiastically, handing the telegram around the table. Ramsay scanned it quickly.

REPORT FROM SWISS BORDER INDICATES CROSSING OF TWO WOMEN, ONE ANSWERING DESCRIPTION SUPPLIED, AT COMO. PASSPORTS IN NAMES GERTRUT OSWALD, AUSTRIAN, AND GRETCHEN REINHARDT, SWISS. DESTINATION UNKNOWN.

"Switzerland!" exclaimed Ramsay. "What possible reason would she have to cross the Swiss border?"

"Obviously because Switzerland is neutral," replied Mrs. Halifax. "It is, however, a curious change in the direction of her travels," she added, her brow wrinkling in thought.

"No matter," said Barclay. "This means she is not yet back to England."

"*If* she is still in Switzerland," said Ramsay.

"I have a feeling she is," rejoined Barclay. "This companion of hers was carrying a Swiss passport. Does the name mean anything to you?"

Ramsay shook his head. "As far as I know, Amanda has never been to Switzerland before. Why do you say *companion*? Perhaps they just crossed the border at the same time."

"Matteos seems to indicate there is more to it than mere coincidence."

"Nevertheless, the other name means nothing to me."

"As long as she does not reach France," Barclay went on, "I think our chances of nabbing her remain excellent. I shall notify Matteos to follow up on this lead immediately. Interrogations at the border and with railway personnel at the Milan station ought to reveal the destination."

"I was just in Milan."

"Yes, and it appears you shall have to return."

"But I did not find a trace of her," insisted Ramsay.

"It would appear she was closer than you realized."

"We don't know that," argued Ramsay, not appreciating the implication.

"If they crossed the border in Como, they had to have taken the train north from Milan. If we can learn their destination, Matteos will see to the rest."

23

New Story and Discussion

♦♦♦

*L*ater that week the sisters and their guest gathered for another evening of reading at the Chalet of Hope.

During the intervening days there had been a great deal of discussion, and most favored the continuation of the story recently completed.

"All right, so is it decided that we will continue on with the sequel?" said Marjolaine.

"Yes . . . yes," chimed in several voices at once.

"I thought so," she laughed. "I must admit, I am in agreement. We did have it in our library, I am happy to say. In fact, I have it right here."

Sister Marjolaine pulled out the volume and opened it to the first page. She began reading immediately:

It was one of those exquisite days that come in every winter, in which it seems no longer the dead body, but the lovely ghost of summer. Such a day bears to its sister of the happier time something of the relation the marble statue bears to the living form; the sense it awakes of beauty is more abstract, more ethereal; it lifts the soul into a higher region than will summer day of lordliest splendour. It is like the love that loss has purified.

Such, however, were not the thoughts that at the moment occupied the mind of Malcolm Colonsay. Indeed, the loveliness of the morning was but partially visible from the spot where he stood— the stable-yard of Lossie House, ancient and roughly paved . . .

"Have you ever noticed how many of the Scotsman's books open with some discussion of the weather?" interrupted Sister Anika.

"I have noticed that, now that you mention it," rejoined Sister Hope.

"I have wondered if it was a means he found comfortable of getting into the mood of his setting, as an author himself, I mean, before actually beginning with his story."

"A plausible theory."

"My favorite is the curate's beginning," Anika went on. "*A swift gray November wind had taken every chimney of the house for an organ-pipe, and was roaring in them all at once, quelling the more distant and varied noises of the woods, which moaned and surged like the sea.*"

"I must say, I am impressed," said Marjolaine. "Do you have the whole book memorized!"

Anika laughed. "No, only the first little bit. I am fond of openings and first lines."

"That is a good one," said Regina. "It sets a mood instantly."

"And Annie's is a great one too," continued Anika. "*—The farmyard was full of the light of a summer noontide. Nothing can be so desolately dreary as full strong sunlight can be. Not a living creature was to be seen in all the square enclosure.*"

"We won't have to read ever again," laughed Sister Gretchen. "Sister Anika can quote our books from memory!"

As Amanda listened, not only to the book itself, but to the tangential and spontaneous discussions that arose, she was reminded how similar the whole mental environment here was to Heathersleigh. Her father and mother discussed everything too, and could never read a story for long without pausing for comment.

"Back to the book," laughed Marjolaine. She began again.

> The yard was a long and wide space, with two-storied buildings on all sides of it. In the centre of one of them rose the clock, and the morning sun shone red on its tarnished gold. It was an ancient clock, but still capable of keeping good time—good enough, at least, for all the requirements of the house, even when the family was at home, seeing it never stopped, and the church clock was always ordered by it.
>
> It not only set the time, but seemed also to set the fashion of the place, for the whole aspect of it was one of wholesome, weather-beaten, time-worn existence . . .

As she read, Amanda took in Sister Marjolaine's features. She was the smallest of the sisters, about three inches less than five feet in height, and of slightly built frame, with high-pitched voice to match. A stranger, first hearing her speak or seeing her from some distance, might almost take her for a child. Yet already Amanda had come to recognize her as one of the most level-headed and mature women at the chalet. In fact, she was thirty-nine years of age and had been here longer than all but two or three others. Her wavy hair of light brown was parted in the middle and combed down on each side, bordering a face of creamy white complexion, out of which shone two expressive eyes of dark brown. Her mannerisms, like her stature, were dainty. Her mind, however, was just the opposite, expansive and always reaching higher. How well-suited indeed she was for this place she had made her home. In her presence one always had the sense of walking through high mountainous mental vistas, from which she was ever peering to see farther and farther. Her mind never dwelt in valleys but made its home in the high places of thought and imagination.

Again Amanda's attention came back to the book and Sister Marjolaine's voice.

> . . . One of the good things that accompany good blood is that its possessor does not much mind a shabby coat. Tarnish and lichens and water-wearing, a wavy house-ridge, and a few families of worms in the wainscot do not annoy the marquis as they do the city man who has just bought a little place in the country. An old tree is venerable, and an old picture precious to the soul, but an old house, on which has been laid none but loving and respectful hands, is dear to the very heart. Even an old barn door, with the carved initials of hinds and maidens of vanished centuries, has a place of honour in the cabinet of the poet's brain. It was centuries since Lossie House had begun

110

to grow shabby—and beautiful; and he to whom it now belonged was not one to discard the reverend for the neat, or let the vanity of possession interfere with the grandeur of inheritance.

Sister Marjolaine paused. Now it was her turn—always the prerogative of the reader—to reflect upon what she had just read.

The discussions which accompanied the reading of most books under the chalet's roof doubled or tripled the time it took to get through them, and doubled or tripled the enjoyment of the literary experience.

"Don't you appreciate the authors who aren't in such a hurry to get on with the story?" she said after a moment. "It is as Sister Anika pointed out—beginning with the weather and setting the mood. I love a nice slow opening. Some might complain, I suppose, at the leisurely pace. But don't you enjoy this diversion he makes, discussing the beauty and value of old things?"

Sister Marjolaine read again the description about old things.

"But it might have to do with the story, you know," said Agatha. "You know how clues planted early aren't recognized for clues until later."

"True enough," rejoined Marjolaine. "Yet at the same time, the men and women who wrote in the last century didn't mind pausing in mid-narrative simply to reflect on something they were interested in, just like we do when we stop to talk about what we read. To my mind it makes their books so much richer and more varied."

"But the Scotsman is a masterful planter of clues."

"Then we shall just have to keep our eyes on these and see if he does anything with them later on," said Sister Marjolaine. Again she continued on, this time reading uninterrupted for an hour.

When at last she closed the volume with a bookmark in place and set it on her lap, the story was well begun. A few contented sighs sounded. Sister Hope rose.

"More tea anyone?" she asked. "I think I shall brew another pot."

"How did these readings and discussions come about among you?" asked Amanda. "My parents used to read aloud in my family too. But then I suppose I sort of outgrew it."

"Outgrew reading?" Marjolaine exclaimed in her high soprano. "Impossible. Some people lose interest, but you can never *outgrow* a good book."

"That wasn't exactly what I meant," Amanda replied. "I think I began to find my father's intrusions irritating."

"Do you mean he interrupted stories to talk about them—like we do?"

Amanda nodded.

"And you didn't like it?" Marjolaine asked. "Why ever not?"

Amanda shrugged.

"It is the discussions that make it so enjoyable," said Anika.

"But, Sister Marjolaine, what about Amanda's question about how we began our reading nights?" Hope called out from the kitchen. "I would like to hear how you would answer it."

24

Heart of a Giant

◆ ◆ ◆

A silence fell through the large room. For a few moments the only sounds heard were the crackling of the fire and an occasional chink of cup or saucer from the kitchen. At last Sister Marjolaine began to speak again, though in a more thoughtful and subdued voice than before.

"You may have noticed, Amanda," she said at length, "that I am quite small."

"You are . . . shorter than average, I suppose," said Amanda. "I thought no more about it than how tall I am, or any of the others. Everyone's different."

"Exactly," replied Marjolaine. "It is no more important than that I have brown hair. But when I was young I considered my shortness a defect. From my earliest memory I thought there was something wrong with me."

"Oh, but I think it's delightful," said Amanda. "You are very pretty."

Sister Marjolaine smiled. "Thank you. I am very thankful for my stature now. But as a child that was certainly not how I felt. You see I came from a family of four boys and two girls. All my brothers are great towering men, as is my father. My sister is of more modest height, though of course she stands a head above me, and my mother is large. So what was I to think when I was young except that I was odd, out of step, the black sheep, the ugly duckling? In fact, I was so tiny as a child that for many years my parents actually considered that perhaps I was a dwarf or midget, though I had none of the other physical manifestations."

She paused briefly as Sister Hope set a pot of fresh tea on the table in front of the fireplace, then returned to the kitchen for another.

"My father was not a mean man," Sister Marjolaine continued, "but he had little use for me. I was an oddity. He had his sons to occupy him. I suppose my mother loved me, yet I knew I was odd in her eyes too. So it could not be helped that I thought of myself almost as not one of the family like the rest. Later, I wondered if I had been adopted and they hadn't told me—adopted, perhaps, from a band of gypsy dwarfs passing through our village. Yet even if that were true, it didn't stop me from thinking of myself as a mistake on the human family tree, an evolutionary blunder. I don't know whether you believe in evolution, Amanda. Actually, I don't know whether I believe in it myself! But if you subscribe to such a theory, that explains how I saw myself— as an evolutionary mistake.

"For one who is not tiny, it is impossible to describe how shortness affects every aspect of life. People cast you odd looks. In a crowd you can see almost nothing. Everyone looks down to talk to you. Shelves are too high. You must crane your neck up to talk to people. You are out of step with *everything* in life. It never dawned on me that God might have made me the way I am *intentionally*. Had someone told me such a thing, I would have laughed in their very face. Nor did I yet know that everyone has *something* about which they feel exactly as I felt about my shortness, something they do not like about how they look, something they would change if they could. I would learn these truths eventually, of course. And how I began to learn them was through books."

Sister Hope appeared again, this time with a second pot of steaming tea, and the story was interrupted once more for a few minutes.

"I always loved books," Marjolaine began again after fresh tea was poured. "I dreamed and imagined myself in the stories I read. But as I grew older, I found that I began to grow from them as well."

"Grow . . . how do you mean?" asked Amanda.

"At first I read just for fun, to escape to faraway places and forget my own miseries for a while. When I was a little girl, books helped me pretend I was someone else. In my dream world I could be happy when reading and forget that tiny little Marjolaine Hedvige was funny looking—a mistake that no one could possibly care about.

"Then came a moment of great revelation, a moment that changed my whole life. I was fifteen at the time and was going through a book of fairy tales. The story I was reading in the book was not exactly a fairy tale, because it was about a young man, French as am I, from a village in the French Alps not so very far from my own hometown. There were no fairies in the story, though perhaps it was a fairy tale after all, because there was a very mean and terrible dragon."

"Tell us the story!" said Sister Anika.

"You have all heard it before!" laughed Marjolaine.

"I haven't," said Amanda.

"Perhaps I shall tell it again on one of our reading nights, then. But it must be dark and stormy."

"Yes, yes!" clamored the others. "You have never heard a scary story like Sister Marjolaine can tell it on a stormy night."

"This night is much too calm for a tale like that!" said Marjolaine. "And I mustn't lose my point. I am telling Amanda *my* story, not the tale of Michel Archenbaud."

"Promise that I shall hear it, then," said Amanda.

"I promise. But back to the heroine of tonight's story—which is *me*." The most delightful giggle erupted out of Marjolaine's mouth as she said the words.

"So I was reading the story of Michel and the dragon," she continued. "I suppose to tell you my story I shall have to tell you a little of Michel's story too. And that is just this—Michel had to save the entire valley from the dragon's wrath because, like all dragons, this particular one was terrible and ugly and wicked. I don't know why there aren't nice dragons in stories from time to time. Perhaps I shall have to write a fairy tale about a nice dragon. But in any case, the dragon bothering Michel's village was a normal and very wicked creature.

"Finally the dragon was about to swoop down and breathe his fire on every house and destroy them all and leave the whole village in ruins when Michel Archenbaud strode up to the dragon's lair on the mountain, drew out his sword, stood in the mouth of the cave, and shouted into the blackness.

" 'I can feel your evil breath, Dragon!' Michel cried out. 'I know you are in there. Come out and prove you are no coward, for today I shall kill you!'

"Before long Michel heard puffs of fire and the tromping of steps from inside the cave. Slowly they came closer and closer. Gradually he felt warmth breezing toward him, not a pleasant warmth as from a cheery fire inside a cottage, but a noxious warmth, and he knew he was smelling the dragon's foul, fiery breath. At length he saw the dragon's two glowing eyes gleaming out of the blackness.

" 'What feeble squeak did I hear!' hissed the dragon. 'Did some little mouse dare threaten me?'

" 'You heard the voice of Michel Archenbaud say he was about to kill you!' shouted Michel into the dragon's face.

" 'You!' taunted the dragon, clomping forward another few steps. The end of his green nose now became visible. Out of its two wide black nostrils puffed grey smoke. 'You are the tiniest man I have ever seen. You are smaller than the boys in your village. You are a mere dwarf. You could not kill a fly!'

"A great roar sounded from the dragon's mouth at these last words. Hot flames spewed out of his nostrils like red waves of water, swirling about the cave and out toward the entrance. They singed Michel's feet. But he bravely stood fast.

" 'Perhaps I am tiny,' he replied. 'But inside my chest I have the heart of a giant because I believe in myself. And inside my head I have the brain of wisdom because I have read the books of a hundred learned men. But you, Dragon, have a heart of stone and a brain the size of a pea. And it is with my heart and my brain that I shall defeat you, not my height. Your size may be fifty times mine, but my sword shall plunge through your wicked skin because my heart and my brain are greater than you.' "

"What happened next?" Amanda asked.

"Michel killed the dragon and saved the village," replied Marjolaine. "That's what happened in the story of Michel Archenbaud."

There was a short pause. Everyone was quiet. A brief gust of wind blew against the window. Amanda shivered but waited, engrossed, for Sister Marjolaine to go on.

"In *my* story, something else happened," she said. "You see, all the time I had been reading, in my imagination I had pictured Michel as a great warrior, as the tallest man in his village. Never in my wildest thoughts did I think he could be a short man . . . like me. When I read those startling words *You are the tiniest man I have ever seen*, I was so shocked I could not believe my eyes. I had to read them over and over again. The hero, the warrior, the dragon-slayer—a tiny little man, the village dwarf. And when the next words came . . . *it is with my heart and my brain that I shall defeat you* . . . I felt a great gong explode inside me. It was an instant when all of life changed for tiny little Marjolaine Hedvige."

Again she paused thoughtfully.

"Suddenly I realized that perhaps I could defeat my own dragon too. My dragon didn't breathe smoke and fire. But he lived deep in a dark place just like the dragon of the tale—the cave of my very own heart."

"What was your dragon?" asked Amanda.

"My dragon was my own doubts and fears, and feeling that I was a mistake. Suddenly I thought that perhaps I might slay those doubts too, with my *heart* and with my *brain*! Why could I not have the heart of a giant, just like Michel Archenbaud? I too had read books. Why could I not have the brain of learned men?

"I did not, at fifteen years of age, suddenly become brave and courageous and strong like Michel. But I *began* to grow, because I determined to believe in myself as he did. I knew there had been a change. I slowly began to believe in myself, because I saw that I could stand *taller* on the inside than I may have looked on the outside, just like brave little Michel of the fairy tale. I saw that my heart and my brain could soar with the birds, could climb the high mountain peaks, could dare open dark caves within myself, could imagine and dream high things, and think lofty thoughts. I saw that my thoughts and imagination *could* be tall. And that was a greater kind of tallness than how big my body was. Who wouldn't rather be an imaginative, tall-thinking, happy tiny person than a dull-witted, clumsy, unthinking giant?"

A few of the sisters chuckled. Sister Marjolaine went on.

"During the next years my reading changed. I wanted to grow and learn—to stretch my brain and heart, so that I could get taller and taller. Taller *inside* . . . taller in my thoughts, in my imagination. And I began to feel taller too—inside, I mean. Gradually I began to see that people around me every day, whose *bodies* were taller than mine, were *not* as tall as I was on the inside, because they had not explored mountain regions of thinking and imagination. They had not read the books of a hundred learned men. They had let themselves become content with their own tiny brains, and thus those brains did not grow and stretch and expand and become taller. Strange as it may seem to say, I began to feel sorry for those I met who were not reading and growing and learning and stretching, who were not taking their hearts and brains on journeys to the high places that minds and hearts are meant to explore.

"And finally, my dear Amanda, would you like to know the miracle that happened?" Marjolaine asked.

"Yes, yes, I would," replied Amanda. She had been sitting on the edge of her seat listening attentively, as had all the others. Sister Marjolaine was indeed a wonderful storyteller.

"I woke up one day to realize that the most astonishing change had taken place. I suddenly realized that I was *thankful* for my size.

"You can imagine how shocked I was. I could not believe it! *Happy* . . . me? Because I was tiny!"

Just to hear her tell it so exuberantly made all the sisters smile as they listened.

"Then I began to laugh!" Marjolaine went on, giggling as she spoke. "And I laughed with pure joy and happiness for several minutes because I realized I was truly *happy* that I was small—physically small, I mean. I would not have traded sizes with anyone. It was my stature that caused me to read in the way I did. It was my shortness that helped me see that bigness of heart and tallness of brain are so much more important. Had I not been tiny, I might never have discovered these things. You cannot imagine how much I now treasure the words 'In my weakness I am strong.' "

"But that still doesn't tell Amanda how you began our literary evenings," laughed Sister Hope.

Marjolaine's face fell playfully, and she tried to frown. "I do turn everything into a story, don't I? Shame on me! Then I shall try to finish quickly.

"I have continued to read all my life," she went on. "Books are so very special to me. Every book I read, every character I meet, I grow and learn from. I love to meet new people in books. They make me think and learn. For you see, I am still trying to grow taller inside, with that part of me that thinks and imagines and dreams and loves. That part of me I hope will keep growing taller and taller to all eternity.

"Naturally I want to share my love for books and characters and growth and getting taller and the imagination of a hundred learned men with my friends. So when I came to the chalet, I asked Sister Hope if I could read a book aloud one evening a week. That was more than ten years ago. Now we do it twice a week, and sometimes in wintertime even more often. I think we have all learned to climb a little higher on our heart-mountains together. Books and stories and characters help us look inside ourselves. They help us decide the kind of people we want to be, and how tall we want to become."

She fell silent. Sister Regina now spoke up. "When I first made Malcolm's acquaintance," she said, "about whom we have recently been reading, you cannot imagine the impact it had on me, just as little Michel Archenbaud did for Sister Marjolaine."

"In what way?" Amanda asked.

"I wanted to be like him," Regina replied.

"But he is a man."

"So was Michel Archenbaud," said Marjolaine. "But from him I learned about big hearts and tall brains."

"I want to be like Malcolm in *character*," Regina added.

"Men of character are equally good role models for women as are women of character," said Marjolaine.

"Who else do we try to pattern our lives after than the Lord Jesus, the perfect man?" added Gretchen.

Again silence fell. A few yawns went around the room, indicating that the pleasant evening was nearly at its end and that cozy feather beds were calling out to their owners.

"Unless I am mistaken," said Sister Hope, "the temperature has been falling as we've been sitting here."

Gretchen leapt up from her chair and ran to the front door. She opened it to the night.

"It's snowing!" she exclaimed.

25

Orphaned Kid

*S*now did indeed fall through the night, though still not in the huge quantities winter would eventually bring. When Amanda awoke and gazed out her window the following morning, a fresh blanket of three or four inches covered the landscape.

A giddy delight seized her. She jumped out of bed, dressed hurriedly, grabbed her coat, and ran downstairs. She saw no one around, although a fire in the stove was already heating up the kitchen.

Amanda ran outside into the cold morning. The sky was a pale blue. The clouds had passed with the night and the temperature was well below freezing. The sun had not yet made his appearance for the day.

But the eastern horizon was bright and he was obviously on his way.

Amanda charged straight into the virgin white, heedless of the cold and her thin boots. She ran recklessly through it, kicking up fresh bursts of powder with her feet, laughing like a child. The spontaneous outburst of giggling enthusiasm, however, proved of short duration. She found both hands and feet frozen within a minute or two. Amanda turned and made a dash back for the house.

She ran inside shivering and laughing all at once.

"Brrr!" she cried. "It's freezing out there!"

"It certainly is," Sister Marjolaine's voice answered. "Come into the kitchen—it's nice and warm."

Amanda stomped her feet to shake off the snow, then hurried toward the stove, holding out her hands over it.

"You look like you could use some tea."

"Y-y-yes," stammered Amanda with quivering lips. "I don't know w-what I w-was thinking."

"Snow always does that. You can't help yourself. You weren't even the first one out."

"I wasn't? I saw nobody."

"Didn't you notice the footprints across the snow?"

Amanda ran to the window. "You're right," she cried, "and heading straight for the barn. Sister Galiana, no doubt."

"There is a mama goat whose time is getting close," now said Sister Hope, descending the stairs behind her. "If I know Sister Galiana, her first order of business this morning was to check on the mother-to-be."

Gradually the other sisters came down in ones and twos until all but Sister Galiana were enjoying morning cups of tea and chocolate, while Sister Marjolaine finished setting the breakfast things on the table.

Galiana did not appear until well after the others had finished breakfast. She walked into the house carrying a tiny white kid in her arms, obviously newly born. She had a finger in its mouth, upon which it was sucking violently.

"Oh . . . it's so tiny and cute and cuddly!" erupted a chorus of feminine exclamations.

Galiana had tears in her eyes. At first the others thought they were from happiness. The sisters jumped up from the table and ran toward the door to cluster about and fondle the new arrival.

"And nearly frozen to death," said Galiana. "Would someone please put a pan of milk on the stove and find one of our feeding bottles."

Hands and feet scurried to the kitchen in response.

"You look frozen yourself. What happened?" asked Hope.

"I don't know," replied Galiana. "When I got to the barn to check on this poor little baby's mother, she was gone. I can't imagine how she got out or why. But that loose latch we've been meaning to fix was the culprit. The door was open—"

Gretchen moaned. "Oh no—I'm sorry. It was on my list for today!"

"The goat must have gotten out just after the first of the snow," Galiana went on. "I could barely see the footprints under the two inches that had fallen since. I searched high and low and just found this little kid about ten minutes ago, buried in the snow, her mother on top of her to give what was left of her body's warmth. I think I reached her just in time."

"And the mother?" asked Hope.

"The mother is dead," Galiana replied.

"Oh . . ." went around a few gasps.

"It's my fault for the latch!" Gretchen wailed, her eyes filling with tears.

"You can't blame yourself," Sister Agatha said. "I have lived in these mountains all my life, and sometimes animals do foolish things."

"But—"

"What's good for the sparrow is good for the goat," added Agatha. "God is sovereign over the beasts, and not even latches or barns can change that . . . or sisters with more to do than they can keep up with."

"I will try to remember. Thank you, Sister Agatha," Gretchen said.

"The mother goat saved her own kid's life," said Galiana. "So we must nurse this little one to health."

"She will now depend on us," said Hope, bringing a bottle with cold milk until that on the stove was warm. "We shall do our best to care for it and feed it," she added, then gently stuck the nipple into the tiny mouth. Galiana pulled out her finger. "Of course we can never replace her parents," Hope added, "but we will do our best."

"Maybe you will even do better," said Amanda innocently.

Sister Hope cast her a look of question. "What can you possibly mean?" she asked.

"You'll feed her and keep her warm and protect her, just like when you found me all alone and took me in."

"You are hardly an orphan."

"But you are all loving me in ways my own parents didn't," Amanda replied. "So maybe it's for the best. I know I feel more love here than I did at home. Maybe the baby goat will too."

Sister Hope spun around. Her face was red. Her eyes flashed with fire.

"Don't you ever consider us a replacement for the greatest gift God has given you!" she said sternly.

Amanda scarcely recognized Hope's voice.

"I only said—"

"I heard what you said well enough, Amanda! I will not—"

Suddenly Sister Hope caught herself. She paused abruptly.

Every sister's eye was riveted on their mentor and older sister with astonishment at the outburst. Hope glanced from one to the other, around the room, speechless, suddenly realizing what she had done. Then just as suddenly she turned and hurried from the room.

"What did I do?" said Amanda. "I meant to say something good."

"You hit a little close to home," said Gretchen. "Certain things are very precious to Sister Hope's heart, and parents are the most precious of all. It is the greatest shame she can feel to be told she is providing something for another that they ought instead to be getting from their mother and father."

"I meant nothing by it."

"Perhaps there was more in your words than you realize, Amanda. There have been those whom Sister Hope has asked to leave the chalet for just that reason. She wants one's time here to be healing in the right way, not a replacement for home."

"But why would she send them away?" asked Amanda.

"She sent them back to their parents."

"I have only seen her eyes flash like that once before in all the years I have known her," said Marjolaine.

"What caused it?" asked Luane, who had never seen such an outburst during her brief stay at the chalet.

"We had a young lady with us," answered Marjolaine, "probably in her early twenties. It appeared she was going to remain for some time. One day she said to Sister Hope, 'My mother and I were not close. I could never feel as comfortable with her as I feel here. I don't even think my mother is a Christian. Would it be all right if I called you *Mother* while I am here?' "

"I remember the day well," Gretchen nodded.

"How did she answer?" asked Luane.

"Her eyes and face lit into the closest thing to rage I have ever seen," replied Marjolaine.

"Righteous indignation, I would call it," Gretchen added.

" 'How dare you even think such a thing!' she cried at the unsuspecting girl," Marjolaine continued. " 'You have been given the most precious gift in all the world, whether or not your mother is a Christian. I will not have you cast that gift in the swine-pit of your youthful blindness. I would *never* usurp that most priceless of all relationships in the world.'

"The girl stood stunned. Yet in a way it was her own fault, wouldn't you say, Sister Gretchen? We had all spoken to her many times about her attitude toward her mother. But her heart was closed. She simply wouldn't listen."

"I take it," Luane asked, "that she did not remain long?"

" 'I want you down the mountain and on a train home by tomorrow, young lady,' Sister Hope said to her after she had calmed down. 'I want you to go home and beg your mother's forgiveness for your ungodly attitude toward her.' "

"What happened?" Amanda now asked.

"The young lady left. We never heard from her again," Gretchen replied. "Not everyone appreciates Sister Hope's bluntness at times, or is able to see the love that prompts it."

Ten minutes later Hope's soft footsteps could be heard descending the stairs. She came back into the room and approached Amanda. Her face and eyes were red with remorse and weeping.

"Amanda dear," she said, taking Amanda in her arms. "I am *so* sorry! I should not have been so harsh. Please forgive me."

She sat down at the table and poured herself a cup of tea.

"Do you remember when our conversation was diverted in other channels when we were walking back from Grindelwald?"

Amanda nodded.

"Perhaps now would be an appropriate time for me to tell you the rest of my own story. Certainly not to excuse my outburst—I would not do that. But what I have to say may at least in part explain it."

The other sisters remained seated around the large table. Sister Galiana, still holding the kid, walked into the spacious room and took a seat in front of the fireplace. Sister Anika followed her and replaced the first bottle of milk with a new warm one, then returned to the table.

When everyone was situated comfortably, Sister Hope began.

26
Unexpected Origins

You remember, I am sure," Sister Hope began, "my telling you about going to the mission office in London, thinking I would be sent off immediately to some foreign land?"

Again Amanda nodded.

"After being, as I thought, rejected by the mission, I was so despondent," Hope said. "I didn't know what was to become of me. Although it was kind of the woman to offer, especially to a stray who had just walked in her door, I couldn't imagine working at the mission office. I had no place to go, no place to stay, no friends in London. Well, there was one place I probably *could* have stayed, but I would sooner have slept on the streets than go back there."

"Why didn't you just go home?" Amanda asked.

A sad smile followed.

"*Home,*" repeated Hope. "You speak as one who has a home. But what does one such as myself do, alone in London, her hopes of the mission field dashed . . . if she has no home to return to?"

"I don't understand," said Amanda, confused.

"Amanda dear," said Sister Hope, "I was an orphan."

———— ◆◆◆ ————

When the baby was brought to the Wigham Street Orphanage in London, not a soul was able to offer the slightest clue as to her origins. Nothing was known but that a child had been left on the doorstep of the parish church of Bromley, whose vicar contacted the administrators of the institution and arranged for them to take her.

Inquiries were made, of course. All of Bromley heard of it, and many were the theories that circulated, some even attributing the child to wayward royal stock.

Eventually word began to spread that there was nothing either so mysterious or sinister about the affair. The rumor had it that the child's father had long since left England for wars in unknown parts and was presumed dead, and that the mother herself had not survived the night of birth. The baby's aunt, who already had more mouths to feed than she could afford, took the child to the church. A note was pinned to the dirty blanket in which she was wrapped with four words scrawled in a nearly illegible hand, no doubt the final dying request from one who had none: *Her name is Hope.*

Certain facts of the case corroborated the evidence. The vicar himself allowed that it was the most credible of all the stories that had been put forward, though nothing more was ever learned of the unknown aunt, or where the story had originated.

That she was an orphan was all but certain. No additional facts ever came to light. The vicar himself, an elderly gentleman, was gone to his final reward before the youngster was old enough to make inquiries herself. The aunt never surfaced. Eventually the incident was all but forgotten in Bromley.

The life of an orphan in 1870s London was neither an easy nor a pleasant one. But the fortunes of those girls who chanced to reside at Wigham Street were especially bitter. There was scarcely enough gruel provided to keep them alive, their labor was arduous, the bottom of a glass could not be seen through the drinking water, rats swarmed the place, which in winter was hardly warm enough to keep the insects in the walls alive, and no adult supervision prevented cruelties innumerable from being meted out on the young and helpless. Many were the nights its more pitiful inhabitants wept and shivered themselves to sleep. They lived not merely without hope, but without hope of ever having hope.

No worse hell could have been imagined for its inmates, and no socialist idealism of forward-thinking liberal politicians in Whitehall could ameliorate its multifold agonies.

In afteryears, Hope's only specific memory, because it recurred with such terrifying regularity, was that of lying awake at night, long after dark when everyone else was asleep, hearing scratching sounds in the walls. Gradually the noises came closer. As night deepened, the rats became bolder and bolder. Presently their busy feet could be heard scurrying all about the floor searching for crumbs of food. It sounded like an army of rats, even under her own bed.

Wide awake, she shivered under a thin blanket, hiding her head under it and drawing her feet up inside at the bottom of her sparse nightgown as best she could for fear the creatures would climb up the endposts and nibble on her toes.

She did not think to pray, like Annie in Bruce's garret, for pussy to come. The only cat little Hope was acquainted with was a mean and mangy alley tom who hated little girls as much as he did rats, and had left far more claw marks on the arms of the unsuspecting girls of the place than ever had the rats' teeth on their toes. So as she lay praying against the rats, she prayed just as desperately against Tom's appearance.

There was no salvation from the terror other than the long, slow approach of dawn, which usually resulted in the rats' disappearance and her own drifting off to sleep—a sleep rudely interrupted with a vigorous shaking and a volley of gruff orders not to sleep the day away.

It was a wonder she slept at all. Yet she did not get enough sleep upon such occasions to avoid getting drowsy at her afternoon work and sometimes falling asleep altogether. Such an occurrence always resulted in an awakening even more cross than the morning's, accompanied by a box on the ear by the female warden of the prison.

Hope grew from a baby to a child. Somehow she survived to become a girl of thirteen. She was one of the few who managed not to be completely embittered by the place, survived by keeping to herself, and, miraculously, somehow kept hoping that a better life would come to her when she was older.

How, she couldn't imagine. But she refused to let the dreams of something better die altogether. Even as a child, her name began to send roots down into the soil of that intrinsic desire toward goodness which has been implanted into every man and woman, but which so many allow to become hard and incapable of sustaining life. Thus did character begin to grow.

Thinking that perhaps her salvation had come, at thirteen she was moved to a girls' home in Birmingham. And it was indeed in certain ways an improvement over Wigham Street. Fires were warmer during the winter months, food slightly more plentiful, rats thankfully less so. But girls of seventeen are equally adept at inflicting cruelty on timid girls of thirteen as her elders had been in London.

Her misery therefore deepened. Where she had allowed herself to hope she might have friends, she now had none. Compassion, however, is a commodity infused into the human character by suffering. Little did young Hope know that she was being prepared even now for that highest calling of mankind and womankind—the giving of cups of cold water to a thirsty humanity. Caverns of compassion were being carved out within her, even as she cried herself to sleep, praying, after what fashion she was capable, for her tormentors.

But whereas her salvation had not come at thirteen, as she supposed, it did in fact arrive during her nineteenth year. She and several other of the girls were given permission to attend the tent meeting of a renowned revivalist being held within walking distance of the home. None were particularly interested, but any excuse to get away from the place for an evening was seized upon.

Her companions sat snickering at the preaching. But nineteen-year-old Hope's heart was seized with something the likes of which she had never known. Hope indeed now arose within her breast, hope of new life.

Only a week later she was on her way back to London by train, a place in which she had hoped never to set foot again. But now she had purpose and vision.

She was going to London to be a missionary!

Alas, it was too lofty a dream, and its shattering therefore all the more painful. As she walked the streets after leaving the Baptist Missionary Society, unconsciously her steps took her in the direction of Wigham Street.

An hour later she stood outside the orphanage where she had spent thirteen bleak and dismal years, gazing up at the stark grey stone walls, hearing an occasional shout or shriek or wail of pain from inside, knowing well what misery stalked its floors. She made sure she kept out of sight. The last thing she wanted was to be seen by someone who might recognize her. So many painful memories were hid behind those walls. She hated the place, yet it was one of the only two homes she had ever known.

Full of thoughts and emotions too deep and painful to think about, slowly she turned and began walking away. She had no place to go other than *away* from the Wigham Street Orphanage. She would sooner sleep in a deserted alley than seek refuge there.

Tears came. She could neither prevent them nor stop their

flow. Her thoughts began to return to the lady she had spoken with at the mission board office. Unconsciously her steps turned again in that direction.

"I will try to be willing, Lord," she prayed. "I will do whatever you want me to . . . but I *hate* London! Isn't there someplace you could use me? Anyplace but *here*!"

It was late in the afternoon when Mrs. Weldon looked up again from her desk and saw the same young woman standing before her from earlier. It was obvious she had been crying.

"Hello, my dear," she said.

"I . . . I have nowhere to go," said Hope, her eyes filling with tears. "I have decided to take the job you told me about. I don't have any training, like you said earlier, for anything—for being a missionary or anything else. But if you'll show me what to do, I will do my best."

Mrs. Weldon's heart smote her with tenderness toward the poor girl. She rose and approached.

"But I'm sorry," Hope went on, "I have no place to stay. I spent all my money just getting here. I was so sure that I would be able to . . ."

She glanced away.

"I understand, dear," said Mrs. Weldon, placing her two hands on Hope's shoulders. Suddenly her heart was strangely warmed to this nineteen-year-old waif who wanted to be a missionary.

"—you will come home with me tonight," she added.

Hope never forgot that simple gesture of hospitality, nor what a ministry was involved in a simple kind word to a lonely heart, especially when accompanied by a roof overhead, a warm meal, and a bed in which to spend the night.

———————— ♦♦♦ ————————

The chalet fell silent.

After a moment or two, Amanda rose, walked around the corner of the table, leaned down, and wrapped her arms about Sister Hope, who opened her arms and returned the embrace.

"I'm so sorry," said Amanda. "I had no idea. I didn't mean to hurt you by what I said earlier."

"Nor I you, Amanda dear. Thank you."

27

At Sea

$\mathcal{A}$ set of eyes hidden behind two cylinders of glass peered across the sea below.

From this vantage point high above the plateau on which the lighthouse was situated, their owner could make out the small convoy of five British vessels clearly enough. It looked like two standard cruisers, a battle cruiser, and two light cruisers.

No U-boats were in the vicinity. There was nothing to do but report the activity at the earliest possible opportunity. He could tell nothing of the destination of the five ships, though from intelligence reports that had come last week, he suspected the Mediterranean.

It would be useful if he could make positive identification of the vessels. These binoculars, however, weren't quite powerful enough.

He rose and walked across the small enclosure at the top of the tower. He would use the telescope.

As the HMS *Dauntless* steamed southward through the North Sea in the dawn hours of the second week of November of the year 1914, Sir Charles Rutherford of Heathersleigh in Devonshire could have no idea toward what fate his destiny was carrying him. Nor could he possibly realize to what an extent the fortunes of his older daughter, as well as his own, were bound up in the isolated stretch of England's eastern coastline they were now passing, from which their movements were being watched by his onetime colleague and friend Chalmondley Beauchamp. Indeed, had Beauchamp's eye been focused with pinpoint accuracy at this moment, he might have decried his former friend, whom the Fountain had not been as successful at recruiting as they had he himself, on deck at the bow of the lead cruiser, gazing ahead thoughtfully in the chill morning air. Commander Rutherford had noticed the unlit lighthouse onshore surrounded by a small cluster of buildings as he walked across the deck a few moments earlier. But he thought nothing of it.

Though Charles' brain was unaware of his fleeting proximity to the Fountain of Light's Yorkshire beachhead for its clandestine spy operation, his heart felt strange stirrings as they went.

Something told him that a dawn in his daughter's life was at hand, that years of prayers were about to strike root within her heart in more direct ways, and possibly had already begun.

Spontaneous prayer often arose within him for Amanda. But for some time it had been accompanied with heaviness of heart that no attempt to drum up praise and thankfulness had been able to combat.

They had been praying for so long, with no visible or apparent change. Faith on Amanda's behalf had become a commodity more and more difficult for him to come by as the years progressed, and nearly impossible since her letter of less than two months ago. The enormous satisfaction and thankfulness and personal friendship he felt with George and Catharine only deepened the discouragement he felt whenever he remembered their sister. If only, Charles could not help thinking, she could be with them now, during these wonderful years of young adulthood, to relish in and benefit from the maturing bonds of family relationship each of the other two enjoyed with him and Jocelyn. Even if Amanda came back someday, she had already missed so much of what the rest of them would treasure all their lives. Thought of it could make him weep. She had sacrificed so much on the fleeting altar of youthful independence.

Word of her hasty marriage had been like the blow of a thousand freight trains crashing into him, crushing what remained of his hope, grinding the dreams of his father's heart to powder beneath their cruel, thundering wheels. He had continued to pray but felt so like the man who cried unto the Lord, "I believe . . . help my unbelief."

Suddenly on this morning, however, as he and George departed Scapa Flow, he felt a new vibrancy of hope coming to life within him.

Hope!

How long since he had felt anything like true hope on Amanda's behalf? Whatever may have been happening within Amanda—and he didn't even know where she was or what impact the war was having on her—all at once God seemed to be answering his "help-my-unbelief" prayer.

"Oh, God . . . God," he sighed, *"what can I pray that I have not prayed a hundred times before. . . ?"*

As was so often the case, his prayers gave over to deep sighs of fatherly affection and entreaty to Amanda herself, which constantly intermingled with his anguished cries to their mutual Father.

"Amanda . . . Amanda," said Charles, "my dear Amanda . . . what will make you awake at last to the love in my heart for you. . . ?

"Wake her, Lord . . . wake her, I beseech you. Bring her home . . . at last bring her home."

He fell silent for a time, continuing to stare into the chilly morning with the breeze of the ship's motion on his face, encouraged to pray again with boldness. He recalled to mind Jesus' words to his disciples, "You have not, because you ask not."

"Continue, Lord," Charles began to whisper again, *"to send arrows of clarity into Amanda's heart and brain, flashes of insight and memory. Help her remember that life was good at Heathersleigh, that we loved her and that there was a time when she loved us. Help her remember the past as it really was, not as she has been told by those who would remold her memories and contort them into a fiction. Give her insight to recognize the wedge they have driven between her and us to lure her loyalty to them and thus satisfy their own pride.*

"Restore her memory accurately, Lord. Rescue her from this deception. Turn her heart toward home. Give her the courage to turn from the falsehood she has embraced. Open her mind with clarity to see that she has only been a pawn in the Fountain's hand."

As Charles prayed, his hope grew. With hope came a commitment to redouble his prayers and not to allow his newfound hope to fade.

"God," he said, praying now for himself, *"give me courage to pray believing that answers are already on the way to my daughter even before the words are out of my mouth.*

"Oh, Lord, I ask that you answer our prayers for Amanda, not on the basis of my own faith, which is so small even now, but on the basis of your faithfulness. I am so weak. Forgive me, Lord, for my unbelief—for my doubting and untrusting heart. But I know you are sovereign, and that your love for your wayward children—myself as well as Amanda—and your determination to bring them all home to your heart do not depend on my tiny faith, but are rooted in your faithfulness in the midst of our weakness."

He drew in a deep breath of the tangy salt air.

"I thank you, Father, for this mounting sense of hope you have given me. I thank you for the conviction that Amanda is already in the process of turning toward home. May it be swift, Lord. Send people to help her in her homeward journey. Send those who would be true friends to her prodigal heart and who would urge her homegoing. Fill her path with your people, Lord.

"Oh, God, cover my weakness with your perfect Fatherhood. May Amanda's recollection of my imperfect carrying out of my fatherly charge be no longer a source of resentment within her. May it turn her the more deeply to you, as all imperfect earthly fatherhood is intended to do.

"And may Amanda not only seek home, but may her heart turn toward you, dear Lord. Above all things, may she seek you as her Father. Teach her to trust you and love you far beyond what she ever will me. My fatherhood was strewn with mistakes, for I am but a weak man like all men, and an imperfect father like all earthly fathers. But you are the perfect Father.

"And I ask you to be the perfect Father to my dear Amanda."

Almost the same instant that his heart filled with peace and his lips became silent, Charles heard footsteps approaching behind him. He recognized their sound.

The form of a young midshipman strode up and stood beside him. The two stood gazing forward for a few moments of quiet contemplation.

"I went to your cabin," said George at length. "When you were not there, I knew where I would find you."

"You do know me well, my boy," smiled Charles affectionately.

"We have twenty minutes before drills begin. I hadn't seen you since we departed. I thought I would see how you are doing."

"Never better, George," replied Charles. "Nothing like the excitement of setting to sea!"

"What have you been thinking about up here?"

"The adventure you and I are embarking on," answered Charles. "And your mother, of course . . . and then I began praying for Amanda. How about you, George? What are *you* thinking about."

"Lieutenant Forbes keeps us too busy to think!" George laughed.

"I told you he was a good man!" rejoined his father.

"I suppose I am excited too," said George. "I cannot know what the future holds. But sailing at dawn stirs one's blood for adventure."

"Spoken like a true twenty-six-year-old!" laughed Charles. "Alas, we are not bound in search of gold on the Spanish main but to fight the Germans. Not so romantic in this modern day, I suppose, but necessary."

Father and son fell silent. Charles stretched his arm around George's powerfully built but slender frame, then gave his back two affectionate pats.

They stood another moment or two, then George spoke again.

"I suppose I ought to be getting back," he said.

"I'll see you this evening, George, my boy. Thanks for coming to find me—I appreciate it."

George turned and strode away, leaving Charles alone again at the bow. He glanced about to the right and left and drew in another deep breath. Nothing in all the world felt like sea air in the nostrils and lungs!

The lighthouse on shore had by now faded from his view.

28

Milan Again

*R*amsay Halifax scanned the menu of the Sans Souci Restaurant at the Eliseo Hotel in Milan. A few moments later he had ordered an expensive bottle of white wine to accompany *abbacchio alla cacciatora*.

He resented this whole business. He didn't know whom to be angrier at—Barclay or Amanda. But here he was at the mercy of both. It could not be helped. So he might as well enjoy himself to what extent was possible so far from anywhere. At least there were not yet too many reminders of the war here in Italy. He had telegrammed Adriane to see if she might join him. Her presence would certainly make the trip worthwhile. But he had heard nothing back.

Forty minutes later, as he was finishing his meal, he glanced up to see a man approaching the table.

"Are you Halifax?" the stranger asked in perfect English.

"I am. You must be Matteos."

"That's right."

He sat down opposite Ramsay and pulled out several papers.

"I have been working on, shall we call it, your difficulty," he said. "I have many contacts, in the governments of all the countries which may concern us, including Switzerland and France. Since notifying you of the crossing by train at the border north of Como, the party you are looking for has not appeared again."

"She is no *party*, you idiot, she is my wife."

"Barclay did not tell me you had a rude tongue," replied Matteos calmly, lifting one eyebrow toward Ramsay in annoyance. "No matter—my best information still places her in Switzerland."

"Where in Switzerland?"

"That you will have to find out on your own, Mr. Halifax. As you will see," he went on, unfolding a map of the region and spreading it out on the table across from Ramsay, "I have noted the likely train routes. From Como north, as you can see, the probable destination is Luzern. At that point they could either have gone north to Zurich or Basel, or south to Bern. I have circled the likely location as things stand at present."

Ramsay scanned the map briefly but was unimpressed.

"What good does a circle covering hundreds of square miles do me?" he exclaimed. "This map is useless."

"All investigations must start somewhere, Mr. Halifax. Yours began with nothing, as I understand it. Now there is this circle on this map. You must narrow it down."

"How?"

"By tracing the Reinhardt woman apparently traveling with your, er . . . *party*?"

He glanced toward Ramsay with another slow upturn of his eyebrow as he emphasized the word. Ramsay let it pass.

"If she is Swiss, in time she will be found," he added.

"Found . . . how?"

"I will arrange a meeting for you in Luzern with a resourceful fellow by the name of Fabrini Scarlino. He is half-Swiss, half-Italian, speaks both languages and every local dialect fluently, and is probably by this time in the employ of both the Entente and the Alliance to spy on one another. He is, shall we say, a very unusual man. He has far more contacts in Switzerland than I. Given enough time, he can find out almost anything. He has already been apprised of the situation, and should be at work on it even as we speak. I have done what I can. Now it will be up to the two of you."

"Is he a member of the Fountain?" asked Ramsay.

"He is a member of nothing," replied Matteos. "His only loyalty is to himself."

"Do you trust him?"

"Of course I don't trust him. He would slit my throat as soon as do me a favor. But as I say, he is extremely resourceful in such matters. For a price he can find anyone, or do anything. You will not be disappointed. You have money, I take it?"

"That will not be a problem."

"And a weapon?"

Now it was Ramsay's turn to eye the man carefully.

"I have a short-barrel nine-millimeter Luger," he answered after a moment.

Matteos took in the fact, nodded significantly, then looked Ramsay in the eye seriously.

"Make no mistake, Mr. Halifax," he said. "The man is dangerous. Watch yourself every moment. Do nothing to anger him. A Luger in your vest pocket must not lull you into a false sense of security."

"I've been around that type plenty of times before," replied Ramsay.

"I warn you—guard your tongue. A careless word to *him*, such as you have spoken to me this evening, and you will find yourself buried in next year's glacial pack in the Swiss Alps."

"Don't worry," insisted Ramsay, still too casually to suit his companion.

"Mr. Halifax . . . believe me, there is *no* one like Scarlino. I urge you, do not take my warnings lightly."

29

Dream Turned Nightmare
♦♦♦

A week passed at the Chalet of Hope. The snow gradually melted but was longer doing so than before.

The Alpine air filled with fragrant reminders that winter was nearly at hand and the next snows to fall would probably lie on the ground until April or May. Final prewinter chores of preparation were set about with increased diligence. The last of the feed and supplies for the animals was brought in and stored away, as well as provision for the human element of the chalet. Everyone worked hard, and most days ended in contented exhaustion. Sister Gretchen chopped several cords of firewood, reactivating several persistent blisters on both hands, but declared she never felt better than when her hands were stiff and her muscles ached from hard physical work.

But with the first major snowfall, which could now arrive anytime, all but the most essential outside activities—the most needful of which would be to keep walkways shoveled between house and barn and other outbuildings—would be curtailed. Then would arrive the season for dressing warm and catching up on reading, sewing, knitting, embroidery, and numerous inside projects. A large workroom they called the dairy, which sat next to the kitchen and opened to the outside in the direction of the barn, would continue to see some activity, namely cheese and butter production for another month.

Amanda contributed to these preparations for the winter months with energy and enthusiasm. Never had she worked so hard or enjoyed it so much. Several of the sisters noted that her strength was improved, and the robust color of health shone on her cheeks. How *good* it felt, Amanda thought, to sweat from honest activity, to push and strain and lift and carry to the limit of strength, then to bathe when the day's work was done and dress in a clean warm housedress, glowing with hard-earned fatigue. It was a new experience. She found herself relishing it.

One evening after supper, the ten sat before the fireplace, a few reading quietly, several others engaged in various needlework projects. Sister Luane, the only other temporary resident at the chalet, though she had now been in Wengen nearly a year, spoke up.

"Sister Hope," she said, "I have been curious ever since you told us last week about the orphanage and your going to work for the mission board . . . how you ended up here at the chalet."

Two or three of the other sisters looked up from their books and laps and glanced at one another. They knew it to be a painful story.

"It has been a long day," said Sister Gretchen. "Perhaps we might read from a devotional tonight and save that for another time." As she spoke, Gretchen looked over just in time to see Hope glance briefly toward Amanda, who was sitting beside her on the couch. Gretchen half suspected what her friend was thinking.

"No, Sister Gretchen," replied Hope. "Thank you . . . I know you are being considerate of me. But I think I would like to explain to Sister Luane how the Lord led me here."

Those who had them slowly set down their books, though several pairs of knitting needles continued busy in their owners' hands. After a minute or two of thoughtful silence, Sister Hope began.

◆ ◆ ◆

The day Klaus Guinarde walked into the office to receive his final missionary training before being sent out into the field was one which would change Hope's life forever.

By then she had been working in the London office of the Baptist Missionary Society for several years and was still living in the extra room in Mrs. Weldon's house. She had learned to find satisfaction in her duties and to be thankful for them. But the foreign mission field remained her dream.

From the border region of southeastern France below Geneva near the Swiss border, Guinarde spoke fluent French and German, with English colorfully tinged with flavors of both. It was not long before the handsome young Frenchman with the blond hair and accented tongue and the orphaned English secretary were in love.

Klaus would happily have delayed his departure in order to court Hope. But as she had no home nor family, neither of them saw reason to delay their marriage. The ceremony took place three months later, with all the mission board and two or three of Hope's orphanage acquaintances in attendance.

At last her dream seemed about to be fulfilled. Hope was a missionary wife and ready to begin her *own* training. She and Klaus would be sent to the mission field *together*, as a husband-and-wife team.

It was one of the happiest days in all her twenty-five years, after their joint missionary training was completed, when Klaus announced:

"Hope darling, they have given us our assignment! We are being sent to New Zealand to establish a mission in the Wanganui jungle among the Maori natives."

"Oh, that is so exciting!" replied Hope, "—to think that we will be establishing a brand-new work!"

"After living accommodations, our first job will be to construct a small chapel."

"How will we do it?"

"With the help of the Maoris. We must earn their confidence and trust."

Klaus paused.

"But there will be dangers, Hope," he added after a moment or two. "It will not be an easy life."

"I know, Klaus," replied Hope. "But it is what I have wanted for so long."

✦✦✦

Sister Hope's voice fell silent. Sitting beside her, Amanda waited. "As you may have guessed," Hope went on after a moment, and her tone was noticeably subdued, "the danger was far greater than my youthful idealism imagined. I was, you must remember, still a relatively new believer, and subject to that normal tendency of young people in general, and of young Christians, to see things in their most utopian manner."

"What happened?" asked Amanda.

"It was a wonderful first couple of years," replied Hope. "The work went well. The chapel was built. The native people seemed to be responding to us. I developed several treasured friendships with the Maori women. It was a marvelous time. I could not have been happier. And to tell people who live in huts and have no conception whatsoever of the modern world—to tell them of God the Father's love, about the cross and the shed blood of Jesus our Savior . . . then to lead them to salvation in Christ . . . to hear them pray in their native tongue—it is like no thrill in the world. And to increase my happiness all the more, I became pregnant. It was truly everything I had ever wanted."

Again Sister Hope paused.

"But then disaster suddenly struck. The witch doctor of the village turned against us. They burned the church and the rest of our buildings. My husband was killed."

Both Amanda and Sister Luane gasped in shock. Neither had expected the sudden tragedy, and Hope uttered the startling words so abruptly and in such a matter-of-fact tone.

"Killed?" repeated Luane. "You . . . you must have been—what about you . . . were you not there at the time?"

"No, I was there. He hid me in a cellar just moments before the attack came."

She went on to tell of the ordeal in more detail.

"And your . . ." Amanda said.

"Yes, and I lost my baby."

Sister Hope smiled. "She would have been just about your age, Amanda," she added softly.

"I am so sorry," said Amanda, recovering from the sudden and unexpected change in the story. She reached out and placed a hand on Hope's arm.

It was a simple gesture, but of great significance in that realm where eternal battles are won and lost in the tiny exchanges which pass during the course of a day mostly unnoticed. The tender heart of a compassionate woman was slowly coming alive within Amanda's soul. She had *reached out* to comfort another living being in her sorrow, the very woman who had given refuge and comfort to her own aloneness. In so doing had she set a new course for her own future.

"What happened then?" Amanda asked.

"Eventually I returned to London," answered Hope.

"But how did you escape from the Maoris?" asked Luane.

"I was in the cellar for two days," Hope replied, "terrified and alone. Finally I summoned the courage to break my way out. Since Klaus had not returned, I feared the worst. I heard him putting a chest or something over the trapdoor after he made me go inside. It took all my strength, standing on the ladder, to dislodge it. I think it was the struggle to do so that sent me into premature labor."

"And when you . . ."

"What met my eyes when I climbed out was so ghastly, I shall never forget it."

◆ ◆ ◆

As the young pregnant missionary woman finally managed to push up the trapdoor, what remained of the chest above it crashed over.

Slowly she lifted the door and climbed up into the light of day. But she did not find herself in her former home as she expected, but in the smoldering ruins of a dream now gone up in smoke.

Mercifully, she did not immediately see her husband's body, dead now two days.

How she managed to survive those next horrifying hours she hardly knew. The natives were already feeling pangs of remorse for what they had done, and for a time their wrath was spent.

There was still food and water in the cellar, by which Hope kept alive. Some of the native women had been watching to see if she might make an appearance. When they saw her, they approached and took her weeping in their arms. They knew well enough that she was in a woman's way, and even the witch doctor was not prepared to murder a white woman in her condition.

The village women assisted her as she gave birth to her child. But the little girl did not survive the night.

The women of the tribe kept her safe until the British troops arrived, who had been called in to put down the uprising—which by then had spread throughout the region—and could take her back to Europe.

In England once again, Hope had to rethink everything about

her faith, her whole basis for conversion, and whether she really believed God was good at all. This was no everyday trial of minor discouragement. This was heartbreak and tragedy the likes of which altogether broke the faith of many.

How *could* she believe in God's goodness after what had happened?

Over and over, she asked herself what kind of God had she given her life to.

Why should she continue to serve him? How could she tell people of God's love? Why should she tell people to dedicate themselves to him when he had taken from her everything she held dear? How could she be a missionary ever again?

Such questions began a serious period of reevaluation. If her own faith was wavering, what basis could she possibly have to think of continuing with the mission? By now the great Charles Spurgeon had gone on to be with the Lord he had served. Hope had no one to whom she felt she could go to help her resolve what was becoming a crisis of faith.

Thus she had to go to her heavenly Father himself and wrestle through her future at his throne, and there alone, in her own private closet of prayer.

Eventually the questions went even deeper than her own missionary future. How could she even continue to consider herself a Christian at all after this? Did she even want to be?

◆ ◆ ◆

"It is impossible to describe," Hope went on, "what it was like for me to sink to such a state. In one way, perhaps, it was even a blacker time of despair than my time at the orphanage. Because now the very thing I thought had delivered me from that earlier hopelessness was destroyed. Inside I felt something slowly ebbing from me, as if the water of life was trickling away and would eventually be gone, and that I would just shrivel up and wither into a pile of dust. For so long I had clung to the hope that someday life would get better. And then I *thought* that hope had been answered in my faith and my marriage.

"Now it was all dashed away. I felt the hope that had sustained me all my life dying in my heart. As it did I almost felt like I was dying along with it. Finally I had to admit defeat, admit that I could hold out no longer, admit that life was cruel and unjust. I came to a point as his friends counseled Job to do, where the only course left was to curse God and die. There was no such thing as hope. Life is cruel ... and then you die. My name was meaningless ... it had always been meaningless."

30

Whence Originates Goodness ... and Why?

*S*ister Hope sighed deeply. Obviously the memory was difficult, as Sister Gretchen had known it would be.

"Thankfully," she continued after a moment, "God had not quite given up on me yet, though I had nearly given up on him. I was out walking one day, in a busy part of London, just walking and thinking and wondering what was to become of me now, not even praying anymore ... just thinking absently and despondently. There in the midst of the crowd pressing about me I looked down on the walk and saw a little boy sitting on the edge of the gutter, his poor little face in his hands, crying. He could not have been more than four or five.

"I paused and stooped down. His little red cheeks were dirty and stained with the tracks of his tears. He cast up at me, with his big wide brown trusting eyes, a look such as pierced my heart with a hundred daggers of compassion. Then he whimpered, 'I've lost my mum.' And in that instant I *loved* that little boy with a new and different love than I had ever felt.

"I stretched my arms around him as if he had been an angel, as perhaps he was, and slowly picked him up in my arms, kissing his tear-streaked cheek, and telling him that I would help him find his mother. And we did find her, too, more quickly than would seem possible. For no sooner had I begun to make my way with him to the policeman at the next corner than a shriek met my ears from a young woman speaking urgently to the man in the uniform. She glanced toward us with such a look of relief. The next instant the boy was scrambling down out of my arms and dashing off toward her.

"I resumed my walk, as you may imagine, strangely warmed by the incident. Gradually my thoughts returned to their previous channels. But now I found my brain debating with itself. If life was cruel and meaningless, and no such thing as hope existed, then where had orig-inated the love I had felt for that little boy?

"Such a thing as love *must* exist . . . somewhere. I had *felt* it, been filled with it even in the midst of my own dejection.

"Furthermore, what I had done now struck me as odd. Was there truly no such thing as hope? Then why did I not say to the boy, 'You stupid little urchin, why do you sit there crying and looking at me with those big brown eyes! Don't you know there is no hope? You will never see your mother again!'"

The sisters began to laugh to hear Sister Hope speak so, knowing that such were the last words she would ever speak to anyone.

"But no," she went on, "I kissed him and took him in my arms, and told him I would help find his mum. Even in the midst of my own despair, *I had given that little boy hope.*

"The realization shocked me. Where had it come from, this act of kindness I had shown? Though only moments before I had been saying to myself that life was cruel and hard and unjust and meaningless, from within my own heart had sprung an act of *goodness*, not meanness . . . of *kindness*, not cruelty . . . of *hope*, not despair. I did not think *myself* a worthy person as a result. Just the opposite, in fact. During those bleak days I felt anything but good. I felt like a wretch. Yet I could not deny that a moment of goodness and kindness *had* sprung forth from within me. And I now found myself questioning what could have been the origin of it. Why had a spark of goodness come out of the heart of a miserable, doubting, self-absorbed wretch? *Where* had it come from . . . and *why*?

"The next thought that came nearly stopped me in my tracks, right there on that busy London street. If goodness existed within me, I said to myself, in the very midst of my despondency . . . then there must be a larger Goodness from which it had come. There had to be something bigger which truly was *Good*, some larger *Love* which had birthed the love I felt for that little boy.

"Then finally came the idea which began to turn everything around. What if, I thought, God's goodness and God's love don't necessarily re-move the cruelty and suffering and injustice and pain from the world?

"What if they were never intended to?

"What if goodness still exists even though life is hard and cruel, and even though people suffer? What if God's goodness wasn't meant to take away the world's suffering, but was meant to provide a refuge in the midst of it?

"It was such a shocking idea. It made me realize that I had been *expecting* life to be good and pleasant and happy because I was a Christian. Now I began to wonder if I had been wrong.

"If these realizations were true, then the only thing that God's goodness would eliminate . . . was hopelessness. Because if God is good, there can *always* be hope . . . *though there may continue to be pain and suffering and injustice and cruelty and heartbreak.*

"These thoughts did not end my doubts all at once. The struggles and long walks and tears continued. But before long I was talking over my doubts with God again, and asking him to give me answers and trying to listen to what he might say. Finally I had to accept—not had to, really . . . I *did* accept because I believe it is true with every fiber of my being . . . I believe the Gospels teach nothing else than this truth—but what I came to accept was simply this . . . that *God is good.*"

A long silence followed.

"Only that and nothing more," Sister Hope added, "—*God is good.*

"It does not mean that things in my life will always be good . . . but that *God* is good. It does not mean that my life will be an easy one . . . but that God is good. It does not mean that my prayers will always be answered in the way I would like . . . but that God is good. It does not mean that tragedy may not visit me . . . but that God is good. It does not mean that the human struggle is not difficult . . . but that God is good. It does not mean that there will not always be suffering in the world . . . but that God is good. It does not mean that there will not be times when I am so overcome by sadness at memories in my life that I must go outside and find a place to be alone and just cry for an hour . . . but that God is good. It does not mean that there will not continue to be many who will deny his very existence because of the pain and seeming unfairness of life they see all around them . . . but that God is good. It does not mean that there will not always be many questions for which we have no answers . . . but that *God is good.*

"God's goodness is the larger truth over the whole, the largest truth overspreading all of life—over cruelty, over suffering, over tragedy, over doubts, over despair, over broken relationships, over sin itself. Why God's goodness doesn't eliminate such things, I don't know. Perhaps we shall ask him one day. For some reason our tiny human minds cannot comprehend, God has allowed suffering in his universe. I don't know why. You and I might have done it differently. But then we are not God, so it is impossible for us to see all the way into the depths of the matter. We therefore cannot perceive the many ways in which the very suffering we rail against may in fact contribute to the overall eternal benefit and growth of God's universe and its created beings.

"We cannot see to the bottom of such things. So we foolish creatures look at the world's suffering and say God must not exist, or if he does he must not care, or must be a cruel God. Yet I suspect that when we are one day able to see all the way into it, we will see that Goodness and Love lie at the root even of all the suffering that was ever borne by this fallen humanity of which we are part. The devil is presently having his brief illusion of triumph, but God's goodness will reign in the end."

She paused, then added, "In short, the circumstances of life do not always seem to be good, but God *himself* is always good. Thus, though there may not always be happiness, there *is* always hope. That must be the basis for our faith—not that God gives us a happy life."

Again there was a pause.

"Once I had resolved the issue of God's goodness in the midst of my own personal loss—which was no easy matter, I assure you—and that my faith could not be based on what had happened to *me*, but in who God *himself* was, I then had another huge issue to resolve—my future. Gradually the Lord began to show me that being a missionary did not necessarily mean in service only overseas. There were many kinds of 'missions.'

"My first thought was that he was preparing me to serve him in London. I assumed that if I decided to continue on as a missionary, I would have to remain at the mission board office the rest of my life.

" '*Oh, Lord,*' I cried out in prayer many nights, '*please not London . . . anywhere but London!*'

"It was a terrific struggle, almost as great as the other. You cannot imagine how deeply I disliked the city. But eventually I had to relinquish my resistance to the idea. I knew he was asking me to lay it down. I knew I had to tell him I was willing to serve him wherever he wanted to place me . . . even right there where I was.

"I will never forget the night I finally fell on my knees and said, '*I give in, Lord. I will serve you anywhere . . . even in London.*' It was no happy decision. I wept after saying the words. It was the greatest sacrifice of obedience I have ever had to make.

"And yet I knew God was good. My faith was now based on who God was, in his character and his goodness, not in what I expected or even hoped he would do for *me*. He was good, therefore I could trust him to do good in all things. So I could relinquish my future into his hands—not because he was obligated to make me happy ... but because he is good.

"A week later a letter came. It was from Klaus's mother, saying that she had fallen ill. She had no one else to turn to but me. Her husband was gone. Klaus was their only child and now he was gone too.

"So I left London for Switzerland. I came right here to Wengen, in fact to this very house, where Klaus's mother had lived alone since the death of Mr. Guinarde."

Sister Hope glanced toward Sister Luane with a smile.

"So you see," she said, "there is really nothing more to it than that. The chalet belonged to my husband's parents ... and here I am."

Again she paused and smiled, this time nostalgically.

"I moved in with Madame Guinarde and cared for her until her death about two years later. We became very close. I truly came to appreciate her as a mother, the only mother I ever knew. On her deathbed she said to me, 'My dear Hope, I never had a daughter when I was young. But in these last brief years, you have been so dear to me that I feel you were always my daughter—' "

Sister Hope's voice broke as she said the words. She began quietly to cry as she continued.

"Can you imagine what those words felt like to one like me," she went on, "one who had never had a mother at all? They pierced straight into my heart. I wept and wept as she was speaking. I knew she was dying, and that I was losing the only mother I had. As traumatic as it had been in the jungle, I actually think losing Madame Guinarde was more difficult. It touched such deep places within me. Losing a mother was almost worse than losing a husband and a baby.

" 'This beautiful chalet of my husband's will be yours now, Hope,' Madame Guinarde said to me. 'We were happy here ... put it to good use. Make people happy here, dear Hope. My son loved you, and you have been so kind to me. Thank you, my dear daughter. Make people happy. Give them hope, as your name says. Give them reason to live.'

"Later that same night she was gone."

By now most of the sisters, as well as Amanda, were softly crying along with Sister Hope.

"You have had to suffer so much heartache," said Amanda through her tears and sniffles. "I can hardly bear it for you."

Hope smiled. "You, dear Amanda—thank you," she said. "I know you mean it, and the fact that you care so deeply means a great deal to me. But the Lord enables us to bear up under our sorrows. It is his means for making us strong, for turning us into his daughters. Therefore, I give him thanks for what I have experienced."

"How can you say such a thing? It has been so awful, so heart wrenching."

"I can say it, my dear, because God *is* good. I finally did learn that most basic of all life's lessons. He is good, he is loving, and he is trustworthy. These are the deepest truths of the universe. These are the ingredients of the soil out of which has grown, and every day continues to grow, our salvation."

"Is not the cross the basis of our salvation?" asked Sister Luane.

"I would say rather," answered Sister Hope, "that the cross is *evidence* of our salvation."

"I don't think I understand what you mean."

"I sometimes envision the cross as a living tree," Hope replied, "with living roots stretching deep down below into the depths of the rich black earth of God's own nature, which is love, goodness, and trustworthiness. I see the very shape of the cross stretching up out of that earth into the air and sunshine of life, reaching toward the sun because it is alive, with arms outstretched in praise for the soil beneath it in which it is planted, and in praise for the Light above which makes all the universe radiantly and eternally alive.

"I believe this is what allowed Jesus to go to the cross and hang there and die in agony for our sins. I believe Jesus hung on the cross in peace because he knew the roots of that living and praising tree of salvation extended down into the rich depths of his Father's goodness. That is why I say the cross *evidences* our salvation, which is based in God's nature itself, and grows up out of it. If I can learn anything from his example during my remaining days on the earth, I want to learn to trust in the Father's goodness as Jesus did, and thus make his death and my salvation come more and more alive in my heart."

A long and worshipful silence followed. The chalet remained in a solemn hush as each of the sisters pondered anew the wonders of their salvation.

"This is what the beautiful Alps of Switzerland have taught me to say above all else," Sister Hope added at length, "—that God is profoundly and always and eternally *good*."

They were all quiet for some time.

"Did you return to England after your mother-in-law died?" asked Sister Luane at length.

"Believe it or not, I have never been back. I remained here at the chalet from that time on."

Again Sister Hope paused.

"Strange as it may be to say it," she continued, "in one way everything I have just told you is only the first half of the story. Once Klaus's mother was gone, I was left much as I had been at birth—*alone*. I was completely alone in the world.

"Except . . . for the Lord, of course, and this chalet. Those were my only two possessions. So I began to pray to the Lord about how he would have me do what Madame Guinarde had said, put the chalet her husband had built to good use. How would he have me steward it? *'What do you want me to do with Chalet Guinarde?'* I asked the Lord.

"What I began to sense in answer to that prayer—to my astonishment—was that he wanted me to put it to use being a missionary right here.

"At first I could not imagine what he could possibly mean, or if I had misinterpreted the answer.

" '*But, Lord,*' I said, '*to whom do you want me to be a missionary?*'

" '*To those I send you,*' came the reply.

"Still I had no idea what this could mean. Who would possibly come to such an out-of-the-way place as this chalet built on the slopes of a mountain? The very idea seemed incredible. A missionary . . . *here?*

"I continued to seek the Lord in prayer. *'But who will you send?'* I asked.

"The answer this time was so simple, yet profound, *'If you pray,'* I sensed the Lord saying, *'I will send those in need of refuge, in need of a home, in need of a smile, in need of the Father's goodness . . . in need of the hope you can give them.'*

"So I did begin to pray. And over the years people have indeed come. And that is how Chalet Guinarde became the Chalet of Hope."

Another long silence followed. This time it was Amanda who broke it.

"Now I begin to understand," she said, turning toward Sister Gretchen, "why, when you befriended me in the train station, you said that you had been sent to find me."

"We are always looking for those whom the Lord is sending," Gretchen nodded. "They are sent to us, and we are sent to them. It is what God has given us to do. Therefore, we are always in prayer for whom he may be preparing to come."

31

Kapellbrücke

*L*uzern's two famous wooden bridges across the River Reuss, the Kapellbrücke and the Mühlenbrücke, had been the site of more rendezvous, clandestine and otherwise, than any other site in the whole of Switzerland.

Something about meeting above the middle of the river, on a covered wooden bridge, with flower boxes and paintings everywhere and people walking back and forth, must have appealed to an innate sense of the dramatic, for politicians and businessmen, lovers and friends, hoodlums and beggars, had all been making use of the city's two bridges to conduct their business almost from the day they were built.

As Ramsay Halifax now stood in the center of the Kapellbrücke awaiting his first meeting with the man called Fabrini Scarlino, he could not help an occasional twinge of trepidation as he recalled the grim words of Matteos. He had put on a brave face in front of the Italian. But in truth he had never pulled the trigger of his Luger except in the direction of a target when learning to use it—a target which he had not once come within two yards of putting a bullet into. And in fact, the Luger was now safely back in a drawer in his hotel room. He didn't want to take any chance of angering this Scarlino fellow, and judged it prudent to be weaponless for their initial interview.

Out of the corner of his eye he saw a man eying him suspiciously—short, balding, dressed in a business suit, with beady eyes. He looked like the kind of man who would kill you and not think twice about it if you so much as—

"You Halifax?" came a gravelly voice at his side.

Startled, Ramsay spun around. There stood a tall man in his midforties, stocky and muscular, staring out across the Reuss, to all appearances paying Ramsay not the slightest heed.

"Yes, I'm Halifax," replied Ramsay.

"Then follow me," said the man, turning and walking away.

With one final glance back in the direction of the short balding man, who continued to observe *everybody* who passed with a suspicious eye, Ramsay obeyed.

"Finding one person in all Switzerland is not an easy task," said the stocky man when Ramsay had hurried up alongside him.

"I was told that you—"

"Forget what you were told. Now it is just you and me, Halifax. Do what I tell you and she will be found. I hope you are prepared to pay."

32

A Walk in the Village

◆◆◆

Since her arrival at the chalet, Amanda had only once been in the village of Wengen, and then only briefly with Sister Gretchen. Today, Sister Hope asked if she would deliver a loaf of bread to the lady who operated the post.

As she was heading out the door, Sister Marjolaine came bounding down from upstairs.

"Oh, Amanda, I heard that you were going to the village," she said. "Would you mind taking this book back to Herr Buchmann? I borrowed it last week."

"Buchmann," laughed Amanda. "Doesn't that mean *bookman*? Is that really his name?"

"Actually . . . I don't know," Marjolaine replied. "That is what everyone calls him. He is the old schoolmaster and now something of a bookdealer, although mostly what he does is lend out his own books. He is a one-man library. I don't know what I would do without him. Someday you will have to hear his story."

"I would like that."

"In the meantime, here is the book. He lives four houses down from the post. Frau Schmidt can point out the cottage to you, but you can't miss it—a thatched roof with garden in front, and with a door knocker in the shape of a book."

"I will find it," said Amanda.

She left the chalet and walked to the village in good spirits, and went into the post to make her delivery.

"So you must be the new young lady at the chalet," said the woman, taking the wrapped loaf and placing it on the counter. "I am Frau Schmidt."

"Hello. I am Amanda Ruther—er, I mean . . . my name is Amanda."

"I am happy to meet you, Amanda," said Frau Schmidt, extending her hand. "I have known dear Hope Guinarde almost since the very day she arrived here in Wengen to care for her husband's mother, God bless her. She is a dear, dear woman."

"Can you tell me the way to Herr Buchmann's cottage?" asked Amanda.

"Of course, dear," replied Frau Schmidt. "Come with me—I will show you."

She led the way out the front door and pointed along a side street to the house.

"I see it . . . thank you very much," said Amanda and continued on.

A few minutes later she approached the cottage, which was exactly as Sister Marjolaine had described it. She lifted the book-shaped knocker and let it bang against the brass plate beneath it.

Ten or fifteen seconds later the door opened. There stood a man whom Amanda judged to be in his early sixties, with a massive crop of unruly hair, mostly grey but with thick remaining patches of black strewn throughout it, and a full pure white beard. He was wearing what appeared to be laborer's clothes—dungarees, a red-plaid flannel shirt, over which were strung a pair of green suspenders.

"Are you Herr Buchmann?" asked Amanda.

"At your service," he replied with a wide smile.

"I am from the Chalet of Hope. I brought you back this book from Sister Marjolaine."

"Oh, the dear girl—finished it already, has she?"

"I don't know. She only asked me to return it to you."

Amanda handed him the volume. He took it, though without any indication that the interview was over.

"Come in, come in," he said, "—what is your name?"

"Amanda."

"Well, Amanda, I am delighted to make your acquaintance. Please . . . come—perhaps there might be something I can do for *you* in the way of a book, since you are here."

The friendly but, to Amanda's eyes, somewhat eccentric man led her into the sitting room of a quaint and old-fashioned cottage. He did not stop there, however, but continued through it into a dimly lit corridor which led to the rear of the home. Books lined every available space, sometimes from floor to ceiling.

"This is my library . . ." he said as they entered what appeared to be the largest room of the cottage, which sat at the opposite end from the door by which she had entered. The four walls of the room were not even visible, for books on the bookshelves literally took up every inch of vertical space, in many places two volumes thick. Books sat upright, were stacked in piles, and leaned against one another at every possible angle between zero and ninety degrees. The dusty aroma of oldness met Amanda's senses as they entered, which she recognized but was not yet quite seasoned enough to love as one of the treasured fragrances of the growing, learning, reading, deepening life. Two or three worn over-stuffed chairs, a couch, and a couple of reading tables—upon which sat several more stacks of books, and one large atlas, which was open to a map of the continent of Europe—took up the remaining floor space. He was either a sloppy librarian or else this room saw a great deal of use that rendered neatness both impossible and unnecessary. Amanda already suspected the latter. On one of these packed shelves he set the book in his hand that Amanda had given him.

". . . and over here," he added, continuing on through a low alcove and pointing into a tiny room that might once have been something like a large closet but was now sort of an anteroom to the library, "is my little workshop and bindery."

"You bind books too?"

"Oh yes, and repair them," he replied. "Anything a book needs I will try to do for it. I am greatly fond of books."

"I can see that," laughed Amanda.

"I love not only their souls, which are obviously the most important parts, but also their bodies."

"So you're a little like a book doctor."

"Indeed, right you are—a good image, Amanda. And occasionally a surgeon, though never an undertaker."

"Why do you say that?"

"Because I do not believe in death."

The statement struck Amanda as odd. She glanced at Herr Buchmann with a curious expression, which he returned only with a mysterious smile in which was mingled a hint of cunning, as if he were attempting to coax from her further question on the matter. The expression indicated worlds of intended significance it would probably take many fascinating discussions to plumb. Amanda did not take the bait, however, and he quickly went on.

"That is to say," he said, "I do not believe that books die. So they have no need of an undertaker. Any book can always be brought back to life from the jaws of death. Although I confess mildew is a disease for which there is no known cure. But even that cannot kill the book's contents and ideas any more than sin can kill the human soul. But mildew *is* something of a trial for one who loves books as I do."

He paused briefly, and a thoughtful expression came over his brow. For an instant Amanda wondered if he had forgotten she was there.

"But as I said," he went on after a moment, "I do not believe that a book ever dies, even if the physical specimen in which the thoughts of the author were housed one day should fail altogether and be cast on the fire, the thoughts that were in the mind of the author live on. Not altogether unlike the human species, if you don't mind a bit of theology thrown in at no extra charge. For wasn't it said that one might kill the body but never the soul? That's how it is with books too, although what role the fire may play insofar as the book is concerned is probably something less eternal than its counterpart in the world of men's souls.—But excuse me," he said, glancing back toward Amanda with a smile of good humor and a return of the mysterious twinkle in his eyes, "I diverge on a tangent that is something of a hobby with me— a theological hobby, that is."

"I've never heard of theological hobbies," laughed Amanda.

"Oh, I have a good many."

"Why do you call them hobbies?"

"Because I indulge myself thinking about them and studying and reading about them and searching the Scriptures for light on them, all for my own enjoyment. But they are not central things to the faith. If I may say it like this—they don't *matter*. Eternally, I mean. They are fascinating, but not essential to what comprises belief."

"What is essential?" Amanda found herself asking.

"What else," replied Herr Buchmann, as if the answer was the most obvious thing in all the world, "—but to do what *he* said."

A brief silence followed.

"But I thought you were a bookseller," said Amanda, changing the subject.

"Upon occasion. When the villagers have need of a certain book, I will order it for them. But mostly I like to lend my own books, and fix and bind the ones people bring me that are in poor repair. So, as you say, I am more physician and librarian than merchant of the written word."

"Sister Marjolaine said you used to be the schoolmaster."

"That I did. Many of my regular—what shall I call them? Hardly *customers* . . . but those who visit me now to read one, now another from my literary storehouse, were once my students. I tried to do one thing above all else—instill a love of books in young people. And over the years, because of my own love of books, I somehow accumulated a good many, as you can see. I hope you will feel free to come back anytime, Amanda. My door is always open, and never locked even when I am not here."

"That is very kind of you."

"I do not think I have ever had a book stolen. Occasionally one comes back a little worse for wear. But I do not mind. Books are to be *used*, not sit on shelves. Mildew never infects a book that is being read over and over and passed from one hand to the next. With the insides of books as well as the insides of hearts, mildew is the result of disuse. It is the disease of staleness and stagnation, the opposite of *life*. Oh, there I go again!" he said, laughing heartily. "Before I die I hope every one of my books is full of smudges and scuff marks and bruised bindings, and even a few torn pages. These are all good and healthy signs to a booklover, as long as they have come from use, not carelessness. Nothing pleases me more when returning home, either from the post down the street or from a day or two down in Interlaken, than to find my cottage occupied with one or more of my friends and acquaintances browsing through my shelves, even sitting in one of my chairs quietly reading. The cottage may be mine, but my library belongs to the entire village."

"That is very generous of you. I shall be sure to come back. Thank you very much."

When Amanda left a few minutes later, Herr Buchmann did not seem nearly so peculiar as she had first taken him for. Theologically eccentric perhaps, but so personable and friendly that who could hold it against him?

As she left the intriguing librarian and physician of books, and with the sun shining down brightly, Amanda decided to explore a little more of her surroundings.

As she walked through Wengen's two or three streets, snow was still to be seen in some of the shadows where it had been piled against the north sides of buildings. Her heart was merry, and gradually her thoughts returned to Sister Hope's remarkable story of the previous evening. She could sense it penetrating into deep places within her, though she had no idea what might be the end result in her own life. She found herself wishing Sister Hope and her mother could know each other.

Ahead of her, coming out of an alleyway into the street, Amanda saw an old woman approaching, bent over and dragging a load of branches. Still in good spirits from her pleasant encounters with Frau Schmidt and Herr Buchmann, she greeted the woman with a friendly smile.

"Would you like some help with your load?" Amanda asked. "It looks heavy."

"Mind your own business, girl!" the woman barked out in a Swiss dialect Amanda could scarcely understand, not even looking up at her as she did, and then continued on.

Saddened and bewildered by the sharp word, Amanda stared after her. She watched as the woman turned into an unkempt and overgrown yard toward a cottage in the middle of it, which appeared in as sorry a state of repair as the grounds.

33

Heathersleigh

*J*ocelyn, Catharine, and Maggie were all standing at the Milverscombe train platform saying their final good-byes. To one side Mr. and Mrs. Sherborne were speaking with the conductor about some last-minute arrangements concerning the luggage. In a few minutes Catharine would be leaving with her former tutor and his wife for Oxford, where they had agreed to take her to visit the women's colleges.

"I wish you were going, Mother," said Catharine. "Maybe it's still not too late."

"Now that the prospect of your actually leaving is here," returned Jocelyn, "I am beginning to wonder if I made the right decision about staying home. But I am afraid it *is* too late to change my mind now."

"Grandma Maggie," said Catharine, turning to Maggie and embracing her, "you will have to visit Mother every day to keep her from being lonely."

"It will be a pleasure," said Maggie, "—oh, but look . . . here comes Mrs. Blakeley."

The three women turned to see Rune Blakeley's wife hurrying along the platform toward them.

"Agatha!" laughed Jocelyn. "You look like *you're* running to catch the train!"

"Not the train but Miss Catharine before she leaves," replied Mrs. Blakeley. Out of breath, she stopped and walked the last few steps. As she reached them, she held a box tied with string out toward Catharine.

"Catharine dear," she said, "would you mind giving this to Stirling when you see him?"

She smiled and her face colored slightly. "You know how mothers are," she added. "It is the first time he has been away from home. I had to send him some fresh bread and a meat pie."

"Of course, Mrs. Blakeley," replied Catharine. "We shall be having dinner together tomorrow afternoon."

Mr. Sherborne now approached, showing an interest in the box. "Perhaps we can encourage Stirling to share his good fortune with us," he said.

"You mind your own business," laughed his wife. "A university student is not meant to share his gifts from home."

"Charles and I both appreciate your taking Catharine to Oxford," said Jocelyn in a more serious tone to Mr. Sherborne.

"I am looking forward to seeing the university myself," replied Mrs. Sherborne. "Just think what opportunities young ladies have now to dedicate themselves to learning. What times we live in!"

A whistle sounded behind them.

"All aboard!" boomed the conductor's voice.

Another flurry of hugs and farewells and handshakes followed. Then the three travelers boarded the coach. In another minute Catharine's head popped out an open window above where the others stood on the platform.

"I'm back!" she said brightly.

"Have a good time, Catharine," said Jocelyn. 'Don't worry about me—you just enjoy yourself."

"I will, Mother . . . although I may worry about you just a little— oops! I feel the train starting to move!"

Inch by inch, Catharine's face, still leaning out the window, began to move away from them. Jocelyn, Maggie, and Agatha Blakeley slowly walked along in the direction of the train's movement. The engine quickly began to pick up speed, and after another few moments they stopped, satisfying themselves with a last lingering round of waving hands as Catharine gradually receded from view.

"I love you, Mother," Catharine called out.

"I love you, Catharine," replied Jocelyn.

And then she was gone.

Jocelyn turned away, dabbed once or twice at her eyes, then drew in a deep breath, turned, and looked up at her two friends with a bright smile.

"Well," she said, trying to buoy up her own spirits as she spoke, "my little baby girl is off to see the university! Who would have thought it!"

The three turned and left the platform together.

"You know, Jocelyn," said Agatha softly, "Rune and I have more to thank you and Sir Charles for than we will ever be able to tell you. We will never forget all you have done for our family."

Jocelyn glanced over at Stirling's mother with a smile. She nodded, as if to say, *I know . . . I understand.* Both knew that no words were capable of expressing the many thoughts and feelings they shared together.

Later that afternoon, Jocelyn moved about in the kitchen gathering a tray of tea things to take into the sitting room. Behind her, she heard Sarah Minsterly enter.

"I can do that for you, Lady Jocelyn," said the housekeeper.

"I can manage, Sarah," replied Jocelyn. "You may go back to whatever you were doing."

"I haven't much to do, Lady Jocelyn. There's no one but yourself to cook for, and Hector is off to Totnes, and you gave the others the week away."

"Yes, and aren't you going to take the time to visit your sister?"

"I plan to, ma'am. I will take the train into London tomorrow."

Sarah paused and stood silently.

"What is it, Sarah?" asked Jocelyn.

"Well, that is . . . will you be . . . that is, here all alone and all—"

"I will be just fine, Sarah," smiled Jocelyn. "I want you to go to London and enjoy yourself."

"Yes, ma'am—thank you."

The following day, after taking Sarah to the train and seeing her off, Jocelyn returned once again to Heathersleigh Hall. She parked the car in front, got out, and went inside. As if by force of habit, she went to the kitchen and began making a pot of tea. When it was ready, she carried the tray of tea things, cup, saucer, and a few crackers, up to the bedroom and private sitting room. As she went the sound of her own footsteps seemed to echo off the walls with desolation. The whole huge house which had once rung with life and activity and laughter and children's voices . . . now stood empty and deserted.

Her step slowed as she reached the top of the stairs, then stopped. For several long seconds she stood.

The house was so quiet and dark. She glanced down the stairway, then along the empty corridors. Silence. Emptiness.

Suddenly Jocelyn felt very much alone. A great wave of sadness swept over her. Never had she felt so alone.

Would this house ever know laughter again? she wondered. Would the happy shouts of many voices ever fill its corridors and ring out across the lawn and garden?

Trying to shake off the doldrums, at length Jocelyn continued on to her rooms. She set the tray down on one of the small tables, then turned to her dressing table. She caught her eye in the mirror. The sight of her own face somehow increased all the more her sense of isolation.

She tried to take a breath, but the effort caught in her throat. Suddenly the floodgates gushed open. She turned, sought her bed, and before she had even managed to lie down, was sobbing from the depths of her being, stomach and throat aching as she wept.

She cried for Charles. If ever she needed his strong arms around her and soothing words in her ears, it was now. But he was gone.

She cried for George, thrust so young into the cruel ravages of war. Whenever she thought of him, she was afraid. Many mothers sent sons off to war and never saw them again, and she did not think she could bear it.

She cried for Catharine, knowing that another daughter might be leaving for a time.

And then great sobs shook her body as she wept for Amanda.

It took many long minutes, but gradually the tempest began to pass. As the heaves and tears slowly subsided, Jocelyn tried to pray for each one of her family. She prayed that she would trust God for the care of them all. But the effort was not particularly successful. She was sad, she was afraid, and she was alone. And no words of prayer—as hard as she tried to be thankful for her present circumstances—could alleviate how she felt.

At last she fell into a peaceful sleep.

When she awoke several hours later, dusk had descended over Heathersleigh Hall. Jocelyn rose, dressed for bed, crawled under the blankets this time, and was soon once again fast asleep.

34

Unpopular Conviction

$\mathcal{A}$s Amanda turned, saddened by the incident with the old woman, and began making her way back to the chalet, Sister Anika came out of the bakery. She ran ahead to join her.

"Hello, Amanda," said Anika. "I didn't know you were in the village."

"I was doing a couple of errands for Sister Hope and Sister Marjolaine."

From her first day at the chalet, Amanda had been struck by Sister Anika's beautiful features. Tall and slender, she carried herself with stateliness and poise, and seemed like a lady who belonged more in some king's court rather than on a farm in the Swiss Alps. Her eyes, the most arresting part of her countenance, were large, blue, and always full of light, and were complemented by thick straight hair of a shade which might be called dark blond. Her pretty smile, never far from her lips, revealed perfect glistening teeth and was capable of melting the most severe grumpiness in an instant. One flash from eyes, lips, and teeth in concert together was to behold the sun suddenly exploding from behind a cloud.

"I just saw an old lady back there who spoke so rudely," said Amanda. "Most of the villagers are very friendly. But she was downright crotchety."

"There are many people living all around in the hills," Anika said as they walked. "They are all so different. When I first came I didn't think I would ever stop seeing new people. Though it was difficult to get to know them. The Swiss tend to keep to themselves. That old woman was probably Frau Grizzel. She is a very unhappy lady. She was unhappy long before you and I came here."

"How long have you been here?" Amanda asked.

"Let me see . . . it would be eight years now."

"Eight years—don't you ever think about getting married and having a home of your own?"

"I was married for several years," Anika replied.

Amanda's reaction as she glanced to her side showed her surprise well enough. It also hit closer to home than she expected. She waited.

"After three years," Anika went on, "I discovered that my husband was involved with another woman."

A momentary gasp escaped Amanda's lips. She had not expected it in the least.

"We had not known each other very well," said Anika. "But I was in love, you see, and thought that was all that mattered before marriage. I was far too young at the time to marry at all."

A look of pain passed over Amanda's face. She began to stammer. "Oh, I'm sorry . . . what did you do?"

Anika paused thoughtfully. Something made her turn and look straight into Amanda's eyes. Amanda turned her head quickly away. She almost felt as though Sister Anika must know about Ramsay, though that could hardly be.

"I was raised in a godly home," Anika said after a few moments. "I never dreamed anything like that would happen to me. I cried and cried. I thought my life was at an end. My husband and I separated for a time. I could not be with him after learning what I had. I felt so betrayed."

"And . . . then what did you do?"

"I didn't know *what* to do. I thought of running away, just disappearing. I felt so humiliated. I talked to many people, my parents and minister. After several weeks had passed, my father and the minister went to my husband and confronted him with what they had learned. They urged him to repent and break off his relationship with the other woman and rededicate himself both to me and to the Lord. I was prepared to take him back. But he was angry toward them and said dreadful things. So upon their counsel, after searching the Scriptures myself, I divorced him."

Amanda gasped again, and her expression registered surprise. "When was that?" she asked.

"Twelve years ago."

"And you never remarried?"

"I never considered it."

"Why?" asked Amanda.

"Because in God's sight, Hörst was still my husband."

"I don't understand. I thought you said you divorced him."

"What he did could never change the fact that in God's eyes we were married . . . I believe married for life."

"But you divorced him."

"Yes, because he had committed adultery. But that sin of his could not justify my taking a new husband."

"But he wasn't your husband any longer."

"Actually, I believe he still was, and still is my husband to this day—in the sight of God. A *divorced* husband, it may be, but still my husband."

"But . . . but that's so . . . it seems contradictory. You are divorced, but you still consider him your husband?"

"To most people what I have said would seem only so much nonsense. But I believe that in the economy of heaven, only death ends marriage. Divorce doesn't *end* a marriage but is only a means God devised for separating a husband and wife who, for various reasons, can no longer live as a husband and wife are meant to live. It separates them but does not *end* their marriage. At least that is how I see it."

"I have never heard such a thing."

"That is why I say we are separated," Sister Anika continued, "—divorced. But in the economy of heaven I believe I still have a husband. Therefore, I am not free to remarry." After a painful yet beautiful smile, she added, "And the experience has helped draw me into a much closer relationship with the Lord."

"I have never heard anything like that before," repeated Amanda.

"I was always taught that divorce is something the Bible allows under certain very specific circumstances, but not remarriage. In my case, I was scripturally advised to divorce. But I did not feel I could remarry. And this is how the minister of our parish counseled me when I was considering the divorce. He said, 'Be very, very prayerful, Anika. If you divorce, you will not be scripturally free to remarry . . . ever.' Our curate, however, disagreed. After that, I searched the Scriptures on my own. I took many long walks along the dikes near Amsterdam pondering what I was to do."

"What did you find?"

"That I agreed with the minister. I found that marriage was for life, even though divorce sometimes severed that marriage in the world's eyes. I could not escape Paul's words to the Romans which say that a woman who marries another man while her first husband is still alive is an adulteress. I could simply find nothing in the Bible about remarrying without twisting the words. I came to realize that I was accountable. I married my husband. I made lifelong vows. The divorce did not break them, it only suspended them. But I remained accountable for not seeing the defects of character which eventually revealed themselves. I believe I have to take permanent responsibility for the failure of the marriage too, because I married him. Sister Agatha disagrees with me. She believes that because my husband was not a churchman, and because he committed adultery that I *am* free to remarry. But I cannot take her counsel above what I think the Bible teaches."

"But . . . did you never wish to be married again?" asked Amanda.

"Of course," Anika replied. "There are many times I am lonely, even now. And I would so liked to have had children. But I would never think of disobeying the Scriptures merely to satisfy my own loneliness. Obedience is far more important than that. As I said, I am accountable too. If occasional loneliness is the price I must pay for my mistake, then that is something I am willing to endure."

"Your mistake. . . ? *You* did nothing wrong."

"I mean my marrying a man who was not going to be faithful to me."

"You could not have foreseen that."

"Perhaps not. Yet perhaps I *should* have tried to know him better beforehand. People don't change as much as one might think. There are always signposts of character indicating what is likely to come in the future. But most people have not made it a practice to look for them, or, seeing them, do not pay sufficient attention to them."

Again, the words bit a little too deep for comfort, and Amanda did not reply.

"Maybe if I had been mature enough to pay closer attention," Anika continued, "I might have seen Hörst's streak of selfishness and pride which revealed itself when my father and our minister tried to speak to him. I might also have seen that his roving eye indicated danger to a future wife. I was young and careless, Amanda. I married carelessly. I am accountable for that."

"But it seems all those are hard things to say. Is God really like that? Does he want you to be lonely?"

"No, of course not. God did not put me in the position I am in. I did it myself. I cannot run away from my own contribution to the failure of the marriage, if only in that I should never have married Hörst in the first place. The Lord helped me come to my decision and I am content, though occasionally lonely. I am content because I feel it is the right thing for me to do. I feel no shame in being divorced. I know it was not my doing. But I would feel shame in remarrying. Divorce is not wrong in itself. Re-marriage when a spouse yet lives *is*, in my opinion, wrong."

"It still seems hard."

"It is only hard because people do not like the idea of taking account for their own failed marriages. They always want to blame the other for the failure, and then interpret the Scriptures in such a way as to justify their remarrying. But in my opinion this is only so much excuse making."

"You are really hard on those who don't see it as you do."

"So some of the other sisters tell me," Anika laughed.

"Like Sister Agatha?"

"Especially Sister Agatha! She and I have discussed this matter for hours and hours on end. She happens to be the daughter of a very happy second marriage, whose mother and father have been married forty-five years. Sister Agatha vehemently disagrees with everything I have just said. And for good reason. She points to her own parents' very happy years together as evidence of the validity of remarriage."

"What do you say to her?"

"Nothing. We disagree but love one another dearly. These things I have told you simply represent my own convictions. I do not insist that everyone agree with me. It is a good thing, too, because most do not!" she added, laughing. "And I *may* be wrong, you know," she added with another smile. "Or it may be a conviction the Lord wants *me* to follow, and to help me do so he has given me strong views on it, yet it may not be an absolute truth that applies to everyone. I don't know. This is how I see the matter. But others disagree, and I have no problem with that."

"If most people disagree with you," said Amanda, "how do they respond when you tell them all this?"

"I don't tell it to many, because people tend to become angry."

"Angry, at whom . . . not angry at *you*?"

"Sometimes. There are those who become angry whenever any view is expressed that is contrary to their own. They say I am wrong to have such a conviction, that I am judging everyone who doesn't agree with me, that I am living under the Law. They say all sorts of things. Why is it, do you suppose, that people so dislike when someone tries to obey a conviction of their heart? It puzzles me. Honestly I do not think I judge others. I love Sister Agatha's dear mother. But mostly people I tell get angry toward the minister to put that kind of burden on a poor young brokenhearted girl."

"What does Sister Hope think?" asked Amanda.

Anika smiled. "You should ask her," she answered. "My plight has caused her to think and pray about it more seriously than she ever did before. And she has not been able to help being drawn into some of the heated discussions that have arisen between Sister Agatha and me. I think Sister Hope sees both sides. To tell you the truth, I do not think she has fully made up her mind on the issue. Obviously, *she* could remarry if the opportunity ever arose because her husband is dead—although, like me, she does not feel that is what the Lord wants for her. But the whole matter of remarriage is a very complicated question. Sister Hope is so aware of God's grace at work that I think she tends to believe that God can work in the midst of second, and even third marriages at times, just as much as he can in one-man, one-woman lifetime marriages. She is a realist, and I think would say that God is a realist too. He knows that in a fallen world, there will be failed marriages and that we must not condemn those involved in them. I hope I am not condemning. I desire to live in God's grace too, and I try to extend that grace to others. Yet I cannot escape my conviction. In any event, I think Sister Hope tends to disagree with my view of remarriage, though I have never heard her say so specifically."

Amanda was quiet for the remainder of the walk back to the chalet.

Sister Anika was used to such a response to her story. It always made people think, whether they agreed or disagreed with her.

35

Deep Intelligence

An interesting association may have fallen into our laps," said a man of dubious tongue. He might have been either Swiss or Italian, though in truth his accent, along with the name by which he was known, was an integral aspect of the constantly changing disguise by which he kept his true loyalties, if he had any, to himself. "Are you still seeking a means for infiltrating the British Admiralty and cabinet?"

"Of course," replied the other, whose uniform gave away his allegiances without any attempt to hide them. "Infiltration is the objective of intelligence. We have contacts in that direction, moles and others we have turned to our cause. But when it comes to spies in the enemy's camp, one can never be oversupplied."

"A young Englishman has recently been sent my way. He is looking for a woman, but that is a minor sidelight to the greater issue. He may be useful to you."

"How so?"

"He is associated with a fringe operation which apparently has roots in Vienna and connections with the Black Hand. But mostly what I find intriguing is that several of them are actually English."

The Prussian nodded with significant expression.

"And they have been active on behalf of the Alliance?" he asked.

"Apparently for some time. The contact I speak of has connections in Britain, carries an English passport, and may be an ideal candidate for an assassination. Perhaps he might even be induced to make the hit himself, although from his looks I doubt he has the stomach for it."

"Can you find out?"

"I might arrange a test of his resolve—to see what he is made of."

"What is your own role in the affair?"

"I have been enlisted, as I said, to help him locate a woman who has apparently defected from their camp. I have the feeling there is more to it, but that is all I have been told. But the links to their organization are what I thought might interest you."

"You did well by coming to me, Fabrini. But it is not the Black Hand itself?"

"No, it is more English than Serbian."

"What is this organization called?" asked the Prussian.

"I don't know yet. My contact, an Italian, has told me little."

"Find out, then contact me. It may be just what we need to penetrate Whitehall. If the double assassination is to be successful, we will have to use their own people. Find out the name of this network."

"I will do what I can."

"Are you handling the affair personally?"

"Don't worry, Wolfrik—I will see the thing through. In the early stages, I will keep to the background. I have an operative, a useful but expendable fellow, who will help in this regard. But I will be nearby."

36

Christmas Plans

••••

$\mathcal{A}$s they sat around the fireplace one evening, Sister Hope brought up the subject of the approaching holiday season.

"What will you all be doing for Christmas this year?" she asked.

"My family will all be together for the first time since I came here," said Sister Regina. "I will be going back to Barcelona for two weeks."

"That will be wonderful for you!"

"My father is gone, as you know, but I haven't seen my little baby sister in years. She is a grown woman now."

"I will be leaving the day after our Christmas party," said Sister Marjolaine. "Three of my brothers are meeting my sister and me in Lyon. We are all going to surprise our mother with a visit for Christmas. It will be her first Christmas without my father."

"Does everyone leave for Christmas?" asked Amanda, suddenly wondering if she would be left alone.

"No, dear, only those who have families to celebrate with," replied Sister Hope. "I will be here, and perhaps two or three of the others. We celebrate Christmas together a week or two early. Then those who are going home leave."

"My family is traveling to the Mediterranean," said Sister Galiana. "So I will stay with you at the chalet. Someone has to care for the animals."

"Well, I am certain I could manage!" Hope laughed. "But I will be happy to have you with me as well."

For the moment, Amanda said no more. Talk of Christmas filled her with strange feelings that she did not want to think about.

Even in the midst of their discussions of family and Christmas plans, none of the sisters asked Amanda whether she might be thinking of returning to her home for Christmas. Most, including Sister Hope, had already begun to suspect that family strife lay somewhere at the root of her occasional quiet moods and the fact that she was obviously in no hurry to leave the chalet. But the time to approach the matter more directly had not yet come.

"What about you, Sister Clariss?" Hope asked.

"I will go home for a week," she answered.

"And you, Sister Gretchen?"

"My sister and I will go to Munich, as long as it continues safe. I do not think anyone will mind two single women crossing the German border and then coming back."

"I would like to go home," added Sister Anika. "But I fear the war is too close. My mother has written to tell me to stay here."

"That is unfortunate. This war is a dreadful thing. I pray it doesn't interfere with the rest of your plans."

As if reinforcing her cautions and reminding them that the world was indeed at war in spite of how sheltered they happened to be from it, the next day a message arrived from one of the nuns at the Catholic church down in Interlaken. Sister Hope told the others about it at their evening meal.

"It seems there is a young Muslim woman down in the valley," she said, "cast adrift by the war—a Serbian from Albania whose husband was killed. I don't know the details of how she ended up here, but Sister Stephanie, from the convent there, said she has no place to go. She spoke with Father Stein, who suggested that we might help. What do the rest of you think?"

"I would be happy to go down and meet her," said Sister Luane. "I speak several of the dialects of that region—at least enough to get by."

"Obviously we will take her in, will we not?" said Sister Gretchen.

"Such was my first thought," Hope replied. "But I thought we should pray about it together. It would be a different situation than we have faced before. In the meantime, perhaps, Sister Luane, you could go down to the valley tomorrow and take the train into Interlaken. If you feel so led after meeting her and talking with Sister Stephanie, and if you think the young woman would benefit from time at the chalet, bring her back with you."

37

Persuaded by the Heart

◆ ◆ ◆

*O*ne morning Amanda arose early. She came downstairs to find a fire already burning in the fireplace, the smell of coffee pervading the room, and Sister Agatha sitting in an overstuffed chair in front of the hearth.

"Good morning!" said Amanda. "You're up bright and early."

"Good morning, Amanda," replied Sister Agatha. "I might say the same of you."

"That coffee smells good—do you mind if I join you?"

"Of course not, there is plenty."

Amanda walked to the kitchen, poured herself a small cup, to which she added a generous portion of cream, then returned to the fire.

"I couldn't sleep," Agatha said. "So I got up and decided to put the time to good use."

Amanda watched her for a moment or two at some mysterious tiny needlework activity with which Sister Agatha's fingers were busily engaged.

Sister Agatha was a round woman, almost as wide as she was tall, the very image of the rotund, robust farmer's wife. Yet she had never married. She was always busy. Amanda had never seen her hands idle, except during a few occasions during their evening story times when she became so engrossed that her hands would unconsciously come to a stop.

"What is that you're doing?" Amanda asked at length.

"It's called tatting—do you know it?"

"Uh, no . . . but it looks familiar for some reason."

"Here, I'll show you how it's done. Sit down beside me."

Amanda stood, then sat down on the couch next to Sister Agatha.

As Agatha began to explain the process, an image came into Amanda's mind as she watched the fingers and shuttle flying along, a mental picture of a cottage in the woods.

As had occurred on several previous occasions, the years fell away. It was now Maggie's voice saying almost the same words as Sister Agatha just had, trying to teach her the intricate process. But Amanda had been prickly and unteachable and had not wanted to learn.

Amanda now recalled the disappointed look on Maggie's face and the rude remark that had fallen from her own tongue.

She hadn't thought of the incident in years. Now the memory stung and she almost felt a tear rise in her eye. She forced herself back to the present.

"... and then you tie it off ... like that," Sister Agatha concluded. "Then the process starts all over again. Would you like to try it?"

"Not now," replied Amanda. "I don't think I could concentrate on it. But I would like to another time." She paused momentarily. "Do you mind if I ask how you came to live here at the chalet?" she asked after a moment.

"Of course not," Agatha replied. "I was born in a small village just over the hills. It is only four or five miles away. I see my parents every few weeks. I am very close to my mother."

"Why do you live here?"

"I love this ministry and wanted to be part of it. My parents are very poor and their cottage is small. My living here saved them the expense of supporting an unmarried daughter. And when I sell my lace and needlework, I give them what it brings to help with necessities. I suppose I will move back to the cottage when their health begins to fail and they need care. Living here is a help to us all financially, and of course I love it here."

"How did you meet Sister Hope?"

"I used to do housecleaning for Madame Guinarde. She and my mother were friends for years. When she fell ill, we did what we could to help. I was the one who first wrote to Sister Hope in London explaining what had happened. When she came, we immediately became friends, but I did not move here until Sister Gretchen and a few of the others were here."

"Do you mind if I ask you another question? I was speaking with Sister Anika about divorced people getting remarried. She told me her story, of course, but also told me about your parents, and that you disagreed with her view on the matter."

Sister Agatha nodded.

"If you don't mind, would you tell me why?" Amanda asked.

"I haven't studied and read the Bible about it," said Sister Agatha. "I am not a great reader. But my heart simply tells me that God is big enough to have room in his heart for people who have been divorced to marry again. Surely it is not like God to tell people that they must remain alone and miserable for the rest of their lives just for one mistake early in their lives."

"Sister Anika does not seem miserable."

"You are right. But even she admits to occasional loneliness."

"She said that it is not God being severe with her, but her taking account for her own mistake."

"Then perhaps I would say she is being rather too severe with herself. In my heart I feel that God does not mind it nearly so much as Sister Anika might think. And when I look at my own father and mother—who are two of the most wonderful people in the world, who love each other like a true husband and wife should—what other conclusion can I draw but that God's blessing can rest upon second marriages as well as first ones. My mother married early, and the man she married was a dreadful man, to listen to her tell about him, who was anything but kind to her. Then she met my father, who had also been divorced. They have had a wonderful life together. And if they had not, I would never have been born. And if God loves me and lives inside me, then he must have blessed their marriage. It is not that I think Sister Anika is wrong in not wanting to marry again. If that is how the Lord is leading her, then who am I to tell her otherwise? But I do confess to thinking she is wrong in saying that divorced people *shouldn't* remarry, and that it is going against the Bible when they do."

Amanda took in everything Sister Agatha said.

As with many of the conversations she was having, the words went into Amanda's soul, awaiting the appointed season when they would be harvested and bear fruit in her own life. She found herself thinking about the comments of both the women, wondering what she would eventually do regarding Ramsay. She wasn't quite ready to think about her own future yet. And thankfully no one here had probed too deeply with personal questions.

She would have to think about it someday. When she did . . . well, she didn't know what she would do.

38
Back to Milan

*R*amsay Halifax and the tall man he had met on the bridge returned from an interview that had been less successful than hoped.

"We seem to have temporarily lost the trail," said the tall man.

"What now?" asked Ramsay.

"I still have some people who may be able to get me the records I need to trace that passport. It is our only hope of finding her current residence. I will continue to pursue contacts here. Meanwhile, I want you to go back to Milan."

"What for?" said Ramsay.

"Contact Matteos. It is a long shot, but it just may be that the Reinhardt woman has relatives there."

"But the name is German."

"Yes, and she was in Italy."

"We do not know why."

"We must explore every lead. If she was in touch with someone there, it may be a link to finding her. We have only two sources to explore—following the ticket and passport, and investigating the Milan link."

There was a short pause.

"There is one other thing," said the tall man. "Matteos tells me you are part of an organization, a network of some kind. You have said the woman you seek is a spy. He says you are all spies."

"Matteos has a loose tongue," said Ramsay.

"He says the same of you. All I want to know is whether it's true."

"Perhaps."

"I must know."

"Why?"

"My reasons are none of your concern. But it may assist me in locating the girl. There can be no secrets between us."

Ramsay eyed the man warily, pondering the odd request.

"It is called the Fountain of Light," he said at length.

"Matteos mentioned Vienna. Is that where the rest of you are?"

"We are everywhere. At the moment some of us find Vienna a safe location for our activities."

"I see. All right then, get to Milan and find out what you can."

"But all this is taking too much time."

The man swore lightly. "Do you want to find her, Halifax?" he said irritably. "It means nothing to me. But here the trail has gone cold. What I need to do does not require your tagging uselessly along beside me. So if it takes a month—"

"Look, Scarlino, I don't have a month," shot Ramsay. "I've got to find—"

The man cast him an evil look and Ramsay calmed.

They continued walking in silence. As they passed a small park, several pigeons suddenly shot out of a nearby tree. The sound startled Ramsay. He glanced toward the sound and saw them flying off.

When he turned his head back in the direction he had been going, he found himself walking along the street alone.

39

Living Miracle

As November gave way to December, a mounting festive atmosphere gradually filled the air. A few of the sisters were beginning to pack and get ready for their journeys home, but mostly the activities of the chalet were in preparation for Christmas and the annual party the sisters put on for the village.

The most recent arrival, Kasmira Tesar, kept mostly to herself. The sisters of the chalet had scarcely seen so much as a glance from her eyes, and had not seen the rest of her face at all except for the few meals she took in silence with them. There seemed more occupying her thoughts than the war and loss of a husband would account for, though none of them had been successful at penetrating the veil of her isolation which she kept drawn down upon her soul as tightly as the black veil over head and face. Though she spoke sufficient German to communicate, she walked among them in a cloud of mystery.

But even Kasmira's silence could do nothing to dampen the Christmas spirit the rest of them felt. Smells of baking emanated from the kitchen. Christmas melodies now on the lips of one of the sisters, now another, filtered through the chalet like intertwining strands weaving in and out among one another, occasionally uniting as three or four broke into song together. One by one, they might be joined by others, until quiet but complex feminine harmonies filled the chalet, from Sister Marjolaine's high, dainty soprano to Sister Regina's deep, rich contralto. Then, after the rising crescendo of a chorus of "Angels We Have Heard on High" or "Joy to the World" or some other carol, the voices would softly fade until each had resumed her own quiet humming or singing and they continued about their affairs, with hints of a Swiss yodel echoing quietly from Sister Agatha's lips occasionally to intermingle melodically with the rest.

No huge snowfall had come, only a succession of small ones, such that about a foot of snow lay on the ground. Well-worn paths existed through it in most directions, and walks to and from the village, even down to Lauterbrunnen, were still manageable.

In the barn, Sisters Galiana and Clariss were putting fresh straw out for the animals.

"I have a great idea!" Clariss burst out suddenly as they worked.

Galiana looked up, hair loose with a few pieces of dried grass hanging from it, as she tossed half a bale of straw into one of the goat pens, surprised by the outburst of the usually quiet Clariss.

Clariss went on to explain what had just occurred to her.

"I think we should do it," Galiana said after a few minutes. "Let's go tell Sister Hope and see what she thinks."

Meanwhile, Amanda had just come upon Hope apparently returning from a walk in the nearby woods. Her face was red, though not from cold. It was obvious she had been crying.

"Sister Hope . . . what is it?" asked Amanda.

Hope smiled. "Oh, nothing," she said. "I have just been out for a sad cry."

"But why?" said Amanda. The words seemed so out of character from the Sister Hope she had come to know.

"Christmas always makes me a little lonely."

"You . . . lonely?" said Amanda, almost incredulous at the thought. In fact, she had been feeling a few pangs of loneliness herself from hearing the Christmas carols inside the chalet, and had come outside as a result. She had assumed that she was the only one among them for whom the season carried difficult memories that as yet she didn't quite know how to resolve in her heart.

Hope nodded. "It is at such times as this that I remember my orphanage years and feel the pangs of sadness a little more keenly."

"But you have a wonderful life here," said Amanda.

"I do indeed," Hope replied as they began walking together, "and I am grateful beyond words. But that does not prevent sadness from sometimes overwhelming me. No one who has not experienced such aloneness can possibly know what it is like not to have a family. Sometimes it sweeps over me, Amanda, and I just have to cry. God is good . . . and he has been so good to me. But there are still times I am sad. Have you seen Kasmira this morning?"

"No . . . no, I haven't," replied Amanda.

"I am concerned for her. She seems more forlorn than nearly anyone I have ever met, yet so unreachable. I wonder if some of it has to do with our Christmas celebration. Kasmira is a devout Muslim, and—"

Sounds of laughter interrupted them. They looked up to see Galiana and Clariss hurrying toward them from the direction of the barn.

"Sister Clariss has a great Christmas idea," Galiana said as they ran up. "—Tell them, Clariss."

"In Italy," Clariss began as they continued toward the chalet, "many of the village churches set up a live crèche on Christmas Eve. It is a tradition that began with Saint Francis of Assisi. He loved animals, you know, just like Sister Galiana. On one Christmas Eve he set up a manger scene using live animals and real people. It occurred to me when we were working in the barn just a few minutes ago that we might do the same thing. We could put together a makeshift stable on the hill in front of the chalet. Sister Gretchen could build it and we could help. Then when we have the villagers to the chalet for singing and treats before Christmas, we could put some of our animals in the scene and could dress up as the wise men and shepherds and holy family."

"I think it is a wonderful idea," Hope said. "It would help them realize how Christ came to each one of us in such a quiet and humble way."

"And make the Christmas story more real to them," Galiana added.

"And perhaps more real to us as well," said Sister Hope. "We will tell the others and begin planning for it immediately!"

40

Chalet Christmas Party

The day of the chalet's annual Christmas party arrived. Everyone except Kasmira was up at the crack of dawn. Soon the kitchen and whole chalet was bustling with activity.

In midmorning, Amanda was in the kitchen helping Sisters Agatha and Anika chop nuts and dried fruits. Several others were also busy in the kitchen baking and mixing and kneading various breads and pastries and cookies. Sounds, smells, and spirits were festive and gay. From the great room came wonderful music from their old piano, where Sister Gretchen sat practicing the carols and hymns they planned to sing that evening.

"How are you three doing?" asked Galiana.

"That depends on how much you need," Anika replied.

"Oh, my *stollen* needs cups and cups," Galiana said. "It is the nuts and fruit that make the bread so sweet and crunchy and delightful."

"And I need some for my steamed plum pudding," Sister Hope put in as she walked by. "We shall keep you three busy all day at the cutting board!"

"I am going out to help Sister Clariss with the last work on the stall," Galiana said. "Then we shall have to bring straw to our manger. But I will be back to finish the stollen before long. It must have time to bake."

The three cutters returned to their work. After some time Amanda left the counter to take a break and stretch her back. Absently she walked to the window. Outside she saw Galiana and Clariss assembling the last bits of wood for the manger stall and shaking straw around on the ground where they had cleared away the snow, then placing some in the little manger Sister Gretchen had built. She could hear nothing of what they were saying, but they were talking and laughing freely. Truly they seemed like sisters.

What would it be like to laugh and talk and have fun with a sister?

Amanda wondered. Her thoughts immediately went to Catharine. She could hardly remember any happy times they had enjoyed together such as she was witnessing right now outside the chalet. Catharine had always seemed so many years younger. But had there been more to it? Had she herself perhaps prevented the kind of camaraderie sisters were meant to have?

The thought was unwelcome. She tried to shake it away. Why did the season of Christmas, which was supposed to be happy, bring so many painful stabs of past thoughts with it?

Amanda sighed, then turned and rejoined Anika and Agatha at the chopping board.

Late in the afternoon the villagers began to arrive, continuing to drift across the snow-covered field to the chalet by ones and twos and family groups, mostly walking but a few in horse-drawn sleighs.

The Christmas party given annually by the Chalet of Hope for the village of Wengen had become for many of the region the traditional beginning to their own Christmas season. For the sisters of the chalet, however, this day represented the climax. Over the next few days, those sisters who were leaving would depart to be with their own families.

As the villagers approached, all were curious about the new addition this year, the live crèche sitting in front of the chalet, complete with a cow, a donkey, two goats—a little too restless for the occasion—and several of the sisters dressed up and standing quietly occupying the roles of Mary, Joseph, and a few shepherds. As the villagers continued to come, they paused quietly, filled with a sense of reverence and awe.

Sister Anika sat in the middle of the scene, holding a small bundle of wrapped blankets and staring down at it. She did not glance up at the visitors. She knew from the whispered comments they made amongst themselves that they were staring at her. But she sat unflinching. Never had her face been more radiantly beautiful, nor filled with such an expression of peace. No one needed to explain the scene. Though most of the villagers had never seen such a thing, even the children understood.

When everyone who was expected was inside, Galiana took the animals back to the barn while Anika and the other participants came back inside the chalet to change their clothes.

Meanwhile, Sister Hope greeted all the arrivals at the door.

"Frau Schmidt . . . Herr Buchmann—how are you?"

More villagers crowded in, feeling the warmth inside from the fire.

"Father Stein," now said Hope, "I am so glad you could make it up the mountain!"

"I wouldn't miss it," replied the priest.

Hot potato soup and fresh rolls followed, then singing with Sister Gretchen at the piano. The evening sped by, as it always did, with food and drink, stories and songs, laughter and even a few games.

Gradually one, now another of the sisters gathered the Swiss children in a circle to tell them how the boys and girls in each of their own countries would be celebrating Christmas.

"In my country of Holland," said Sister Anika, "Saint Nicholas will arrive not many days from now, and he may be there already, on a big ship. He will be accompanied by his assistant, who is called Peter and who carries the gifts. Then Saint Nicholas and Peter will mount great white horses, and ride through the Dutch countryside giving candy and toys to all the good children of Holland. He will leave their gifts in wooden shoes. Sadly, I will not be there this year, but on Christmas Eve here you may be sure that I will put out my wooden shoes in hopes that Saint Nicholas and Saint Peter will not forget *me!*"

All the children watched her and listened with even more than usual interest, for they were still somewhat under the spell of having seen her earlier in the crèche. And now her expressiveness in the matter of the gifts brought high-pitched laughter to their lips.

Now came Sister Gretchen's turn.

"In Germany," she began, "as in many other countries, we put up and decorate a Christmas tree. My mother and father are very old now, but you may be sure that when I arrive at their home in Munich, they will have a tree. But they will wait until my sister and I arrive, and we will all decorate it together. All the children of Germany look forward to the visit of Kriss Kringle. He has long blond hair and wears a white robe and gold crown. He is helped by Saint Nicholas, whom Sister Anika told you about. Saint Nicholas carefully watches all the children of Germany through the year to see if they have been bad or good. If they have been good, there will be toys and gifts under the tree on Christmas morning. But bad children will find switches and twigs and nasty things like that, and they will know that they must try harder to be good during the coming year."

"In Spain," began Sister Regina, "all the children wait for the arrival of the three wise men. These great kings of the Orient never fail to come to Spain at Christmastime, bringing gifts just as they did when they visited Bethlehem many years ago."

"Will *you* be there for Christmas?" asked a tiny girl, looking up into Sister Regina's brown face with wide inquisitive eyes.

"Yes I will, Anke. I am leaving by train tomorrow," replied Regina. "All the boys and girls of Spain will fill their shoes with straw and place them out on their doorsteps on the night before Christmas. The straw is for the camels that carry the wise men on their long journey. When the children awake early the next morning, they find to their amazement that the straw is gone. In its place are toys and fruit the wise men have left for them during the night."

"In Italy," now said Sister Clariss, "children believe that on the night before the twelfth of Christmas a kind old lady arrives at all the towns and villages of the country. But she is really a witch who loves little children."

"A *witch*?" said little Anke in amazement.

"Yes, dear, but a good witch," replied Clariss. "Her name is La Befana. All the little girls and boys prepare for the arrival of La Befana by placing their shoes next to the miniature manger that every Italian family displays at Christmastime. During the night, La Befana flies through the window and fills the children's shoes with toys and candies, or maybe with a few pieces of coal if any of them have been naughty."

As they sat listening, the children's eyes were big and round, and their mouths hung open at the thought of a witch, even a good one, flying right into their homes.

"But these are all just stories," Clariss said, breaking the spell. "They remind us that baby Jesus came to earth and was born in a manger. That is why we made the little stable outside, to help us remember that Christmas is not really about toys and candy, but about the birth of the Savior, our very own dear Lord Jesus."

She paused and now glanced around the chalet at all the rest of the villagers present. As Amanda sat listening, she too glanced about as if in unconscious response. Out of the corner of her eye she saw the black-shrouded form of Kasmira Tesar at the upper landing of the stairway, obviously listening as Clariss spoke but trying to keep out of sight. Amanda had only seen her briefly all day, and she had not participated in the party since its beginning. Her presence reminded Amanda of the few Serbs whom she had met at the house in Vienna, and it filled her with unpleasant memories. She could not help being a little afraid of her.

And what did she think, Amanda wondered, of such things as she was now hearing, so very different from Muslim belief?

"As you know," Sister Clariss went on, "many of us will be leaving Wengen to enjoy Christmas with our families. I will be visiting the family of my younger sister. But we are going to leave our stable and manger out in front of the chalet. Each morning Sister Galiana will put the animals out, that is if it is not snowing. And we would like to invite you all to come to the chalet as often as you like, and stand in the different places of the nativity scene. One day you may wish to come as a family and all take different positions and talk together about how you think the shepherds might have felt on that holy night, or Joseph, or the innkeeper. You might want to sit where Sister Anika sat this evening and think to yourself what might have been going through dear Mary's mind and heart after giving birth to the baby Jesus. We want you to enjoy this Christmas as never before, by understanding a little more personally what Jesus' birth means to you. This is our Christmas gift to you, our dear friends of Wengen. Please ... not only enjoy it, but let the living stable and the miracle of the manger make Christmas a living miracle in your heart."

As the story time now broke up, more refreshments, cookies, stollen, and hot cider were served. Herr Buchmann was in rare form, laughing and visiting with everyone. Some of his former pupils, which included half those present, began to clamor for a story. At length he agreed, took a seat, and once again the chalet quieted.

"Let me tell you a tale," he began, "of an old doll maker and a queen. It happened long ago in a distant land, though in a village not so different from our very own Wengen. . . ."

The mere sound of his voice immediately had all the children mesmerized. They were well accustomed to Herr Buchmann's stories, and none were ever disappointed.

As Amanda listened, however, suddenly she was overcome with sadness. Tears struggled to rise. She blinked them back. She didn't want to get nostalgic now. She didn't want to remember how devoid of meaning Christmas at the Pankhursts was. She didn't want to feel pangs of loneliness. She didn't want to remember Christmas hymns from the Milverscombe church, or a childhood carol her mother taught them. She didn't want to remember their baking day at Heathersleigh, when she and Catharine and George and their mother had filled the kitchen with pans and bowls and trays, laughing and singing as together they made raisin shortbread, almond candy, gingerbread men, and molasses candy....

But once begun, the memories came back like a flood. Amanda scarcely heard any more of Herr Buchmann's story. The next time she happened to glance around, Kasmira's dark form had disappeared from the landing above, and Herr Buchmann was rising from his chair, the story of the doll completed.

41

Dark Night

$\mathcal{T}$he night was late.

A chill breeze blew off the Wohlensee toward central Bern. The two men who were speaking in low tones in the shadows beneath a tall deserted brick church felt the cold. But the heart of the one was colder than the air and he hardly noticed. And the other would be home in his bed before long.

"Look, Scarlino," said the latter, "what you ask will not be easy. Those records are closely guarded. I could lose my job."

"What is that to me? You will be well paid. The time has come when the people who put you in your job expect compensation."

"What do you know of that?"

"I know. That is all that is important."

"Does this have to do with the war? Which side are you spying for this time?"

A low laugh sounded in the darkness.

"You know me better than that."

"Yes, I do. You would kill a German just as soon as an Englishman or a Serb."

"Or a Swiss bureaucrat, if it came to that. Let me just say that there are certain people high up on both sides who are very interested in a contact who stumbled across my path recently. There are rumors of an independent network with connections in Austria, and an English-woman who infiltrated them and is now making a run for it. It is even said a high-level assassination is planned. You would not want your name somehow linked to all that, would you?"

The Swiss man squirmed. He should have known better than to get involved with these people.

"What would your dear wife and children say?" continued the man whom he had called Scarlino. "The stakes are high. To fail me now could, shall we say, be a fatal miscalculation on your part."

"Don't worry," he said finally. "I will get the information. Just keep my name out of it."

42

Frau Grizzel

*E*ven in the midst of her own melancholy, Amanda had noticed that Frau Grizzel was noticeably absent from the chalet Christmas party. For several days following, her thoughts continued to turn toward the grumpy old woman she had met in the village. Maybe, she thought, she could try to cheer her up. No one ought to be miserable at Christmastime.

The day after Sister Gretchen—the last of the chalet's departing sisters—was gone, Amanda set off for the village with a parcel of fresh cookies, bread, and some Christmas candy.

Her own spirits brightened considerably as she walked. The mere resolution to try to do something for someone else took her mind off her own troubles. But the closer she got to Frau Grizzel's run-down cottage, the weaker her knees began to feel and the slower her step.

But there was no turning back, she told herself as she made her way up the walkway. She must not lose heart now. Amanda stopped, drew in a last breath of courage, then timidly knocked on the door.

Inside she heard nothing. She waited for what must have been a whole long minute in silence. Suddenly the door slowly creaked open to a distance of about six inches. Out of the black void peered a wrinkled old face, out of the middle of which glared two mean-looking eyes. The mouth displayed no sign of intended movement. The eyes, however, roved up and down skeptically over the unwelcome visitor who had interrupted their solitary misery.

"Hello," said Amanda, "I don't know if you remember me. I saw you just down the street there several weeks ago. My name is Amanda. I live up at the chalet. I brought you a loaf of stollen and some other sweets. I wanted to wish you a happy Christmas."

"Christmas, bah!" retorted the old woman, her lips springing into action and her eyes narrowing as they stared out of the opening, which did not widen a millimeter. "What happiness does Christmas have for one like me whose family has left her?"

"I . . . I'm sorry . . ." stammered Amanda. "I didn't—"

"Go away, girl," interrupted the woman.

"I just thought you might like—"

"Take someone else your alms. I don't need them."

"But, please—"

"Wait till you're my age, little girl! You'll see what old age brings them as has no family, whose loved ones are gone and care for them no more."

The words sent a pang into Amanda's heart. The next sound she heard was of the door slamming in her face.

Saddened, she turned to walk away. She paused at the street still holding her parcel, then turned in the direction of Herr Buchmann's cottage. How very different was the answer to the knock she gave upon his door a minute or two later.

"Amanda, my dear!" exclaimed the bookman, the very whiskers of his beard seeming to come alive from the smile radiating out from the center of it. "How delightful to see you again. Please come in!"

"Would you like some Christmas bread and sweets?" said Amanda as she followed him inside.

"What a thoughtful thing—why, thank you!"

This time Herr Buchmann closed the door behind them and offered Amanda a chair in his front sitting room rather than proceeding straight to the library.

"Actually," said Amanda shyly, setting the parcel down on a low table in front of her host, "I came to the village intending these things for Frau Grizzel. But she shut her door in my face. So I didn't *really* bake them just for you."

"You are a straightforward young woman as well as thoughtful!" laughed Herr Buchmann. "Believe me, I am not insulted in the least. I shall appreciate the goodies no less for being secondhand gifts. You may recall, I am fond of secondhand things!"

"I think I remember!" laughed Amanda. "Books at the top of the list."

"Right you are, my dear!"

"I had hoped that Frau Grizzel would see my gift as a gesture of friendship," said Amanda. "She seems so sad and lonely."

"Many have tried," said Herr Buchmann sadly, "including myself and all the dear sisters of the chalet. But the poor woman is so consumed by her bitter and unforgiving spirit, she will let nothing in—not gifts, not flowers, not smiles, not a kind word."

"Was she always like this?" asked Amanda.

"Actually no," answered the former schoolmaster. "It is the most curious thing. She used to be one of the most highly thought of ladies in all Wengen, with a happy family and children the entire village enjoyed. They were all pupils of mine."

"What happened?"

"To tell you the truth, I don't know. Her husband died some years ago. But she seemed to handle his passing with the special strength given to women for such occasions. At least I saw no immediate change. One by one her children all left. I don't know when the sourness of her present disposition began, or why. I suspect creeping resentments gradually got the best of her—although concerning what I haven't an idea. They are like that, you know—unseen resentments that prowl around in the hidden places and dark shadows within us. They can take us over if we do not conquer them. Obviously poor Frau Grizzel did not root them out, so they grew and grew in her mind, and gradually conquered *her*."

"It is so sad. Why would anyone *want* to be so miserable?"

"There is a certain pleasure the soul takes in self-centered misery," answered Herr Buchmann. "Wallowing in such gloom is easier for some people than swallowing their pride over some assumed offense they have been dealt by another, or by life's circumstances, or by God himself. Many sad souls find it a better thing to remain angry and unforgiving than to lay down the offense and let forgiveness wash their soul with the sweet-smelling water of God's roses and violets and hyacinths. I don't understand it myself, but I see many who are the sad victims of their own pride. It seems to be a disease especially lethal among the aged."

"Do you really think so?" said Amanda. "It seems to me that young people are more foolish and prone to—"

Suddenly she stopped. Where had such a thought come from! She had been about to land the implication of her own observation straight down on her own head.

If Herr Buchmann suspected the truth about her sudden silence, he gave nothing away by his expression.

"I admit," he said, "that there is a foolishness in the heart of the youth that later years do tend to cure. However, the foolishness of old age is sadly one for which there seems no cure but death. My own theory is that old age brings to the surface what has been invisibly growing from thousands of hidden seeds one has been planting in the garden of his or her own heart all their lives, either seeds of sweetness and graciousness, or seeds of irritability and grumpiness. As life slows down, those seeds sprout for all the world to see."

"It is a fascinating theory," said Amanda.

"It answers the curiosity," Herr Buchmann went on, "that old age seems to make some people sweeter and others more crotchety. The sad truth is, Amanda, my dear, many people are not able to see the character traits they are building within themselves day after day, year after year. Then they grow old. Some of the natural defenses and barriers of personality fall away, the second childhood of life comes, and suddenly blossoms a lifetime's character patch of ugly weeds, or a nicely trimmed garden of sweet-smelling flowers. You are young, Amanda, so take care what you plant, because you will reap your own harvest in the end. But come," he added, rising, "enough of all this serious talk. I want to show you a book that came into my hands just a few days ago, an absolute treasure. I think you might like to read it."

Only too glad to avoid any further conversation in the direction this one had been going, Amanda jumped up and followed him through the cottage toward the Buchmann library.

43

Miraculous Birth

*H*ope Guinarde awoke early Christmas morning.

It was still dark outside, though hints of dawn were visible. She thought she had heard a sound, like the door opening downstairs.

She listened. The chalet was completely quiet. Gradually she dozed back to sleep.

When Hope woke again, another hour had passed. It was yet early and the house still quiet, but the light of morning filled her room.

Some compulsion made her rise. She put her robe about her and went to the window, then gasped in astonishment.

Out in front of the chalet, in the freezing cold of morning, Kasmira Tesar was kneeling in the snow staring at the empty manger of their makeshift crèche. Her black veil was down from her head, hanging from her shoulders. If was the first time Hope had even seen her full face and neck and flowing black hair, and a beautiful picture it was. Even from this distance, Hope could tell that the girl's cheeks were wet with tears.

Hurriedly she dressed and ran downstairs.

As Hope ran out the door and across the frozen ground to the empty stable, gradually her step slowed. The radiant tearful expression on Kasmira's face was such as she had never beheld in her life. She stopped and could do nothing for a moment or two but gaze upon it.

Still the veilless young Muslim woman stared weeping at the manger, in which still lay the folded blanket Sister Galiana left in it every day for the villagers to make use of.

Slowly Kasmira glanced up.

"I don't know why," she said softly as Hope now approached, in broken but intelligible German, "something seemed to tell me to come out. I fell on my knees and was filled with such wonder as I remembered what I heard the other night about the stable. . . ."

Her eyes glistened, her lips parted in a smile of mingled bewilderment and awe, and with also the dawning hint of a smile from some new well of joy inside that was unlike anything she knew.

Hope went forward, knelt in front of her, then slowly wrapped her arms about the cold shoulders from which hung the veil this precious new daughter of God would no longer have to hide behind. Kasmira fell into her embrace and wept like a child.

For a minute or two they remained in each other's arms, then slowly parted. By now Hope was no more aware of the morning's cold than Kasmira had been earlier.

"But . . . why is this happening?" Kasmira said. "What is the power of this . . . what is it called, this *Futterkrippe*—"

"That's right," smiled Hope, "a *manger*."

"What is the power of this manger? Why did the story make me weep? Why am I filled with new feelings I cannot understand? Why do I no longer think I must shield my face? Why do I no longer want to hide any part of me? I feel . . . so . . ."

Her voice stopped as her mouth remained open in wonder.

"My dear sister," said Hope with a heart full of tender love, "the power of the manger is that the little baby that was born in it was the Son of God. Because of that, he *changes* people, as he is now changing you."

"Do you mean the man Jesus? I have heard of him."

Hope nodded.

"But I do not believe. . . . I am a Muslim, not a Christian. How can *he* have power . . . over me?"

"Do you think it matters to him what you call yourself? His love for you is no less than it is for me, or anyone else. That is what the manger means, Kasmira dear, that his love has come to the whole world—you and me . . . and everyone."

"You . . . you call me sister. But I am a Muslim . . . you are a Christian."

"Yes," said Hope, "and we have the same Father. That makes us sisters of the universal humanity to whom he has given life. You may not yet know him as I do. There is a closer family as well as a universal one. He wants you to be part of that family too. He wants to know you intimately, and that is why he called you out here on this Christmas morning to show you the meaning and power of the manger . . . to touch your heart with the new life he has for all."

"*He* called me out," repeated Kasmira in astonishment. "Do you mean it was *his* voice that woke me?"

"I believe so, my dear."

"That . . . that Allah would speak . . . to me . . . why would he do so?"

"Because he loves you."

"*Me* . . . a mere woman?"

"The true God, the Father of Jesus Christ, loves all equally—women, men, rich, poor. And speaking to individuals is the kind of thing our Father does when a heart is searching for its home."

"I . . . I don't understand what you mean."

"He is always waiting to speak, waiting to wake, waiting to reveal the manger. That is no doubt why he sent you here, so that you could hear about Christmas and so that he could wake you and bring you on your knees before the manger."

"Oh . . . there are so many things I do not know what to think about," said Kasmira, beginning to weep again. "It is all so strange to my ears. Do you mean that I can be a Christian too?"

"Of course, my dear," replied Hope tenderly. "The Father draws men and women to the manger from every nationality and culture—Muslims, Africans, Serbs, Chinese, Americans, Russians, Germans, Buddhists, Hindus, those who believe, those who do not believe. God brings *all* to the manger eventually, just as he brought you on this morning. The manger is where life begins."

"It is all so new . . . there is so much I do not understand."

Hope rose and now helped Kasmira to her feet.

"Come inside, my dear," she said. "We shall build a warm fire and have a long talk. I shall tell you all about the man who was born in this manger, and how you can take him for your very own Savior."

44

Christmas Morning

When Amanda awoke on Christmas morning, she lay in bed a long time.

The chalet was quiet, though she heard what might be voices somewhere outside. But she thought nothing further of it. Something made her reluctant to rise, sensing that the day would contain memories she wasn't sure she wanted to face.

But as on the night of the party, she was not able to stop them. Gradually images and scenes, sounds and sights and smells began to tumble out of the past into her consciousness. . . .

———— ◆◆◆ ————

Christmas morning at Heathersleigh Hall was always fun and filled with laughter and presents, song and food and stories and rides in the country. Charles and Jocelyn Rutherford spared no effort to make every Christmas more memorable than the last.

On this occasion, seven- or eight-year-old Amanda bounded

down the stairs at the crack of dawn, followed by her brother, George, older by two years. They scampered to the Christmas tree, the floor underneath it spread with brightly colored packages and presents. Yelling and talking both at once, they could scarcely contain their excitement, or wait for their mother and father and baby sister to make an appearance.

"The stockings, George!" cried Amanda. "Look!"

The next instant they were off in the direction of the fireplace. There hung three huge knit stockings with the three names AMANDA, GEORGE, and CATHARINE knit into the pattern, all fat and filled and spilling out with candy and tiny toys, and with three small stuffed animals peeking their heads out from the tops of each. On either side of the three hung two others, not stuffed so full, it is true, but completing the picture of the whole family of five, with the names CHARLES and JOCELYN embroidered into them.

Moments later Amanda's and George's stockings were in their laps on the floor. Amanda hastily picked hers up from the bell on its bottom and dumped all the contents into a heap on the floor. She grabbed the first piece of candy her fingers could seize, stuffed it quickly into her mouth, then proceeded to rip open every present in a frenzy of unbounded energy.

George, meanwhile, who had had the good sense to move a little way across the floor from her, began methodically to examine each item in his stocking with interest, slowly opening one tiny package after another, not beginning another until he had given each the attention it deserved.

"Hurry up, George!" clamored Amanda as he began carefully to open a second little wrapped box. "I'm already done.—Here, I'll help you with that . . . I know what it is!"

"Get away, Amanda. I want to do it myself."

Amanda turned and ran back in the direction of the tree.

On the landing above, seen by neither, stood Jocelyn Rutherford in her robe, watching the scene in silence with a contented smile on her face. . . .

Years sped by and the three young Rutherfords grew, and now the scene shifted to another Christmas. Amanda was fifteen, George seventeen, Catharine nine. How very different was the atmosphere in Heathersleigh Hall now as the five members of the family sat in front of the tree on Christmas Eve listening as Charles read the Christmas story from the Bible. As teenage Amanda sat listening, she could feel the quiet annoyance rising in her heart. Christmas used to be so fun, she thought, before they started making it so religious and . . .

———————— ♦ ♦ ♦ ————————

In the midst of her reflections, Amanda heard the front door of the chalet open downstairs. Voices were entering from outside. It was time she got up.

Slowly Amanda rose. She was in no hurry to go downstairs. She moved about her room slowly, gazing absently out the window for several long minutes at nothing in particular, then began to dress.

Some time later she slowly made her way along the corridor toward the stairway. She wasn't sure what to expect. Suddenly she felt almost like the child of her memory again, though cautious and timid now rather than eager and energetic. There was no tree, no presents, no pony with ribbon tied to its mane awaiting her. Why did she feel so peculiar on this Christmas morning?

As she reached the landing she heard voices downstairs. She began to descend the stairs, sensations from many past Christmases deepening within her, paying little attention to the conversation in progress below. She glanced toward the fireplace as it slowly came into view, almost expecting to see stockings hanging from it with hers, Catharine's, and George's names on them.

But there were none.

A pang of nostalgic sadness swept through her. She could almost sense at this moment that her mother was thinking of her. What was the rest of her family doing right now? Amanda wondered. Were they all celebrating happily around the Heathersleigh Christmas tree? A lump tried to rise in her throat. . . .

"You dear girl . . ." Sister Hope's voice now penetrated into Amanda's hearing, "our Father is a good Father. . . ."

Amanda now paused to listen as the present pushed out memories of the past. Hope, Galiana, and Anika were all in the big room, apparently talking with the young Serb, Kasmira. As she stood halfway down the stairway, Amanda became aware of the fragrance of sweet rolls coming from the kitchen.

"God will not be angry with you," Sister Hope continued, "because you voice doubts. His heart is tender toward you."

"But we are taught that Allah is angry toward all his enemies, toward those who doubt him."

"Many believe that of the God we call Father too," Galiana now said.

"As well as many Jews of ancient times," added Anika. "That is why God sent his Son Jesus, to tell men and women the truth about their heavenly Father, to tell us that he is good and loving, and that we may trust him."

"As you learn to accept his love and forgiveness and kindness toward you, Kasmira dear, you need think no longer of God's anger. You have a Father who loves you and a Savior who wants to be your friend and companion all the rest of the days of your life. I realize it is all new and must seem strange and different from your Muslim tradition. But you will learn, and you will soon discover how very patient and forgiving and understanding God is."

Amanda now continued down the final few steps of the stairway, then entered the large room where the others sat. Sunshine streamed in the windows. It was a bright, cheery day. Sister Hope glanced up.

"Good morning—Happy Christmas, Amanda!" she said. She rose and gave Amanda a warm hug. "We have just been talking about the Christmas story with Kasmira. She has not been familiar with it. Make yourself some tea, then come join us."

An hour later, after one of the most unusual discussions of spiritual things Amanda had ever been part of, during which Sister Hope had knelt with Kasmira and the former Muslim had offered an extraordinary prayer of grateful conversion from one faith to another, the five women took chairs around the large table. In front of them stood platters of what could only be described as a Christmas breakfast feast— bread, cheeses, sliced meats, yogurt, butter, and fresh cheese danish still steaming from the oven. Two fresh pots, one of tea, the other coffee, added the pleasure of their aromas to the whole.

"Why don't you all help yourselves and begin," said Sister Hope, "while I read the Christmas story from the Gospel of Luke. Sister Galiana, would you give thanks for us on this wonderful morning of new birth?"

45

Heathersleigh Christmas

*C*hristmas morning at Heathersleigh Hall could not have been more different than Amanda envisioned it, or more distinct from that in which she herself was participating at that moment.

The spirit over the estate of her former home had grown more subdued and quiet as Christmas approached. Upon Catharine's return from visiting Oxford, she and Jocelyn had begun thinking of Christmas and wondering what to do to keep from becoming too depressed at the thought of Charles', George's, and Amanda's absences.

"You know what we should do, Mother," said Catharine one day in the middle of December. "We have to try to make Christmas special for *others*. If we are alone, that does not give us the right to be sad."

"You are exactly right," rejoined Jocelyn. "What would our Lord do? Obviously he would think of others, not himself. Many women are without their husbands and fathers and brothers just as we are—we shall try to cheer them up rather than be lonely ourselves. What do you suggest . . . that we go visiting, that we bake things for people?"

"Why don't we do both, Mother? It would be fun. We could load up the car just like Father Christmas's sleigh, full of breads and jams and sweets, and then go round to everyone in the village."

Jocelyn laughed with delight at the image.

"We shall do it! I propose we set to work planning and baking this very day."

They had done just that, such that by Christmas Eve the kitchen and pantry were piled high with loaves of breads and candies, cakes and cookies and puddings, biscuits and scones and preserves, and all manner of dried fruits and nuts. The list of potential recipients had grown steadily since the inception of the project, and now included the name of nearly every family in Milverscombe and for several miles around.

When Christmas Day came, Jocelyn awoke early. She could not help it. It was Christmas morning, and she was a mother.

Her thoughts immediately filled with Amanda. Little did she dream that at that moment Amanda lay in a comfortable bed in the care of dear sisters in the Lord thinking of her. Had Jocelyn known it, she would have wept for joy. As it was she wept quietly for sadness. But her years of prayers for her eldest daughter were being answered to a greater degree than Jocelyn could have imagined. Many good influences toward home-going were being planted in Amanda's heart, and the memories stirring within her were doing their healthy work of disconcertment. Much movement in the right direction was vigorously under way.

Jocelyn rose, dressed, and went downstairs alone to have a walk through the quiet house, praying for each of her family. As always, she had placed their five stockings on the fireplace. But she and Catharine had agreed to let even their two remain empty this year with the rest. It was a little sad and brought a few renewed tears to see them hanging limply from the hearth.

That was where Catharine found her when she approached from behind and placed a gentle arm around her shoulders. Jocelyn glanced to her side and up into the face of her youngest daughter.

"Hello, dear—Happy Christmas," said Jocelyn, smiling through her tears.

"And to you, too, Mother. Thinking of the others?"

Jocelyn nodded.

"We will all be together again, Mother," Catharine said. "One day the stockings will be full again."

"I know, sweetheart," replied Jocelyn softly. "I'll be all right. I've had my cry for the day. And now you and I are going to have a wonderful Christmas!"

The two Rutherford women enjoyed a quiet Devonshire breakfast together, then set upon the last of their baking with enthusiasm, planning to leave the house on the first of their Christmas rounds, as they had come to call them, around nine.

Their first call was to Maggie's cottage to give her their gifts and spend half an hour enjoying a cup of tea with their dearest friend. They well knew after leaving Maggie's and driving into the village that they would be invited for tea at every home they entered. But neither time nor their constitutions would permit the acceptance of every such request. According to Catharine's calculations, accounting for travel time between stops—and an hour's break for the morning's service at the Milverscombe church, where they would see and visit with everyone a second time—ten or fifteen minutes in each home was the maximum they could afford to budget.

When Jocelyn and Catharine arrived back at Heathersleigh Hall late in the afternoon about thirty minutes after the sun had set behind the western hills, they were exhausted with the pleasurable fatigue of having given of themselves to the limit.

"I don't know how I will sleep tonight," sighed Jocelyn as she turned off the car's engine in front of the Hall and laid her head back against the seat. "I've never had so much tea in one day in my life. But I am so exhausted all I can think of is my bed."

"You can't go to sleep yet, Mother," said Catharine. "I still have my present to give you. I've been saving it all day."

They got out of the car and wearily walked inside. The house was empty and quiet. The staff had gone to be with their own families for several days. Jocelyn was especially glad on occasions such as this for the electricity Charles and George had installed. She switched on several lights as they entered, and immediately the great house did not feel nearly so desolate.

"I have something for you too, Catharine," said Jocelyn.

"I didn't see anything under the tree."

"I didn't put it under the tree—I wanted to surprise you. Do you feel like something to eat?"

"Perhaps just a light snack ... a roll and a glass of milk, perhaps ... but no tea!"

They both laughed.

"That sounds good to me too. Then we shall exchange our gifts."

As they sat down thirty or forty minutes later, it was with the contented feeling of a day well spent. Jocelyn handed Catharine a small wrapped package across the table.

"Thank you, Mother—what is it?"

"Open it, dear. You don't think I'm going to *tell* you!"

Catharine did so, pulling out a small, exquisitely hand-painted watch pin.

"Mother ... your watch!" exclaimed Catharine.

"My father gave it to me when they were leaving for India and I remained in England to begin my nursing training. It is one of my most treasured reminders of him. You are twenty now and will be going off to Oxford to study next year—"

"Perhaps," said Catharine. "I haven't entirely decided."

"Nevertheless," Jocelyn went on, "I want you to have it now."

"Thank you, Mother. I shall treasure it always. Now I have something for you."

Catharine jumped up from the table, left the room momentarily, and returned a minute later with a small rolled parchment scroll tied with a thin red ribbon. She sat down and handed it to her mother.

Jocelyn untied the ribbon and unrolled the parchment, then cast up at Catharine a look of puzzlement.

"It is a little story, Mother," said Catharine. "I wrote it for you."

"How special dear! I can't believe it."

Slowly Jocelyn began to read the hand-lettered words on the page, her eyes slowly filling with tears.

God's Woman

I went out today and found myself tracing steps through the grass. Though I knew not whose they were, something caused me to ask, "What makes a woman of God?"

A hunger arose within me, and I wondered, "Will it ever be said of me that I am she?"

Then came an answer. "The path toward what you seek is trod by few. The cost is high, the way marked not through grassy meadows of contented ease but across byways of sacrifice, grief, doubt, prayer, and tears. Through such are my women made strong, and their hearts enlarged to house my presence."

Suddenly I knew they were your steps I was following on just that very journey. With a pang I realized that even my love could not allow me to know all you have felt as you walked that course, or the pain that came as you trod avenues of life you did not anticipate. But setting my feet in yours let me share it briefly, and for that moment I rejoiced.

Then I saw you coming toward me from a small wood ahead. Your face was radiant and alive with great joy. I knew that you had seen the Master.

I tried to speak. Fain would I ask what wondrous thing your countenance revealed, that I might partake in it. With all my heart I desired to be God's woman too. But no words came from my lips. You held your hands out to me in embrace. I saw in their palms the holes of the Savior's own death. All my questions were swallowed up in the radiance of your face, and I knew that your joy came because you had partaken in his suffering. And I saw the truth you had discovered in your prayer closet, that suffering carves out within God's women the very cistern of soul into which he pours his presence. And I knew that the deeper the well, the more of himself it is able to contain.

Then the vision vanished, and I was alone. I turned back the way I had come. I looked down. The imprint was no longer in the grass beneath me. I wondered, had it all been a dream?

In the distance I saw you walking toward me again. Now it was no mere vision but was really you, the friend I love. And I knew where you were going. You were bound for your prayer wood where the Master waited to fill you with the joy your faithfulness had made you ready to receive, and which my vision had foreseen.

You smiled as you passed. Your hands were unblemished. For what I had beheld earlier was but a symbol of the scar of that deeper cavity you now carried within your very own soul. You had suffered with him. You had wept in the seasons of your aloneness. He had privileged you to feel the pain of love and the agony of loss. He had gathered up the droplets of your weeping and poured them into the deep reservoir within you, which was the shape of his own being. Your tears had become the perfume of precious nard with which his dwelling place was anointed. And I knew that you were his woman.

I loved you anew as you passed. I longed to follow, but knew I could not. For my time was not yet, and I must walk the path he had chosen for me.

I watched you go, knowing how blessed I was to be allowed to share a season of life's pathway with you. And now came the answer to the question I had asked in the beginning.

"Follow the example you have seen."

And I knew the meaning of my vision, that it was said of you: "She has allowed me to carve out my depths within her, and in her heart I dwell."

When she had completed it, the paper fell from Jocelyn's hands. She rose and walked around the table. She had no words. All she could do was take Catharine in her arms and weep.

46

Christmas Dinner With Meat for Discussion

◆ ◆ ◆

*L*ate in the day, Herr Buchmann arrived at the Chalet of Hope for Christmas dinner. After carving the Christmas turkey, he and the five women took their places around the large table.

"Herr Buchmann," said Sister Hope, "would you be so kind as to offer our appreciation to the Lord on this special day of thanksgiving and rejoicing."

"I would be honored," replied the schoolmaster. *"Our loving heavenly Father,"* he began, *"our hearts are full of gratitude on this day for what it means to those who know you, and for all those who are yet to know you.*

"Thank you for this season, for the life you have given us, for the ministry of this chalet, and for your great gift most of all. Thank you for the reminder of that very special day when you gave your Son that mankind might know you as it had never known you before. Through him you revealed that deepest aspect of your nature that you had not shown fully until that moment—that you are our Father.

"Thank you, God. Because of the miracle of Christmas, we now know to call you by that wonderful name. On this day especially let us dare address you as Jesus did, as our very own and personal Abba. For Fatherhood is the message of Christmas, as your own Fatherhood is your greatest gift to us—exactly as Jesus told us. Amen."

Herr Buchmann turned to Kasmira sitting beside him as the platters began to make their way around the table.

"How long have you been with the sisters here at the chalet, my dear?" he asked.

"Three weeks," she replied timidly, still somewhat shy of this outgoing, gregarious man who seemed to treat women as respected human equals, and was therefore different from any man she had ever met in her own culture.

"I understand your husband died in the recent fighting?"

"Yes," answered Kasmira, lowering her eyes.

"I was very sorry to hear of it. But I trust that you will find good in life in spite of it. Our Lord told us that death was not the end, you know. We still have much to hope for."

She nodded.

"And what do you think of it here?" he asked.

"I am learning many new things."

"I have always found that the atmosphere of the chalet tends toward that," said Herr Buchmann. "Would you not agree, Sister Hope?"

"Such indeed is my prayer."

"You know, Sister Hope," said Anika thoughtfully, after a temporary lull in the conversation, "what Herr Buchmann prayed a few minutes ago was exactly what I might have expected to hear from you."

"I confess," smiled Sister Hope, "I did find his words resonating within my own spirit."

"To what are you referring?" asked Herr Buchmann, intrigued.

"About God's Fatherhood being the gift of Christmas," said Anika.

"Ah yes, one of my scandalous theological notions."

"I don't find it scandalous in the least," said Hope. "I might not have used those exact words, but it is that very thing, in principle at least, that I have been explaining to Kasmira today, that because of Christmas we can more fully know of the Father's goodness. She has grown up in a tradition where an angry God rules the universe. I have told her that the manger shows us God's love. It is the culmination of his many acts of mercy and goodness toward his children."

"I have always thought that God's greatest gift to us was Jesus," now said Sister Galiana, "and that *he* was the gift of Christmas."

"Jesus is certainly a dear and precious gift to man," rejoined Herr Buchmann. "But I have to say that I believe God's *most* priceless gift to us is himself. Of course it is impossible to separate Jesus from that. When God sent Jesus to be born, he was giving himself, wasn't he?"

"What do you mean?" asked Sister Galiana.

"Just this—that he sent Jesus, not as a gift to us merely in himself as the Son, but for the purpose of telling us that God is our Father. That is the one thing Jesus talked about above all else—the one thing he tried most persistently to get through to his disciples ... that God was their Father, a *good* Father, their loving and tender *Abba*."

Amanda listened with fascination. She had not heard a theological conversation around a meal table like this since Heathersleigh. And yet, she supposed, today *was* Christmas. What better subject to discuss than what the day signified?

"What do you think, Sister Hope?" now asked Herr Buchmann, glancing toward his hostess.

"I would agree that when God sent Jesus to live among us on that first Christmas back in Bethlehem, more than anything he was revealing himself to us as Father."

"That was the reason Jesus came after all, wasn't it?" added Herr Buchmann, "—to tell us about the Father."

"I thought Jesus came to bring salvation," said Galiana.

"He did," rejoined Herr Buchmann. "Jesus came to show us the way to salvation, which exists nowhere else but in the Father's loving heart. What is a cross but two slabs of wood? Only a Son who knew the Father's love could take us, through the cross, *to* that love. Without God's Fatherhood there is no salvation. It is because he loves us with a Father's love that *he*—the Father—saves us. Such was Jesus' sole purpose for living, to take us by the hand and bring us to the Father's heart of love."

"Now he sounds exactly like you," said Anika, turning toward Sister Hope.

She laughed and Herr Buchmann joined in. "I want to hear more," he said.

"Perhaps another time," she said.

"But isn't what you say making less of Jesus' role in salvation?" persisted Galiana, who had never heard these ideas expressed quite so succinctly, even from Sister Hope.

"Is it? I don't think so," replied Herr Buchmann. "Jesus never exalted himself, but only exalted the Father," replied Herr Buchmann. "I sincerely hope what I have said is not to diminish the Lord Jesus, but rather to obey him."

"So what is his role in our salvation, then?"

"Just what he himself said it was—the role of a loving Son carrying out the will of his loving Father. Such makes the atonement more beautiful to me, not less. The Father forgives our sin. Jesus leads us by the hand to that throne of forgiveness. It is a beautiful picture to me, and makes me feel like such a loved and secure little child when I place myself in it along with the Father and the Son."

Again it was silent for a few moments.

"What you have said sheds an entire new perspective on what happened that night back in Bethlehem," Hope said.

"I think I have always thought of this day only in connection with the baby Jesus," said Anika at length. "But God's gift at Christmas is so much larger than I had ever considered."

"That can be said of everything God does and all he gives," added Sister Hope. "*Everything* of his is so much larger than we think—especially salvation."

"How do you mean . . . *larger*?" now asked Amanda, joining the discussion for the first time.

"I mean," replied Sister Hope, "that men and women are so prone to place limitations upon what God does, or can do, or *might* do, so that they can explain his ways and means to the satisfaction of their small intellects."

"I couldn't agree more, Sister," said Herr Buchmann. "God's work has fewer boundaries than we generally think. Limitations speak of fi-niteness, but God is infinite. And especially are God's love and salvation not limited by man's interpretations and by the boundaries man would place around the extent of their reach."

47

New Year and Changes

*O*ne by one the sisters of the Chalet of Hope returned to Wengen as the days of the year 1915 opened.

Changes were in the wind, and not only from the blustery black clouds swirling about the Jungfrau and other peaks that were now mostly lost to sight.

All immediately beheld the change on Kasmira Tesar's radiant unveiled face.

But they sensed an alteration in Amanda's spirit as well, not so visible yet perhaps extending as deep in different ways as the transformation that had come to the young Muslim. For though the pilgrimages of the two young women whose lives had intersected high in the Swiss Alps were very different, they were both learning to turn their faces toward Fatherhood, which is the central necessity of the universe.

Meanwhile, a hundred miles to the southeast, a young German teacher in a Catholic school in Milan resumed her duties after the Christmas holiday. As her class of little Italian girls filed from the room on their first day back at school, Elsie Reinhardt was surprised to see two men standing in the corridor outside the classroom, apparently waiting to see her.

She did not recognize either of them. Neither did she like their looks.

"You are Elsie Reinhardt?" said the smaller of the two in Italian.

She nodded, glancing at the other man as she did.

"Have you or someone in your family been traveling recently by train to Switzerland?"

"I have recently returned from a Christmas visit to Munich. I traveled through Innsbruck."

"No—before the end of the year . . . weeks ago."

"I . . . my sister Gretchen visited me two months ago," she answered slowly.

"And did she return to Switzerland by train?"

"She was on her way back to Inter—"

The young teacher hesitated. Something in the man's eye caused her to stop. The sense came over her that these two were not here in any official capacity.

"Inter . . . what?" said one of the men.

"I think I should say nothing further," replied Elsie, on her guard yet the more.

"Was a young Englishwoman with her?" now demanded the other man in a tone Elsie did not like.

"I know nothing about an Englishwoman," she said. "My sister visited me and left . . . alone. What is this all about?"

"We are looking for the Englishwoman. She is a spy."

"I know nothing about her."

"Where does your sister live?"

"I really think I have said enough. Please . . . you will have to excuse me," she added, now walking past them and down the hall toward the headmistress's office. She was relieved when she did not hear their footsteps following behind her.

48

A Bad Father

A week later a letter arrived at the chalet for Gretchen. She was surprised to see the return address so soon after they had been together for the holiday, for her sister was not a frequent correspondent.

Dear Gretchen, she read,

I had the most peculiar and unnerving visit yesterday from two strange men whose looks I did not care for at all. They were aware of your visit to Milan and wanted to know your whereabouts. I may have said too much, though I did not tell them where you lived. It was spooky. They spoke of spies. What could it be about, Gretchen? They also asked about a young woman, apparently English, they thought you were traveling with. They said she was a spy. I don't know how they got your name, but I said you didn't know anyone like that and had left Milan traveling alone. Whatever it was all about, Gretchen, I cannot help being worried. Be careful.

Love,

Elsie

Concerned, Gretchen showed the letter to Sister Hope. After serious thought, they judged it best to say nothing to Amanda for the present, though the situation obviously bore watching.

Ever since her return, Sister Marjolaine had been quieter than usual. One evening around the fire Sister Gretchen asked if something was troubling her.

"You know my father died last year," said Marjolaine.

Gretchen nodded.

"This was my mother's first Christmas without him. I was never close to my father. For many years I did not even think he loved me. But being home for Christmas made me realize that I miss him. Whatever he felt toward me, I realize how much I loved him."

Softly Marjolaine began to cry. Gretchen reached out from where she sat and placed a reassuring hand on her arm. Only the crackling of the fire broke the silence for a minute or two.

"Losing one's mother or father is one of the painful transitions of life," said Gretchen at length. "I have not faced it yet, but I am trying to prepare myself. It must be very painful."

"The only thing worse is not to have them at all," said Sister Hope. "I would give anything to have a father, or perhaps I should say to have been able to know my father, even if it meant one day having to lose him."

"Even an uncaring father?" Amanda asked.

"Yes, Amanda—I would give anything even to know a bad father. You cannot imagine going through life with no one whom you can call by that name. Those who complain about their fathers have no idea how fortunate they are."

Another pause followed.

"But in all honesty, dear," added Hope at length, "I doubt your father was so uncaring as you might think, if I am reading into your words accurately."

The words stung.

"Why would you say that?" said Amanda, a slight edge of annoyance revealing itself in her tone. "You don't know a thing about my father."

"Because in my experience, those who complain loudest about their parents usually do so to mask wrongful attitudes within themselves."

Amanda's face flushed with momentary anger.

"Sister Hope is right, Amanda," said Clariss. "Most parents are more loving than people realize. Take it from one who knows."

Amanda said nothing. But Sister Luane now spoke up. "I take it, you are such a one?"

Clariss nodded.

"I would be interested to hear about it," said Luane, "if you don't mind."

"Not at all," Clariss replied. "I can talk about it now—though it was difficult for a long time. My very earliest memories are happy ones," she began. "My mother was loving and kind. But when I was about four, my father began to drink. He was very stern by nature, and the drink only made it worse. He drank a lot, and we were often hungry because there was no money for food. He spent most of his wages on drink. When he was drunk he would hit my mother. When I was twelve, my mother died in childbirth. Her dying words to me were a plea to look after my little sister Gabriella. After my mother died, my father turned even more to drink. He neglected us when he was sober, and when he was drunk he would—"

Her voice caught in her throat. Clariss glanced away, her eyes filling with tears.

As she spoke, Amanda was reminded of Rune Blakeley and the anger she had always felt toward him for his treatment of his family. As she sat listening, she took in Clariss's features. Her complexion hinted at the olive shades of Italy, though was by no means dark. Her eyes and lashes, however, were pure black, as was her hair, adding to what might be described as a general air of quiet sadness, a constant expression of Mediterranean mystery. Her mouth was small, and, perhaps because of her past, not prone to much smiling, though when her thin lips did part in occasional subdued laughter, the wait was always worth it.

"Excuse me, I'm sorry," Clariss continued after a moment. "I had so many fears from those years that sometimes they still come over me. Even now I often hear sounds in the night and am filled with terror, imagining that my father is coming into my bedroom drunk. It paralyzes me with fear. A thunderstorm can still terrify me.

"One night when Gabriella was four, I woke to find him lifting her out of my bed. I went wild with all the rage of a mother bear. I jumped out of bed and attacked him and hit and screamed at him, although he hit me so hard in return it knocked me to the floor. But at least he left us alone for the rest of the night. The next morning I hid myself and Gabriella at a neighbor's house. That same day, when he was gone, I snuck back to the house to gather our clothes. Then with the little money I had, we took a train to an aunt's, who took us in."

"Have you seen your father since?" Marjolaine asked.

"A few times," replied Clariss. "My neighbor wrote to me at my aunt's to tell me that he had stopped drinking. Later he remarried and asked Gabriella and me to come back. But when we arrived, it was clear to me that our stepmother wanted nothing to do with us. She had her own children and had no use for two more, especially as I was by then nineteen. We only stayed a day or two and then returned to our aunt's. I eventually grew old enough to find work to support Gabriella and me. She is now married and happy, and I am here."

"Is your father still living?" asked Agatha.

Clariss nodded. "I visit him occasionally," she said. "He is old and grey now, and his temper calmed. I think he has forgotten the past, or if he remembers, he does not want to talk about it. I suppose that is how many people deal with past wrongs. Perhaps they think a little change makes up for the past, so they look ahead and refuse to look back. But I don't know . . . my father has never once in his life said he was sorry. I do not hate him, though I still have many fears and hurtful memories, for I know what drink can do to a man. I think I have perhaps forgiven him, though he has never asked for it. To ask forgiveness requires admitting having hurt someone, and some men never seem to be able to do that. At least my father never has. So he has changed, but I do not think he has repented."

Clariss paused sadly and thoughtfully.

"I cannot say whether all in my heart is right toward him," she went on at length. "Perhaps I will never know. I try to forgive. But it is difficult."

She glanced toward Luane and smiled a sad smile. "I am afraid my story does not have a very happy ending, does it?"

"It has been my experience that not all stories can," she replied. "But God is still God in spite of sad endings. And he can make sad endings happy in the end."

49

Sister Regina's Story

"What about you, Sister Regina?" said Luane after a brief silence, turning toward her. "I have not heard how you came to the chalet."

Regina smiled. Her face, perpetually brown even in winter, always wore a look of inner contentment and calm, as if she was in the midst of some inner conversation either with herself or with the Lord. The peacefulness of her countenance gave her what could only be described as a compelling beauty, though more of the spirit than of the flesh. In her case, however, the two could hardly be distinguished, so thoroughly did the various components of her nature blend into a harmonious whole. Her beauty might have made the first words out of her mouth seem strange to one who did not know her.

"Even when I was a little girl," she began, "I never thought of marrying."

"Why?" Luane asked. "I would imagine that an attractive young lady such as you would want to marry."

"I was drawn from an early age to a life of solitude and contemplation," Regina replied. "From before I can remember I enjoyed being alone, to walk, to think, to talk to the animals, even to pray. I suppose I was different from the beginning, and my parents thought I was somewhat odd and out of step. But I was content to be alone with my thoughts. I was never happier than when alone in the woods or by the sea. We lived near Barcelona, and I was fortunate to have both nearby."

"Sister Regina is our resident mystic," said Gretchen, and a few smiling nods went around the room.

"As I grew older," Regina continued in her deep rich voice, "my quiet side became more spiritually sensitive. By the time I was eighteen I knew that the desire of my heart was to devote myself to the Lord's work. Of course I thought that meant becoming a nun. And I might well have done so, for my family was Catholic. In fact, I assumed that I would eventually join the convent in Barcelona, where I knew many of the sisters. They had always seemed to me to be happy and at peace, and I hungered for just such a life. But on the other hand, I did not want to be cloistered away and separated from people. I liked to be alone. Yet I wanted to live a contemplative life of service and ministry in the midst of and involved with people too. I might have joined a teaching or perhaps a nursing order, but I had no inclination toward medicine, nor, that I could see, a gift for teaching.

"I prayed for several years, asking the Lord to reveal to me how and where such a life as I envisioned might be possible. When I came to this area as a lady's companion, I fell in love with the mountains of Switzerland. As much as I loved the sea, I came to love the mountains even more. Sister Hope and I met quite by accident down in Interlaken, at the fountain in the middle of town. I was standing there enjoying the sunshine and the water of the fountain and gazing up at the Jungfrau, when I became aware of someone looking at me."

Sister Hope laughed to hear Regina tell it. "I could tell there was something different about this young Spanish girl who had caught my eye," she said. "I couldn't help staring. Suddenly I came to myself and found that she was staring back at me."

"What did you do?" laughed Luane.

"We both laughed with embarrassment," Regina replied. "Then we began talking and introduced ourselves. I think we were drawn to each other immediately. We agreed to meet again. To make a long story short, when my duties with Señora Peña were completed, I came here to the chalet."

"You have been here ever since?"

"Yes, and I have never been happier. I feel that I have the best of all things. Life here resembles some of what it might have been like for me in the convent. But I am free to do whatever I feel and to minister to those whom the Lord sends in many diverse ways. I keep busy in and around Wengen helping some of the older women with their work, substituting in the village school when the schoolmaster is ill or must be away, sometimes minding one or another of the village shops in Wengen or down in Lauterbrunnen, even helping Frau Schmidt at the post. I have tutored some of the children who have had special needs or difficulties. And when there is not something to do for one of the villagers, I am always kept busy milking cows or tending our goats or chickens."

"And thinking!" added Anika.

"Yes," smiled Regina, "I enjoy my walks in the hills. I must have time to think and pray and be alone or I would die. As much as I love every one of you, I have to be alone some time every day too. Too much talk tires my spirit. And now having said that, I think I have said enough and will be silent." She glanced around the room with a sweet smile and said no more.

Sister Luane returned her smile. "Thank you for sharing your story with me," she said.

50

Narrowing Circle

◆ ◆ ◆

*Y*ou say the same name turned up crossing the border at Schaffhausen into Germany?"

"Yes, and also north of Innsbruck coming either from Austria or Italy."

"It appeared twice—the same name?"

"Reinhardt."

"Germany . . . that makes no sense. Why would she be going to Germany? And was there any sign of—"

"There was no trace of the Oswald name."

"I don't understand."

"They both returned a week later, crossing the same borders again back into Switzerland and Austria. Undoubtedly some connection to the sister in Milan. But I'm afraid there is no hint whatever of the other young woman."

"So what good does the information do us?"

"We have managed to trace the movements of the one south to

Milan, the other to Interlaken in central Switzerland."

"*Interlaken*, of course! That is where the Bern trail must have been going before, and what the sister started to say."

"But there is no indication the Englishwoman is still there."

"It is all we have."

"Interlaken is an odd place for a nest of spies."

"They hide wherever they can."

"Then it seems the circle has just narrowed considerably. I believe we are getting close. It is time to concentrate our efforts in the region of Interlaken, and find this Reinhardt woman once and for all."

51

Significant New Book

𝒯he sisters of the chalet had completed the Scotsman's sequel just before Christmas, but they had only now resumed their reading nights. According to one sister's expressed wish from several months earlier, *Robinson Crusoe* was now chosen, though they did not gather in front of the fire until somewhat later in the evening than was their custom.

"Whose turn is it to read?" asked Sister Marjolaine as the unofficial moderator of reading nights on the rare occasions when any exercise of leadership was required.

"I have not read for ages and ages," answered Sister Gretchen, "and to be perfectly honest, I am in the mood to do so."

"Then you shall read to us of the adventures of young Crusoe," Marjolaine said. "But first we must know the background of the book. Does anyone know about it?"

She glanced around, but her question met only silence.

"I shall tell you this much, then," she went on, "—it was written by Daniel Defoe, an Englishman, in the year 1719. *Robinson Crusoe* was Defoe's first novel, but he had been writing political pamphlets for twenty years before that, some of which got him into so much trouble that he was actually imprisoned for a time for his views. Do you know the style in which *Robinson Crusoe* was written?"

"In first person narrative, isn't it?" replied Agatha.

"Yes, it is, like many works of fiction of that period. It is a technique employed by many novelists, the Scotsman among them, and Dickens and many others. But rarely are such stories actually autobiographical, and neither is *Robinson Crusoe*. To our knowledge, Mr. Defoe himself was never lost at sea."

"Why are so many stories told that way?" Regina asked.

"You must remember that fiction in the early 1700s was still a relatively new genre, except of course for theater plays. Novelists were just beginning to learn their craft, and at first the public was somewhat skeptical of the new form."

"I didn't know that," said Sister Hope.

"Casting stories in the first person," added Marjolaine, "in the guise of true-life adventures, made them easier for the public to accept. Jane Austen, you may remember, employed this method in the early 1800s, and was—"

A sudden shriek from Kasmira brought the discussion to an instant end. Every head turned toward her and saw that she was staring at the window in terror.

"There is . . . someone is there," she said trembling, "—looking in at us, from outside . . . I saw two huge eyes."

The others looked around, some faces now displaying a little trepidation of their own. The night was cold and black outside, and they could not imagine who might be spying on them through the window.

"Is anyone feeling brave?" asked Agatha. "Speaking for myself, I plan to remain right where I am!"

"I'm sure it is nothing," said Gretchen, setting down the book and marching toward the window. "I will settle this mystery once and for—"

She did not finish the sentence. All at once her voice broke into laughter.

"Sister Galiana," she said, "I think it may be you who are wanted. It seems one of your children is having a fit of sleepwalking."

Galiana jumped up and ran to the window, pressing her face against the pane. Hearing Gretchen's laugh immediately alleviated their worry, and all the others were after her in a flash and now crowded about the window.

"Kasmira did indeed see two large eyes," said Gretchen, "but of the bovine variety, not the human."

"Toni, how did you get out!" Galiana exclaimed. "Don't you know that cows freeze in the snow?"

Already she was bound for the door. "I just hope no one else is loose."

Twenty minutes later, still laughing over the incident and with Toni safely back in the barn and all its doors secure, everyone gradually resumed their seats in front of the fire.

"Well, Sister Gretchen," said Marjolaine when they were all seated again after the exciting misadventure of the curious calf, "it is already late, but what do you say—shall we at least get a beginning made?"

"Let us indeed!"

Sister Gretchen opened the old volume that had come from the Buchmann library and began to read aloud.

> I was born in the year 1632, in the city of York, of a good family, though not of that country, my father being a foreigner of Bremen, named Kreutznaer, who settled first at Hull. He got a good estate by merchandise, and leaving off his trade, lived afterwards at York; from whence he had married my mother, whose relations were named Robinson, a very good family in that country, and after whom I was so called, that is to say, Robinson Kreutznaer; but, by the usual corruption of words in England, we are now called—nay, we call ourselves, and write our name—Crusoe; and so my companions always called me.
>
> I had two elder brothers, one of whom was lieutenant-colonel, to an English regiment of foot in Flanders, formerly commanded by the famous Colonel Lockhart, and was killed at the battle near Dunkirk against the Spaniards. What became of my second brother, I never knew, any more than my father and mother did know what was become of me.
>
> Being the third son of the family, and not bred to any trade, my head began to be filled very early with rambling thoughts. . . .

The very words reminded Amanda of her own visions of London and activity and getting away from Heathersleigh.

"It is not much," said Sister Gretchen, closing the book, "but we have at least made a beginning, and we can get much further next time."

It was late, and the yawns all around the room indicated clearly enough that the evening was over. Gradually they all rose and made their way upstairs.

As Amanda closed the door to her room, an undefined grumpiness crept over her. She had been feeling it all evening. The instant Sister Gretchen had begun reading from that book she had grown unsettled.

Where had such feelings come from?

Things could not be more perfect here, she told herself. Yet for some reason she could not account for, she was feeling irritable and testy. Little things about some of the sisters were starting to annoy her.

52

Ramsay Sinks

The words had grown hostile, the voices raised.

"I don't care what you say—"

"I tell you, we're going to do it my way!" interrupted the other.

Suddenly a gun appeared.

But Ramsay had by now become accustomed enough to his tall, gravelly voiced counterpart since their first meeting on the Luzern bridge that he was no longer intimidated. He had also quit leaving his gun in his hotel.

Ramsay stared back at the weapon, not exactly smiling but neither trembling in his boots. An inner conviction told him, despite the warnings he had been given, that the man did not possess courage to pull the trigger.

By a small succession of bad choices over a lifetime, Ramsay Halifax had slid lower and lower down the slope of character. And now a moment of climax in that progression had come.

Virtue cannot be attained in a moment. Sin, however, can be turned from in a single instant of decision. The road to virtue may be a long one, but it must begin with a single step. Even now it was not too late for God's grace to reach down and pull Ramsay up. But the downward trend of sin could only be stopped by his own choice.

That crossroads of truth had come. It was a crisis, not of life or death, but of the will.

Would he reverse the slide of his character toward the hell such people have unknowingly made their destination? Or would he hasten all the more his eventual fall into it?

For the briefest moment Ramsay seemed to hesitate. His eyes flinched, almost as if some corner of his being apprehended that an eternal choice lay before him. Was he having second thoughts about Amanda? Did he care more about her than he realized? Had he grown concerned for what might be her ultimate fate in this messy affair?

If so, such thoughts flitted through his brain in but half a second and were gone. The moment was all that mattered.

Then just as quickly the decision was made and the die cast. On this day he would not reverse the slide.

Ramsay ripped the Luger from his vest pocket and in the same motion did what he correctly assumed the other would not. An explosion deafened his ears. Before the tall man could recover his astonishment at the unexpected turn of events, he slumped dead to the ground.

Almost in shock at what he had done, Ramsay's arm dropped to his side. For several long seconds he stood staring forward, smoking pistol hanging limp in his hand.

A moment or two more the silence lasted.

Suddenly a voice sounded in the night behind him.

"So, Mr. Halifax," he said, "you have more guts than I would have expected."

Ramsay spun around, nearly frightened out of his skin. Standing some ten feet away, face barely illuminated by the tiny flickering light of the end of a cigarette, stood the short, balding man he had seen staring at him on the Kapellbrücke in Luzern.

"You!" he exclaimed. "What are you doing here?"

"I have been watching you all along, Mr. Halifax."

"But . . . but—who are you?"

"My name is Scarlino," replied the man.

"But what about . . ." began Ramsay in sudden confusion.

An evil chuckle sounded at the end of the cigarette. "One of my operatives," replied the man. "I keep myself out of sight unless absolutely necessary. Now I suggest you put that gun away and come with me before the police arrive. You have passed your test. We now have more important things to do."

In a daze, Ramsay complied, casting but one glance down at the body of his erstwhile colleague as they stepped over it and then disappeared together in the night.

53

Becoming a Daughter

♦♦♦

*A*ll the following day, Sister Gretchen prayed for Amanda. She had detected the subtle shift in spirit. That evening they were all seated around the fire with books or needlework in their laps. After some time, Gretchen broke the silence.

"Tell us *your* story, Amanda," she said. "What circumstances led you to the train station where I first saw you?"

"Oh ... you wouldn't be interested."

"Surely you know us better than that by now. That is the reason we are here, the reason we bring people to be with us. We ask the Lord to send us people who have lost hope."

"So, you think that about me," snapped Amanda sarcastically.

Several of the sisters glanced up. Eyes met as they seemed of one accord to sense a sudden dropping of the spiritual barometer.

"I was not referring specifically to you, Amanda dear. I did not mean to offend you. Although I must say," added Gretchen, "when I saw you in Milan, you had a look of hopelessness such as I have rarely seen."

Amanda sat in silence. As is the pattern with many, now that the unpleasant circumstances in which she had found herself earlier were alleviated and the temporary crisis past, she had begun again to consider herself an island who neither needed nor wanted anyone else's help.

"Our mission in life is to give hope by encouragement and hospitality," Sister Hope now added. "We try to help people to see that however bleak their circumstances, they yet have a Father who loves them, and is doing his very best for them."

At the word *father*, Amanda bristled yet more. Her unsettled annoyance was growing more pronounced by the minute.

Both Gretchen and Hope saw it clearly enough.

"Amanda," Gretchen began after a moment or two, "I would like to tell you a story about a young lady who was here at the chalet a number of years ago. She had been the most compliant little girl in the world growing up. She hardly ever did anything wrong and never needed to be spanked.

"But deep inside this girl carried a secret. More than just a secret—it was a secret *sin*. One of the worst sins imaginable. It was the kind of sin that rarely hurts anyone else because it is a very private sin. But if it is allowed to remain, it can destroy the person herself. And it almost destroyed her."

Amanda wasn't interested, but she supposed she didn't have much choice but to sit and listen. She sensed that the sisters were closing in on her. It had begun to feel like years before at home.

"This little girl positively *hated* being told what to do," Gretchen went on. "She did what was expected, but always on her own terms. She had a temper, too, but she learned to control it. She pretended to be obedient, to smile at the right times, and to wear a mask to hide what she was feeling down inside. In her own way, I suppose, she wanted to be good, but she didn't want to be *told* to be good. All the while, as she grew, she became more and more determined to get away from her parents at the first opportunity, so that she could be free of their rules and ways of doing things. More than anything, she wanted to dictate her *own* affairs. She wanted to make her *own* decisions. She never wanted anyone telling her what to do again.

"That's what made it such a serious sin—because that kind of attitude can prevent a person's entering into the relationship with God we're supposed to have. This girl thought about God sometimes. She even prayed. But she never realized that her independent spirit prevented God from being able to say anything back to her.

"Finally when she was twenty-one she had the chance she had been looking for. She was offered a job as a professor's secretary. You see, this girl was very intelligent and had made the most of her education. The pay was very good, and she could easily afford to live on her own as she had dreamed of doing.

"She left home and worked at the new job for three years. But inside she was not as happy as she had always expected to be. Then she met another young lady several years older than herself. Immediately they became close friends. But the independent girl of twenty-four realized her friend had something she did not have."

"What was that?" asked Amanda, gradually finding herself interested in the girl of the story.

"A meaningful relationship with God," answered Sister Gretchen. "The younger girl saw immediately that it was much different than her own shallow belief. Her new older friend had invited her to come and live with her one summer when the professor in the city did not need her. She came to assume that the idyllic surroundings of her friend's country home must be the cause of her peacefulness and spiritual maturity. If she could just stay there forever, she thought, she would eventually develop the same faith her friend had. The more she was around her friend, the more she hungered after intimacy with God too. Yet she didn't know how to attain it."

"Why didn't she ask about it?" asked Amanda.

"That is exactly what she did. But her friend's answer surprised her. Actually, at first it made her a little angry."

"What did her friend say?" asked Amanda.

"She said that living in a peaceful setting would not bring her close to God."

" 'Why?' the girl asked.

" 'Because there is something wrong in your soul,' answered the other, 'something preventing the intimacy you seek.'

" 'What could that possibly be?' asked the first.

" 'A spirit of prideful independence,' answered the older.

"Sudden anger rose up within the younger of the two. *Pride . . . independence*—how dare her friend say such things! You see, beneath a very calm exterior, she still possessed her silent temper. She did not like to be criticized any more than she wanted to be told what to do."

"What did she do?" asked Amanda.

"She stormed off," Gretchen answered. "She smoldered and pouted and was silent for days. Eventually, of course, she calmed down. Actually, she was a little ashamed of herself. So she went to her friend and apologized. Then she said she was ready to listen.

"The older of the two young women became very thoughtful. 'Are you certain you want to hear what I have to tell you?' she asked. 'It may be painful.'

"The younger said she was certain. She was ready to grow, she said, no matter what it took.

"So the older spoke very bluntly. 'You have been resisting authority all your life,' she said. 'When you were younger and you could not run away from it, in your heart you silently resisted your parents, doing things your own way even though you pretended to obey.'

" 'How do you know that?' asked the other.

" 'Am I right in what I say?'

" 'Yes, but how could you know?'

" 'It is not so hard to see. You still carry the same spirit. For those with eyes to see such things, it is as plain as the nose on your face. I see it all about you. Until it is dealt with, it will forever keep you distant from your heavenly Father.'

" 'What should I do?' asked the younger.

" 'You must learn what you should have learned as a little girl. You must learn to rejoice in being a child so that you can learn to become God's daughter.'

" 'Surely . . . you don't mean I should go back to *live* with my parents. You don't mean literally . . . a *child*.'

" 'I mean a child in spirit, one who does not resent authority over them—parents or anyone.'

" 'I am a grown woman. I have not lived with my parents for over three years.'

" 'Twenty-four is not really so very old.'

" 'But do you actually suggest that I . . . go back and live with them?'

" 'That is not for me to say. Whether with them or alone, somehow you must put right within yourself what you refused to learn early in life. You must learn to be happy and content under authority. Only then will you be able to discover the true independence of adulthood— the humble freedom of maturity rather than the prideful independence of childhood. It is what being God's daughter is all about.' "

Sister Gretchen paused thoughtfully.

"What happened? What did she do?" asked Amanda.

Gretchen remained quiet for another few long moments.

"I quit my job and went back to live with my parents," she replied at length. "I remained with them for five years, seeking to honor them and submit to them in my heart as I should have many years before. Believe it or not, they were the happiest years of my life. My parents treated me respectfully like an adult, yet I was able to honor them in a new way, even serve them and help them far more than I ever had when I was younger. I tried to live for *them*, rather than only for myself. My mother and father became true friends. My pride and self-centeredness gradually fell away—or, I should say, *began* to fall away. And I found myself beginning to understand many things about God in a new light. My dear friend had been right—the doorway to intimacy with God was through my very own parents. Not because of anything they did or said, but because of the change God wrought within me as a result of my decision to put myself willingly under them. *My* heart was wrong, and it could only be made right as I dealt with my wrong spirit toward authority. After five years, with my parents' blessing and encouragement, I went back to live with my friend, and I have been here ever since."

She smiled at the other sisters, though Amanda was silently beginning to fume at the trick she now felt had been played on her.

"I would have been content to remain with my parents even longer," Gretchen continued. "But by then, I think I was ready to leave. And, of course, this time I sought their counsel in the decision. They, too, thought it was time for me to establish my own life apart from them, now that I had discovered what I had been put under their care and authority to learn in the first place. I now visit them every chance I get. Along with the sisters here, and my own sister Elsie, my mother is my best friend. My father is old, and if he should die, my mother will come to live with us here."

"Why didn't you tell us it was about you all along?" said Amanda stormily.

"I wanted you to hear my story," replied Gretchen. "I thought that was the best way of telling it."

Amanda rose and walked off under a cloud.

54

Against Entreaties and Persuasions
◆◆◆

*T*he next evening the sisters gathered again in front of the fireplace for the second installment of *Robinson Crusoe*. They had seen little of Amanda all day. She had been down for lunch but had not participated in any of the day's chores, keeping to herself all afternoon in her room. She had not spoken a word at supper.

When the dishes were done and the kitchen clean and a nice fire crackling, they all took chairs in the big room. Amanda sat to one side, expressionless.

Sister Gretchen picked up the book, opened it to where they had left off, and began to read.

My father, who was very aged, had given me a competent share of learning, as far as house-education and a country free-school generally go, and designed me for the law; but I would be satisfied with nothing but going to sea; and my inclination to this led me so strongly against the will, nay, the commands of my father, and against all the entreaties and persuasions of my mother and other friends, that there seemed to be something fatal in that propensity of nature, tending directly to the life of misery which was to befall me.

"It seems that many young people set their sights contrary to what their parents want for them," Regina commented. A few nods went around the room. Sister Gretchen continued.

My father, a wise and grave man, gave me serious and excellent counsel against what he foresaw was my design. He called me one morning into his chamber, where he was confined by the gout, and expostulated very warmly with me upon this subject: he asked me what reasons, more than a mere wandering inclination, I had for leaving his house and my native country, where I might be well introduced, and had a prospect of raising my fortune, by application and industry, with a life of ease and pleasure. He told me it was men of desperate fortunes, on one hand, or of superior fortunes, on the other, who went abroad upon adventures. . . .

He pressed me earnestly, and in the most affectionate manner, not to play the young man, nor to precipitate myself into miseries which nature, and the station of life I was born in, seemed to have provided against . . . and that he should have nothing to answer for, having discharged his duty in warning me against measures which he knew would be to my hurt . . . and though he said he would not cease to pray for me, yet he would venture to say to me, that if I did take this foolish step, God would not bless me; and I would have leisure hereafter to reflect upon having neglected his counsel, when there might be none to assist in my recovery.

I observed in this last part of his discourse, which was truly prophetic, though I suppose my father did not know it to be so himself; I say, I observed the tears run down his face very plentifully . . .

and that when he spoke of my having leisure to repent, and none to assist me, he was so moved that he broke off the discourse, and told me his heart was so full he could say no more to me.

Gradually Amanda was growing uneasy.

She saw the parallel clearly enough with what her own parents had tried to do in urging her not to go to London. But this was just a story, after all, she tried to reason. Let this fellow Robin Crusoe, or whatever his name was, be as stubborn and rebellious as he wanted—what was that to her?

What was any of it to her!

She had a good mind to get up and leave. Yet still she sat for a little while longer.

. . . I took my mother at a time when I thought her a little more pleasant than ordinary, and told her that my thoughts were so entirely bent upon seeing the world . . . and my father had better give me his consent than force me to go without it; that I was now eighteen years old . . . and if she would speak to my father to let me make but one voyage abroad, if I came home again, and did not like it, I would go no more, and I would promise, by a double diligence, to recover the time I had lost.

This put my mother in a great passion; she told me she knew it would be to no purpose to speak to my father upon any such a subject; that he knew too well what was my interest to give his consent to anything so much for my hurt; and that she wondered how I could think of any such thing after the discourse I had had with my father, and such kind and tender expressions as she knew my father had used to me; and that, in short, if I would ruin myself, there was no help for me; but I might depend I should never have their consent to it; that for her part, she would not have so much hand in my destruction; and I should never have it to say that my mother was willing when my father was not.

Though my mother refused to move it to my father, yet I heard afterwards that she reported all the discourse to him, and that my father, after showing great concern at it, said to her, with a sigh, "That boy might be happy if he would stay at home; but if he ever goes abroad, he will be the most miserable wretch that ever was born: I can give no consent to it."

"He was a true prodigal, wasn't he?" said Sister Marjolaine.

"Obstinately deaf," rejoined Sister Agatha, "—what an apt description of the prodigal mentality."

It was not till almost a year after this that I broke loose, though, in the mean time, I continued obstinately deaf . . . and frequently expostulated with my father and mother about their being so positively determined against what they knew my inclination prompted me to. But being one day at Hull, whither I went casually, and without any purpose of making an elopement at that time . . . I consulted neither father nor mother any more, nor so much as sent them word of it; but left them to hear of it as they might, without asking God's blessing or my father's, without any consideration of circumstances or consequences, and in an ill hour, God knows.

"The age-old story," remarked Sister Gretchen, "—no one is going to tell *me* what to do. How well I know. He sounds just like me!"

"I realize it's only a story," said Regina, "but why do young people like Robinson Crusoe find following counsel so difficult to heed? I know what you have shared about your past, Sister Gretchen, but I confess, I do not entirely understand it, never having felt such things toward my parents."

"It would have kept young Crusoe out of a good deal of trouble," said Marjolaine, "if he hadn't resented the good advice of this father."

"How do you know?" asked Anika.

"Oh, I forgot," she giggled. "I've read it before!"

By now Amanda had entirely had enough. She was certain everyone was thinking of her. Finally she rose in the middle of the discussion, left the room, and walked toward the stairs.

"Are you coming back, Amanda?" Marjolaine asked, glancing after her.

"No, the story doesn't interest me."

She did not intentionally slam her door, but she made sure the others knew she had closed it tight and would not be listening to anything more that was said.

55

Unpleasant Reflections

*T*he night was late.

Amanda lay in her bed awake. She was more irritated than ever and ill at ease. Many confusing and conflicting thoughts were spinning through her brain.

They probably planned the whole thing, she thought. Why had everyone around here suddenly turned against her!

Her resolve of a few months earlier to get away from Ramsay and seek refuge at home was all but forgotten. The danger past, old annoyances had resurfaced and were quickly regaining the upper hand.

Independence . . . why was everyone talking about that all of a sudden!

What was wrong with being independent anyway? What did they expect, for people to remain little children all their lives? It was ridiculous! Everyone had to grow up and get out from under their parents' thumb sometime!

All that nonsense Sister Gretchen said about going back home—it was absurd. She would *never* do something like that!

Suddenly in the midst of her reflections, Amanda awoke to the thought *Where was her home?* as she faced again the horrifying fact that she was married.

The reminder sent a throb of physical nausea through her body. She felt herself gag momentarily. She had almost forgotten! It was like a bad dream. There were times she almost managed to convince herself it had all never happened.

But it had! She was no longer Amanda Rutherford at all but Amanda Halifax! The very idea was revolting. It made her so sick she wanted to die.

What was she going to do? She couldn't return to Ramsay! She could never do that either.

What *was* she going to do?

If only she had listened to her father's cautions, she thought, drowsiness gradually coming over her. Maybe she *was* like Robinson Crusoe. The words came back into her mind from the story in Sister Gretchen's voice—*"if he ever goes abroad, he will be the most miserable wretch that ever was born."*

That was her, she thought sadly and sleepily—a miserable wretch.

Amanda felt herself starting to cry. Quickly she took a deep breath and stopped it. She wasn't ready to collapse. It was still her father's fault for landing her in this fix in the first place!

If only, she thought again as she had so many times, she might awake in the morning and find that it all had been a bad dream.

She closed her eyes and slowly drifted off.

Hazy images of the Devonshire countryside floated like clouds into her dreams. Something was chasing her . . . someone . . . she was running, looking back. She was trying to get to Heathersleigh before they caught her. She had to get home . . . her mother and father would help her. They would know what to do. They would protect her, hide her from the danger. She looked back again. Terror seized her. She tried to scream. But her lips were silent. The great stone Hall of her childhood was just ahead. On she ran. At last she found her voice . . . *Mummy, Daddy!* she cried as she went, *Help me.* She reached the door. It was locked! She glanced back again. Now she saw Ramsay's face, clearly now, an evil grin of triumph on his face. *"I have found you at last!"* he shouted. *"You are mine again, Amanda . . . mine . . . mine. You will never leave me again . . . never again."* She screamed in terrible panic and turned back and began pounding for dear life on the door . . . pounding for anyone to hear . . . anyone to help her. *Help, help!* she cried. Another frightened glance behind her . . . Ramsay was to the top of the drive now and coming for her. He carried a rope . . . he was going to tie her up and drag her away! Desperately she pounded. But the Hall was empty and silent. She heard the echoes of her knocks inside, but there was no one to open the door. They had waited and waited for her return, but finally could wait no longer. Now they had gone . . . they were all gone. There was no one to help her . . . she had waited too long . . . and now the Hall was silent and empty as a tomb. *Mummy . . . Daddy . . . please—help me!* But there was no one to hear her plea, no one to help . . . for she was alone . . . alone . . . alone. . . . Behind her Ramsay came closer, his menacing footsteps crunching on the gravel. . . .

Still whimpering and with the words *Mummy* and *Daddy* on her lips,

Amanda suddenly awoke. She found herself cold, sweating, and breathing heavily in the blackness of a wintry night among the Alps of Switzerland.

Unconsciously—heart still pounding as if her knocking on Heathersleigh's door had become the beating within her chest, and with weird images of both dream and Sister Galiana's calf mingling in her confused brain—she glanced toward the window, almost expecting to see Ramsay's face leering inside at her.

But it had only been a nightmare. She began to breathe more easily.

For now she was safe . . . but she felt more desolate and alone than ever.

56

Bold Confrontation

Sister Hope awoke early.

Almost the same instant she was at her bedside on her knees praying for Amanda. The moment she awoke she knew what she had to do, and she knew that today was the day.

"Lord, do I *have* to?" she argued as she prayed. "It is so unpleasant to have to speak to people about their weakness."

"That is why I sent her to you," she felt the Spirit reply.

"But I get weary of being the one."

"Did you not pray to be used in people's lives?" came the Spirit's soft voice again. "Now you ask not to use the gift I gave in answer to your own prayer."

"But it is a painful gift."

"The girl's heart requires surgery. Prodigals need friends who will speak the truth, not justify their rebellion."

"But, Lord . . ."

"I want you to be Amanda's friend."

"But, Lord, it is *so* hard."

"Do you love her?"

"You know I do."

"Do you want what is best for her?"

"You know it, Lord."

"Then you must speak. You must fulfill the role of the prodigal's friend."

After breakfast on the morning following the second Crusoe reading, Sister Hope found Amanda alone in the sitting room. The other sisters had quietly dispersed. They sensed that the crossroads time which inevitably came for many of their guests had now arrived for Amanda.

"You seemed quiet last evening, Amanda," Hope said, sitting down opposite her. "I might even say you seemed annoyed with us."

"I'm getting sick of all this talk about independence, that's all," Amanda replied grumpily. "Why is everybody picking on me all of a sudden?"

"I didn't realize we were."

Amanda tried to laugh, but the sound which came out was more a perturbed grunt.

"I would say it's rather obvious," she said. "Sister Gretchen with her ridiculous story, trying to make me think *she* was rebellious. I don't know if I believe a word of it."

"You didn't know her back then. She was stubborn as could be. If anything, she downplayed that element of her story. She is greatly changed."

Amanda was silent.

"What do you think, Amanda, that she would make it all up just to irritate you?"

Amanda shrugged.

"We talk, we share, we are open and honest with one another," Hope went on. "You have seen that. If the Lord wants to accomplish a work within one of us, we want to get to the bottom of it."

It was silent a moment or two.

"How can you be so sure I am full of these things you're all talking about?" said Amanda finally. "Listening to all of you, you'd think I was Robinson Crusoe himself."

"Did any of the sisters hint at such a thing?"

"I'm not like Robinson Crusoe," Amanda said, ignoring the question. "I never went off to some ridiculous desert island!"

"I shall ask you a question, Amanda," Hope said. "There is a simple test to see if the spirit of young Robinson Crusoe sits on the seat of your will ... or if you prefer, call it the spirit of Gretchen Reinhardt before she decided to change it. I asked Sister Gretchen this same question the summer she spent here away from her job. Oh my, did she fume. So, Amanda dear, I am not, as you say, picking on you. I am asking you the same thing I asked her, and the same thing I often ask myself.

"Here is the test—how do you make decisions in your life? Do you automatically do whatever *you* want to do, or do you consult someone else? For example, do you say to one who is above you, *What would YOU have me to do?*"

"Who are you to ask me such a question?" said Amanda. "Have you set yourself up as my judge and jury?"

"I do not judge you, Amanda. I love you. I offer these words in prayerful hope that they will bring you understanding."

A noise something like *humph* sounded from Amanda's mouth.

"Did you ever say this to your father, Amanda, or to God?" Hope persisted. "Whenever it was that you left home, Amanda, did you say to father or mother, *What do YOU think it is best for me to do?*"

"What does it matter? It was all so long ago," said Amanda irritably. "Maybe I don't feel like answering your silly question."

"Nothing else matters so much, Amanda," rejoined Hope. "Amanda dear, *laying down* the right of self-rule is the business of life—the *only* business of life. To learn this one lesson is what we are here for. It is what our Lord came to teach us. Of course in the natural we seek our *own* will. But to train ourselves in opposition to this natural tendency is why we have been given a certain number of years on this earth. There is no other thing in life that matters than to learn to say, *Be it unto me, Father, according to YOUR will.*"

There was another pause of silence.

"I believe this is why God sent you here," Hope continued. "We all need help, Amanda dear. Humble yourself and let us help you learn this important truth."

"Stop!" Amanda suddenly cried, rising to her feet. "I won't listen to any more. *Independence ... independence ...* ask everyone else what to do! Can't any of you make up your own minds about anything! You don't give a person an inch to breathe, do you!"

"I heard Mr. Spurgeon say long ago," replied Hope calmly but seriously, " 'Men do not get better if left alone. It is with them as with a garden. If you let it alone and permit weeds to grow, you will not expect to find it better in six months—but worse.' "

"I am no garden!" snapped Amanda.

"Perhaps you are, Amanda," rejoined Hope calmly. "And there are weeds growing in your heart. To yank them out may cause pain. But better that than let them take over the whole garden."

Amanda was silenced again briefly, but anger was visible enough in her red cheeks.

"Why were you so tender and loving to Kasmira?" she said after a moment. "She wasn't even a Christian, but you are as nice as can be to her. I haven't heard you say anything like this to her. And now you talk to me like this!"

"Kasmira came to us lonely, confused, aching from loss of her husband, and knowing nothing about her heavenly Father. But you *should* know about him, Amanda. You do not need what she needed. You do not need to be coddled, you need to repent of bad attitudes. Some of your weeds have been growing a long time. They are weeds that will destroy you unless you root them out—the weeds of pride, rebellion, and unforgiveness."

"I don't have to listen to any more of this!" said Amanda.

"You will have to listen sometime," Hope said, her voice now taking on the tone of command.

"You're talking to me like I'm a little girl. I'm twenty-four years old!"

"That is not so old. In some ways, you are but a child, Amanda. It is only children who still think they have a right to self-rule. Grown-ups know better."

"So you *are* calling me a child!"

"Yes, but you can become a daughter. An obedient daughter of God."

"Who wants to be!"

"I do," said Hope. "In your deepest heart I think you do too."

"What do you know about my deepest heart!"

"I know that as a woman the highest privilege of that heart is to allow God to make a true daughter of you."

"Maybe I don't care! Maybe I have the right to make up my own mind, to make my own choices."

"The only right you have is to *lay down* the right of rule in your life. That is the only right any of us have. What we call our rights are illusions, Amanda. They do not exist. That is what childhood is for, to teach us how to lay down what we imagine is our right to independence, so that we will be capable of stepping into the greater freedom God wants to give. Without laying down the one, we can never enter into the other. Sadly, Amanda, it appears that you did not learn this lesson from your own childhood."

"Well, maybe that's too bad for me! I'm not a child anymore, so I suppose it's just too late!"

"It's never too late, Amanda. We *must* learn it. Otherwise we will never be our true selves. If you refuse to learn it, then a crisis lies ahead. When the battle will come, I cannot say. But come it will. For this purpose was the Son of God born, and for this purpose did he die—to save men's wills from self-rule, and to show us how the Self might be yielded to God's highest will."

Amanda walked to the window, turning her back as Sister Hope continued.

"That's what following God is—taking his will for our own," she said. "There is an independence into which we must all grow that is part of the maturing process. But the independence that is making you miserable, Amanda dear, is something else, and is nothing but pride. Every prodigal has to go home eventually. As was the case with Sister Gretchen—"

"I'm not a prodigal!" shouted Amanda, spinning around.

"It may be painful to admit, but that is exactly what you are."

"What gives you the right to preach to me!"

"What gives me the right is that I love you, Amanda. I want the best for you."

"It is hardly the kind of love I care about. If this is what you call love around here, then I think it is time for me to leave!"

Amanda turned from the window and left the room.

No one saw her the rest of the afternoon. She did not appear for supper.

57

Departure

$\mathcal{T}$he chalet remained subdued all evening.

Every one of the sisters had heard portions of the heated discussion. When, after silence had fallen, one by one they began to return downstairs to find Sister Hope alone and in tears, they knew well enough what had been the outcome of the exchange.

Sister Gretchen tried to comfort her friend, telling her she had had no choice but to speak. But to Hope Guinarde's grieving heart it was little consolation even to see Gretchen herself in front of her, to whom she had once spoken nearly identical words, knowing that Amanda had angrily rebuffed her attempt to help.

"If only I had been more gentle..."

"Hope, listen to me," insisted Gretchen, "there are times when firmness in the face of such attitudes is the only course. I am one who knows."

"But perhaps I should have been less confrontational—"

"I thank God," said Gretchen, "that you had the courage to expose my own self-centeredness. I shudder to think how long I might have gone on had you not looked into my eyes and said, 'Gretchen, you will never be happy as long as *Self* is ruling your life.' That took courage, and I am thankful for those words. They changed my life. A person's response to the truth is theirs to make before God. Yours was yours, mine was mine, and so is Amanda's. She must face what she has made of herself, and decide what to do about it. She is in God's hands now."

Sister Hope nodded, and her friend left her.

For the rest of the day the sisters went quietly about their business, each praying silently that Amanda would be able to find it within herself to heed Sister Hope's exhortation.

The following morning, after most of the others were seated around the table for breakfast, Amanda slowly walked downstairs and took a seat at her usual place.

"Good morning, Amanda," said Sister Regina in a quiet and loving voice as befitted the somewhat somber situation.

Amanda nodded. Greetings were extended by the others without reply.

After thanks had been given and tea was poured, at last Amanda spoke.

"I have decided that it is probably best for me to leave the chalet," she said in a calm voice.

"Amanda, I want you to know—" began Sister Hope.

"Please," interrupted Amanda, "don't apologize or try to talk me out of it. I think it is obvious that I will never fit in here. I'm not . . . like the rest of you."

"Oh, Amanda dear—" now began Gretchen in an imploring voice.

"My mind is made up," said Amanda. "Maybe people like me can't stay in a situation like this forever. I appreciate what you have all done for me, but it is time I considered what I ought to do next."

A brief silence followed. A few chairs shuffled.

"Where will you go?" asked Anika.

"I don't know, but right now it feels that anywhere would be better than a place where—"

Suddenly Amanda caught herself. Even her residual anger from yesterday's events could not prevent a momentary pang of hesitation for what had nearly popped out of her mouth.

She paused. The sisters continued to stare down at their plates in embarrassment and heartbreak. Most of them had at one time or another been exactly where Amanda was this moment—at a critical crossroads of character where pride and humility intersected, and where only one road led toward the future. It was so small, so simple, so *right* a thing to humble oneself and heed the precious counsel of wisdom. They had each faced their own such turning points and had had to painfully relinquish that which had bound them in their own maturity-inhibiting bondages.

But they could not help Amanda now. This was her crisis. Every man and woman must face the decision such a moment brings in the solitude of their own souls. They had told their stories, but would Amanda learn from them? They could only wait silently to see which of the character pathways she would choose to take.

"I don't know exactly what I will do," Amanda said after the brief, awkward silence. "I only know I must go."

Another period of quiet settled around the table, this time more lengthy. The sounds of forks and spoons and a few cups of tea being poured were the only indications that breakfast was continuing, though no one was very hungry.

"I promised we would help when you were ready to leave us," said Gretchen at length. "What can we do for you?"

The question took Amanda off guard. She glanced up with a look of bewilderment on her face. She seemed stunned by the words.

"You mean . . . after what I have done and said . . . you would still help me?"

"Of course," said Galiana.

"We love you, Amanda," added Hope. "Sister Gretchen speaks for all of us. Yesterday and what you have said just now changes nothing in our commitment to help you however we can."

"Just help me get back to England," said Amanda after a moment. "If you can lend me enough money for a train and boat to London, I will send it back as soon as I can."

"Of course, we will be only too glad to give you enough to get you home."

The rest of the day remained quiet. Amanda returned to her room. Subdued by the unexpected offer, she quietly began making preparations to go, packing her few things, and trying to convince herself in the face of gnawing unease that she had no choice other than to leave. She was not yet strong enough to admit herself wrong and reconsider her plans. She was especially not yet mature enough to ask for anyone else's help or advice.

After breakfast the following morning, as the entire household, including Kasmira, stood by the front door, a series of awkward hugs went around the somber group.

Sister Hope embraced Amanda tightly, but Amanda's pride was still too wounded to offer more than a stiff response.

"Dear, dear Amanda . . ." began the older woman. But she could say no more. She pulled away and broke into tears. "Good-bye, Amanda," she managed to add, kissing Amanda on the cheek, then turning and disappearing into the chalet.

Sister Gretchen and Amanda, both heavily bundled, walked crunching across the snow and got into the small waiting wagon where Amanda's bags already sat. Gretchen took the reins and urged the single horse forward toward the tracks through the snow down the slope toward the valley. A few more waves and good-byes came from the group of women clustered by the door. Amanda glanced back once more, lifted her hand in a final halfhearted wave, then turned away and did not look back at the chalet again. One by one the rest of the sisters followed Sister Hope back inside.

By the time the wagon disappeared in the distance, every one of them was weeping with her.

58

Lauterbrunnen

*U*nder the shadow of the Jungfrau range, situated in the long narrow valley extending from Interlaken to the base of the Jungfrau herself, Lauterbrunnen was not a large village. Fortunately on this occasion, it proved just large enough to keep Amanda from the danger that was stalking her much closer than she had any idea.

As Amanda and Sister Gretchen entered the village and made their way to its small station, the husband whom none of the sisters knew about had at last narrowed his search to the Lauterbrunnen valley. He and his treacherous companion, in fact, had arrived only twenty minutes earlier on the very train whose scheduled return trip his wife planned to take, not knowing that she would be doing so under his very nose. He was at that moment questioning the man whose name their contact in Interlaken had given them.

"Look, old man," an angry Ramsay Halifax was saying, "the name is Reinhardt. She lives somewhere around here."

"If she were one of the villagers," the man insisted, "I would know it. I tell you, I have never heard the name."

"You old fool!" cried Ramsay. "She is here, and I think you—"

"Let's go, Halifax," said Scarlino. "This is useless. He knows nothing."

"I think he does."

"Then you are a fool too, Halifax. His eyes would betray him. I can tell. He knows nothing. We will try the church."

"The church—that's it!" cried Ramsay glancing about. "There it is, over on the other side of the station. I remember seeing it when we got off the train. Of course the priest will know."

"Perhaps I should handle the interrogation," returned Scarlino sarcastically. "You are too hotheaded. We can't have you losing your temper and killing a priest."

It was quiet between the two women as they awaited the time for Amanda to board the train into Interlaken. How much had changed since their first meeting in Milan! Across the tracks rose the steeple of the Catholic church. Amanda glanced toward it and was reminded nostalgically of the Milverscombe steeple.

The time finally came. The train was preparing to depart back down the valley. A strained embrace followed.

"Thank you again," said Amanda. "You helped me when I had no one to turn to. I won't forget it."

She turned and walked toward the train.

The moment she was out of sight, Sister Gretchen began to cry. She searched the windows, but Amanda had taken a seat on the opposite side.

Gretchen could bear the wait no longer. She turned and hurried back to her waiting wagon.

The two strangers to the peaceful valley entered the church gate and made their way through graves and tombstones toward the empty church building. Scarlino led the way to the rectory behind it. If he was intimidated by the sacred tradition and intimations of eternity around him, he did not show it. Whatever his warning to Ramsay, he himself would not hesitate to kill a priest if need be. Although on this occasion, necessity probably did not extend quite that far. His plans involved larger fish than anyone in this little village, or anyone in Ramsay Halifax's scheme either.

"Good day," said Scarlino with a smile as the door of the rectory opened to his knock. "We are looking for someone and hope you might be able to help us."

Immediately on his guard, the priest eyed the two carefully. How deeply a spiritual man he was, his eyes did not immediately reveal. But that he was a better-than-average judge of character was clear from the imperceptible squint accompanying his first glimpse of these suspicious visitors.

"For what purpose?" returned Father Stein.

"She is believed to be harboring a spy."

"*She?*"

"That is, we *think* it is a woman—the name is Reinhardt," replied Scarlino. "The individual we speak of is extremely dangerous."

"Switzerland is neutral. I am neutral. I have no allegiance one way or another in this conflict. Whoever it may be is no spy to me. I am afraid I cannot help you."

He attempted to close the door.

"I realize the war is none of your concern," said Scarlino, preventing the door from closing with his foot. "Yet she could be a threat to your parishioners," he added with a subtle tone which was not lost on the good priest, "if not found."

The point was well taken, though Father Stein was still reluctant. The eyes of the two men locked momentarily. Father Stein knew the words he had just heard were a threat to him as well as to the people of the village. He was not overly anxious about his own safety. But it would be better to be straightforward than confrontational, and hope the men would simply leave without causing any trouble.

"There is no one by that name in Lauterbrunnen, I assure you," he said. "You can confirm what I say with anyone in town. Your information is obviously wrong. I know only one Reinhardt, and she lives at the chalet in Wengen, not Lauterbrunnen."

"Chalet . . . what chalet?"

"She could not possibly be the person you are seeking."

"Why do you say that?"

"It is a house of unmarried sisters."

"Sisters?"

"Sisters, women of God . . . *nuns*, if you like," he added, stretching the truth just a little, hoping it would dissuade them. He already had the uncomfortable feeling he may have been a little *too* straightforward. "Believe me, the last thing you will find at the chalet is a spy."

"We will be the judge of that. Where is this Wengen?"

"There . . . on the mountain," he answered reluctantly.

The two followed his pointing hand.

"Up there! But how does one get there? Is there a train?"

Father Stein smiled.

"I tell you, whoever it is you are looking for is not there. Even if they were, you will not get there at this time of the year. No, there is no train."

As a train whistle sounded behind them, Ramsay turned quickly toward it. A premonition swept through him. He had not realized the train was pulling out behind him on its return from where it had come an hour before. He stared after it for several seconds as it picked up speed and gradually disappeared down the valley. His thoughts were interrupted by Scarlino's voice.

"But I see a wagon that appears on its way up the mountain right there," he said, still looking off in the opposite direction toward the mountain.

"A few people make the trip," said Father Stein. "But unless you found one of the villagers willing to take you by wagon or donkey, I do not think you will get there at all. On foot you would never make it. And unless I am mistaken," he added, glancing over his shoulder toward where the peak of the Jungfrau would be had they been able to see it, "a storm is on the way."

"Then who is that there!" finally exclaimed Ramsay impatiently, pointing toward the wagon pulled by a single horse that was just disappearing into a thicket of trees.

"From this distance, I really could not say," answered the priest.

59

Strangers in Wengen

As if the skies over Switzerland had been roused to blustery fury in response to Amanda's departure from the Chalet of Hope, within a few hours—as she now rode northward toward Bern and Basel on a course that would eventually take her to France, and just as Father Stein had foretold—great black clouds continued to approach from the south.

It was late in the day when two strangers, whose feet were nearly as cold as their hearts, made their way along Wengen's deserted main street. They had arrived only a short while earlier on a hired donkey cart whose unbelievably slow pace had infuriated Ramsay nearly to rage. As yet they had not seen a soul.

"This is a small enough village," shivered Ramsay. "Surely we will be able to—"

He glanced around as they reached a side street.

"There is an old woman up ahead!" he exclaimed, pointing down the lane to his left. "—Hey, Hausfrau!" he called, running forward toward the bent form struggling against the wind with bag in one hand and walking cane in the other.

She continued on, giving no reply or other indication that she had heard a thing, which in this wind she may not have. The ground was frozen enough, however, to make certain the footsteps running up behind her sounded clearly.

Ramsay caught up and ran in front of her to block her way.

"Get out of my way, you young—" she began.

"Didn't you hear me?" said Ramsay rudely. The long day, intolerable ride, and frigid cold had long since laid waste any patience he might have possessed, which even on his best days was not much. "I'm talking to you."

"I heard you and I didn't like what I heard," she returned in kind, brushing her way past him. But again Ramsay stepped forward and blocked her way.

"Keep your temper, old woman," he said. "All we want to know is where someone named Reinhardt lives."

"Mind your own business and leave me be!" she retorted. "The chalet concerns me no more than you do yourself. Now let me pass."

"What chalet?" said Ramsay.

Bitten by a sudden whim of concern, not so much for the sisters themselves but for any inhabitant of her village over this rude stranger, the reply which now met Ramsay's ears was more cryptic than he had patience for.

"Ow, there's chalets here and chalets there," she said, still struggling to get by. "The Alps is full of chalets."

"What do you mean?"

"I mean nothing, only that you'll get no more out of me."

She shoved past again, this time giving Ramsay a sharp whack with her cane.

He winced in pain, his anger now roused to fury. He took yet another step forward, reaching out and grabbing hold of her shoulder.

Momentarily, however, he had met his match. She spun around, fire in her eyes, and attacked him with her cane more vigorously than before. A volley of abuse poured from her lips. Before Ramsay knew what was happening, he had received two more blows, one to his shoulder, one to his midsection.

Incensed, he lurched sideways, then grabbed at the swinging weapon. After two or three tries, he latched on to it, wrenched it from her grasp, and threw it across the street. Reacting on impulse rather than thought, the next instant a blow from the back of his hand slapped against the side of the woman's face.

She fell backward onto the frozen ground with a shriek, more of wrath than pain, unleashing a torrent of profanity at her assailant. Had she possessed the Luger that was inside Ramsay's coat at that moment, he would have been a dead man within seconds. As it was, the rapid fire of her verbal assault met only Ramsay's cruel laughter in the howling wind.

"Let's go, Halifax," said Scarlino, pulling him away. "You are growing more mad by the second."

Already darkness had begun to set in. By now the entire Jungfrau region was blowing a tempest and the temperature had dropped ten degrees. The two returned in the direction of the main street.

In the warmth of his own cottage, in spite of the wind Herr Buchmann heard his neighbor's cry of pain. He glanced out the window, saw nothing, then grabbed his coat and hurried out the door.

It did not take him more than a minute or two to discover Frau Grizzel's form lying in the street halfway between their two cottages. The tussle with Ramsay, the blow to her face, combined with the wind and the cold, had rendered the poor woman powerless to regain her footing. Had not Herr Buchmann arrived when he did, she would certainly have frozen to death within the hour.

"Frau Grizzel . . . Frau Grizzel!" he exclaimed, hastening forward and stooping down beside her. "What has happened!"

Exhausted, well aware of her danger, and thus feeling an overpowering sense of what had not stirred her heart for years, that is *thankfulness*, Frau Grizzel was not inclined to hurl unkind and accusatory threats toward both attacker and rescuer altogether as might have been her inclination at any other time. For once she held her peace and allowed the strong arms of the schoolmaster and librarian to assist her.

"It's some gash you've got on your cheek, poor woman," said Herr Buchmann, pulling her to a sitting position, then managing to get an arm under her shoulder. "We'll get you to my cottage, where a warm fire and a cup of tea and a dab of salve will help get the strength back in your legs."

Remarkably, the old woman did not argue. When Herr Buchmann had her on her feet and began leading her away in the direction of his home rather than hers, with his arm still around her to steady her wobbly feet, even then she did not resist.

In truth, for the first time in more years than she could remember, tea and a fire in the company of another human being sounded to her heart as a very balm sent from heaven.

60

Stormy Night

*L*ater that same evening, the mood in the chalet continued tearful and quiet. It was reading night. They gathered around the fire, though no one was talkative.

"I don't think I could bear to read *Robinson Crusoe* tonight," said Sister Marjolaine. "It would remind me of Amanda and I would start to cry all over again. I am so afraid for her, that she may be embarking on her own season of shipwreck."

"Just the thought of her out on a night like tonight," added Sister Luane, "on the train or in a lonely station somewhere, or in some lonelier hotel in Basel . . . I can hardly bear it."

"Especially when she could be here with us," added Sister Agatha.

"We mustn't lose heart," said Sister Hope. "Or stop praying. Though she is obviously still trying to run away from her problems, it may be that she is more homeward bound than she realizes. At least such is my prayer. She is on her way toward England, and I pray the Lord will use that fact for good."

Sister Hope's words seemed at last to buoy their spirits and enable the sisters to see how good might yet come of Amanda's leaving.

"So ... what shall we read?" Hope asked, herself in more hopeful spirits than she had felt all day.

Just then a fierce gust of wind blasted against the windowpanes, nearly setting the whole house to shaking.

"Something stormy," suggested Galiana.

"Yes, yes—read us one of your stormy stories, Sister Marjolaine," said Gretchen. "It will take our minds off Amanda and help us enjoy the tempest."

"What do you suggest, Sister Anika?" Marjolaine asked. "If I know you, you probably have another of the Scotsman's on the tip of your tongue to fit the occasion that you could probably quote from memory."

"Not exactly," laughed Anika. "But I do remember the openings ... let me think ..."

Already they were feeling much better. Twenty minutes later, with fresh tea before them, and two new logs crackling in the fire, they again found seats. In the meantime, Anika had made her selection.

"So here is another of the Scotsman's stories," she said. "Perhaps we shall not finish it all, but we shall at least enjoy it this evening." She opened the book and began.

On the night when my story opens, the twilight had long fallen and settled down into the dark. Presently there came a great and sudden blast of wind, which rushed down the chimney and drove smoke into the middle of the room. The howling wind could not shake the cottage, for it lay too low, neither could it rattle its windows—they were not made to open. But it could bellow over it like a wave over a rock, and as if in contempt, blow its smoke back into its throat.

It was a wild and evil night. The wind was rushing from the north, full of sharp stinging particles, something between snowflakes and hailstones. Down it came, into the face of the solitary walker who was still out on the darkness of the moor in a chaos of wind and snow. The young man fighting against the elements did not despair. Rather his spirit rejoiced. Invisible though the wild waste was to him through the snow, it was nevertheless a presence, and his young heart rushed to the contest.

As Anika read, the wind continued to beat upon the chalet, if anything with increasing force. It seemed as if the very words of the book were whipping up their own wind to correspond with the sister storm of the story.

"I hope no one is out like that in *our* village tonight," remarked Regina.

"No one will be," Agatha replied. "No one who lives in these mountains would venture out at this time of year at night with a storm blowing in."

Sister Anika went on.

> The walker fought his way along across the open moor, the greater part of which was still heather and swamp. Peat bog and ploughed land was all one waste of snow. Creation seemed nothing but the snow that had fallen, the snow that was falling, and the snow that had yet to fall.
>
> Back at the cottage, the snow was fast gathering in heaps on the windowsills, on the frames, and every smallest ledge where it could lie. In the midst of the blackness and the roaring wind, the tiny house was being covered with spots of silent whiteness, resting on every projection, every rough edge of wall and roof. All around the wind and snow raved. The clouds that garnered the snow were shaken by mad winds, whirled and tossed and buffeted to make them yield their treasures—

Suddenly a knock sounded. Half of the listeners nearly jumped out of their seats.

"What was that!" exclaimed Gretchen.

"One of your cows again?" said Agatha, turning toward Galiana.

Again came the sharp rapping.

"Someone is at the door," now said Luane.

They all glanced around. Several shivered. The chalet seemed all at once to have grown very cold. For a moment it was deathly still.

"Who could it be at this hour, and on such a night?" Gretchen wondered.

Again silence fell.

At last Hope rose and walked slowly to the front door. The eyes of the others followed her. Something about the strange knock on such a stormy night had filled them all with a sense of trepidation.

Sister Hope opened the door. She saw two unlikely strangers standing before her in the darkness. The reflection of the light from inside revealed a few snow flurries beginning behind them. From where

Gretchen sat in the big room, she could see one of the faces plainly. Her eyes opened wide in recognition.

It was the man she had noticed in the train station in Milan!

Instantly she realized the presence of these men meant danger. She knew just as surely that her friend was likely to reveal too much, and perhaps even invite the men in out of the storm. She was on her feet the next second and moving toward the door. Out of the corner of her eye, Sister Hope saw her approaching and turned.

"Sister Gretchen," she said, "these, uh ... gentlemen are asking about you ... and Amanda."

"I see," said Gretchen, coming forward. "What can I do for you? I am Gretchen Reinhardt."

"The priest from down in the valley sent us," began the shorter of the two.

"Father Stein?"

"Yes, yes ... of course—Father Stein. He assured us that you might be able to help us."

He smiled a toothy, insincere smile. Gretchen knew he was lying.

"We understand you were traveling with a young woman called Amanda," now said Ramsay, squeezing forward, "and that she might still be with you."

As he spoke he peered behind her and into the chalet.

"I am sorry, gentlemen," Gretchen answered, realizing it would probably be useless to deny it. "I did meet a girl by the name of Amanda when I was in Italy and brought her home with me for a while. But she left us some time ago."

"Where was she going?"

"I don't know exactly—France, I believe."

Ramsay eyed her menacingly. Sister Gretchen returned his gaze.

"You had better be telling the truth," said Ramsay. "The woman is a spy, and it will not go well for you if I find out you are lying."

"She is not here, I can promise you that," said Gretchen. "You are welcome to come in and search if you think I would lie to you."

"That will not be necessary," now said Scarlino. "Come, Halifax—she is not here."

They turned and departed. Quickly, before they could change their minds and before Sister Hope could offer them refuge from the cold, Gretchen shut the door behind them.

As she turned back inside, a look of question on Hope's face greeted her.

"They are bad men," said Gretchen. "They were lying about Father Stein. I only pray they did not harm him. One of them I have seen before. I believe he is the one who is after Amanda."

"But, Sister Gretchen," said Hope, "you did not tell them the truth."

"I did not *exactly* lie," she returned. "I said she had been gone for some time, which is true. Twelve hours is *some* time, is it not? And none of us knows exactly where she is going either, and she *is* going to France."

They walked back into the room, where the eyes of all the other sisters were wide. They had heard every word of the dangerous exchange.

"It appears that it is more important than ever that we keep Amanda in our prayers," said Gretchen. "That man has been following her since before she came to us. I doubt very much if he will give up now."

"We must bolt every door and window securely tonight," added Hope.

PART III

England

1915

61

Attack

*A*n explosion only a few feet off the port bow sent a plume of white spray into the air.

The HMS *Dauntless* rocked slightly. It was the nearest miss yet.

Even a British battle cruiser was no match for the German U-boats. Every man on board knew it. If they didn't knock this one out right now while it remained a little too near the surface and was visible, it would dog them underwater and out of sight until it found the mark and they were on their way to the bottom. On the main deck, midshipmen and officers were scurrying together making lifeboats ready and breaking out the supply of life vests. On the bridge, Captain Wilberforce and his officer corps kept watch with binoculars and waited. There was nothing much they could do now except zigzag between their own firings and hope for the best. The sub was out of range for their large surface artillery.

At the torpedo station, the headset crackled with the coordinates relayed from the tower above into the ears of the radioman.

"Port torpedo two, heading two-nine-three," called out Petty Officer George Rutherford at the radio controls, passing the information along to the gunnery crew.

"Heading two-nine-three . . . locked," barked back the confirmation.

Commanding the torpedo squadron, Lieutenant Forbes quickly checked chamber and heading and then gave the order. "Torpedo two . . . fire!" he called.

"Torpedo away."

Even as new torpedoes were being prepared for chambers one and two by other of Forbes' men, and as the lieutenant was moving on to chamber number three, from the lookout above now came another frantic message to the bridge.

"Incoming . . . incoming torpedo!" sounded a frantic warning.

"All hands—" cried the captain into the address system. But it was too late.

Another explosion rocked the ship. This time it was obviously more severe.

"Damage?" shouted Wilberforce into the microphone.

"Minimal, sir," came the answer from below.

"Are we hit?"

"Checking, sir."

"Engine room . . . damage?"

"None, sir—still at full power."

More messages came shouting back and forth between deck and bridge and other parts of the ship.

"No penetration . . . glancing blow," finally came the word.

Below, the torpedo squadron under Lieutenant Forbes had recovered its footing and readied for another firing.

"Petty Officer Rutherford," called Forbes, "do you have the new coordinates?"

"They're coming now, sir."

Forbes waited.

"Torpedo three," George called out in another few seconds, "heading two-seven-nine."

"Prepare to fire," called Forbes.

"Heading two-seven-nine . . . ready."

Again Lieutenant Forbes gave the command to fire.

"Torpedo away," said the first gunner.

As the British fleet under the command of First Lord of the Admiralty Winston Churchill had dispersed from Scapa Flow in the Orkneys throughout the months of fall and early winter, gradually the threat to the coast of Great Britain itself lessened. The Fleet's engagements with the German navy had during those months spread around the entire circumference of Europe into the North and Baltic seas, the Atlantic and Adriatic. The Mediterranean, where the HMS *Dauntless* had encountered a stray U-boat and was now battling for its very survival, had become the most strategic area of naval activity, just as the region of northern France and Belgium was for ground troops.

From all three of Europe's seas, Allied ships, the *Dauntless* among them, were converging upon the Aegean, where an offensive was planned against the Central powers of Germany, Austria-Hungary, and Turkey in support of Greece and Serbia.

A dull underwater explosion sounded some two thousand yards across the water. A bulging bubble of blue capped with white slowly rose from the surface of the sea.

"It's a hit!" cried several officers' voices on the bridge.

"I think we got it!"

On deck all those running about among the lifeboats stopped, their gaze riveted across the water. As the bubble rose, then exploded itself into the air, the tip of the submarine's hull crested the surface momentarily at a dangerous angle, then disappeared.

A great cheer went up from the deck. They would not need the lifeboats today.

"Torpedo room . . . torpedo room," came the message from the bridge, "stand down. You did it!"

Above, Captain Wilberforce glanced around at his officers and exhaled a long sigh. A few congratulations and handshakes went around, but mostly more sighs of relief. "I would rather it not be communicated to the men," he said with a relieved smile of his own, "but I don't mind telling you . . . that was what they call a little too close for comfort. All right—resume your stations, send a crew to check for minor damage, and set course for the Dardanelles. We must be there on schedule."

62

Intelligence in the Alliance

$\mathcal{I}$t was not often that the German military confided in the Prussian Intelligence Service. Especially at these levels. Rald Wolfrik knew something big was in the wind the moment he was summoned to Berlin.

But why him? he wondered. Unless the information he had passed on from Scarlino had paid off.

Even he did not realize the level of the meeting to which he was bound until he walked into the room and saw Generaloberst von Bülow himself along with two or three others.

They wasted no time getting to the business at hand.

"I have been informed," began the generaloberst to Wolfrik, "that you are involved in the covert British operation."

Wolfrik nodded.

"Something has come up which may affect our plans—a defection ... a serious one, at the highest level."

"How high?"

"My own top assistant," replied von Bülow. "He knows of the assassination as well as our invasion plans."

"You are, I assume, taking measures to prevent him from reaching England."

"Unfortunately, it is too late for that. He is already in enemy hands."

"In England?"

"He slipped out of sight in Greece. We suspect that he is still on the Continent."

"Then he must be intercepted."

"Our orders are to eliminate him, along with the others. That is why we brought you here. We want you to handle the affair. Your Swiss contact, I believe, is serviceable in such matters."

"As might be our young English friend. He recently passed an important test, and we believe he will suit our purposes perfectly. In addition, we have learned more about the organization of which he is part. It is called the Fountain of Light."

"I am well acquainted with one or two of its principles," rejoined von Bülow. "They operate out of a large house in Vienna. This is excellent. They will be able to help you. I will arrange to have you briefed in a few important matters tomorrow. Then get down to Vienna and contact a man called Barclay. He has helped me set up what has been a very effective link across the Channel. Tell me, is the young Englishman personally acquainted with the prime minister?"

"Not to my knowledge. But he is said to have sufficient contacts to enable him to walk straight into Downing Street without raising suspicions."

"Does he know?"

"Of course not. With such types, it is always best not to divulge too much until you have them caught in such a tight squeeze they have no alternative but to go along."

"And your Swiss colleague?"

"I will contact him immediately. He is presently in Zurich. I will tell him to leave the other matter for now and meet me in Köln the moment I have arranged things with this Barclay."

63

War Closes In

$\mathscr{A}$manda sat in a train staring out the window at the passing countryside, considerably subdued since her departure from the chalet two days before. Moving across northeast France after crossing the border from Switzerland, she was bound for Paris.

Her route had already taken her closer to the fighting in northern France and Germany than she had anticipated. She had been so insulated from the events of the war during her months at the chalet that she had had little idea how close it actually was. The moment she crossed the border, instantly the war—if not actual fighting, then certainly its effects—was all around her. France was not only one of the principal powers involved, unlike neutral Switzerland and Italy, this region between Basel and Metz represented the French-German border, and along it, included in the 400-mile entrenched line from the English Channel to the Swiss border, both sides were dug in and the fighting was severe. There were times they had been so close to the border yesterday that she could hear the sound of artillery fire in the distance. In every town or village they passed she saw signs of the conflict—soldiers in troop trucks, wounded men with slings and bandages and crutches, nurses and doctors, and columns of new recruits on their way to the front.

Suddenly the reality began to dawn on her that she might be heading toward even more trouble than she had intended to leave behind. Not that she wasn't relieved to be in France. It was almost like being back in England after all the long, frightening months in Austria. She was more comfortable with the French language than she had been with German. Yet still the war was all of a sudden so close.

Mingled with Amanda's observations were questions at last coming into focus of what she would do if and when she did get back to England alive.

Where she would go, what she would do, she wasn't exactly sure. She hadn't really thought much about her prospects. Would she get a job? What was she suited for? What could her future possibly hold?

She would probably look up Sylvia Pankhurst. She was the only friend she had. Actually . . . what else *could* she do? Maybe she could stay with Sylvia until she got on her feet.

Perhaps Cousin Martha would help her again. She hadn't thought of the lady in months, maybe in a year. She was reminded of Geoffrey, but then quickly put the London Rutherfords out of her mind.

Then again came the horrifying, sickening reminder—something like waking up from a bad dream—that she was actually married!

Married!

How could she have been so foolish as to rush into something so important on a whim?

That was the biggest question about the future of all—what was she going to *do*!

Divorce Ramsay? Would she be able to do that in England when they had been married in Austria? The thought brought Sister Anika and Sister Agatha to Amanda's mind. It was all too confusing. She didn't want to think about the chalet right now. She didn't want to think about Ramsay. She didn't want to think about whether divorce was right or wrong. She didn't want to think about the future. She just wanted to feel English soil under her feet.

A soldier came walking down the aisle toward her, limping, one leg heavily bandaged and with a soiled white bandage wrapped around his forehead. Amanda glanced from the window toward him.

Suddenly with horror she realized that his right arm was missing!

The sight of the empty sleeve of his uniform hanging from his shoulder filled her with strange revulsion and she turned away. The look in his eye—he was younger than she, a mere boy of nineteen or twenty—was of lostness, aloneness, sadness, and pain.

Who was he? she wondered. Was he going home?

Amanda's thoughts turned to her brother, George. She had not thought of him in so long. She was glad *he* didn't have to be in this war. The thought of George involved in the fighting was too awful. She could not hold it in her brain for long.

The young man sat down just in front of Amanda. She could not keep from staring at his misshapen and armless body. She wanted to weep for him. But the season for Amanda's tears had not yet come, and though her heart ached, her eyes remained dry.

Beside her as they approached the station in Troyes, a man got up to disembark, leaving behind the day's newspaper in his seat. Amanda picked it up. It was full of war news about troop movements and U-boats, ships and battles, the Schlieffen Plan and the Battle of the Marne, the Russian invasion and the trench warfare in Belgium. Amanda understood a little of what she read and skipped about among the headlines and leading captions.

FIGHTING INTENSIFIES NEAR RHEIMS, read one. GERMAN AND ENGLISH SHIPS SUNK IN MEDITERRANEAN, read another.

A short article about German submarines located in the North Sea between Scotland and Norway interested her and she read half of it.

ALLIES BEAT BACK GERMAN LINE, PARIS SAFE FOR NOW, read one of the large captions. Amanda began to read the text of the article.

"After penetration by German infantry troops in September, the Allied trench line roughly along the French-Belgian border now appears secure. The inhabitants of the great French capital are breathing much more easily now than during the panic of only a few short months ago. . . ."

Paris, thought Amanda. Had France really been so nearly overrun and defeated!

An article about spies now caught her eye and she began to scan it. As she did, words and phrases jumped off the page into her brain with a strange sense of familiarity, ". . . infiltration into France and Britain, apparently a network capable of moving spies in and out of Britain at will. It is thought that some coastal location . . . British Army and Royal Navy command continues mystified how their messages are being intercepted. . . ."

Memories of the Fountain and her hazy and unpleasant days in Vienna began to rise into Amanda's consciousness. Why did something seem familiar here . . . what was the connection between this article and Vienna?

Now came back to her words and phrases she had overheard at the house on Ebendorfer Strasse, ". . . said he knew about the lighthouse operation . . . might know about the signals."

What kind of *signals*? she wondered. But there was more. As her consciousness slowly awakened she found echoing in her brain confusing reminders and bits of conversation she overheard when no one thought she was paying attention.

"... change the code ... Morse ... U-boats ... land an invasion ... the lighthouse cannot be compromised ..."

The *lighthouse*, thought Amanda. What lighthouse ... and where?

Didn't she remember hearing Ramsay mention something like that too ... or was it his mother?

Was it connected—the spies infiltrating England, and what she had heard in Vienna?

And why not? The house on Ebendorfer Strasse had been associated with the very assassins who had started the war—whether directly or indirectly she still didn't know. But there must be a spy network along with it. Gavrilo Princip had hinted to her about such things. That must have been what she had overheard Muhamed Mehmedbasic talking to Hartwell Barclay about.

Why had she not paid more attention? How could she have allowed herself to fall into such a state? What was it she had heard Mehmedbasic say?

Yes, now she remembered!

He had said to Barclay, "... and I know about your lighthouse."

And Barclay had instantly become serious at the words. It must have been important.

Whatever was going on, a lighthouse somewhere must be at the bottom of it!

She had to get back and tell English authorities what she had heard.

But then Amanda's thoughts sobered. What would she tell them? What did she really know? She didn't know where this supposed lighthouse was. Great Britain had thousands of miles of coastline and hundreds of lighthouses.

Maybe it wasn't on the coast of Britain. For all she knew, it might be a lighthouse in Greece. Now that she thought about it, she didn't really have any information that would do anybody much good at all.

64
A Letter and a Nightmare

*C*harles Rutherford awoke early. He had been doing so frequently these days, it seemed. It was still dark out. He turned on his light and glanced at his watch. Five-forty. That would make it between three and four in the morning back home.

It was nearly time to be up anyway. He needed to tell Jocie what had happened two mornings ago. He might as well get started on it now. The ship would be reasonably quiet for another hour.

He rose, dressed, and within ten minutes was seated at the small writing table in his cabin gazing at the small framed photograph of his wife in front of him.

My dear Jocelyn, he began,

I don't know when you will receive this—we have not put in since passing Gibraltar and entering the Mediterranean, and already we have passed Malta and expect to see Crete soon. I have begun at least ten letters since we last saw England's coastline, but as time passes I feel the constant need to begin anew, since what I may have written yesterday, or last week, no longer seems so immediate as the now. I shall probably post them all at the first opportunity, giving you a long string of letters begun ... but all remaining unfinished!

Christmas was particularly difficult for me. I am certain it was for you and Catharine as well. How I missed you and longed to be home! I relived every Christmas we have ever had together, I think, and the day was filled for me with visions of trees and stockings and your delectable rice pudding ... but mostly just with thoughts of you and wanting to be with you. I love you more than ever!

At least there were no enemy ships about, and we took the day to quietly remember our families. I led the men—I feel like calling them boys, as most of them are to my eyes—in the singing of some Christmas carols, which we concluded with sharing and praying together. It was quite extraordinary how men will open themselves to other men if given the opportunity, aided by a holiday and a little fear of what may lie ahead.

All in all, under the circumstances, I felt it was a good day, one that drew the officers and men closer together, an important component of ship life. But what am I repeating this for? It is all explained in great detail in the letter I began the day after Christmas!

In any event, George and I managed to have some time together as well and it was rich. We even squeezed in two epic games of chess—though I am no longer his match. He is so mild mannered, but ruthless with his bishops, knights, and rooks. I have never encountered so persistent and cunningly dangerous a queen! He is growing into a fine man to make both of us proud. His companions look up to him, and gradually I see leadership qualities emerging in him. I'm sure I have told you already that he is a petty officer now, in charge of all the radios on board, and second in command of his squadron. Though it is a severe grief to me to be away from you, to be close to him during this learning, maturing, critical time in his life makes it almost worth it. Nothing really makes it worth it, of course, but if there must be sacrifices, it is so good of the Lord to give us corresponding blessings along with them.

As if the intensity of his thoughts in her direction had forced themselves into her own brain, terrifying visions and images began to rise within Jocelyn's dreamy consciousness where she slept in her own bed at Heathersleigh. But they were not happy images of Christmas....

A ship was slicing through dark waters, tilted to one side. The sky was nearly as black as the waters, the only illumination coming from occasional bursts of fiery explosions in the air ... silent bombs that gave no sound, only brilliant, terrifying light. Aboard the vessel were what seemed ten thousand men running to and fro in confused panic, resembling more ants than men ... they were trying to scream for help, but their voices made no sounds and there was no one to help them. The explosions overhead closed in around them ... now crashing upon the ship itself and exploding it apart ... some of the ants were thrown into the air and overboard into the black sea ... others scurried over the sides ... the ship was aflame now, engulfed in its own certain death ... over the side poured streams of the ant-men, crawling down the sides of the ship by the thousand, clinging to its lurching sides like insects. Back and forth the ship rocked violently, as if it were trying to shake them loose ... more explosions ... fire, fire everywhere. Into the water the ants poured ... swimming now like tiny fish, but not fish who could live in water ... fish-men who needed air and land ... but without hope, for there was no land in sight, no land anywhere ... only water ... water. Gradually they began to sink, overcome by the turbulent black waters ... struggling, gasping frantically for breath ... sinking out of sight into the black—

Suddenly Jocelyn's own screams awakened her. Her head jerked off the pillow. Her brain was bewildered and flooded with confusion. She glanced about, panting, perspiring, her eyes unable to focus.

"Mother ... Mother, wake up!" came Catharine's voice. But the sound was distant, along with the gentle shaking that went with it.

"But they're ... the water is all around ... sinking ..."

"Mother ... Mother, it's me," came the voice again.

For a second or two Jocelyn probed the face. Her eyes were huge, searching for some correspondence between what lingered in her brain and this form in front of her. Gradually the dream faded. By degrees she realized she was sitting in her own bed with her daughter's strong arms around her.

"Oh ... oh, Catharine ... it's you...."

"You've had a nightmare, Mother," Catharine was saying in a soothing voice. "It's gone now ... I'm here ... everything's fine...."

"Oh ... oh, Catharine ..."

Then the dream returned and Jocelyn began to cry. Catharine pulled her tight.

"I'm afraid, Catharine ... afraid something terrible has happened."

"It was only a nightmare, Mother. I'm sure everything is fine. We'll pray for them.—*Dear Lord,*" Catharine prayed, *"we ask for your special protection on George and Daddy right now. Keep them in your care, and in your heart. I pray that you would take away Mother's fear. Thank you, dear Father, that in all that happens we know you are good and care for all your children."*

As she fell silent, Jocelyn continued to cling to her, almost as if she were the child and Catharine were the mother.

"I'm still afraid, Catharine," she whimpered tearfully. "I can't help it. It's like an awful premonition. I ... I don't know ... I don't think I could live without Charles. Catharine ... I'm afraid."

65
Revised Plans

◆◆◆

𝒯he telegram delivered shortly after daybreak at Nr. 42 Ebendorfer Strasse in Vienna was brief. It aroused a wrathful response as Hartwell Barclay read it. He then shoved it across the breakfast table to Amanda's purported mother-in-law. She read it somewhat more calmly than her white-haired and red-faced companion.

> ZURICH. SHE IS GONE. WAS CLOSE IN SWITZERLAND BUT ABSOLUTE DEAD END. SUSPECT FRANCE, THEN ENGLAND. WILL AWAIT REPLY HERE. R. HALIFAX.

The reply sent back by the waiting delivery to the Zurich hotel was equally terse.

> MEET ME PARIS. L'ATELIER DES PRÉS. WILL USE NETWORK TO GO TO ENGLAND. SHE MUST BE STOPPED. BARCLAY.

Ramsay set down the single sheet of paper. He could almost feel Barclay's annoyance in the very abruptness of the communication. But for once their mutual animosity had played right into his own hands. *Paris*—the very sound of the word was music to his ears!

His last conversation with Adriane a week ago was from Paris, where she still had another three weeks to play at the theater!

Wherever had that lunatic Scarlino disappeared to?

Not that Ramsay cared.

He hoped he never saw him again. He was a bad one. Barclay and his imbecilic contacts—the fellow had proved less than useless at finding Amanda and now had suddenly disappeared without a trace.

Well, good riddance. He wasn't about to hang around waiting for him to show up again.

Paris ... he would leave immediately!

66

Sharing a Corner of God's Heart

*U*naware of Jocelyn's fears concerning him, Charles paused briefly, sat back, and glanced at her face in his photograph again. He smiled to himself, then whispered, "God bless her . . . take care of her during this time, Lord."

A moment or two more he sat, then began again to write.

I do not mean to make you sad, my dear Jocie, he continued, *but I know you will want to know my heart during these times when we are apart. So I will share with you an experience I had two mornings ago. It was sad, I have to say, and I found myself nearly overwhelmed with grief. Yet I cannot help but think it was a significant revelation the Lord gave me through it.*

We had been engaged the day before with a German U-boat. It was our closest call yet. We were actually hit by one of the torpedoes, but without sustaining damage. Shortly afterward we sunk the U-boat. It was an event which had a marked effect on many of these boys who are turning into men perhaps more rapidly than is desirable under normal conditions. War does that. These are not desirable conditions, and we are at war.

For a brief time there was great elation at the sinking of the U-boat. But then in some of the younger midshipmen the realization set in that, in saving our own vessel, we had actually sent a submarine full of German youths to their own deaths. For the first time since sailing from Scapa Flow, the war suddenly became very personal.

I noticed a marked change in George the next time I saw him. I think he felt it acutely, as he was in charge of the radio in the torpedo command room itself where they actually launched the weapon. I could see it weighing heavily on him. Had we been at home, I think he may have fallen into my arms and wept manly tears of youthful confusion and uncertainty and grief. But he must be a man too. And though I sensed a slight quiver in his lip as we looked one another in the eyes, I knew they were feelings he had to keep inside for the present.

I immediately went to my cabin, however, and wept in his stead. That

brief quiver of his nearly grown-up lip, as I remembered holding him in my
arms when he was no more than two, nearly broke my heart. . . .

As he wrote the words Charles could not prevent renewed tears. He
had no choice but to set the letter aside and briefly turn away. He
picked up his pen again the moment his eyes would allow him to see
and resumed.

A child never knows a hundredth of the things a parent feels on his
behalf, or the depths of love that swell the heart, sometimes over the tiniest
things. How quickly they grow, how fond do those childhood reminders be-
come in the parental storehouse of treasured memories.

Does a child ever know? Perhaps not. Did my own father and mother
feel the same things I now feel for our three dear ones? It is hard to imagine.
Yet perhaps that is part of the eternal parental sacrifice—to love a hun-
dredfold more than that love will ever be known.

I wax philosophic! Forgive me, my dear Jocie. When a man is alone like
this, feelings rise that can only be relieved by attempting to put them to
paper.

Perhaps it was in part the tears I shed for George on the afternoon of
the U-boat sinking, and the stab in my heart every time the image of that
quiver of his mouth came back to me, followed by his having to force the
anguished feelings inside rather than release them, that kept me near tears
all the rest of the day. The feeling persisted that night. I slept poorly and
awoke as dawn was just about to break.

An overpowering sense of what I can only call sadness nearly engulfed
me. I don't remember ever being so sad in my entire life. Everywhere I
ached, with almost the physical sensation of pain, for sheer dejection and
utter despondency. My heart was so heavy that I literally did not think I
could pull myself out of bed.

But I did. For activity of any kind was the only possible relief. I thought
that if I could just feel the wind and salt spray on my face, and take a few
deep breaths of it, perhaps I could allay this melancholy that had so filled
me and made me feel as if I were just going to give up and expire from it.
Is it possible literally to die from sheer sadness? I do not know. But after
this experience I wondered if there may actually be such a thing as a "bro-
ken" heart capable of crushing the very life out of a human soul. I do not
say that I was close to that point. Yet I can say that never have I felt such
abject despondency.

I dressed and went up on deck, where a thin light was just beginning
to make the Mediterranean visible. Even before I was standing at the bow

I knew what had caused the sadness, though it had only just come to my conscious mind.

It was this—I had the overpowering sense that I would never see Amanda again. And it was just too much to bear. The agony of the thought was like a thousand knives piercing my heart. How much I loved her, and love her still. The thought of never again holding her in my arms and feeling her arms around me, and hearing her tell me that she loves me too . . . the idea of it was more than I could bear.

I burst out crying like a baby, right there on the bow of the Dauntless as we ploughed through the sea and as my burning face rushed through the cold, damp, dark morning air. I was thankful for the early hour. I felt such hope for Amanda only a short time ago. I had the sense that her homecoming had begun. Now this. I did not understand why.

How long I wept, I have no idea. I don't even exactly know what I thought about. But when I came to myself and realized that my eyes were drying, it was fully daylight and I could hear voices about me in indication that the ship was coming to life.

Then came the revelation which prompted this letter. I found myself thinking about the cross, about the agony of what it must have been that our Lord suffered. The thought of the pain he felt as he hung there brought tears to my eyes again. For I realized how minuscule was the pain I had just been feeling moments earlier in comparison with the agony of his suffering. For a moment I felt in a small way privileged to have felt the anguish I had on that morning, for it caused me to reflect on that far greater anguish he felt on our behalf.

Then further came the realization that the Father himself suffered, too, on that crucifixion day—suffered in a way perhaps even greater than the physical torment of the Son. For the Father had to suffer the loss of a Son whom he loved. And perhaps my losing of a daughter—though I pray it is but temporary—is a price I should be willing to pay, maybe even be glad to pay, that I should rejoice to suffer, that third portion of my fatherly dreams and ambitions gone—in order that I might be able to identify with one tiny corner of God the Father's heart.

He lost a son. And perhaps blessed are those who are called in this life to experience such a loss, that they might yield the anguish and sadness of that parental loss up into his Father's heart even as Jesus, the perfect and sacrificing Son, yielded up his own anguish into his Father's heart, that the world might be saved.

Not only that, the Father lost his only Son. We have not suffered near so great an agony. We still have our dear George and Catharine—God bless them!—and pray daily that our dear Amanda will be restored to us as *well—and God bless her! So how tiny, really, is our suffering compared with his. Were we to suffer even a millionth the pain man's sin causes the Father-heart of God, we would surely die! Yet by such glimpses as our own suffering affords us of that greater divine suffering of eternal Love do we perhaps apprehend God's heart a little more directly.*

Periodically I recall that sermon I preached in Timothy's church so many years ago about intimacy with God and the universal need to become children and return to our Father. I suppose in a way Amanda is only living out a microcosm of that universal human prodigality of which we are all a part. In my own way I am just as in need as she of learning to be my Father's child. It is the one thing we are put on this earth to learn—childness—yet the one thing we most resist submitting to. It is curious, is it not, that God made our greatest need that which we strive most fiercely against?

After all these thoughts had gone through my mind, I then tried to find comfort in the fact that in the Father's heart is nothing ever lost—not one of a mother's tears, not a second of a prodigal-father's grief as he waits gazing down the empty and silent road. I resolved, whenever I am in any kind of pain or mental anxiety, to remember the suffering Jesus endured for us, and to thank God for the privilege he allows us to suffer, that we might in this small way partake in the reality, and the ultimate victory, of the cross.

And I tried to give my own heartsick condition over to him, to place in his Father's heart—remembering that I am his son too, and a prodigal one at that as I suppose we all will remain to some degree while in this life—to hold in his heart until that day—

A knock sounded on Charles' cabin door. He glanced up. How long had he been sitting at his desk? It was light out.

He rose to answer it. There stood Captain Wilberforce.

"A private communication for you, Commander Rutherford," he said. "It was relayed by wireless and received only minutes ago. It is from the First Lord of the Admiralty."

He handed Charles the envelope, then turned to go.

"Just a moment, Captain," said Charles. "There may be something here we need to discuss."

Charles opened it.

To Charles Rutherford.
For your eyes only.
Dauntless not to participate in Dardanelles offensive. Captain will be ordered to put in at Salonika. You will be met and taken ashore. Major

defection to Allied cause has occurred to be placed in your care. When se-
cure, set sail for Scapa Flow immediately. Imperative top secret. Informa-
tion in his possession could end war within months. None aboard must
know mission. Keep identity and presence absolutely unknown. Security
breach feared. Must remain isolated from all crew. You must be only con-
tact until I see you. Give my apology to Wilberforce. All for his safety and
that of crew. He will be fully briefed at Scapa. Be assured all being done
by my direct order. You will be given further orders onshore.

W. Churchill

Charles folded the paper and glanced up at the captain.

"Mr. Churchill asks me to apologize personally to you," Charles began, "for keeping you in the dark. He says it is a matter of your safety and the crew's, and that he will brief you fully at the first opportunity."

"What's it all about, Commander?" asked Wilberforce.

"Actually," smiled Charles, "I don't know much more than you. The message is rather cryptic. Apparently you will shortly be receiving orders to put in at Salonika—"

"Yes, they came at the same time as this communication to you."

"I see—well, apparently once we dock, I am to meet a liaison onshore from Mr. Churchill who will give me further instructions. I believe at the same time you will be given new orders as well."

Captain Wilberforce nodded.

"Well, it does appear to be something of a mystery," he said. "I suppose we shall know more when we reach Salonika day after tomorrow. And putting ashore," the captain added, "will allow us the chance to collect all the men's mail and get it on a transport back home."

"Right," rejoined Charles. "I shall have a whole sheaf of letters for the packet myself! I am just finishing up another right now."

67

Paris

◆◆◆

*A*s Amanda arrived in the station in Paris, she was tired and growing more and more apprehensive. She could tell the war was close. The city was not exactly somber, but it certainly was far from gay and lively. She had never been here before, but this was not what she expected. Soldiers were everywhere.

As much as at some other time she might have wanted to visit the city, now all she wanted to do was get the next train to the Channel. In her present state of mind, Paris was too huge and intimidating.

She looked around on the schedule boards but saw no indication of trains bound for Calais. She walked toward a ticket window.

"Excuse me," she said to the agent. "I want to go to Calais."

"Calais, miss—you can't get there without crossing the German line. There's bad fighting going on between here and there."

"But . . . but then how can I get to England?"

"The safest way is from Cherbourg, miss."

"Then give me a ticket to Cherbourg."

"Only one train to the coast a day, miss, and it's already gone. The next will be tomorrow."

Amanda turned away with a sigh. She walked to an empty bench and sat down with her two bags. She was so tired of traveling. Now she was going to have to spend another night in a strange city.

She glanced up at the big station clock. The hands read three-ten. She would rest just a few more minutes before going out and trying to find a hotel.

She closed her eyes and before she knew it had begun to doze off. She caught herself after a few minutes before she had fallen completely asleep and forced her eyes open. She couldn't go to sleep now. It would be getting dark soon. She had to get out and find a hotel for the night before—

Suddenly Amanda's eyes shot wide open. In a split second she was wide awake, with sleep the farthest thing from her mind.

Across the station only some fifty feet in front of her was walking none other than Ramsay's mistress—Adriane Grünsfeld, or Sadie Greenfield, or even Annie McPool, for all Amanda knew who she really was!

Amanda's heart began pounding both with fury and revulsion. Momentarily she turned away to hide her face. The next instant she was ready to jump up and run straight up and clobber her over the head with one of her suitcases. So many emotions surged through her that all she could do was sit and stare at the retreating form as Adriane, alias Sadie, alias Annie, left the station.

Suddenly coming to herself, on an impulse Amanda jumped to her feet, picked up her bags, and followed. As she emerged into the outside air, she was just in time to hear the beautiful woman giving instructions to a cab man. "L'hôtel Atelier des Prés," she said, then got inside. The cab sped away.

Without pausing to think what would come of it, Amanda signaled the next cab in sight and repeated the same destination.

A hundred thoughts flooded her during the ten-minute drive, approximately the ninety-eighth of which was the question what was she doing this for? Unfortunately, before she had managed to come up with an answer, the cab had stopped in front of the hotel. Amanda got out, paid the driver, and cautiously walked toward the door, keeping a wary eye roving about. She didn't want to run into Grünsfeld face-to-face! She just might clobber her for real and wind up in jail.

Slowly Amanda entered the lobby. There she was, approaching the main counter!

"Oh, Miss Sadie, you have a message," said the desk clerk. He handed her a piece of paper.

She read it quickly.

"Can you place a telephone call for me, Charlot?" she asked.

Amanda crept closer, keeping to one side of the lobby and shielding herself from view behind a couple of large potted plants.

All at once her ears perked up. The next moment they became bright red as if to match her anger. Whatever intimidation she may have had about the consequences of following Ramsay's mistress, it was now entirely vanquished at fury over his betrayal.

"Oh, Ramsay darling . . . you're coming here!" she heard Grünsfeld say, "—that's wonderful! But why?"

Amanda tried to catch a peep of the actress through the palm. Obviously Ramsay, wherever he might be, was speaking as she held the receiver to her ear and nodded intently.

"But what makes you think she's here?" she said.

Amanda gasped. They were talking about *her*!

"Will you go to England, then?" asked Grünsfeld.

Again she was silent a moment.

"But how will you—"

A pause.

"Of course. I had forgotten ... until tomorrow night, then, darling."

She hung up the receiver and handed the telephone back to the clerk. "Thank you, Charlot. I will take the key to my room now."

"Yes, Miss Sadie. Will the gentleman be requiring a room when he arrives?"

"You were listening, Charlot!" teased the actress with flirtatious tone.

"Only in hopes of serving you more thoroughly, Miss Sadie."

"You are a charmer, Charlot. But no, I believe Mr. Halifax will find my room quite suitable."

"Of course, miss."

Amanda's eyes narrowed in wrath. If she had tried to speak now, it would have been through clenched teeth. How *could* he ... how could they both! Didn't she care that he was married? Had she no more scruples than Ramsay?

Already the actress had turned and was ascending the stairway. Amanda waited until she was out of sight, then drew in a deep breath, tried without much success to calm herself, and walked toward the counter.

"*Bonjour, monsieur,*" she said in perfect French. "*Je voudrais une chambre, s'il vous plaît.*"

"Will it be just for yourself, miss?"

Amanda nodded.

"For one night?"

"I, uh ... actually I am not sure exactly how long I will be staying," she replied.

68

High-Ranking Defection

The HMS *Dauntless* anchored off Salonika on the eastern coast of Greece in midafternoon.

Charles had heard nothing more since the strange communication from Churchill. When night fell, however, he kept his uniform on, halfway expecting a summons.

Around ten o'clock he set aside the book he was reading and lay down on his bunk. Soon he dozed off.

A knock came on the door. Charles roused himself and stood to answer it. The hour was one-thirty.

"Commander Rutherford," said a stranger standing before him in the corridor. "I am Colonel Rawley. I have orders to take you ashore. I believe you have been apprised."

"Yes, Colonel," replied Charles. "Just give me a minute to dash some water on my face, make sure I am thoroughly awake, and get my coat and hat."

Minutes later they were leaving the silent, sleeping ship, climbing down the rope ladder in darkness to a small waiting transport vessel of some forty feet. Once aboard they headed across the calm black surface toward the harbor. Besides the skipper of the small boat only one or two others were present. No one spoke.

An hour later, Charles stood waiting with the colonel in silence under the dim shadow of a bridge over the Vardar.

Ahead out of the darkness, three men approached.

"Commander Rutherford," said one of the newcomers, "I am General Payne. The army and navy are cooperating on this matter. I have orders here for you from the First Lord of the Admiralty."

Charles nodded.

"I have been instructed," the general went on, "to turn over to you, shall we say, our new friend here. You are to take him back to the *Dauntless*, keep him secure and out of sight, and return to England immediately. Mr. Churchill will be waiting at Scapa to take charge of the matter personally. All is explained in your orders."

"I understand," said Charles.

"I have been told you speak German?"

"Well enough," answered Charles. "Not exactly fluently."

"It will be sufficient to communicate with your ward, as it were. I also have orders here signed by Mr. Churchill for Captain Wilberforce."

"Very good, sir."

General Payne handed him the two sealed envelopes. They saluted and shook hands. The general and his assistant turned and disappeared in the night. Colonel Rawley now led Charles and the newcomer away. The man was dressed in civilian clothes but bore the demeanor—which the thin light accentuated occasionally in his eyes—of a military officer, probably of high rank.

They reached the *Dauntless* a little after three-twenty. Rawley saw them safely on board, then disappeared back down the rope ladder. Charles was left alone for the first time with the man whom he judged to be a German officer. He led him along the deck, then down into the ship, careful to avoid the night crew, and to his small lodgings, where quarters had been prepared in a connecting officer's cabin.

Once safely inside, speaking in German, Charles offered the man something to eat or drink. His guest replied, however, that it had been a long day and all he wanted to do was sleep. Charles showed him briefly around his quarters, then left him.

Once alone Charles sat down on his bed and opened one of the envelopes he had been given under the bridge.

Commander Charles Rutherford, he read,

This will introduce you to Colonel Klaus Spengler, assistant to Generaloberst von Bülow of the German high command. He has come over to our side. The information he possesses could bring this war to a close before summer. He will be in your care to get to Britain as quickly as possible. Keep him in the private quarters next to yours. He is to be seen by no one, not even Captain Wilberforce. Security leaks have already been a problem. I told you when you sailed that you were one of the few men I knew I could trust implicitly. I am more glad than ever that I persuaded you to take up your commission. Little did I know what a significant responsibility I would find myself placing in your hands. I will see you at first opportunity once you are safely back in British waters.

W. Churchill

69

Rising Determination

$\mathcal{F}$atigue at last overpowered Amanda's distraught emotional condition, and she managed to sleep tolerably well under the circumstances.

When she awoke, her anger of the previous evening, while by no means gone, had been replaced by a growing determination to turn the tables on Ramsay rather than cower in fear of him. Whatever was going on, she would get to the bottom of it. Let Ramsay try to take her back to Vienna with him—she wouldn't go without a fight! And now *he* was behind enemy lines, not her. *He* was the spy now, and she would start shouting blue murder if he tried anything.

And just maybe she could make up for some of her earlier stupidity by helping to foil whatever it was they were up to. If they got hold of her and killed her in the end ... well, what did she have to live for anyway? But she had no intention of making that easy for them!

Amanda lay in bed a few minutes revolving these things in her mind. Suddenly she realized she was famished. She got up, bathed and dressed, and went downstairs to the hotel dining room, where the buffet breakfast was laid for the hotel guests. Keeping an eye out, she loaded her plate higher than she would have thought possible, then found a table at the edge of the dining area from which the door would be clearly visible. She proceeded to enjoy three cups of tea and eat her fill, more than she had eaten since leaving the chalet. Her appetite was finally back, and with a vengeance! And she felt a little of her feisty childhood vigor returning along with it.

Thankfully there was no sign of the Grünsfeld woman anywhere. Amanda may have been feeling a little more spunky than before, but she wasn't ready for a face-to-face confrontation just yet. Although what was she worried about? The good *Miss Sadie* would probably never recognize her from their brief encounter in her dressing room anyway. So why not walk right up to her and slap her across the face!

Amanda returned to her room and sat down to think. She didn't have a lot of money. But the sisters had been generous to her, and between the French francs they had given her and what was left of her Austrian schillings, she had plenty to spare above what would be necessary for passage to England and a train to London from Portsmouth. She would go out and see if she could exchange the schillings for francs, if not at a bank perhaps back at the train station, and then buy some clothes to help her disguise herself.

Returning to l'Atelier des Prés after a successful outing a little after noon, Amanda walked into the hotel lobby with three packages in her arms.

Suddenly her heart leapt into her throat.

There stood Ramsay at the counter!

Her first thought was not, *There is my husband,* but *There is a spy and a louse and an enemy of all that is right and good and true . . . and of England as well!*

The shorter version came soon enough on the heels of the latter, however, and with it a return of the nausea she always felt in her stomach at the reminder. To have described her feelings with the word hatred might have been too strong, but anger and revulsion and contempt would all have fit the bill.

She felt like walking up and slapping him in the face too! But instead she slowed her step and drew in a deep breath, trying to keep hold of the cargo, which had nearly dropped to the floor at the sight, and slunk behind a wide column in the lobby.

So, Ramsay Halifax, she thought to herself, *we meet again. Well, this time we shall see who outsmarts whom!*

How different he now looked from her first sight of him when he had swept her off her feet. He didn't look the least bit handsome now. The duplicity she finally saw so clearly was written all over him. Why had she not been able to see it before? How could she *ever* have thought she loved him!

"Yes, Mr. Halifax," the clerk was saying, "I believe she is expecting you. I shall have your bags delivered to Miss Greenfield's suite."

"Thank you," replied Ramsay, then turned and headed for the staircase.

Casting reason to the wind, after a few seconds Amanda followed. Keeping her head down so that her face would not be visible from above, and sneaking a cautious upward glance every few seconds at the pair of legs half a flight ahead of her, she managed to keep loose contact with his retreating form. Her onetime pursuer had unwittingly now become Amanda's prey.

Ramsay left the stairs on the third floor and walked along the corridor.

Amanda hurried the rest of the way up to the landing, slowed and tiptoed the final few steps, then cautiously sneaked a peek, first to the right, then the left.

There he was, his back disappearing down the hallway!

Quickly she turned her head away, retreated a few steps behind a corner, then inched an eye back out around it. Ramsay continued to the end of the hall and turned left.

Amanda walked out into the corridor as fast as she dared and after him, her packages beginning to make lead of her arms and rustling as she went. She reached the end of the hall, slowed again, and peeked once more around the edge of the wall.

"Hello, darling," she heard the slimy voice of the actress say, now stepping out from an open door about halfway down the corridor. "I have been counting the minutes."

A kiss followed. The sight did not sting Amanda as it might have had she been in love with Ramsay. It only infuriated her yet more.

"When do you have to leave for England?"

"Not for a day or two. I'm meeting—"

The door closed behind them.

Heart pounding, Amanda remained where she was a moment longer, then hurried out from behind the wall and ran down the hall to see what room she had been watching. The number on the door read 369.

She turned and quickly ran back the way she had come, slowing to a walk the moment she was around the first corner and out of sight. She continued up to her own room on the fifth floor, finally depositing the three packages on the bed with a weary sigh.

70

Number 42

The arrival at Nr. 42 Ebendorfer Strasse in Vienna was the last thing Ramsay's mother expected. Suddenly standing in the parlor, where the real Gertrut Oswald had admitted them and to which she had been summoned, were four men who obviously had nothing resembling a social visit on their minds.

She vaguely recognized one but had never met him, so she couldn't be altogether sure. Two wore high-ranking uniforms of the Austro-Hungarian army. They were accompanied by a German officer of like importance. The long black leather overcoat and wide-bill hat of the fourth might have been sufficient indicators in themselves, but it was the eyes which said most clearly of all that here was a spy if ever there was one. It was this latter who spoke the moment the matron of the house entered the room.

"Mrs. Halifax," he said, "I am Rald Wolfrik, with Prussian Intelligence. We have a situation. I need to speak with Hartwell Barclay."

"He is not here."

"I gathered that. I am asking you where he is."

"On his way to Paris," answered Mrs. Halifax.

"Paris—why?"

"We had a certain breach of security. He and my son are attempting to put an end to the problem."

"Yes, I am aware of the—"

A light clearing of the throat was added briefly for effect.

"—the, uh ... activities of your son," said Wolfrik. "We have had him under scrutiny for some time."

"You have been watching my son?"

"We watch those whom we judge useful," replied Wolfrik.

Mrs. Halifax thought it best to say nothing further. She held her ground stoically.

"In any event," the man went on, "we must contact your colleague,

Mr. Barclay—immediately. There has been a major defection from the very ranks of the high command itself. You are, I believe, acquainted with Generaloberst von Bülow."

Mrs. Halifax nodded. "He has been here several times."

"Yes, so he informed me. His assistant, one Colonel Spengler, has recently disappeared near the Balkans. Our intelligence sources indicate the worst. Generaloberst von Bülow personally sent me here."

"What is it you want us to do?" asked Mrs. Halifax.

"Steps are being taken to locate Colonel Spengler. Transport, we believe, is by sea. I may need to get to England as soon as possible. These orders from the generaloberst," he said, indicating a folded paper in his hand, "instruct Hartwell Barclay to get me there."

"You are the assassin?" said Mrs. Halifax.

"I carry out my orders," replied Wolfrik. "I will only add that we have a very resourceful individual already on his way north should his services be required. We may also recruit your son's assistance. Where can we notify Barclay?"

Feeling suddenly short of breath, but realizing she had no alternative, Mrs. Halifax gave them the name of the hotel in Paris.

71

Mademoiselle Très Chic

◆◆◆

*A*manda sat in front of the mirror in her hotel room with a pair of scissors in her hand.

With a grimace she took hold of a small strand of brown, then clipped it to a length of three or four inches.

That first snip was the hardest, she thought. She followed with another . . . then another.

Twenty minutes later she stood up and took a few steps back, turning her head first one direction, then the other.

Not the best job, she thought. But the short-clipped hairdo had a distinctively French look. She had seen several girls wearing similar cuts in the shops. Amanda now set the red beret she had bought atop her newly coifed head, tilted it to one side, first to the right, then the left.

Hmm . . . it might work, she thought.

Now for a little makeup around the eyes, and some red lipstick . . .

Of course Ramsay would know her if they met at point-blank range and stared at each other. But she didn't intend to let that happen. As long as she could blend in among a crowd, she ought to be safe. He wouldn't be expecting her in a million years.

Another thirty minutes later, Amanda took stock of herself in the mirror—red beret, pale chartreuse scarf, draped over a loose-fitting blouse of somewhat darker green, fashionably slinky black French skirt with black stockings and boots. Along with the lipstick and dark eyes, it was bold and brash, like nothing Ramsay had ever seen on her before. And so very French! She could have stepped out of a fashion show!

"Ah, mademoiselle," she said aloud, *"vous êtes très chic!"*

Amanda squinted slightly. "I admit," she added, "the colors are a little loud and clashy . . . but even I don't recognize you!"

She turned away and started for the door.

"I think it's time I found out if this is going to do any good."

Amanda left her room and descended to the lobby, where, with magazine in hand, she took up a seat in one of several chairs scattered about a spacious sitting area to await the appearance of the man who, a few short months earlier, she had considered her husband. What she considered him now . . . she couldn't say. She hadn't figured that out yet.

A long and uneventful hour passed. She began to think the whole thing ridiculous. For months she had been doing her best to get *away* from Ramsay. What did she now hope to accomplish by trying to *find* him?

Amanda grew sleepy. Actually . . . this was a stupid idea. Spies and plots and lighthouses . . . she had probably been making the whole thing up. What was she thinking—that *she* was single-handedly going to help England win the war?

And this silly outfit!

Why didn't she just get on a train to Cherbourg before any more time went by and get away from Ramsay once and for all?

She started to stand up, glancing around absently as she did, when all of a sudden, not more than ten feet in front of her, the tall form of Hartwell Barclay walked past.

Amanda's eyes widened to saucers and she froze halfway out of her chair. She could almost feel the hair standing up on her arms and head. Her whole body chilled at sight of the white hair, the tall thin form, the eyes that had exercised such a magnetic, mesmerizing power over her. All her confidence of an hour earlier when alone in front of the mirror in her room instantly vanished. Her knees quivered and her stomach lurched slightly in the direction of her throat.

Barclay was striding across the lobby toward the stairs, looking about casually. She saw his eyes roving in her direction. They lit momentarily upon her . . . then continued on.

Her paralysis lasted but a second or two. Then he was gone. She eased back down into her chair, heart pounding.

What was this, she thought, a convention of the Fountain of Light!

Next thing she knew, Ramsay's mother would show up! A little makeup and haircut would not deceive *her*. She would see through it in an instant. She had better watch herself, thought Amanda, gradually getting her breath back. For all she knew, Mrs. Halifax might be here already.

But Mr. Barclay had seen her and had looked right through her. Seeing his eyes again had terrified her. Amanda knew he would never be able to exercise the same mind-control over her as before. But he was still a forceful presence whom she would just as soon avoid.

After a few minutes she rose and returned to her room. With Hartwell Barclay now on the scene, she had to rethink her strategy.

If she even had one!

72

Questions

At the Admiralty in London, the First Lord of the Admiralty listened to the report that the exchange had been made with success, and, it was all but certain, without detection. Churchill nodded, obviously pleased, though with grave expression.

"Where is the *Dauntless* now, Lieutenant Langham?" he asked.

"Hopefully safely through the Greek islands and approaching

Malta," replied a young man of confident bearing, blond, tall, and with a rich baritone voice. He carried himself as one who would one day himself be a leader and commander in the military ranks of which he now occupied the bottom rung on the officers' ladder.

"That should put her in the Orkneys in three or four days," said Churchill. "Have we made more progress in penetrating the Prussian Intelligence Service?"

"No, sir—unfortunately not," answered Churchill's assistant. "But they do appear to be operating from somewhere on British soil."

"Have you spoken recently with the Secret Service?"

"I met with Mr. Whyte last week, sir. They are just as much in the dark as we are."

"We've got to find their headquarters!" exploded Churchill in an uncharacteristic moment of anger as he slammed his fist down on the table. "There are still far too many moles among us. They will be our undoing if we do not root them out. What about our friend Beauchamp?"

"Still no trace of his whereabouts, sir," answered Langham, "nor sign that he has left the country."

"Then he is still either in Britain or has been smuggled out through their network. We've got to penetrate it!"

Churchill paused briefly, then glanced seriously toward his youthful aide.

"I want you to devote even greater attention to this matter than previously, Lieutenant," he said. "Pull out every file. Start over. Investigate everything we have on this security problem . . . the moles, the apparent spy network, the M.P. Beauchamp and his disappearance. Meet again with Jack Whyte. Whatever files of theirs he can open to you, ask him to do so. I want to know what they've got. And you are acquainted with Colonel Forsythe—the army's intelligence expert. Talk to him as well. We have to regain command of the seas and put a stop to this U-boat infiltration. Somewhere there have to be clues we have missed. I want you to make this your personal mission on my behalf."

"I understand, sir," said Langham.

"No one else has been able to find where they are coming in, or how the messages are wreaking havoc with our communications. Maybe you will have better luck."

73

Overheard Schemes

♦ ♦ ♦

*A*manda went downstairs to breakfast early the following morning.

She had to try to find out what they were up to. And she wanted to be safely in place at her table in the corner before either Ramsay or Barclay made an appearance, and with a copy of the day's newspaper to hold up in front of her face if need be.

She had been sitting at the table almost an hour, and had drawn out her own breakfast about as long as was credible, when the two men walked in together, absent the presence of either female member of the potential trio, Greenfield or Mrs. Halifax. Amanda thought she detected Ramsay's eyes resting upon her for the briefest of seconds. Trying to act nonchalant, though her heart began to pound the moment she knew he was looking at her, she took a slow sip from a cup of lukewarm tea, then casually raised the paper in front of her up just to her eyes. Slowly Ramsay looked away.

Whew! she thought. She had apparently passed the first test of the new mademoiselle look with flying colors.

Her self-congratulations, however, were a little too hasty. The men proceeded to serve themselves, then began walking her way.

Oh no! thought Amanda. *They've seen me . . . they know . . . they know!*

She was about to spring to her feet and make a dash for it, when they sat down two tables away. She relaxed, collected herself again, and strained to listen.

" . . . still convinced she's in England?" Mr. Barclay was saying.

"Of course," replied Ramsay. "Where else would she be?"

"Then you need to get over there as quickly as possible."

"And you?"

" . . . can't risk it," said Barclay, ". . . recognize me."

"I can handle Amanda," said Ramsay.

"Like you've handled her up till now?"

Ramsay shot the older man an angry glance.

"In any event a telegram came in for me just moments ago," Barclay went on, "that may require my attention on another matter. The services of the lighthouse are needed. So unfortunately I have no choice but to let you deal with the girl on your own. I hope you can keep from bungling it again."

Swallowing his mounting annoyance at Barclay's barbs, Ramsay took a drink of coffee. "What kind of matter?" he asked.

"Another defection. But of a considerably higher level of importance than your wife's."

"What are your plans, then?"

"I am being met by an operative in Prussian Intelligence who needs to intercept the defector. I have to catch a train north after breakfast tomorrow. I must take him to England."

"I can still get through by normal channels," said Ramsay. "I've got double citizenship and passports. I know Amanda's places. If she has returned to London, I'll find her."

"I'll meet you at the lighthouse," said Barclay ". . . and make sure you have the girl this time."

"I will leave tomorrow as well."

"Why not today?"

"What's the rush? You won't be to the lighthouse for several days. I want to make the most of my time with Adriane. I will be in London by tomorrow night."

"Unfortunately, I will be somewhere between here and Antwerp."

Both men were silent a few minutes.

"Come to think of it," said Barclay at length, "don't bother bringing the girl to the lighthouse."

"What are you implying?"

"I think we both know well enough what I mean. Just take care of it."

"Do you realize you're talking about my wife?" sneered Ramsay.

"I didn't think you were the sentimental type, Halifax. I think it's time you started thinking of yourself as a widower."

Amanda sucked in a shocked gasp. So, they *were* planning to kill her!

For another twenty minutes she kept her face securely hidden behind the newspaper, but could not concentrate on anything other than what she had heard. When Ramsay and Barclay finally rose to leave, she waited another minute or two, then followed them from the room.

If they were both leaving after breakfast tomorrow, she had twenty-four hours to decide which of the two she was going to follow.

Depending on her plan, she might also need another brief shopping excursion into the city.

74

Surprise Intruder

When Ramsay Halifax walked into the dining room of l'Atelier des Prés early the following morning with Adriane Grünsfeld on one arm and Hartwell Barclay walking along on the other side, his thoughts inexplicably turned briefly to the colorfully attired young French-woman he had noticed about the hotel, and wondered why she wasn't seated at her customary table in the corner. Perhaps she had finally checked out.

The reason for her absence, however, was of quite another nature. She was, in fact, at that very moment carrying out a scheme she had been going over in her mind since yesterday for gaining entry into the room he and his mistress had left only minutes before.

"Excuse me, miss," said Amanda to the maid in her practiced French. "I am Miss Sadie's stage assistant. She is on her way to the theater and left behind one of the most important parts of her costume—the hat in which she sings the finale of the last act. She needs it desperately, but she was already late and asked me to bring it. She told me to hurry back and find Fayette."

"I am Fayette," said the maid.

"Good. Miss Sadie said you would be so kind as to let me into the room. It is 369."

"Yes, I know Miss Sadie's room."

"Will you let me in, please—I am in a hurry to get to the theater myself."

Amanda now pulled out a twenty-franc note.

"Miss Sadie asked me to give you this for your trouble," she said.

Persuaded perhaps by the fact that she had seen Amanda several times the day before in this same corridor apparently just leaving room 369—an occurrence which Amanda had carefully orchestrated to coincide with both Ramsay's and Adriane's absence from the room, and no doubt likewise induced by the sudden appearance of the bill—the maid called Fayette took the bill from Amanda's hand, turned, and led the way toward the room in question. In another thirty seconds Amanda was safely inside with the door locked behind her.

Now she had to work fast.

Meanwhile, downstairs in the breakfast room, the trio was making plans to depart the French city, Barclay for his rendezvous with the Prussian, Ramsay for his hoped rendezvous with Amanda in London, and the actress Sadie Greenfield for an appointment with her afternoon's audience at the theater.

"When will I see you again, Ramsay darling?" she asked.

"Mere days, my dear," he answered jovially, "mere days. After my return I shall be all yours."

Hartwell Barclay had had enough of such talk. He rose.

"Don't be too confident of that," he said. "We may yet have other work to do after this little episode is over."

75

North From Paris

---◆◆◆---

𝒧eaving Ramsay's room, Amanda hurried down the hall, then quickly up the stairway.

She walked straight to her room and began hurriedly changing clothes. The next phase of her plan required an altogether different fashion statement, one which she hoped would draw far fewer eyes than had Mademoiselle Très Chic.

She had made arrangements to keep some of her things at the hotel until she returned. She had already left them at the desk. She needed to travel as lightly as possible. She was ready to go and would await Barclay on the street outside the station, watch and listen to find out where he was going, and make use of Gertrut Oswald's passport one last time to follow him.

She left her room and started toward the lobby.

Halfway down the first flight of stairs, suddenly she heard the voices of the three coming up from the ground floor.

"...all goes well ... see you in the north ... or perhaps Vienna...." It was Barclay's voice.

"...may need to use the lighthouse myself," said Ramsay, "...how it develops."

"I'm off, then," said Barclay, "...train to Brussels ... thirty-five minutes."

The next thing she heard, two sets of feet began to ascend the stairs along with Ramsay's and Sadie's voices. Amanda slunk back out of sight on the landing of the fourth floor. Closer and closer came the voices, then turned off the landing at the third floor. The instant they were down the hall toward their room, Amanda flew down the rest of the way. There was not a second to waste. She couldn't lose Barclay now.

She exited onto the street just in time to see him disappearing in a cab in the direction of the station. She hailed another and was soon on her way after him.

She reached the station less than a minute behind the white-haired Englishman and hurried inside. The sights and sounds and bustle of the station reminded her of the terror of the Vienna station when she had just barely escaped his clutches. Now the tables were turned—she was following *him*. And she wouldn't be so easily recognizable now!

She glanced quickly at the schedule board.

There it was—Brussels, nine-thirteen.

Where was Barclay? She'd lost him!

Frantically she looked all about. There he was, stopped briefly at a kiosk. Perfect—she would board the train ahead of him! He would suspect nothing.

Amanda ran for the ticket window.

76

Ramsay's Fury

*N*otwithstanding that they too would be parting in another couple of hours, Ramsay and Adriane entered their suite leisurely and in bright spirits.

Ramsay took off his coat, tossed it over a chair, sat down on the couch, and opened the newspaper he had brought up from the lobby. He did not notice anything amiss until twenty or thirty minutes later as he began thinking about his own preparations to leave.

Chatting with Adriane, he walked to his bureau to gather up his personal things. There, on top of his own wallet, sat a very strange, yet somehow familiar-looking, red beret. He looked at it, momentarily confused. Beside it, neatly folded, was a silk chartreuse scarf.

"Darling, this isn't *yours*. . . ?" he began with a bewildered expression, reaching out and picking up the beret. "I'm sure I've seen it, but don't recall—"

Suddenly he stopped. What was that paper beneath it . . . that oddly familiar handwriting!

"What the—" he exclaimed, throwing down the beret and grabbing up the single sheet of hotel stationery with the sinking feeling of having been duped.

Just a couple of little items to remember me by, Ramsay dear, he read. *I won't be needing them again now that they have served their purpose. At first I thought you recognized me, but the more I saw of you these last few days, the more I realized you had eyes only for another. Under the circumstances, I didn't think you'd mind giving me a little money, especially in that it does not appear that providing for me is high among your concerns of the moment. Call it a sharing of assets between husband and wife. Give Adriane my regards, but don't try to follow me. You couldn't find me in Milan, and you won't find me in Paris.*

Even before he was finished, her name was again on his lips with nearly as much venom as it had been in Vienna.

Amanda! he shouted angrily as he now rifled through his things.

"My money!" he cried. "The minx has stolen every franc I had ... and my passport is with them!"

"You can't mean she was actually in our room," said Adriane. "How could she have gotten in?"

Ramsay shook his head, spinning about in a rage, tearing through every drawer in the bureau.

"Must have been when we were at breakfast," he said, gradually calming. "I can't tell ... she may have taken more too. I had some papers...."

Even in the midst of his search, he felt almost a begrudging admiration for Amanda's spunk.

"How did you do it, you shrew?" he said half to himself, sitting back down to take stock of the suddenly changed situation. "Barclay may have misjudged you, Amanda my dear. But I never did. Maybe I knew you had it in you all along."

A thin smile broke across his lips, and he added silently to himself, "It's too bad, Amanda. We might have had something together, you and me, if it wasn't for your blasted English morality. Unfortunately, it's too late for you now. You have gone too far this time ... and now I shall have to kill you."

"Where do you think she is?" asked Adriane. "Maybe she's still in the hotel."

"Oh no, she's gone by now," said Ramsay, the momentary smile disappearing from his face. "If I know Amanda, she is long gone."

"Where, then?"

"On her way to England, no doubt. But I'll be on the ship from Cherbourg this afternoon. Of course, she'll expect that, and you can bet I won't see *her* on board."

"What about your passport?"

Ramsay smiled and pulled back his coat to reach inside its vest pocket.

"Fortunately," he said, "I have duplicates."

He paused and grew pensive. "I don't know where she is at this moment," he said. "But one thing is for certain. She'll be back in London before the week's out. And that's where I will get my hands on her again. She may be feeling herself very clever after this little game with the scarf and the hat, prancing about under my nose. But she won't outsmart me again."

77

Spy vs. Spy

◆ ◆ ◆

*H*artwell Barclay sat in the northbound train toward Brussels.

Most travel in the war zone had been curtailed, though his Austrian passport and high connections made the transfer out of France into German-occupied Belgium easy enough.

A stooped woman dressed in black from head to foot with a black scarf around her neck shuffled down the aisle with a limp and brushed rudely past him, knocking his elbow from its armrest.

"Watch yourself, old woman," he said irritably, half glancing toward the figure.

A surly grunt of response sounded. She continued on and sat down two seats behind him.

Paying her little heed, his thoughts returned to the approaching journey which had become necessary across the Channel. He didn't like this business of returning to the land of his birth. Too many thoughts and reminders of the past filled him. In his deepest heart he was a man haunted by a host of private fears. He was able to exude confidence and impose his will on others when in comfortable surroundings of his own choosing, and when bolstered by the presence of his loyal subjects. But if challenged man to man in the absence of such, he might wilt like a schoolboy threatened by the class bully. Though he did his best to hide it, he was actually a timid man hounded by guilt for a past he could not face even in the privacy of his innermost heart. That guilt had in no way been assuaged by the betrayal of his native homeland, and he was not especially anxious to set foot on its soil again. He had at one time been a man of relatively high profile and could not help being nervous that he might be in more jeopardy than he realized.

The train had filled as they neared Brussels. Gradually the seating grew crowded. Barclay did his best to keep to himself but found the press of disgusting and smelly human flesh repulsive.

Behind him a loudmouthed Belgian, who had apparently had too much to drink before boarding, was attempting to strike up a conversation with his neighbor, who was not inclined in the least to engage with him in dialog.

"What's your problem, old woman? Cat got your tongue, or are you deaf!" he said after she had said nothing in response to a string of loud questions and attempted off-color anecdotes. "Can't you see I'm talking to you?"

The woman continued not to reply, trying yet again to turn away, an attempt made difficult by the fact that they were seated beside each other, and she had only the window on her other side to keep her company.

"What's the matter," he said, "am I not good enough for the likes of you?"

His attempts grew louder and louder, gradually filling the entire coach. Unconsciously Barclay turned around and looked to see what sort of fool was causing the ruckus. His gaze, however, was diverted toward the old woman in black who was the object of the drunken man's abuse. Though he could only see one side of it, for she was facing the window, her aspect and complexion seemed remarkably youthful for a woman who otherwise appeared sixty or more. Not only that, though he couldn't quite place it, there was an uncannily familiar—

"Brussels, five minutes!" called out the conductor, coming through the coach. "Next stop . . . Brussels."

Barclay turned back around at the sound. The train immediately began to slow. Now commotion filled the coach as bustling passengers began gathering up suitcases and bags, parcels and umbrellas, and putting on coats. One by one they stood and some began moving toward the doors. Whatever became of the loud man's further efforts with his unfriendly neighbor, they were drowned out in the hubbub occasioned by their arrival in the station.

Barclay himself stood as the passengers made their way down the aisles to exit the train. Once the coach was mostly empty, he eased into the aisle, glancing around for one last look at the curious old woman. She still sat unmoving, her face turned away. He stared at her another moment or two. As he did his gaze narrowed slightly and he took a step toward her, his brain trying to place what it was about her that seemed to draw his eyes.

All at once the bothersome man who had been beside her came lumbering up the aisle, bumped straight into him as he proceeded toward the exit, nearly knocking Barclay off his feet.

"Get going, man!" he shouted, his foul drunken breath nearly causing Barclay to swoon. "Didn't you hear the conductor? We're in the station. Get moving . . . you're in my way."

Barclay stepped aside, let the belligerent fellow by, then followed him out and into the station.

Behind him, a minute or two later, the silent old woman in black slowly stepped out of the train, glanced about cautiously, then ambled off after Barclay's retreating form.

78

A Visitor to Heathersleigh

It was Jocelyn who opened the door to the visitor who arrived at Heathersleigh Hall.

"Stirling!" she said, greeting him warmly. "How nice to see you."

"Hello, Mrs. Rutherford. I wanted to stop in for a visit sooner, but my holiday from university has gone by more quickly than I could have imagined."

"You've been busy, then?"

"My father and I have been building an addition to our barn. The work goes quickly with two. I'm enjoying being home and working with him on it. But every day has gone by so fast I've hardly done anything else. We should finish tomorrow."

"Can you come in—do you have time for some tea with us?"

Stirling smiled. It wasn't the timid smile of the boy, but the playful smile of a confident young man. "I was hoping you might ask, ma'am," he said.

"You just make yourself comfortable while I go tell Sarah to add some of those cakes you like to the tea tray. Then I'll fetch Catharine from the library."

"Always in the library," laughed Stirling. "What do you say about my fetching Catharine while you're talking with Sarah?"

"An even better plan," rejoined Jocelyn. "The two of you just stay up in the library, then, and I'll join you. We'll have Sarah bring the tea there."

They parted for their separate destinations, Jocelyn for the kitchen, young Blakeley limping toward the stairs.

Jocelyn entered the library a few minutes later to find the two young people poring over an atlas lying open on the table.

"What are you looking at?" she said as she approached.

"I'm sorry, Mrs. Rutherford," answered Stirling. "I hope you don't mind. I asked Catharine to show me where Amanda was living."

"Not at all, Stirling. That's why the atlas is on the table. We've been following the travels of the rest of our family. Charles and George were on their way to the Mediterranean the last we heard, though there has been no mail for some time. It's very difficult. Somehow the maps help a bit."

She stopped briefly, shaking off the mood that threatened. "So, did you see where Amanda is?"

"Actually," said Catharine, "we don't *know* that she is in Vienna. That was the postmark on the last letter we received after she left. You remember, don't you, when she visited a year ago?"

Stirling nodded. "The whole village was abuzz with it. I was away at the time, but Mum told me all about it. I had hoped she would stay long enough for me to see her again, but then Mum said she was gone again within a few days."

Jocelyn's eyes began to fill. Catharine quickly offered the platter of cakes and breads to their guest. Soon the three were laughing and drinking their tea as Stirling told one escapade after another about the young men he was with at Oxford.

"I hope the young ladies are not so rowdy," said Jocelyn.

"If not, they're sure to be once Catharine arrives," joked Stirling.

"What!" exclaimed Catharine. "Stirling Blakeley, how can you say such a thing?"

"I remember plenty of scrapes you led George and me into, and not so very long ago either."

"I did not!" laughed Catharine.

"You did, and you know it."

"Well . . . I just had to make sure you two didn't leave me out because I was a girl."

The conversation continued gay and lively, and the afternoon passed quickly. Gradually shadows brought an end to the visit.

"I need to be going," said Stirling. "Father and I agreed to take a break from the barn this afternoon, but if I know him, he is probably back at work. And I want to go home through the wood so I can stop by briefly to see Maggie."

He rose, stretched his bad leg a moment or two, then turned toward the door.

"Thank you so much," he said. "This has been a lovely visit."

Jocelyn rose to accompany him. "I'll go with you to the edge of the woods, Stirling. Just wait for me at the bottom of the stairs while I get my shawl."

Jocelyn left the library and walked down to her room. When she returned a minute later, however, she heard Stirling's voice still coming from the library. She went back up the flight of stairs to the second floor. There were the two young people, both leaning against opposite sides of the doorframe into the library, chatting easily and freely.

"Why don't you join us, Catharine?" asked Stirling.

"I'm ready to go back to my book," she replied. "Rebecca is being tried by the Knights Templar and has called for a champion to save her. I must find out if it is to be Ivanhoe, Robin of Locksley, or King Richard."

"Maybe it will be none of them," said Stirling with a sly smile.

"No, no—don't tell me! I have to find out for myself," laughed Catharine, covering her ears and running back into the library to the window seat where the copy of *Ivanhoe* awaited her.

79

Jocelyn and Stirling Blakeley

❖❖❖

*J*ocelyn and Stirling walked down the stairs and left the house through the rear doors. When they were beyond the trim lawn northeast of the Hall and were starting across the wide expanse of grassy meadow between it and the wood where lay the McFee cottage, Stirling spoke in a more serious tone than before.

"I am so sorry about Amanda, Mrs. Rutherford," he said. "I think of her often at university."

Surprised, Jocelyn turned her face toward him questioningly.

"You are wondering why I would think about Amanda?"

"Yes," replied Jocelyn, "I admit, that is what I was thinking."

"You see," said Stirling, "it seems that so many of the young men in the lodgings where I live in Oxford complain about their parents, how they don't send them as much money as they want, or that they pester them about not studying hard enough. But mostly they just complain about what seem to me trivial matters. It reminds me of some of the terrible things I have heard Amanda say about you and Sir Charles. And yet people who live in the village, especially such as myself and my parents, see you in a completely different light. It seems to me that you have given your three children nothing but love, just as you have shown to all the rest of us. I can't imagine any two people being more loved than you and Sir Charles. And it is because you always give so much of yourselves."

"Thank you, Stirling," replied Jocelyn as they walked slowly along. "You cannot imagine how much your words mean to me."

They walked awhile longer, when the young man broke the silence again.

"Mrs. Rutherford," he said, "do you remember the day when Amanda tried to come to my rescue in the village? It was a day when Papa had been drinking."

"Yes, I remember, Stirling. It seems that is when Amanda began to despise me. I am afraid it is not a good memory."

"That is too bad—I'm sorry. It is a good memory for me. She seemed like an angel. I'll never forget how she threw herself between Papa and me to try to protect me from his blows. It wasn't long after that when he stopped drinking—thanks even more to Sir Charles than Amanda."

Jocelyn smiled and nodded.

"It puzzles me how Amanda can be like an angel in my memory, and yet have become so hurtful and critical toward you. I find myself wondering what made her change. And that makes me wonder what the young men at school would think if they knew how my papa had once behaved toward me. Yet now I love him more, it seems, than they love their own fathers, who never did anything like what Papa did when he was drinking. It is all very puzzling."

Again Jocelyn nodded.

"It is interesting, is it not, Stirling," she said, "how people view things so differently? That day you speak of was a very hard one for me. Amanda was furious with me for not stepping in and stopping your father from hitting you. She said when she got older she would stand up for people's rights more than I did. I think that's why the suffragette movement so appealed to her. But I knew anything I did to come between you and your father might interfere with the relationship Charles was trying to establish with your father."

She paused thoughtfully.

"I suppose, as I look back now," she went on, "it may be that we were too strict in some ways. But at the time you never know exactly where the balance lies. You do the best you can, trying to weigh the constantly shifting needs of leniency and discipline. You'll find out just how hard that balance is when you're a father, Stirling."

He laughed. "That's hard to imagine, Mrs. Rutherford," he said. "I'm barely old enough to figure out how to be a grown-up. I can't envision myself as a parent."

"How old are you now, Stirling?"

"Twenty-four, ma'am."

"Hmm . . . the same as Amanda—though she will be turning twenty-five this spring. But the years will go by faster than you realize, Stirling, and one day before you know it you may just have a family of your own."

"If you say so, Mrs. Rutherford," laughed Stirling.

"Well, we are to the edge of the wood—here is where I will turn around," said Jocelyn. "It has been wonderful to see you, Stirling. Give my love to your parents."

"I will, Mrs. Rutherford. And—"

He paused and glanced away briefly.

"And if I could just say, ma'am," he said after a moment, looking back into Jocelyn's face, "thank you for being such a friend to my mother. I know you mean a great deal to her, in the same way Sir Charles does to my father."

"Of course, Stirling—thank you."

They shook hands, then Stirling turned and limped off a few steps, then turned back once more.

"I still pray for her," he said. "Amanda, I mean."

"Thank you, Stirling."

He continued on in the direction of the cottage in the descending dusk and was soon lost to Jocelyn's sight.

A remarkable young man for all he has been through, thought Jocelyn.

She turned and began making her way back to the Hall, whose windows were lit in the distance across the meadow.

"I still pray for her too," she whispered with a smile as she went. "I still pray for her too."

80

Missing Clue

Antwerp was not high on the list of places Hartwell Barclay would have desired to visit.

Especially tonight. It was miserably cold and a light rain had begun to fall. A storm appeared likely, and he did not relish what lay ahead—an underwater channel crossing beneath a turbulent sea.

He pulled his coat up tightly around his neck, walked across the street from the hotel, and lit a cigarette as best he could in this drizzle. They ought to have thought of some better signal.

Behind him a black stooped figure exited the same hotel he had just left.

An impulse caused Barclay to glance back.

What was that old woman there about? It couldn't . . .

But it looked uncannily like the old hag he had seen in the train a day and a half ago. Come to think of it, he had seen a remarkably similar woman even before that . . . all the way back in Paris. It couldn't possibly be the same woman, although . . .

As he looked, the striking similarity seemed more and more than could be accounted for by mere coincidence. What in blazes could she be doing in a first-class hotel like this!

The sound of an automobile approaching interrupted his thoughts. He spun around. He had apparently been seen. There was no more use for the cigarette. He threw it into the street. The auto slowed and stopped in front of him. The back door opened. He got in, and the car sped off.

"I take it you are Barclay," said a figure out of the blackness.

He nodded.

"I am Wolfrik. Are the arrangements made?"

"We will depart within the hour. Tell the driver to take us to the south harbor."

The remainder of the twenty-minute ride was silent. When the car stopped again, Barclay got out, followed by the man called Wolfrik, then another. Barclay glanced warily at the silent man, who was apparently accompanying the Prussian, short of stature and slightly balding. He did not look physically imposing, but the glint in his eye was menacing.

"I was told to arrange transport for one other than myself," said Barclay.

"He is with me," replied Wolfrik. "One extra man will change nothing. It would not be advisable to leave him behind."

Barclay took in the words with silent annoyance. He did not like being left out of a change of plans like this, but judged it better to say nothing further.

They walked toward the docks in silence. The rain had by now begun to come down in earnest. There was no wind, however, and in the quietness of the night their voices carried farther and with greater clarity than they might have expected had they paused to consider the possibility that someone might be listening. The engine of another automobile sounded somewhere a block or two away, but they paid little attention, nor to the footsteps coming their way in the shadows a few moments later from the same direction.

"Has Colonel Spengler been apprehended?" asked Barclay at length.

"Not yet," replied Wolfrik, "but the trap is set. It is vital we get across the Channel ahead of the *Dauntless*."

Barclay stopped and glanced about. They were at the edge of the quay. He had to get his bearings briefly to see which pier was the one he had been told. A few silent ships were about and hundreds of fishing vessels were moored nearby, but this was not the main section of the Antwerp harbor where most larger oceangoing vessels and naval ships docked. It was nearly entirely deserted at this time of night.

Confident of the direction again, Barclay led the way, moving along to the sound of the water slapping against shoreline, hulls of boats, and quay.

"A U-boat is waiting to take us to England," he said as they walked across the quay toward the pier. "We will arrive at Hawsker Head."

"I may need to go to London to carry out the remainder of our assignment," added the Prussian. "I have been told you have contacts that will enable us to move freely."

"It can be arranged," rejoined Barclay. "But why London? I thought you only needed to retrieve Spengler."

"There is one other matter involved. That is why my friend here is along."

"What kind of matter?"

"It is top secret. Can your people get him to London?"

"The Fountain has friends," said Barclay, liking the direction of this mission less and less. "Our network can take you anywhere in England with relative anonymity."

He certainly had no intention of taking them there himself, thought Barclay silently. London was the last place he was about to show his face!

They walked out across the planked decking toward the waiting vessel, which had put in only two hours before for the express purpose of this clandestine rendezvous. Behind them they still saw nothing. But they were not alone.

Minutes later they stepped onto the deck of the sub. Barclay took once final glance back.

There was that old woman again, standing halfway out on the quay! Just standing there staring at him! Had she followed them all the way from the hotel? What was the old crone's game?

His eyes narrowed. But he could do nothing. Already a German officer was shoving him along to the hatch and pushing him down into the bowels of the undersea craft.

On the pier, Amanda waited until he had disappeared, then turned and hurried away. It was time to retrace her steps and get out of this city. She had finally heard the missing clue she had followed Barclay to learn. They were on their way to someplace called Hawsker Head, with some other secret matter to follow involving London.

She wouldn't even go back to the hotel. She had told the cabdriver to wait out of sight. She would go straight from here to the station and make for the coast of France by whatever route would get her there.

Hawsker Head ... she had never heard the words in her life. And what was the *Dauntless*?

Whatever it was all about, one thing was clear—this part of her work was done. She had to get to London as fast as she could. It was time to get the information to England.

From here, maybe she might be able to go to Calais and cross from there. It would be much faster than going all the way back to Paris and then to Cherbourg.

What about the things she had left at the hotel in Paris?

She couldn't worry about that now. She would contact the hotel later.

They needed this information in England and fast. If a trap was set, it meant someone was in danger.

There wasn't a moment to spare.

81

Beneath Channel Waters

◆◆◆

*H*artwell Barclay was no seaman.

It was the middle of the same night and sleep was useless. He would get all the sleep he wanted in the comfortable bed in his own room in the house with the red roof at Hawsker Head. They would arrive at first light of day.

If only the seas weren't too rough to prevent their being able to put ashore. At least beneath the surface the movement was minimal, although still sufficient to keep him awake and his stomach queasy.

The craft lurched starboard a few degrees. Negotiating a channel crossing on the surface, with the wind blowing twenty to thirty knots, would have been impossible. The rough water above, however, did little to disturb their crossing down here, which thus far had been as smooth as he could have expected. That didn't mean he had to enjoy it.

Knowing he was on his way back to England again filled Hartwell Barclay with strange sensations as it had earlier, reminders of his former life, and with them a growing unease about all this he had allowed himself to get involved in. It was not his conscience that was speaking. He had shut that up for good long ago, and its voice hadn't bothered him in years. But English blood was in his veins after all, and it was impossible altogether to dismiss the inconvenient nagging of duty, decency, loyalty, and all the similar attributes which stir in the inbred soul of the English psyche.

He had planned simply to run this fellow Wolfrik across to Yorkshire, spend a day or two at the lighthouse until the Spengler defector was taken care of, however he planned to do it, and then bring them back across and be on his way returning to Vienna—over and back under the Channel undetected—along with the young fool Halifax, who had better have taken care of that greater fool of a wife by this time.

Now Wolfrik was talking about London!

Barclay didn't like it. That's where he would put his foot down. He would absolutely refuse to leave Yorkshire.

What could be the other mysterious assignment? These two he had brought on board with him were a couple of rum customers, that much was certain. He could see it in their eyes. Who was this other seedy character with Wolfrik anyway? Why was he along? He had the eyes of an assassin if he had ever seen one. He reminded him of the madcap Princip, who had started this whole bloody war back in Sarajevo.

Gradually Barclay fell into an uneasy sleep.

When he awoke, he glanced at his watch. It was morning. They should be sitting off the Yorkshire coastline and getting ready to surface by now.

He would be in McCrogher's dinghy within the hour, and on land again shortly after that.

82

Channel Reflections

*A*manda stood on deck of the channel ferry waiting for the lines to be cast off and to begin the voyage over the twenty-one miles of sea separating Great Britain from the mainland of Europe.

She had traveled most of the night between Antwerp and Calais, taking what trains were available and snatching catnaps while she waited in deserted stations. She was exhausted and still had a whole new day ahead of her.

Getting back out of Belgium and into France had proved a little difficult, especially with the war front so close. She doubted the French officers in charge believed a word of what she said about possessing vital information and needing to get to England right away. But it didn't matter. They let her through, and now here she was on board the first ship of the day.

She squinted through the morning's cloudy sky, as if hoping she might, even now, be able to catch a faint glimpse of the Dover cliffs. But it was no use. The storm had passed, but lingering haze and clouds still obscured the vision. Yet just knowing that England lay over there, and that in less than two hours her feet would feel English soil once again beneath them, was enough, in spite of the fatigue, to send tingles of excitement through her whole body.

Maybe she could find a chair inside and catch an extra few winks once they set off. But right now she wanted to savor the scent of the channel waters in her nostrils, and the thought of returning to her homeland.

She hadn't anticipated feeling this way. National pride was the last emotion she expected to rise in her breast. But after all she had been through, and the horrible months in Vienna, and the terrifying flight across Austria and Italy . . . all of a sudden she very much wanted to be back . . . back in *England*.

The very word rang in her mind with safety and hominess.

Her thoughts turned to her father. Why, she couldn't say, but she did not resist them. Strangely, for the first time in a long while, no anger or bitterness came with them. He was a patriot, she thought, who loved his country—more than she had in recent years.

What had come over her to allow her mind to be so clouded by all that ridiculous Fountain of Light talk? And that caustic pamphlet she had let them put her name on. What in the world had she been thinking!

Her father was ten times the man Hartwell Barclay would ever be. A hundred times!

She had been gone from England not quite a year, and from her home for eight years. She had no one to blame but herself for all that had happened to her. Her parents had tried to warn her, but she hadn't listened.

What have I done with my life? thought Amanda.

Over and over, it seemed, she had done one stupid thing after another, always leaving when the going got rough. She left home, she left the Pankhursts', she left Cousin Martha's, she left Vienna, she left the chalet. Always leaving . . . always running away.

Again her father's face came into her mind's eye.

Actually, now that she considered the idea, it might be all right to see her father again. It might even be *good* to see him. Perhaps she was finally ready.

Maybe it was time she started growing up and facing some things. Like *herself*. Facing what she had let herself sink to . . . and maybe facing what she wanted to become.

Before her thoughts could go farther down that road, Amanda felt the boat jerking beneath her and the waves of the Channel beginning to rock it in a gentle, swelling motion.

They had cast off. She was on her way back to England!

83

What Next?

♦ ♦ ♦

$\mathscr{A}$manda arrived at Charing Cross Station about eleven that same morning. She was filled with so many thoughts and emotions she could hardly think what to do with them all.

Over and over she was reminded of Ramsay's words, *I know where Amanda goes. I'll find her.*

Even as she departed the train and walked into the station, excited to hear English being spoken everywhere and to see the familiar sights of the station again, unconsciously she glanced about nervously, as if any second Ramsay might appear from out of the crowd to nab her. He had turned up in every train station she had been in for months!

But she mustn't forget the urgency of her mission. And the foremost question in her mind was: What to do now?

Now that at last she was back in London, she had to get in touch with *somebody* and tell them what she knew.

But who?

Whom should she tell what she had overheard in Vienna and Antwerp? She couldn't just walk up to Westminster Palace or Ten Downing Street and announce, "I have important information. Please let me in to see Mr. Asquith immediately."

Maybe she should march up to the gates of Buckingham Palace, she thought with a smile, and say, "Hello there, King George. I met Queen Victoria when I was a little girl, and now I'm here to help you win the war!"

The thought of such a sight almost made her laugh out loud.

She would never get within a mile of the prime minister or the king. She would be turned away on her heels with the words, "Shoo, little girl ... don't bother us!"

Who did she know who might be able to help her figure out what to do?

Her thoughts suddenly turned to the only person in London who fit the bill—Rev. Timothy Diggorsfeld, the man who had led her father toward his conversion to Christianity.

For so many years she had resented the very thought of the London minister, blaming him, as she saw it, for the disruption of their family. But now she realized he might just about be the only person in the city she could completely trust. And there was no way Ramsay could know anything about him. With him she would be safe from Ramsay.

She would go see Rev. Diggorsfeld immediately.

84

Surprise Caller

*W*ithin the hour Amanda found herself walking along Bloomsbury Way from the corner where she had asked the cab to leave her.

There was the sign and name exactly as she remembered—NEW HOPE CHAPEL, T. DIGGORSFELD, PASTOR.

She took a deep breath, then walked to the door and tried the latch. It was open. Slowly she walked inside. She had not been inside a church for so long, the very atmosphere filled her with inexplicable feelings she could not describe. There was no sign of life, only cool, dark silence. For several seconds she took in the peaceful, quiet ambiance, then began looking about. She saw a small placard reading PASTOR'S STUDY, and followed in the direction indicated by its arrow. A minute later she was knocking on a door which stood slightly ajar. From inside she heard movement.

The door swung open. There stood Timothy's tall, lanky form. A bright smile of welcome, disbelief, and a host of other emotions only he could have identified immediately broke across his face.

"Amanda!" he exclaimed, as if he wasn't quite sure whether he was gazing at an apparition or the real thing.

"Hello, Rev. Diggorsfeld," she replied.

"Come in . . . come in!" he said exuberantly. "It is so wonderful to see you again!"

"I'm not really here on a social call," she said, following him inside.

Not to be dissuaded of his enthusiasm, nor the inward rejoicing of his heart for this answer to prayer, he offered Amanda a chair.

"You are welcome for whatever reason you have come," he said cheerfully. "And if it is not social, why have you come, then? What can I do for you?"

"I know it may be somewhat awkward," Amanda began, "and that I haven't been the kindest to you. I've been out of the country, you see . . ."

As she spoke, Timothy nodded. He knew far more about her sojourn in the far country than she realized.

"In fact, I only arrived back this morning," she went on. "I came to you immediately. I haven't even had anything to eat all day."

"Oh, then by all means," said Timothy rising and starting for the door, "I'll have Mrs. Alvington prepare us some lunch."

"There's no time for that," said Amanda.

"No time . . . why?" asked Timothy, pausing and turning back.

"I've been involved with some people, you see, who are on the side of the Austrians," said Amanda. "Actually, I think they are spies. One of the men is English, and . . . I know it sounds crazy, Mr. Diggorsfeld, I think I may have information that the War Office needs. But I don't know where to go or whom to see."

"I see," said Timothy, his tone immediately serious. "I'll get my coat and hat right away."

"What do you think I should do?" asked Amanda, not quite understanding him.

"Just give me a minute. I'll grab something quickly for you to eat on the way."

Before Amanda could say anything further, Diggorsfeld disappeared. He returned two or three minutes later with a small bag and wearing coat and hat.

"Your father is acquainted with Mr. Churchill," he said, gesturing for Amanda to follow. "I have never met him myself," he went on, leading her out of the church, "but perhaps he will see you. If it is important information, we might as well go to the very top."

"We?"

"I will take you straight to the Admiralty myself," said Timothy.

Already they were on the street and he was urgently waving for a cab.

85

The Admiralty

*A*fter a good deal of searching about, inquiries, and red tape, the unlikely duo of Amanda Rutherford Halifax and Rev. Timothy Diggorsfeld at last reached that portion of the Admiralty they hoped might be in the vicinity of the office they were looking for.

They had come down a long, wide corridor, luckily without being stopped as they already had at several previous junctures, and now stood before two large closed doors, upon which in bold black letters were painted the words FIRST LORD OF THE ADMIRALTY.

"I think we have found it at last," said Timothy. He opened one of the doors for Amanda. She entered and he followed.

"We would like to see Mr. Churchill," said Timothy when the door was closed behind them.

"And you would be—" said the receptionist, gazing up from her desk to look upon the most unmilitary and unmatched pair of individuals she had ever laid eyes on, with an aloof expression of humorous scorn.

"Rev. Timothy Diggorsfeld," replied Timothy. "It is really most urgent that we speak to the First Lord of the Admiralty."

"In the middle of the war? Surely you can't imagine that he can—"

"What we must see him about concerns the war," persisted Timothy. "I have with me here Miss Amanda Rutherford."

"Really, Mr. Diggorsfeld, I am afraid your seeing Mr. Churchill is absolutely out of the—"

"Rutherford . . . did I hear the name *Rutherford?*" now sounded a gravelly voice somewhere. It appeared to have come from an adjacent room whose door stood ajar.

A moment later the massive form of the First Lord of the Admiralty filled the space between the reception area and his inner office. He looked over the two visitors without betraying his thoughts by any change of expression.

"I am sorry to disturb you, Mr. Churchill," said the secretary. "These two people were just leaving. I have explained that you are extremely busy and just making plans to—"

"Who is the Rutherford around here?" interrupted Churchill.

"I . . . I am Amanda Rutherford," said Amanda, who could not help being intimidated by the presence of the man.

"What Rutherfords? You're not by chance the daughter of Sir Charles?"

"Actually, yes . . . I am."

Churchill took in the information with a knowing nod.

"So you're the young lady who wrote that troublesome political pamphlet a while back," he said.

"I am sorry to have to admit it, but I'm afraid I am," replied Amanda. "Much has changed since then. All I can say is that I feel very badly for my part in it, and I am no longer associated with the people who put me up to it."

"I am very glad to hear it, Miss Rutherford," intoned Churchill. "It was a grief to your father to see how they were using you to retaliate against him."

"I'm sure it must have been," said Amanda. "I will apologize to him later. But there's no time for all that now. The reason we are here concerns those same people, and something far more serious than just a pamphlet."

"In what way?" asked Churchill, growing steadily more intrigued. Gradually he approached from the doorway.

"I am almost certain they are involved in a spy network against England. And I think I may have information that will help you uncover it."

"I brought her to see you, Mr. Churchill," Timothy spoke again, "because I was aware of your acquaintance with Charles. He is a dear friend of mine as well."

"Well . . . you came to the right place. What did you say your name was?"

"Timothy Diggorsfeld."

The two men shook hands. Churchill now shook Amanda's hand also.

"Come into my office," he said. "Mrs. Templeton, get Lieutenant Langham and Admiral Snow in here immediately."

"Yes, Mr. Churchill."

"And contact Colonel Forsythe of the army and Jack Whyte. Ask them to come over as well. They both need to hear this. Tell them it's urgent."

86

Change of Plans Aboard the *Admiral Uelzen*

*B*arclay roused himself from the bunk where he had spent the fitful night. As he made his way forward the main deck buzzed with activity.

Commands and conversations in German surrounded him. The commander of the *Admiral Uelzen* had just ordered the periscope up.

As he thought, they were no doubt preparing for final rendezvous maneuvers off the Yorkshire coast. He walked toward his temporary colleague, the Prussian Wolfrik, who stood at the captain's elbow, with a certain feeling of pride to observe in use the system of communication he had himself helped establish.

"Where are we?" asked Barclay in German.

"About three miles offshore, east by northeast," replied Captain Dietz. "I'll take it now, Corporal Ubel."

He took the periscope from his officer, leaned heavily on the two horizontal bars, and peered into its lenses.

"What are the seas like?" asked Barclay.

"It has calmed down," said Dietz, still looking through the glass.

"Good. Why haven't we surfaced yet? By my watch it's well past dawn. We need to get ashore. Has McCrogher been sent out for us?"

"We will remain in position here until the information comes we are waiting for," now said Wolfrik.

"What information? If the seas have calmed, it's time we were ashore."

"We won't be going ashore for some time," said Wolfrik. His tone now took on the ring of command.

"Why in blazes not?" exclaimed Barclay. "I want off this tub and on solid ground. We should have been in contact with the lighthouse long before now."

"We have been in contact with the lighthouse for several hours. As I said, they are relaying information to us. We have other business to attend to before we can—"

Before he could finish, the commander was interrupted.

"Signal coming through," he barked. "Lieutenant Altman, take down new coordinates."

He stood back and the young lieutenant replaced him at the periscope with pad and pencil.

"What coordinates are they talking about?" asked Barclay.

"The location of one of your nation's battle cruisers."

"What! A battle cruiser ... what possible—"

"I told you, Barclay—Colonel Spengler is aboard the *Dauntless*, and our assignment is to eliminate him. To accomplish that, we have arranged a little trap."

"I thought you were going to take him back to the Continent."

"For what purpose? He is a traitor. He deserves but one thing. To that end, we will send him to the bottom of the Channel."

"You can't do that! He is just one man on an entire ship."

"Look, Barclay, I have my orders," insisted Wolfrik, growing impatient with the conversation. "They are to arrange for the sinking of the ship. Two other U-boats are on their way. When they are in place and we have relayed the information to them, but not before, then we will put in."

"That wasn't part of the bargain," said Barclay. "I only agreed to get you across the Channel so that you could get your hands back on your defector. You can assassinate him for all I care, but not sink an entire ship."

"This is war, you fool," replied Wolfrik with an evil sneer. "Do you actually think a pawn like you can dictate events and tell Alliance intelligence how to do its job?"

"I will not be responsible for sending hundreds of innocent Englishmen to their deaths."

"You and your conscience can deal with it any way you want."

"I tell you, I won't have their blood on my hands."

"The blood is already on your hands," Wolfrik spat back. "You betrayed your country long ago. It is a little late for you to turn soft. Events are in motion. You can't stop them. My orders are to sink the

Dauntless if it arrives before our sister vessels are in position. I am telling you one last time that this submarine is under my command, and that we will remain here monitoring signals from the lighthouse on the position of the *Dauntless*, whether it takes twenty-four, or even forty-eight hours. So make yourself comfortable, Barclay, and get out of our way."

"If you sink it, why do you need to get ashore at all?" Barclay said with bitter sarcasm.

"I told you before, there is another matter we will then attend to."

"You mean there is *more*?" said Barclay in disbelief.

Wolfrik laughed, beginning to enjoy the Englishman's discomfort.

"You don't think we would divulge all our plans to a known traitor. I told you, my colleague and I must get to London once the other U-boats are in place," he said. "We need to get ashore and about our business."

Wolfrik's lips parted in an evil grin, then he laughed again.

"Barclay, you are unbelievably naive. I must say I misjudged you. Yes, there is more. You will personally take us to London. If you cause any further difficulties, we will leave you there for the authorities to find, along with your colleague, the young Halifax who has been so agreeable thus far. All the evidence will point to the two of you. They will shoot you both for what they discover you have done."

"Evidence, what the blazes kind of evidence! What is it supposed to point to?" said Barclay, not believing a word of what he was hearing.

"To the assassination of Churchill and Prime Minister Asquith," replied Wolfrik with another grin.

"What!"

"Just think—the name Hartwell Barclay will go down in English history books as the traitor and spy who snuck back into England on a German U-boat to carry out one of the most treasonous assassinations in the history of his country."

"I won't do it!"

"It doesn't matter, Barclay," laughed Wolfrik. "They will all think you did, and the evidence will be compelling."

Barclay was too overwhelmed to say another word. He staggered backward as one stunned and crumbled onto a nearby stool.

"Come, come, Barclay," laughed Wolfrik as if talking to a confused child, "don't tell me you are going to become a patriot now, after you've given us so many of your country's secrets. It is too late for your conscience to start worrying you. You're a fool if you act surprised."

Barclay said nothing. His betrayal had now returned to land upon his own head. He himself had become a pawn in the larger game which he had always persuaded himself was such a noble cause.

87

Deciphering the Clues

❖❖❖

*N*ow, what's this about, young lady?" asked Churchill, his eyes animated, the moment they were all seated in his office twenty minutes later.

"I was in Vienna last summer," Amanda began. "The people that had to do with the pamphlet—"

"What's it called . . . what was it, Jack—you and Admiral Snow were looking into those people . . . something about illumination?"

"The Fountain of Light," replied Amanda. "I didn't know it at the time I sailed from England, but they have a house in Vienna, and it was there I began to overhear things."

"Who was involved?" asked Churchill.

"An Englishman named Hartwell Barclay—"

"The blackguard formerly with the Secret Service—of course! I remember rumors about the fellow.—Whatever turned up about him, Jack? He was one of your people. Didn't he turn up missing?"

"He dropped out of sight about a year and a half ago," replied Secret Service Director Whyte. "There were rumors, as you say, but nothing solid. We looked into it but were never able to turn up anything of substance."

"And Lady Hildegard Halifax—" added Amanda.

"Right . . . now that I hear the name again I recall there being some question what became of Lady Halifax," said Snow. "Nobody's seen her for months."

"Or her son," added Langham. "I met the chap a time or two. Knew him at Cambridge, then he wrote for the *Mail* . . . and then suddenly he too disappeared."

"It's Lady Halifax's house in Vienna that is the headquarters," Amanda said. "At least I assume that. That's where all three of them were. There were all sorts of people always coming and going. The assassins of the Black Hand were there before the war started."

"The Fountain people were involved in the assassination!" exclaimed the army's Forsythe.

"I don't think they knew about it ahead of time," Amanda replied. "But later, one of them called Mehmedbasic was talking about secretly getting to England so he could disappear."

"He is one of the seven who is still at large, I believe, sir," Lieutenant Langham said.

"What else, Miss Rutherford?" asked Churchill.

"I overheard talk about bringing people in and out of England."

"How were they doing this?" Whyte asked.

"I think using a lighthouse, sir. I heard frequent mention of a lighthouse."

"Have you ever heard the name Spengler, Miss Rutherford?" asked Admiral Snow.

Amanda shook her head.

"Colonel Spengler is assistant to Generaloberst von Bülow," added Churchill. "He is the head of German naval operations. Colonel Spengler has recently defected to the Allied cause."

"The other name, the long one you just said, von Somebody . . . that is a name I remember," said Amanda. "I think he was at the house in Vienna once too."

"Could they be planning an invasion?" Colonel Forsythe said to Churchill.

"If so, they would certainly stop at nothing to silence Spengler. He would know the whole plan.—But you say they talked of signals to England. Where?" said Churchill, turning again to Amanda.

"I didn't hear anything about a location as long as I was in Vienna, just signals from a lighthouse," she answered. "But then just two days ago, when I was following Mr. Barclay in Antwerp—"

"You were in Antwerp!" exclaimed Forsythe. "That's behind the lines."

"I have an Austrian passport," said Amanda.

"How did you get it?"

"Actually, I stole it when I escaped from the house in Vienna," she answered sheepishly.

"It sounds like *you* are the spy, young lady," said Churchill with a wry grin.

"I need to recruit her in the service," laughed Whyte.

"But go on," Churchill said. "You have certainly succeeded in getting our attention."

"In Antwerp I heard the words Hawsker Head," Amanda said. "It sounded like they were talking about the location of the lighthouse."

"That's got to be it!" exclaimed Churchill. "That just may be the missing link we've been waiting for."

"I also heard the word *Dauntless*," added Amanda.

The three naval men glanced at one another, taking in this new piece of information with serious expressions.

"Hawsker Head is up north, isn't it?" said Whyte, looking about at the others.

"Somewhere on the east coast, I believe," said Timothy, speaking now for the first time. "Yorkshire, I believe."

"Is there a lighthouse there?"

"I'm afraid I don't know, sir."

Churchill glanced over at Langham. "Find out what you can, Lieutenant."

Langham rose and left the room. When he was gone, Churchill turned to Amanda with a more serious expression than before.

"Your father may be in danger," he said. "That word you heard—*Dauntless*—is the name of his ship."

"My father—what is he doing on a ship?"

"I assumed you knew," answered Churchill. "When the war broke out I asked him to resume his commission in the Royal Navy. He and your brother are both aboard the *Dauntless* at this very minute. They are bringing Colonel Spengler to Scotland. They are probably somewhere off the coast of Norfolk or Lincolnshire by now. We have maintained radio silence because of the delicacy of their mission, so I don't know their exact location. I am scheduled to leave for Scapa Flow tomorrow to meet them when they put in."

This new information noticeably sobered Amanda and Timothy.

Lieutenant Langham returned in about five minutes.

"There *is* a lighthouse on Hawsker Head, sir," said the young lieutenant. "Disused for some time, finally sold twelve years ago to a private organization. As far as the records indicate it has not been in use since then."

"The name of this private concern?"

"The name on the transfer document reads simply 'The Fountain,' sir."

"That's it, then!" boomed Churchill, nearly exploding out of his chair. "Let's go. We've got to get to Yorkshire and put a stop to this before these traitors can do any more damage."

He was already halfway out of the office, with Snow, Forsythe, Whyte, and Lieutenant Langham on his heels, leaving Amanda and Timothy looking at each other in bewilderment.

Churchill paused in the middle of the doorway for the second time that day. This time, however, it was to turn back into his own office.

"Well, come on, young lady," he said, gesturing impatiently to Amanda. "You don't think I plan to leave you behind now after you've nearly solved the case that has kept us baffled for months? I may need you to identify some of these rascals.—Rev. Diggorsfeld, thank you for bringing her to me," said Churchill, shaking Timothy's hand once more. He then turned again to Amanda. "Let's go, young lady—we're off to Yorkshire!"

88

North Hawsker Head

*D*awn had just begun to break over the Yorkshire moors when several automobiles and a single army transport and communications truck drove the last few miles along the narrow deserted sea road between Whitby and Scarborough on the east coast of northern England. Half of those present had come from London by train, where they had met the army contingent arranged for by Colonel Forsythe at Whitby.

Immediately after the previous afternoon's meeting in his office had broken up, Churchill, Forsythe, and Whyte had coordinated plans for today's dawn raid, which was now a joint operation between the army, navy, and Secret Service, with the First Lord of the Admiralty in charge. Churchhill had put Amanda in the care of Lieutenant Langham, who had arranged for her to have a hot meal, bath, and several urgently needed hours sleep in a guesthouse while final arrangements were being concluded. He returned for her later that evening. Once they were en route she slept most of the night in private quarters aboard the train. By the time morning came, and they had eaten breakfast at the hotel in Whitby, where the force met at dawn for final briefing, she felt reasonably rested and refreshed.

A mile or so from their objective, as the road crested a small rise next to the bluff of the shoreline, Churchill ordered his driver in the lead vehicle to stop. His eagle eyes thought they had spotted something in the distance down on the water.

"Hold here just a minute, Sergeant," he said. "I want to take a look." He got out of the car and was joined a moment later by Lieutenant Langham. From his vantage point on the bluff, Churchill peered down onto the ocean, then sent his binoculars panning the horizon.

"What is it, sir?" asked Langham.

"A small boat," replied the First Lord. "I would say it is carrying several people. I see no sign of ships or other activity."

"The lighthouse appears to be sending signals too," Langham said, looking along the bluff toward the white tower about a mile away. Two automobiles were parked in front of the house, and smoke came from the chimney. Despite the early hour, the place was already up and about its clandestine activities. "There are flashes coming from the tower on and off in bursts."

"Obviously they are signaling something out there," said Churchill. "A sporadic light pattern like that is not for keeping ships off the shoals. Although all I see is the little dinghy."

"Do you suppose we're observing the method of infiltration we've been looking for?"

"We just may be, Lieutenant."

"Do you want me to tell the others to move in, sir?"

"Not yet," replied Churchill. "We'll maintain positions out of sight here for now until this boat is ashore. I don't want to tip off whoever this is coming in. I want them all in custody before we leave. We'll let them get inside, then make our move."

Twenty minutes later the dinghy was docked. Churchill watched from the same vantage point as the newcomers made their way up the bluff. When they were safely inside the house, he headed back to the lead car, raising his arm to the small waiting convoy to again begin moving slowly forward.

"It is a brave thing you are doing for your country, Miss Rutherford," Lieutenant Langham said as they sat together in the backseat riding the final mile.

"Thank you," she replied. "That is very kind of you to say. But I don't feel brave. Actually I feel like something of a nincompoop for causing so much trouble. And right now I have to tell you I'm a little afraid. My heart is starting to pound."

"Perfectly natural in these circumstances," smiled the lieutenant. "To be honest, my heart is beating a little more rapidly than usual too. I think it started when the First Lord asked me back at the hotel if my pistol was loaded. Until then I don't think the danger of what we're doing had really sunk in."

"I hope there is no shooting. I think I would be terrified."

"We will do our best to prevent it coming to that. You know another thing I wanted to tell you," the young lieutenant went on, "in case I don't have the chance later, is that I have always admired your father."

"How do *you* know him?" asked Amanda, glancing over in surprise.

"My father and he served together years ago," replied Lieutenant Langham. "He always spoke highly of him. My father followed his career even after they parted ways and said how much he admired your father years later, too, when he resigned from the House of Commons. I remember my father telling me what courage that took, to go against convention and popular wisdom and step aside right at the height of his popularity. I had the chance to meet Commander Rutherford myself before the *Dauntless* put to sea."

"When was that?"

"Mr. Churchill sent me down to Plymouth to deliver a personal message to your father. I was also in Scapa briefly later and met your brother ... George, I believe."

"Yes ... yes, that's him."

"I found what my own father said was true. The exchanges between the commander and me were brief, but he treated me with the utmost respect."

While Amanda was trying to think how to reply further, she felt the automobile slowing again.

"This will do fine, Sergeant," said Churchill to the driver.

"It looks like we've arrived," said Lieutenant Langham.

"Everyone out," said Churchill, "but quietly."

89

Unexpected Visitors to English Shores

*I*nside the house, Ramsay Halifax had arisen about half an hour earlier.

He had arrived at Hawsker Head late the previous night. A nicely lit fire was already ablaze as he came downstairs, thanks to Doyle McCrogher, though Ramsay found himself alone. McCrogher was at sea in his trusty vessel bringing ashore what Ramsay expected to be a single additional guest—an arrival, it might be noted, that he was not especially looking forward to seeing on the basis of the fact that he had himself made the drive north from London alone. There would be purgatory to pay from Barclay's mouth, and he was already trying to plan how to respond to the anticipated caustic barbs from the latter's tongue.

Chalmondley Beauchamp, meanwhile, was atop the lighthouse at the controls, a function in the operation of the network which he now handled almost entirely. The two or three others present were all still asleep.

Ramsay made himself a small pot of tea and had just completed his first cup in front of the fire when the door opened. The astonishment which registered on his face was instantaneous. He sat for a moment gaping at the figure who followed Hartwell Barclay inside.

"Scarlino . . . what are you doing here?" he finally exclaimed, more confused than anything. "You didn't find—"

"No, I didn't find her," interjected Scarlino testily, showing no inclination toward conversation with Ramsay.

Behind him another stranger walked in.

"But if—"

"Forget the girl," said Scarlino, removing his coat as the door closed. "That was just a ploy. We are here on another assignment—one that requires, shall we say, talents of which you have proved yourself capable. The girl means nothing anymore.—Is there any coffee around here?" He glanced about, then walked in the direction of what he took for the kitchen, where a kettle of water still stood steaming on the stove.

"*We*—what we?" said Ramsay, rising from his chair. "I'm not sure I like the sound of that. What kind of talents?—Barclay," he said, now turning to his mentor in the ways of the Fountain, "what's this all about?"

"That's what I should be asking you," Barclay rejoined, finding a cup and pouring himself what remained in Ramsay's small pot from the table in front of the chair where he had been sitting. "*You* were supposed to have taken care of the girl by now, if you recall."

"Unfortunately, she has continued to elude me."

"She's not dead?"

"No, she's not dead."

"Why not?"

"It didn't work out. What are these other two doing here?" he said, returning to the subject at hand. He gestured toward the newcomers in the kitchen, who were investigating coffee makings and scarcely paying attention to the conversation about them in the adjacent room.

Barclay took a long sip from the tea in his cup, then eyed Ramsay intently.

"It seems they have orders from Austrian and German Intelligence to assassinate the good Mr. Asquith and his colleague Churchill," he said.

"What!" exclaimed Ramsay. "That's further than we've ever gone."

"Perhaps," replied Barclay. "Unfortunately, they left me little choice but to bring them to England for precisely that purpose."

"That may be. But what the deuce does it have to do with me?"

"The most fascinating part of their scheme," replied Barclay, the hint of a smile now revealing itself in his expression, "is that they seem to think *you* are the man to pull the trigger."

"What! That's the most insane—"

"It seems they have been setting this whole thing up for months."

"What are you talking about?"

"Once Matteos put you and Scarlino in touch, you were a marked man, Ramsay. They knew all about us. They infiltrated our network."

Barclay's only consolation in the affair—for the past miserable hours in the submarine had caused him to hate Scarlino and the Prussian even more than Ramsay did—was in seeing his irritating and cocky young colleague squirm. "Seems as if we've been beaten at our own game," he added with an ironic smile.

"How is that possible?" exclaimed Ramsay.

"The other fellow there is a high-ranking member of the Prussian Intelligence Service. They have contacts throughout Europe that make us look like amateurs. It would seem, my dear young Halifax, that we are working for them now."

"Well, I for one have no intention of working for them!" said Ramsay irascibly.

"You have no choice, Halifax," said Scarlino with a sinister smile as he walked in from the kitchen holding a cup of very bad and hastily assembled coffee. "We are in charge of this operation now. And its code name is Halifax Kills Churchill."

An evil laugh now filled the room. The sound of it grated on Ramsay's ears so stridently that for a moment his hand twitched in the direction of his gun.

If he was going to kill anyone, he thought, this maniac ought to be at the top of the list!

90

Moving In

*A*s they hatched their plot inside the house, none of them had an idea that less than half a mile away one of the two men they had come to England to assassinate was invisibly closing a net around them.

Churchill motioned to the vehicles that had stopped behind him. Silently about two dozen uniformed men in the colors of the British Army and Royal Navy, along with five or six plainclothes Secret Service agents, came forward on foot. More signals and a few whispered instructions followed. Under cover of the rolling hills, brush, and a few trees, the band began slowly moving toward the lighthouse and other buildings, gradually spreading out to surround the compound against the bluff overlooking the sea.

Her heart pounding even more than before, Amanda walked between Langham and Churchill, beginning to wonder what she had gotten herself into. She didn't mind a little adventure now and then. But these men were carrying guns! Somebody could get hurt around here!

Slowly the combined strike force crept from the three landward sides toward the house with the red roof. The buildings all sat relatively exposed near the bluff. So far they had not been seen. They would have to run the last fifty yards without benefit of cover.

When everyone was in place Churchill gave the signal.

Bending low, they hurried stealthily from their positions toward the first of the outbuildings, then, when it was safe, to the base of the lighthouse, spreading out again around two or three other small structures.

At last they slowed. Following Churchill's signal, they crept toward the main house, crouching as they moved into position. Two teams would enter simultaneously by front and back doors. The rest would remain outside to keep the house and buildings surrounded.

Churchill motioned to Amanda and Langham to follow him. They ducked low beneath a window off the sitting room. Catching a breath or two, Churchill now rose carefully and peeped over the sill of the window. Most of those inside were apparently seated in the main lounge after the arrival of the newcomers. He crouched low again and motioned for Amanda to sneak whatever peek she was able.

Up in the gallery of the lighthouse, Chalmondley Beauchamp happened to glance down toward the ground.

Were his eyes playing a trick on him in this morning mist?

He saw . . . there it was again . . . someone running. What was that figure doing down below? Now he was running toward the base of the lighthouse. What were all those figures about! There were people everywhere.

Dozens of them! Wearing uniforms!

Seized with sudden panic, he grabbed his binoculars and ran outside the small glass-enclosed room to the catwalk. He looked straight down to the ground.

It couldn't be! Was that actually . . . it looked like that young assistant of Churchill's, the son of that naval officer, whatever his name was. What the devil—

Good heavens, there was Churchill himself! And Colonel Forsythe of the army and Jack Whyte from the Secret Service. What was happening!

Obviously the jig would seem to be up!

He had better change the message immediately. As for his own future, suddenly it looked very seriously in doubt.

Amanda clutched the sill and slowly rose to the edge of the window and peeped through into the seemingly innocuous room where so much mischief had been hatched. At last this place was about to be revealed for the den of falsehood it was.

"Do you recognize anyone, Miss Rutherford?" Churchill asked.

"It's Mr. Barclay!" she exclaimed in a whisper. "I don't know any of the others—"

Suddenly a gasp escaped her lips.

"What is it?" asked Churchill.

"Ramsay Halifax is there too!"

"What about his mother?"

"No, I don't see her."

"Anyone else you recognize?"

Amanda glanced around the room, shaking her head.

"Well, those two will be enough to put an end to this espionage ring and shut down this lighthouse for good. That's what I wanted to know. I didn't want to move until we could be confident of nabbing the ringleaders."

"Wait," said Amanda, "—another two men just entered from another room. But . . . no, I've never seen either of them before."

"Let's go. Langham, you take three men and climb the lighthouse and arrest whoever's up there and put a stop to those signals."

"Yes, sir," whispered the lieutenant, motioning to several of the men kneeling behind them.

"The rest of us will bust up this little party inside."

91
Break-In

$\mathcal{M}$eanwhile, unaware of their danger, the group inside the house continued their discussion.

"And the trail in Switzerland?" Ramsay had just asked Scarlino.

"That was on the level," replied Scarlino, taking a seat and sipping at the bitter brew in his cup. "I did my best. Had we located the girl, putting a bullet in her would simply have been a bonus for you. But *you* were my quarry all along, Halifax. Why do you think I let you live through all your stupid moves and the insults that came out of your mouth? If we hadn't had more important plans, you would have been dead long before now. You're the kind of arrogant young fool it is not my custom to put up with."

"And your friend?" said Ramsay with scorn, nodding haughtily in the other man's direction.

"I am Rald Wolfrik with the Prussian Intelligence Service," now said Wolfrik. "My own identity is unimportant. What is important is that we are all on the same side here. This petty arguing is pointless. Our objective is to be rid of Churchill and Asquith and sabotage the Allied cause. And you, Mr. Halifax, because of your background and the freedom you have moving throughout England and especially in London circles, not to mention your newspaper contacts which we plan also to use to our advantage, are ideally suited for the assignment."

"I will be no part of it," said Ramsay irritably.

Wolfrik smiled. "As my colleague said a moment ago, you have no choice, Mr. Halifax. You will be leaving with us for London first thing tomorrow mor—"

Suddenly two doors at opposite sides of the house burst open with a loud shatter.

A dozen uniformed soldiers crashed through and tramped quickly into the lounge.

"What the—" exclaimed Barclay, leaping to his feet.

The rest of those seated inside were so taken by surprise that for a second or two no one moved a muscle. The hands of Scarlino and Wolfrik, both experienced assassins, as if in simultaneous reflex, gradually moved to the guns resting inside their coat pockets. But the rifles trained straight on them caused both to reconsider without need of verbal persuasion.

"Everybody just stay where you are and remain nice and calm," said Colonel Forsythe, moving to the center of the room. "There is no need for anyone to get killed here. As you gentlemen can see, you are outnumbered. There are more of us outside."

Suddenly Ramsay's eyes widened in disbelief to see the figure entering beside the tall form he recognized as that of First Lord of the Admiralty Winston Churchill.

"Amanda!" he exclaimed. "How in the—"

Instantly he caught himself.

Realizing there was no chance of escape, suddenly Ramsay's brain performed a cunning about-face. The transformation was so swift that even one as experienced in chicanery as the Secret Service's Jack Whyte did not see the 180-degree turnabout that had occurred. A wide smile now spread across Ramsay's face.

"Why, Amanda, my dear," he said smoothly, rising and walking toward her. "I am so relieved to see you at last."

"Stay away from me, Ramsay!" said Amanda.

"Is that any way for a wife to talk to her husband? I've been so worried about you."

"*Wife!*" exclaimed Churchill.

"Of course, didn't she tell you?" said Ramsay innocently. "I assumed you knew.—You are, I believe, Mr. Churchill." Ramsay approached and extended his hand. "I am happy to meet you at last, sir. I am Ramsay Halifax, stepson of Lord Halifax, with whom I believe you were acquainted."

"Yes . . . yes, I knew him," said a bewildered Churchill, shaking the offered hand. "But—"

"I have been working undercover with the British Secret Service for some time," said Ramsay. "My colleague and I, Mr. Barclay, who has been with the Secret Service for years," Ramsay went on, nodding in Barclay's direction, "have been on the Continent for some time—Vienna, actually. Our orders were to infiltrate Austrian and German intelligence operations, which we have successfully done. We have just returned and were on our way to London to report our findings."

Churchill glanced at Jack Whyte with wrinkled brow, then turned toward Amanda. "What's this all about, Miss Rutherford?" he asked. His voice did not sound amused.

"Rutherford ... oh no, I'm afraid you're mistaken," interposed Ramsay. "Her name is Halifax—Amanda *Halifax*. Although I cannot say as I am surprised. My wife sometimes has difficulty telling the truth. With all the espionage and counterespionage contacts with whom my work involved us, she occasionally became confused about which side was which. They were understandably perplexing circumstances, I grant you. Yet we had no alternative but to continue with our investigations, for the future of England, even though in time I realized I should probably not have brought Amanda into it so quickly. Unfortunately, in the end, my dear Amanda became so confused she actually thought we were working for the Austrians."

Ramsay smiled with a sadly humorous expression and shook his head two or three times.

"That's when she ran off," he went on. "I've been looking high and low for her ever since. I've been worried sick about you, Amanda dear," he added, once more moving to approach her.

Amanda took a step backward, fuming and speechless.

"What in thunder is going on here!" bellowed Churchill.

"It is obvious she has said some things to you," Ramsay continued, "that are greatly exaggerated, if not outright lies. It would not surprise me to learn that she has told you many things which are simply fabrications of a very vivid imagination, including whatever she may have concocted about this house of ours where we often entertain friends. I don't blame her, however, Mr. Churchill. She has just been very confused."

"Ramsay, how dare you say such things!" cried Amanda, the storm finally exploding. "Everything you are saying is completely distorted. You know it! You have twisted it all to make it sound exactly backwards from the way it really is. You know as well as I do that you're all spies."

"Spies!" laughed Ramsay as if he were humoring a child. "Heavens, Amanda, where do you come up with these things! Just what have you been telling these gentlemen about us?"

It was now Hartwell Barclay's turn to speak up. Very slowly he walked toward the scene. He glanced toward Secret Service Agent Whyte, who was as bewildered as Churchill.

"Hello, Jack," he said, then turned and riveted his eyes upon Amanda's face.

"Ramsay," he said slowly and methodically, his voice smoother and softer than Amanda had ever heard it, "ask *Mrs. Halifax* to come over here with us where she belongs."

As he intoned the words deliberately, his eyes bored into Amanda's with the penetrating gaze that had always succeeded in gaining mastery over her.

"Amanda," said Ramsay in a soft tone of command, "come over here with us, just as Mr. Barclay says. You are one of *us*, remember."

Ramsay took another slow step toward her, extending his hand as if to gently lead her toward him. "You are my wife, Amanda. My *wife* . . . you are one of us."

Amanda tried to pull her face away. For a moment she could not free herself from Barclay's mesmerizing gaze. A reminder of the old drowsiness tried to envelop her. With great effort she forcibly shook her head, as if to knock loose the cobwebs of doubt. All at once she found her voice.

"No . . . no, I won't!" she exclaimed. "You can't befuddle me with all that anymore. You controlled me and twisted my thoughts for too long. It's time I thought for myself. I don't know what is before me, but I am not going back to that life with you."

"Your only life is with *us* now, Amanda," said Barclay, still speaking smoothly, and desperately trying to connect with her eyes. "You cannot go back."

"Don't forget, Amanda," added Ramsay, his eyes narrowing imperceptibly. "You are Mrs. Ramsay Halifax."

The tone of command had now become laced with an undercurrent of threat.

"It was never a true marriage," rejoined Amanda. "I was under a spell. I wasn't myself. But I am now, and I am telling you for the last time—you *will not* control me ever again."

She turned toward Hartwell Barclay and at last allowed her eyes to lock on to his. She gazed straight into them with an intensity equal to his own.

"Mr. Barclay," she said, "I renounce you and your hold over my mind. And I renounce the Fountain of Light and whatever power it once had over me. You can stare at me and talk in the most quiet tones, and say all your tosh and nonsense till your face turns red, but it won't do any more good."

At the words, indeed did Hartwell Barclay's face begin to turn several shades of crimson.

92

Frantic New Message

*B*y now Lieutenant Langham had reached the bottom of the lighthouse, entered the small door to the tower, and had begun running up the steep, winding stairway to the top. He was followed by three uniformed soldiers.

Whoever was up there sending those signals, thought Langham, they could not escape now. There was only one way down, and he had it blocked.

Out at sea, a frantic new message was just coming in as the *Admiral Uelzen,* having deposited its three passengers, was now speeding toward the last coordinates it had been given. But even as it ploughed through the waters off the English coastline, periscope officer Ubel continued to watch for any final signals from the lighthouse as it receded behind them.

"Captain!" he suddenly shouted. "Captain Dietz . . . a new message is coming through."

"What do you mean, Corporal—*new*?" said the captain, turning toward him. "I thought we were through here."

"I'm . . . just taking it down now," replied Ubel.

A brief pause followed. The captain waited.

"It says they are being raided, sir," said the corporal. "We're . . . being asked to stand by to take aboard—"

He paused.

"Go on, Corporal."

"It's broken off for now, sir."

93

Hostage

❖❖❖

*A*manda turned her gaze away from Hartwell Barclay and back toward Ramsay.

"At last I am awake, Ramsay Halifax," she said. "It may have taken me longer than it should have, but I have finally come to my senses. I see what I should have seen in the beginning, what you and your mother and all of you truly are."

As she spoke, Ramsay's eyes glowed with a wrath as red as Hartwell Barclay's neck.

Amanda turned to address the First Lord of the Admiralty, who had remained standing silently along with the rest of the men, not knowing what to do other than listen to the drama being played out before them.

"I am sorry, sir," she said. "Technically what he says is correct. Mr. Halifax and I were married in Vienna last September in a hastily arranged civil ceremony. All I can say is that I was not myself. To say that I was brainwashed is the closest thing I can think to call it. But that really has nothing to do with everything else I have told you—about them and the Fountain of Light—which is entirely true. I don't know how to respond to all he said about me. Yes, I was confused—but not in the way he represents. It was my confusion that made me trust them, when now I see that they are the most untrustworthy people I have ever known. These people are spies against England."

Still temporarily baffled by the sudden turn of events, and not quite knowing where to place the fact that Sir Charles' daughter was the wife of one of the apparent ringleaders of this network, Churchill continued silent a moment longer trying to sort through his options.

Sensing his opportunity, Ramsay suddenly lunged for Amanda, grabbed her about the shoulders, and pulled her quickly to him. The same instant his Luger was in his hand. She was tightly in his grip before anyone could react, gun pressed into her temple. She started to cry out, but a jab from Ramsay's gun silenced her.

"You fool!" seethed Barclay to Ramsay. "What are you—"

"Shut up, Barclay," spat Ramsay, then turned toward the others.

"It does not appear," he said, "that you intend to believe me over this lying vixen. That being the case, I will just make my exit here . . . and I will take my *wife* with me."

"You absolute imbecile!" said Barclay. "Couldn't you see that—"

But by now Ramsay was backing away and toward the door. Scarlino, Wolfrik, and the other two were on their feet the same instant, those who had them with guns drawn, and easing toward the door. Realizing Ramsay's foolhardy ploy had undone any chance of talking their way out of this, Barclay said nothing more. He now slowly moved to join the others.

A dozen rifles and pistols slowly followed their movements.

"Hold your fire!" shouted Churchill, still not sure what to make of it, but certainly not willing to risk Amanda's life. "No one gets killed here. Otherwise we will never get to the bottom of this."

The moment they were clear of the door, the five sprinted for the bluff up which the three recent arrivals had come less than thirty minutes earlier. With difficulty, for she was resisting his every step, Ramsay dragged Amanda after them.

In the house, Colonel Forsythe suddenly came to his senses.

"After them!" he cried.

"That fellow Barclay was with the Secret Service, I can vouch for that," said Whyte as he and Churchill dashed for the door. "As for the rest, I don't know what to make of it."

"No gunfire until we sort this thing out," Churchill ordered when they were outside and saw the getaway taking place in front of them. "Sir Charles' daughter must not be harmed."

The figures neared the bluff. A puffing Doyle McCrogher was just climbing to the top of the plateau after securing his dinghy when Barclay reached him.

"Back, McCrogher!" cried Barclay.

"What the—" began the bewildered Irishman.

"Get down there—we're casting off immediately!"

94

Lights Out

*A*bove in the lighthouse, Chalmondley Beauchamp frantically flashed one last message out to sea.

He knew it was over. They would hang him, shoot him, or imprison him for life for treason. Below he now heard the clanking echo of footsteps running up the stairs.

Frantically he repeated his final communication to the *Admiral Uelzen*. Maybe some of those below could get away.

Then he would do what he had to do.

"If they are in trouble, we have to turn around," shouted Captain Dietz to his crew in the German submarine. "They may need to get away. We've got to pick up whoever makes it out of there."

"What about the English cruiser?" asked his second in command.

"The other vessels can take care of it," replied Captain Dietz. "Colonel Wolfrik's mission is vital and must not be compromised. We have to rescue him if possible. If we are delayed, the other U-boats have the coordinates."

"I have a further message coming in now, Captain," yelled Corporal Ubel—"... stand by ... prepare to take aboard survivors ... major raid appears—"

He stopped.

"What is it, Corporal?"

"I'm looking, sir," he replied, still peering through the lenses of the periscope, "but there's no more—the lighthouse just went black. This time it looks like for good."

"That must be it, then. They must have got to him," said Captain Dietz. "Full speed astern!"

95

Face-Off

◆◆◆

$\mathscr{R}$amsay and Amanda reached the bluff. Amanda was squirming with all the strength she had. But Ramsay was holding her tight. She was pressed too close to his body for those following to get a clean shot at Ramsay.

"I don't know what you're thinking, Ramsay," panted Amanda indignantly. "But I will never—ouch! Stop that!—I will never go back with you! You'll have to kill me first."

"You *are* coming with me, Amanda, you little weasel," Ramsay snarled angrily in her ear. "You've caused me a great deal of trouble."

"You may have frightened me before, Ramsay. But my days of running—especially from you—are over."

"We are married, remember, *my dear*!" He yanked at her arm in a twisting motion. Another cry of pain escaped her lips.

"You tricked me and used me," Amanda shot back, "not to mention were unfaithful to me within two weeks of our marriage. I don't know what will become of me, but I have no intention of returning to Vienna, or anyplace else with you. Besides, haven't you forgotten what Mr. Barclay said to you in Paris, that you should think of yourself as a widower now?"

The reminder that she had spied on him in the hotel, and gotten the best of him, enraged Ramsay anew. He jammed the gun against her head again to remind her of the threat, then slowed to take the first step down the pathway toward the sea. But with the unsteady footing, Amanda felt the grasp of his arm around her waist momentarily relax. A sudden sharp jab of her elbow into his stomach followed.

"Ow—Amanda, you little—!"

But she had lurched free. She gave him a quick shove, then scrambled up onto the firm footing of the grass. Ramsay stumbled briefly but quickly righted himself and ran back after her.

"Amanda . . . stop!" he cried. "Don't make me shoot!"

She paused. In front of her the soldiers and agents stopped in their tracks. Amanda slowly turned and stood facing Ramsay at a distance of about ten yards. He raised his Luger until its barrel was pointed straight toward her face.

The hint of a smile came to the edges of Amanda's lips. She continued to stand unmoving, looking Ramsay steadily in the eye without so much as the flinch of an eyelash. It was clear from her expression that she was not afraid. Their eyes held. In that moment Ramsay knew he was beaten, and that he would never be able to dominate her again.

"You won't shoot me, Ramsay," said Amanda calmly. "I'm not sure I know you, or ever did. But I do know that you're not going to pull that trigger."

Slowly she turned again and calmly walked toward the waiting agents, leaving Ramsay staring at the back of her head along the barrel of his gun.

"Shoot her, Halifax!" cried Barclay from below, but the contest was over, and Amanda had emerged the victor. Only a moment more Ramsay stood. The next instant he was over the bluff and running down the path toward the water's edge.

Scarlino, Wolfrik, and the others had already scrambled into the dinghy, with Barclay close behind, and were pushing off.

"After them!" shouted Churchill the moment Ramsay disappeared from view.

But the sound of his command was suddenly drowned out by a horrific scream that filled the morning air.

The soldiers and agents stopped and turned toward the sound. They were just in time to see the body of former M.P. Chalmondley Beauchamp flailing helplessly through the air from the top of the lighthouse.

96
The Fog Lifts

*A*t the sound of the wailing death plunge, Churchill paused. Over the bluff down at the water's edge, the dinghy was putting out across the waters.

"See if there's another boat around here!" ordered Churchill.

Now he spun around and ran toward the lighthouse.

What he found was not a pretty sight. At the base of the slender column of white lay the broken and battered form of his erstwhile colleague, onetime respected member of Parliament turned traitor against brothers and nation.

Churchill stood for several moments, shaking his head in revulsion and sadness.

The echo of steps reverberated from inside. Churchill glanced up just as Lieutenant Langham ran out the door from the tower. He wobbled slightly as his legs of lead tried to reacquaint themselves with level ground.

"I'm sorry, sir," he said. "There was nothing I could do. He was over the side the moment I entered the gallery."

"I know, Lieutenant," replied the First Lord to his young assistant, still shaking his head in disbelief. "I thought I knew the man. I considered him a friend. How could it come to this? What a tragedy—a waste of a good life. How could he let such a worthless cause as this turn him so far from the things he once believed in?"

"War does strange things to people," replied Langham, in an uncharacteristic moment of reflection in the presence of his superior.

They heard footsteps approaching from behind them.

"So do deceptions like the Fountain of Light," added Amanda, walking up and joining them. "I speak as one who allowed it to do strange things to my whole outlook."

One quick glance at Beauchamp's body and she turned away in disgust.

"Ugh ... that's so awful—oh, I can't bear the thought of it!"

Lieutenant Langham hurried to her side and led her quickly away from the scene.

"How are you otherwise, Miss Rutherford?" he asked as they walked back toward the now desolate house.

"I think I will be fine. But it doesn't look as if we did any good."

"On the contrary," said Churchill, now joining them. "We will shut down this operation for good."

Colonel Forsythe ran toward them from across the plateau.

"They're gone, Mr. Churchill," he said. "They've taken the only craft available."

"I was afraid of that. But they won't get far in that little dinghy.— Lieutenant," Churchill added, turning toward Lieutenant Langham, "it doesn't look like we're going to be able to pursue it from here. You had better radio the base at Whitby immediately and have the Coast Guard dispatch a vessel."

"Yes, sir."

Langham ran off to the communications vehicle, while Forsythe instructed some of his men to take care of the body.

Churchill led Amanda back toward the house.

"Once we get back to London," he said as they walked, "where will you be, Miss Rutherford—er, Mrs.—what *should* I call you anyway?"

"I don't know, Mr. Churchill," answered Amanda with a sigh. "I will have to sort it all out later. I do apologize for not telling you everything. It didn't occur to me to think all that business about my involvement was important."

"No harm done," rejoined Churchill. "I suppose I will just call you Amanda, then. But I feel I need to apologize as well."

"You ... whatever for?"

"For doubting you in there," said Churchill. "I should have known that, however mixed up she might have been for a time, the daughter of Sir Charles Rutherford would come right in the end, and would be a young lady whose word I could trust. But I have to say, I was momentarily quite confused with everything being said. They were so convincing I didn't know *what* to make of it."

"Ramsay and Mr. Barclay have a way of making anything they say seem plausible," nodded Amanda. "They twisted my perceptions around so badly I didn't know black from white—as you know only too well from that outrageous pamphlet I helped them write. I am deeply embarrassed by that now. At the time they had my brain so mixed up."

"I begin to see just what you were up against. In those few moments in the lounge back in there, that young Halifax blackguard had the thing turned upside down and their whole network sounding completely reasonable. If he hadn't grabbed you, who knows how it might have ended up? They might have had *me* joining the Fountain of Light!"

"I doubt that, sir," laughed Amanda.

"It hardly matters now. The minute he pulled a gun on you, suddenly the fog cleared and I saw that you had been telling the truth all along."

"Unfortunately, it took much longer for the fog in my brain to clear."

"Well, apparently it has now. So, *Amanda,* back to my original question—where will you be in London?"

"Uh, I don't really have any immediate plans," she answered. "I hadn't thought past just getting back to warn you about what I had heard."

They reached the now deserted house. Churchill led the way inside. The fire was still burning. Amanda walked into the lounge and glanced about pensively.

"You know," she said, "this really is a comfortable place. I can see how easy it would be to sit here with a nice fire, enjoying pleasant conversation and tea, and get lulled to sleep by the warm and cozy atmosphere. I wonder if all deceptions begin like that—seemingly innocent, even pleasant and friendly and enjoyable. That's certainly how they wooed me. The deception creeps over you in ways you never see coming. And they were especially clever in never making a full disclosure about what they believed. So I did not have to face squarely what I was slowly becoming part of until I was all the way inside. By then it was too late. It was just all so . . . *comfortable* that I never paused to look beneath the surface for what sorts of things they stood for."

"Well, I don't know about all that," said Churchill. "But I do know that it would be a shame to waste a good fire. What do you say we enjoy a cup of tea, like you said, while we are waiting for Lieutenant Langham and the others to wrap it up?"

"It will be my pleasure," said Amanda, walking into the kitchen. "I'll see what I can find."

"You know," Churchill added as he followed her, "there will no doubt be a commendation in this for you, possibly from the prime minister himself. It is impossible to know, of course, but shutting down this channel in and out of England, not to mention destroying the method they were using for signaling German U-boats . . . it may have a significant impact on the outcome of the war. There may still be some submarines lurking along our coast. But I would think that once we get those subs out of our waters, things could begin to turn for us."

"I am glad my experience—miserable though it was—may serve some use in the end."

"In any event," said Churchill, "we will make arrangements for a place for you to stay the moment we arrive back in the city. I will need to be off to Scapa Flow myself. But Lieutenant Langham will handle the details and will see to whatever you need. At some point we will want to talk to you further and get a more detailed statement about exactly what went on in Vienna. We need to make as many identifications as possible. Hopefully by then we will have nabbed all the scoundrels in that little boat out there and have them behind bars."

97

Father and Son

$\mathcal{T}$he seas had calmed considerably in the North Sea as the battle cruiser HMS *Dauntless* steamed toward its destination north of Scotland. The calm was only on the surface, however, for intelligence had it that German U-boat submarines were still prowling the entire British coast.

Several British cruisers had been destroyed by U-boats early in the war. And just two months ago, on the first day of the year, the British battleship *Formidable* had been sunk right in the Channel. So the threat of German submarine activity was real enough. But the urgency of their mission in the end weighed most heavily in Captain Wilberforce's decision to make a run for it in spite of the reports. Traveling in convoy, as well as the use of aeroplanes and dirigibles to spot U-boats from the air, had greatly reduced Allied casualties. On this occasion, however, there was no air support, and their mission demanded stealth. They would have to negotiate these familiar waters alone.

They had successfully navigated through the entire Mediterranean with the secret cargo they had picked up in Salonika, past Gibraltar, and north into the Channel without so much as sight of a German vessel. Now they were off southern Scotland and could breathe easier. They should be in Scapa by tomorrow.

The attack fell without warning.

The first hint that enemy submarines were anywhere within a hundred miles came with the explosion of the lead torpedo against the port hull—about two-thirds of the way fore.

The *Dauntless* rocked dangerously to starboard, sending half the unprepared crew off their feet. Black smoke poured into the sky from somewhere belowdecks. Every man on board knew instantly they had been hit.

The ship righted itself as all hands regained their balance. A second torpedo ricocheted off the starboard side dangerously close to the propeller. The opposite angle of approach indicated that they were under attack by at least two U-boats positioned on both sides of them. The situation was precarious.

The shrill announcement of general quarters blared over the loudspeakers. On the bridge, frantic orders followed to the lookout and torpedo room, and a barrage of messages requested damage assessment from various key positions throughout the ship. There was no command the captain could give in the meantime other than full power and a change of direction, until they managed to locate the enemy and begin discharging their torpedoes. Whether they would have time to do so was a dubious question in the captain's mind. Meanwhile, the moment they were on their feet, every man of the torpedo crew was scrambling to their stations to await firing coordinates.

Commander Charles Rutherford, who had been walking near the port rail, picked himself off the deck where the first blast had thrown him. One knee had been badly smashed against a steel ventilation lid. As he struggled painfully to his feet he knew the injury was severe. But he couldn't worry about it now.

His first thought was for George. He had to find him. Immediately he limped off and made for the torpedo room.

Smoke was blackening the sky from fires deep in the ship. As Charles hurried down the metal stairs, cadets and officers were climbing up them in the opposite direction, squeezing past, yelling and running, some for their posts, others to loosen lifeboats from their riggings. After descending two more noisy, crowded stairwells, with great effort Charles reached the corridor at the third level.

Another blast shook the ship. This was no glancing blow like the last, but a direct hit thirty feet below the water line. A dull, thundering echo rippled through every section of the ship, followed by a shuddering tremble. Charles felt the walkway tipping beneath his feet. Within a minute the entire vessel was listing fifteen degrees. Groping for the handrails, he struggled forward, wincing terribly from the pain in his knee. The lights flickered briefly, then resumed power. How long the ship's generators would hold was doubtful.

Charles arrived at the torpedo room.

It was only half manned. Those who remained had begun deserting their posts with the second blast. He saw George at the radio, as he knew he would, awaiting instructions from the bridge. He was only able to nod a brief acknowledgment in his direction before he was nearly knocked off his feet by the commander of the small squadron hurrying his way.

"Everybody out . . . up on the deck!" cried Lieutenant Forbes. "Commander," he said, seeing Charles enter and running toward him, "help me get them out of here!"

"It's only general quarters, Lieutenant," replied Charles, trying to remain calm. "No evacuation has been sounded yet."

"But we don't have a chance, Commander. We've got to get—"

He was interrupted by a blaring command over the speakers.

"Evacuate ship! This is Captain Wilberforce—evacuate at once!"

"There it is!" said Forbes. "Clear the torpedo room!"

In that moment, even the most inexperienced of the sailors knew the hits were mortal, and that the *Dauntless* was sinking.

Another shaking trembled beneath them. Lieutenant Forbes fell. His head slammed against torpedo chamber two, which had seen its last duty of this war. He slumped to the floor.

George jumped from his post with the evacuation order and now ran toward the scene. He and his father met on the floor where Charles had stooped to pick up the unconscious form of Lieutenant Forbes.

"I'll get him, Father," said George. "It will be easier for me to carry him than you."

"I won't argue with you, my boy," replied Charles, rising. "Get him topside. I'll see what I can do to help some of the others."

In seconds George had hoisted up Forbes' form and draped him over his muscular young shoulders. Quickly he made for the door.

Five minutes later George dropped Lieutenant Forbes into the nearest lifeboat which was about to be let overboard. In nearly the same motion, he turned and ran back in search of his father. Instinctively he knew he would find him amid the worst of it, trying until the very last second to help whomever he could get to safety.

George sprinted for the stairwell he had labored up with Forbes moments earlier, this time not touching so much as a single stair. He seized a moment when the walkway was empty, gripped the smooth handrails firmly in both hands and glided to the first landing below-decks in a single motion. The instant his feet landed, he dashed off again in the direction from which he had recently come.

"Rutherford . . . Petty Officer Rutherford!" came an urgent cry as he ran past a lieutenant moving in the opposite direction. "Get out! Our orders are to evacuate. Don't go—"

"I've got to find my father!" cried George without pausing.

"But it's—"

Already George had turned into another corridor, making for the next stairwell down, and was gone from the lieutenant's sight.

The lights dimmed again. Suddenly darkness engulfed the corridor. George slowed. He could not go far in total blackness.

"Father . . . Father!" he called. "Commander Rutherford, can you hear me . . . Commander Charles Rutherford!"

Suddenly came a flicker . . . then on came the lights again, but only to about half strength. Smoke began to infiltrate the corridor now, pouring up from below. The clanking echo of footsteps on metal, accompanied by continuous yells and shouts throughout the ship, sounded from all directions in mingled panic, confusion, and desperation.

With the return of the lights, George darted for the next stairwell.

On level two, just below where George was searching desperately for the only face among hundreds he now cared about, the eldest man aboard and third in command stood in one of the main corridors near the base of a narrow flight of stairs. The calm on his face contrasted noticeably with the panic of the few sailors left around him, half his age and less, who were running in terror but seemed to have lost their sense of direction. Amid the confusion, the older man was pointing the way to the stairs in the decreasing light, calmly giving directions what to do and which way to go.

Suddenly behind him a young petty officer flew down the stairs. His boots clanked onto the grate of the landing. The two men met in the corridor two seconds later.

While still outwardly calm, the panic around him, along with the smoke and yelling and continued rumble of explosions below, had taken their toll on the younger of the two. His eyes could not hide the fear in his pounding heart. A sigh of anxious relief crossed his face at sight of the older man.

The next moment they were in each other's arms.

"George," whispered the elder, "I love you."

"I love you, Father."

They stood a moment. Then again the ship shook dangerously. Charles felt his son tremble in fear.

"We are safe, son," he said. "Our heavenly Father is with us."

"I am afraid, Father."

"As am I, George. But you remember what he said about sparrows. We are in the palm of his hand even at this moment. But let us go. There yet may be time."

They fell apart. Even in the moment they stood together, two or three more sailors squeezed past. The echoing steps of the last of them sounded up the stairs. It grew ominously quiet around them.

"Come, Father," said George, pulling him toward the stairs.

"You, go, George—get up to the deck before it is too late."

"Not without you, Father."

"I will be right behind you. Go."

Hesitantly, George turned and made for the stairs. Glancing back, now for the first time he saw that his father was injured. Halfway up, he paused to wait. Charles was behind him, though moving slowly, taking each rung of the steep climb with gritty deliberation.

"Hurry, Father ... please hurry!"

"George—don't wait for me. Go, my boy ... get up there! I'm right behind you—go."

Torn with such emotion as he had never felt in his life, George climbed to the landing, stopped, got to his knees, then flat on his belly, and stretched his hand down as far as he could reach it.

"Just a little more, Father . . . you're almost there—take my hand, I'll pull you—"

Suddenly another great convulsion rocked the ship, throwing all those who remained aboard off their feet.

As their hands met, Charles' footing gave way. Immediately he disappeared from sight, bumping and clattering down the steep stairs. It was too obscure to see what had happened, but from the landing above George heard a cry of racking pain from the smoky darkness below. He was on his feet the next instant clamoring back down the stairs. Charles lay in a heap at the bottom.

"Up, Father . . . here, take my hand."

"My knee is broken, George," panted Charles in agony. "Go, my boy—get up on deck!"

"No, Father, not without you."

George's eyes were weeping freely. He stooped and gently took his father in his arms.

"I'm going to drape you over my shoulders, Father," he said. "I have to keep one hand free to get up these stairs. Here we go!"

With a great thrust he hoisted Charles over his shoulder, extending his right arm firmly around his torso, then began struggling up the narrow stairway. But it was tilting badly, and George could barely keep his feet.

Above in the outside air, the final blast had tossed many of those near the edge of the deck like helpless ants into the sea.

For a few seconds a great silence replaced the sounds of explosions. Then came a deep lurching groan, as of some monstrous inanimate giant giving up and exhaling its final breath.

Slowly but with awful force the crippled vessel rolled the rest of the way onto its side. The last of the lifeboats were struggling desperately to get away before being sucked down with the mother ship.

It did not take long for the end to come. Within minutes the bow of the *Dauntless* disappeared into the chilly waters of the North Sea.

PART IV

Shock and Grief

1915

98

A Bomb at Heathersleigh

◆◆◆

The moment Jocelyn opened the door and saw the uniformed military escort wearing somber expressions, with First Lord of the Admiralty Winston Churchill walking toward the door, in her heart she knew why they had come.

That portion of her face capable of it whitened. Unconsciously her hand went to her mouth. Cheeks and lips began to quiver.

"Lady Jocelyn . . ." Churchill began. The tone of his voice confirmed her worst fears.

Jocelyn burst into tears and glanced away. Churchill waited patiently. This was the deepest of human agonies which the senseless war had fated for them to share in this moment.

Jocelyn tried to turn back to face him, eyes nearly as red as the birthmark on cheek and neck.

"I am sorrier than I can tell you," said Churchill. "Your husband was one of the finest men I knew. You cannot imagine my personal grief for bringing Charles into the war effort. He was a patriot and a fine man."

Jocelyn nodded, tears pouring from her eyes in a torrent.

"The prime minister sent me personally," Churchill went on, "to extend the government's deepest sympathy and sorrow. . . ."

Jocelyn could say nothing. The words entering her ears sounded distant and foreign and hardly registered meaning.

"We learned the news in the middle of the night—only hours ago. . . ."

She wanted to scream in agony, but her heart was constricted in her chest. She gasped for breath.

"At the prime minister's request I was on a special train to Devon at daybreak."

Churchill now handed her the single sheet of paper in his hand. The telegram from the minister of war was brief.

CRUISER DAUNTLESS TORPEDOED AND SUNK BY GERMAN U-BOAT
OFF COAST OF SCOTLAND. ONE THIRD OF CREW LOST. COMMANDER
SIR CHARLES RUTHERFORD AND SON, PETTY OFFICER GEORGE
RUTHERFORD, AMONG CASUALTIES. CONDOLENCES TO ALL FAMILY
FROM ADMIRALTY, WAR OFFICE, AND GOVERNMENT.

The paper dropped from Jocelyn's hand and at last a great wail
burst from her mouth.

"And George!" she shrieked in disbelief. *"God—oh, God!"*

By now Catharine was approaching from behind. Jocelyn heard her
footsteps and turned.

"What is it, Mother—" Catharine began. But already Jocelyn was
running to her youngest daughter.

"It's your father . . . and George—" she cried, then broke down in
a passion of weeping.

Catharine's large frame and wide embrace swallowed her mother
like a child.

Churchill stood gravely waiting. Twenty or thirty awkward seconds
passed, during which nothing could be heard but the sounds of sobbing. Sarah and Kate came from the kitchen and were now crying with
Jocelyn and Catharine.

At length Jocelyn remembered they were not alone. She tried with
difficulty to compose herself, released herself from Catharine, and
turned back to the First Lord of the Admiralty.

"I am extremely sorry, Lady Jocelyn," said Churchill, "but I must
return to London without delay. There are many arrangements to be
made. Your husband will of course be given full military honors. You
will be notified."

"Yes . . . yes, thank you," sniffed Jocelyn, lurching shakily for a
breath. "It was kind of you to come all this way."

"Your husband was a friend."

"I . . . that is . . . our . . . my other daughter . . ." began Jocelyn.

"Yes . . . Amanda—actually we've met," said Churchill. "I felt you
needed to know first. But she will be the first person I will see when I
return to the city. I intend to go straight to her hotel. I will be speaking
to her within hours."

"Thank you," said Jocelyn, not realizing at first the implications of
what she had just heard. "But I'm afraid I don't know where she is or
how to help you contact her."

"That will be no problem. I saw her only two days ago. She is in London."

Suddenly the bombshell broke into the mother's seared brain.

"London!" exclaimed Jocelyn. "Amanda . . . in London!"

"You've not been in touch since her return?"

"Not for a very long time.—Oh, poor Amanda!" exclaimed Jocelyn, breaking into tears again.

"I will do what I can to ease the pain," said Churchill.

He shook Jocelyn's hand, uttered a few more words of sympathy, then turned and strode back to the waiting automobile which would return him to the Milverscombe station.

In another minute the women were alone again. Heathersleigh's desolation had suddenly increased a hundredfold.

"Sarah," said Jocelyn when she was able, "please find Hector and send him for Maggie. Tell him to bring her to the Hall as quickly as he can."

The moment she was gone, mother and daughter embraced again, wept several more minutes, then Jocelyn went upstairs to Charles' study.

She had to use the telephone.

99

A Friend's Devastation

Timothy Diggorsfeld's face was ashen as he held the telephone receiver to his ear. For the first moment he was too stunned to move, to respond, to weep, to speak. As marvelous an invention as it was, what good was a telephone when there were arms that needed to hold and be held, and shoulders that needed to absorb the mutual tears of suffering.

His every instinct was to rush out immediately and board the first train for Devonshire. He must be with poor Jocelyn and Catharine at this horrifying time of tragedy.

The telephone line was silent for several long seconds. It was Jocelyn who finally broke it.

"Timothy," she said. "Mr. Churchill tells me Amanda is in the city."

"I didn't know she was back from the north."

"What north?" said Jocelyn, confused. "Do you mean in Britain? I had no idea she had come back to the country."

"I was with her just three days ago."

"You were with her!"

"She had just arrived from the Continent," replied Timothy. "She came to me immediately. Mr. Churchill needed her to go to Yorkshire with him. She had information about a spy network."

"What . . . Amanda . . . spies!"

"The people she was involved with," explained Timothy, "—all that business with the Fountain or whatever it was called. I intended to telephone, but I thought I should wait until she returned."

"But Amanda . . ." began Jocelyn, then her voice trailed off.

"Yes, she must be told," said Timothy for her.

"Mr. Churchill said he would notify her at the hotel the minute he arrived back in the city."

"She needs to hear it from a friend. I will take care of it."

Again came a long silence. Now finally did the tears in the pastor's eyes begin to flow.

"Jocelyn . . . my dear, dear Jocelyn," said Timothy at length, "—I cannot tell you how sorry I am."

"I know, Timothy. He was your friend as well as mine."

"How is dear Catharine taking this dreadful news?"

"Much as I am. She is sick and can only weep. But she is strong, Timothy. Thank God for that—she is a strong young lady."

"God bless her—I will come as soon as I am able. I promise, I shall be there as quickly as circumstances allow. And I will find Amanda."

"Thank you, Timothy. You are a true friend."

Timothy put down the telephone and slumped as one lifeless to the nearest chair, and wept as he hadn't since he was a boy.

He tried to pray. But not only no words—not even *thoughts* of prayer would come.

Why, Lord . . . why! was the only prayer his devastated brain could form. He knew the words were not uttered by a heart of faith. He could not call them words of prayer at all. They were the cry of a grief-stricken heart to the great unknown of the universe that men and women have been crying out to in their seasons of agony since the beginning of time.

Why . . . why . . . *why!*

He could not say that he was angry at God . . . but so very, very confused. Horribly confused. How could this be!

How, Lord, could you allow such a thing! suddenly burst from his lips.

The next instant he thought to retract the faithless outburst. But he could not. He was devastated and confused, and the words mirrored what he felt.

His only thought was that he had to comfort Jocelyn and Catharine. He must get to Heathersleigh without delay.

His mind suddenly returned to Amanda. What was he waiting for! He had to go to her. This was no time to worry about the past or what she thought of him. Nor to wallow in his own grief. If ever Amanda needed someone, it was now.

Timothy was out the door before the realization struck him—he had no idea where Amanda was staying!

But Mr. Churchill knew. He had said as much to Jocelyn. He would go straight to his office.

Thirty minutes later, Timothy walked into the office of the First Lord of the Admiralty for the second time that week. On this occasion the receptionist recognized him and gave him a cordial smile and greeting.

"I am Rev. Diggorsfeld," said Timothy. "I must see Mr. Churchill."

"I am sorry, Rev. Diggorsfeld," she replied. "Mr. Churchill had pressing business in Devon early this morning. He left at dawn and has not returned."

Of course, what was he thinking? thought Timothy—the First Lord couldn't possibly be back in the city yet. Jocelyn had called him only half an hour ago.

"When do you expect him?" he asked.

"I really don't know," the lady replied. "Not until much later this afternoon, if at all. I do not actually know whether he will return to the office. We have lost another one of our battle cruisers, you see—"

"Yes . . . yes, I know," replied Timothy. "Thank you very much."

"Is there a message you would like to leave?"

"Uh . . . no . . . no, thank you," mumbled Timothy, stumbling out. He wandered in a new stupor toward the stairs, tears filling his eyes again. How was he going to find Amanda!

Once outside, no thought of a cab came to his mind. He had to walk. He would walk back and try again to come to terms with this devastating news, which all at once seemed yet the more crushing in that now he had nothing before him to *do*.

What was he going to preach on during tomorrow's service? he thought. How could he possibly preach at all!

On he walked, hardly conscious of direction . . . thinking of Charles, thinking of Amanda, thinking of Jocelyn, and vaguely continuing to despair from the hopelessness of attempting to preach in a mere twenty-four hours.

How could he possibly take the pulpit and offer anything to his people, when his own faith was so shaken, and when he was filled with such turmoil?

100

The Streets of London
◆ ◆ ◆

*A*manda slumped to a chair in her London hotel, face ashen, the thin yellow paper falling out of her hand to the floor. It was the same communication that had been delivered hours before to her mother at Heathersleigh Hall.

Winston Churchill had just left.

How long she sat in a stupor, Amanda had no idea. Finally she rose and stumbled in a daze out into Saturday afternoon London.

Somehow—she could not have said how—the rest of the day passed.

Timothy Diggorsfeld sat despondent in his study. He had not eaten so much as a half dozen bites of Mrs. Alvington's supper.

"Lord, how can I possibly face tomorrow?" he said to himself for the fiftieth time. "It is hopeless. I have nothing to offer my people, because I have nothing to offer myself."

All afternoon and evening, the smiling, laughing, exuberant face of his friend Charles Rutherford had loomed in the eye of his brain, suddenly so much larger than life—such a true friend and man who had had such an effect on his own life and ministry.

Dear, dear Charles! he thought, eyes filling again with tears that refused to stop.

What could he do in remembrance of Charles? What legacy could he leave his friend?

Suddenly came the idea. Why should he not preach the very sermon Charles himself once gave from his pulpit?

He had asked Charles, after he had been a Christian for some time, to speak a message that was dear to his heart. With fondness he recalled the long talk they had had about intimacy with God and how such closeness could be attained between men and their Creator. At the time, Charles had been reflecting on much that had been in his own heart prior to his conversion.

In a sense it had been Charles' own personal testimony of faith couched within the structure of a sermon. As Timothy recalled, the message had been hard-hitting and direct. That was the sort of man Charles Rutherford was—forceful, straightforward, intellectually honest, and unafraid to look himself in the eye.

He would deliver it again, thought Timothy. Tomorrow . . . in remembrance of Charles!

The resolve that some tiny good might come from this hour of such intense personal agony enabled Timothy to take a deep breath—his first of the day.

Where Amanda's feet took her as afternoon gave way to evening, she hardly remembered.

She walked miles through streets and parks, her mind senseless. She was unable to think, unable to focus her brain on anything definite.

Motion became the sole determinative feature of her being. Movement did not console her, but it kept her limbs busy enough that she did not have to confront that most dreaded enemy which had suddenly begun to make its true nature known—the *Self* she had almost begun to look at after arriving in Switzerland.

But she would be able to hide from herself no longer. Suddenly everything was changed.

Tears had not yet come to Amanda's eyes. She was too deep in shock to cry.

She would weep in time. When she did, bitter indeed would be the sting from the hot tears down her cheeks. For they would be the anguished tears caused by the eye-opening truth that she had never been a true daughter to her father . . . and that her chance to become one was now gone forever.

The telephone in Timothy Diggorsfeld's study rang. He leapt for it.

"Rev. Diggorsfeld?" said a familiar voice.

"Yes."

"It's Winston Churchill. My secretary told me you were in earlier. I am sorry for not getting to you sooner, but it's taken some doing to track you down. I apologize for ringing so late, but I'm afraid I have some terrible news."

"Yes, yes, thank you for calling," said Timothy. "I've heard. Lady Rutherford rang me earlier."

"Ah, I see."

"I am concerned for their daughter, however—Amanda. That was the purpose of my coming to your office. Jocelyn, er, Lady Jocelyn said that you—"

"Yes, she's been notified. I called at her hotel the moment I arrived back in the city."

"Can you tell me, then, where she is?" asked Timothy.

"At the Hotel Clairmont," replied the First Lord.

"Right, thank you—I'll go out and try to see her immediately."

"If there is anything else I can do, for you or any of the family," said Churchill, "please do not hesitate to contact me."

Timothy had scarcely put down the receiver when he was out of the house again on his way to the Clairmont.

He arrived twenty minutes later. Amanda was not in her room.

Timothy descended to the lobby pondering what to do. He went back out into the evening air and walked briefly in the nearby streets, then returned. Still she was gone.

By now it was getting dark. Perhaps she had gone somewhere, thought Timothy. She might not be planning to return tonight at all. Perhaps she had even left the city.

He left a message at the desk, requesting that Amanda get in touch with him, then returned to the parsonage of New Hope Chapel.

Amanda hardly noticed when darkness came. She continued to walk and did not arrive back at the Clairmont until sometime after ten o'clock. She had eaten nothing since lunch. She did not check for messages.

Eventually she was swallowed up in that simplest, yet in some ways most miraculous, of the Creator's gifts to his creatures—sleep. Now she had but one Father, and he watched over her most tenderly in these hours after the loss of the other he had given her, and blessed her with a deep and restful slumber.

101

Autumn Rains and Memories

◆ ◆ ◆

*A*bout the same time that evening when Amanda stumbled back into the lobby of the Clairmont Hotel—as one deadened to all around her—and up to the room Lieutenant Langham had arranged for her, Timothy Diggorsfeld arrived home from his unsuccessful attempt to locate her.

As he had walked he had been thinking more and more about Charles' sermon.

He entered into his office before even removing his coat, went straight to his file, and quickly flipped through papers and envelopes and folders. There it was just as he remembered it—the handwritten copy of the text. Charles had given it to him at the end of the same day, saying he no longer had need of it.

Timothy pulled it out and eased into his favorite chair. His eyes and cheeks revealed the gradual signs of advancing age. He was a few years past fifty. His hair was thinning and receding rapidly above the forehead, though he still possessed a good wavy crop up to a distance of three or four inches above both ears, and most of the top and back of his head was still moderately thatched. He had retained his lean frame through the years, for he walked a good deal, and rapidly whenever alone, conducting nearly all his pastoral calls, even occasionally to a distance of an hour each way, on foot. He tended to go through boots rather more quickly than most of his profession, but his health was robust and his face well tanned as a result.

The mere sight of Charles' handwriting—with various marginal notes and a multitude of scratchings and deletions and additions, then the clean-written final draft—brought a renewal of tears to the sensitive pastor's eyes. But the hurricane of initial grief had passed, and the tears had now gradually become as a lingering quiet rain, pouring forth no longer as a flood but rather a steady, almost peaceful, drizzle.

A rush of nostalgic reflections filled him ... Charles' first visit ... the incident with the rabble-rousers ... the sight of him as he walked into New Hope Chapel hardly knowing why he had come, his first questions about faith, their discussions, their many prayers together through the years ... the friendship that had developed, his own many visits to Heathersleigh.

He had seen many things in his life, thought Timothy, and been acquainted with many people. But never had he known a man so obedient, one who so resolutely determined to change the whole course of his life, whatever the cost, because of what he had come to believe.

Most of those in his experience, Timothy reflected, overlaid their belief on top of a lifestyle that continued unaffected by it, as a coat they took on and off once or twice a week, or when a discussion turned toward matters of religion.

Not Charles, he thought with a smile. He had made *belief* the fundamental thing, and had set out to order his priorities and relationships, his family and career, according to it. It was no cloak on top of but separate from the real him ... his belief became the *essence* of the real Charles Rutherford. He was the first to admit having made mistakes in that process. But Timothy admired the effort, however imperfect, in a way that he had never admired anything he had seen a man do in his life.

Slowly Timothy began to read the words in Charles' hand. He reread the entire message for the first time since he had heard the words spoken out of his friend's mouth as he stood behind his own pulpit. Even though he was the one who led Charles to the Lord, he found himself convicted anew by his words.

Charles should have been a preacher, not a politician, Timothy thought, smiling again.

He recalled how earnestly Charles had prayed prior to summoning the courage to deliver this message. He had, in fact, been in fear and trembling beforehand. He had spoken before his nation's political leaders many times. But to rise into the pulpit of a small London chapel and speak to thirty or forty people about being one with their heavenly Father—that was far more fearsome.

Who was *he*, Charles said, to speak to anyone else about rightness with God when he had ignored him most of his life? Perhaps, Timothy had argued, that fact, along with the additional fact that he was ignoring him no longer, gave him the right to speak. In the end, Charles had realized that he must obey the Voice.

Timothy recalled Charles' warning to the congregation at the beginning of the sermon that he would call on them to examine their hearts with an honesty seldom required of listeners to sermons in England these days. But, he assured them, it was by such straightforward honesty that he had himself come to believe—honesty from the mouth of their very own pastor. From him he had learned, Charles said, to ask difficult questions and to point their difficulty first of all upon himself. Thus he would examine his own heart anew with them.

Timothy brushed away a renewal of tears. Less than forty-eight hours after his death, already the memory of Charles Rutherford's life and faith had begun a new work which in time would impact many— that greater work which the seed falling into the ground of the faithful lives of God's servants often produces.

"Lord," Timothy began to pray in the quiet chamber where Charles Rutherford had first come so many years ago to ask about what belief meant, *"may this dear man's life live on. May his faith, his character, his obedience, and his good deeds as he walked the earth continue to draw people to you though his physical presence is gone from us. Use his life, Lord . . . and continue to use him."*

His voice caught as he prayed, and he paused for a moment.

"And may you somehow miraculously use the memory of his character and faith in his daughter's life. What she was unable to see in life, may she apprehend with tenfold clarity in his death. May she truly learn to arise and go to her father, both you and our dear friend Charles. Work a miracle in her life, Lord. Do a work within her that will spread out to influence many for good. May this tragic loss in the end reap a hundredfold harvest for your kingdom.

"Give me strength to speak Charles' words and to forget for those brief moments my own grief. Grant that some soul, Lord, may hear Charles' heart tomorrow, and may his words be what that individual needs at just that moment."

By the time he was through praying, Timothy was again weeping freely. The tears now falling down his cheeks as he gazed upon the treasured sheets in his hand were the gentle showers of a warm autumn's evening, capable of bringing out of the human soul—as the rains of autumn lure from the soil of the earth—many fragrances too subtle to be detected during the happier seasons of blue sky and red roses when high summer reigns over the land.

If his heart could not yet be said to be at peace, the knowledge that Charles and George were in the presence of their heavenly Father was some comfort. And he took quiet consolation in that fact.

It is at such moments that Christians discover how deeply they believe in eternity, Timothy reflected. And perhaps the loss of his best friend shook the foundations of his own belief a little more vigorously than he might have liked. If he took to heart the words of Jesus about eternal life in their fullness, he *should* now be rejoicing.

But he could not rejoice. All he could do was let the autumn rains of grief fall down upon him and drink in the subtle messages they carried from the Father's heart, who invented life and death together and linked them mysteriously as one.

Nor would he chastise himself for his grief. If he could not rejoice, he could be content in knowing that he was but a weak human being, after all, and to suffer and weep at such times was intrinsic to the human experience.

His belief in the eternal life of his two friends would rise again to conquer this present anguish. And the day would come when he would rejoice that they were with the Lord Jesus and his Father. For now he must be free to weep and grieve, that his belief, when it did rise up to quell these doubts of his human weakness, might in the end carve deeper wells of trust within him.

So Timothy continued to weep, and eventually wept himself to sleep, still dressed, with his coat still over his shoulders, and with Charles' handwritten sheets still in his lap.

102
Sunday Morning

*A*manda awoke the following morning feeling weak and numb.

It was Sunday, though she hardly realized it at first. She had but rarely attended church with the Pankhursts during her first years in London, and not once since then. The sisters had had informal services at the chalet, but that was different. On this day, however, when she arose and the day of the week dawned on her, the idea of a church service seemed the only appropriate response to the devastating news of the death of father and brother. She still hardly knew *what* she believed, even *whether* she believed. Yet before she knew it she was dressed and, after half a cup of tea and an attempt to eat a little breakfast in the hotel dining room, prepared to set out for morning services at St. Paul's.

The day was bright, the air pleasant. As she drew closer, however, finding more and more men and women bustling around her on their way to the great London cathedral, she began to feel out of place. The city whose crowded activity and energy had once drawn her had become impersonal and unfriendly.

Up the steps she moved with the masses, then inside the great doors and into the majestic place whose huge dome towered over the city.

Amanda stopped. The throng continued to push past her. But she could not do it. There were too many people, too much commotion. A church service was not what her heart needed right now. She wanted quiet. She wanted to be alone.

For what, she couldn't have said. To *do* what . . . to *think* what . . . to *pray* what—none of this Amanda considered. She just had to get out of there.

She turned and left the way she had come, moving against the human flow out the doors, then down the steps.

As the human river thinned and she found herself on a quieter street, the paralysis of her brain suddenly gave way to a rush of mental activity. Unwelcome and painful memories assailed her. She continued heedless of direction.

All at once her mind was clear and focused. Images, words, faces plagued her . . . her father's voice, the words of parental counsel as she had contemplated coming to London:

You are making a serious mistake, Amanda.

Then words of warning from his letter several years later:

Please, for your good not my own, listen to my cautions. . . . There may be dangers that you are unaware of . . . people you have become involved with are not what they seem. . . . You are an adult now. I urge you to stand tall and mature and to exercise sober adult judgment.

But they had fallen on deaf ears. Sister Hope was right. Amanda had always done only what she wanted to do, heeding no other, asking no other.

Where had it led her in the end but into the very dangers her father had warned of? He had been so right . . . so right about everything! How could she have been so immature and stupid, and yet think herself so wise and grown-up?

Then the cruel words she had written to her parents after leaving Heathersleigh came back to haunt her:

. . . I cannot endorse anything about the life you have chosen. . . . I see no basis for us to have a continuing relationship or friendship. . . . I am not interested in your God, in your prayers, or in either of you.

At last a few hot tears began to sting at her eyes. How *could* she have been so mean, so childish . . . so utterly foolish!

Now more recent words . . . Sister Hope's voice pleading with her to listen . . . *There is an independence into which we must all grow . . . but the independence that is making you miserable is something else, and is nothing but pride. Every prodigal has to go home eventually.*

From her own mouth she could still hear herself shouting back—

I'm not a prodigal!

Then came Sister Hope's pointed reply—

It may be painful to admit, but that is exactly what you are.

More words to haunt her! She had been given sound advice for years. But she had refused to listen to any of it.

She clasped her hands to her ears to try to stop the tormenting flow of memories. But they came from inside, and nothing she did could prevent their piercing accusations bombarding her brain like a waking nightmare.

If only . . . if only she had come back sooner! Maybe she might have been able to make it right with her father and ask his forgiveness.

If only . . .

But what was the use now?

What was the use of anything now? None of it mattered anymore! She could *not* be reconciled to her father. He was gone . . . dead.

It was too late!

Pictures and memories from childhood floated in and out, fragmentary pieces of conversations, harsh words she had spoken. Through it all were images of the two happy, smiling, forgiving, patient, unselfish, loving faces. The best brother, the best father a girl could have!

Their smiles haunted her, refusing even in death to be angry at her, refusing to speak harshly. Smiling . . . only smiling.

Silently they whispered out from some watery grave. She knew well enough what they were saying—that they *loved* her, despite what she had been to them.

How badly she had misjudged them. Suddenly she saw so clearly what wonderful men they both were.

Now she would never see either again!

A lump filled her throat. She forced it down, then drew in several deep breaths, telling herself she must regain her composure.

She continued to walk, she hardly knew where.

103

The Call of Intimacy

◆ ◆ ◆

All the streets where Amanda found herself were lonely and cold, the faces she encountered impersonal. The great metropolis she had once longed for had lost its life.

As Amanda walked along a nearly deserted part of the city, voices of singing caught her ear. She had turned in so many directions by now she had scarcely an idea where she was.

She glanced along the street. There was a steeple.

She was walking along Bloomsbury Way! There was New Hope

Chapel in the next block! How had she come here? Had her steps unconsciously been leading her here all along?

From inside, peaceful melodies of song drifted gently out into the street. The hymn drew her. Slowly she approached.

The singing stopped. Amanda paused and waited. After another few minutes, a man began to speak. Inside she heard the familiar voice of Timothy Diggorsfeld.

"The great crying need of our time, my friends," the pastor began, "is intimacy with God, our Father and Creator and Maker."

He paused briefly to allow the simple yet profound words to sink in.

"What prevents this intimacy we so desperately need?" he went on. "Many evangelists of our day will say it is sin, and then proceed to rail against this or that evil of society. They are right, of course—sin is the great curse that prevents us from what God would give, and especially all that he would have us to be."

Strangely moved, almost warmed by the words which several years earlier would doubtless have angered her, Amanda began to walk forward again, curiously drawn to the message. The doors stood wide open to the fair morning, and Timothy's voice carried clearly out into the street.

"But what about otherwise good people," Diggorsfeld was saying, "even Christian believers, whom the world would look upon with favor? Perhaps some of you men and women listening to my voice are such. And before I gave my own heart to the Lord, such was I—respected and admired by all ... but far from God in my heart. I do not say that evangelists ought not to preach to sinners who need to repent. Their hellfire messages and salvationary fervor are perhaps much needed for some. But they did not rouse me out of the complacent and contented stupor I supposed was my goodness and respectability. Something else was needed.

"So I find myself compelled to ask—what of good people who are in church many a Sunday? Good people, as was I myself? What about young boys and girls, teenagers, young adults with believing parents, who have been in church Sunday after Sunday throughout their lives and who are well familiar with the gospel, perhaps even who believe in its message?"

Amanda was nearing the front of the church now. She continued to walk slowly toward the door.

"Does the heavenly Father not desire intimacy with such individuals just as greatly as with the worst sinner in the land? Does he not desire intimacy with *you*—believer that you are—no less than with a thief or a murderer? Yet it may be, though we are unaccustomed to think so, that this intimacy is actually as *lacking* in the hearts of good respectable Christians as it is lacking in the hearts of the worst sinners listening to a rousing message about the dangers of hell.

"I *know* that such intimacy can be missing in the midst of outward respectability. How can I say such a thing? Because I was just such a one myself. I was a contented, respectable prodigal. I had no idea what I was at all. I would have recoiled from the merest suggestion.

"What—*me* a prodigal! *Outrageous*, would have been my reply.

"You see, my friends, I had no idea that my prodigality was not evidenced by wicked crimes against society . . . but rather lay in my own prideful independence. Thinking myself a fine man, I was in fact living in my very own private far country just like the young man who went to eat with pigs. But I knew it not."

Timothy paused. Amanda could not but recall again, as she had when walking yesterday, her bitter argument with Sister Hope of only a week ago. How much had changed in such a short time.

"Intimacy, therefore, may be lacking in *your* heart as you sit listening to my words this morning," Timothy continued. "I cannot know such things, nor do I judge any man or woman. I only say that perhaps the Spirit of God has drawn you here because he has been calling your heart to deeper intimacy with him."

Amanda slowly sat down on the steps of the chapel outside. She would not have said she *wanted* to listen. Yet somehow she knew she *had* to, feeling compelled to remain.

She knew the words were being spoken to her, even though the preacher could have no idea she was even there. From the energetic tone of his voice, she could only assume that Rev. Diggorsfeld had not yet been informed about her father.

"What is to be gained," Timothy had by now resumed, "by condemning this or that evil, if we neglect that region where lies our first business of life? Indeed, one of the greatest of the last century's preachers said that we could rid the world of *every single one* of its wrongs and still neglect that most important of all life's callings. What will it accomplish if we set *all* the world's evils right, if we rid it of poverty and alcohol and inequity, if we bring justice to every creature, if we give

every man and woman the vote, if we eliminate the scourge of war—
what good will it do, I say, to remove *all* these from the world . . . if we
as a people yet in our hearts remain distant from the God who made
us?

"And, you may rightfully ask, what about me? What about one who
has given his professional life to combating the evils of our society
through government? That is why, as I said, there was a time when I
had to ask these questions first and foremost to myself."

Amanda's ears perked up. These were curious words coming from
Timothy Diggorsfeld. What could he mean?

"And as I asked them," the sermon went on, "I had to face at length
the primary question: What is the calling to which we should aspire if
it is not to rid the world of evil? Many would consider this the highest
calling of man—especially politicians—to rid the world of wrong. But
I say no. I say it is elsewhere we must look for the *summum bonum*, the
highest thing of life.

"Where then? What *is* the highest of life's ambitions, that worthiest
goal to which the human creature may strive?"

The voice stopped. Timothy was glancing back and forth through
his rows of listeners. This was the most difficult sermon he had delivered in his life. Tears struggled to fill his eyes, blurring the page of
Charles' handwriting on the lectern in front of him. Though these were
not his own words, insofar as it concerned one particular individual
whom he did not know was listening, it was also the most important
sermon of his life. Already his prayer of the night before was in the
process of being profoundly answered.

"*Intimacy*, my friends," said Timothy after a moment, "—a personal
and daily walk of trust and reliance upon God our Father, and with
His Son Jesus, our Savior. *That* is the highest thing.

"I speak not only to the so-called *sinners* among you, but to *you*,
Christian man, to *you*, good believing woman, to *you*, young person
raised and trained in a gospel-believing church, to *you*, good citizen
who have dedicated your life to worthy causes and to the elimination
of inequality and injustice and evil in our society. I speak to *you* as well
as to the thief and adulterer and murderer—and I say to you, *Your Father desires to live with you in intimacy*. And because for years I did not
know this intimacy either, I speak to myself.

"Salvation may be all that is required for entrance into the heavenly
kingdom," the compelling sermon went on. "But alone it will not pro-

duce the abundant, fruitful life Jesus came to reveal to his brothers and sisters. The Son of God came that we might walk in close fellowship with his Father. Such he became a man for. Such he died for.

"He did not die on the cross only to save us from our sins, though of course he did do that. He died on the cross also that we might be drawn into and thus share in the relationship he had with his Father— that we might too become fully sons and daughters of God."

104

Respectable Prodigality

$\mathcal{A}$manda had never heard the likes of such a sermon.

Something about the words themselves, even an occasional phrase, sounded oddly familiar. But she knew she had never heard Timothy preach like this. In some peculiar way, it did not even sound like him.

And what was the compelling aura about it that drew her so? Why did the sensation of familiarity make her heart flutter and momentarily make her forget as she listened that her father was dead?

She continued to sit spellbound on the steps outside, heedless of the occasional stares of passersby. The pause in the midst of the message, though Amanda could not know it, came now because Timothy at last had had no recourse but to bring out his handkerchief and attempt to dry his eyes.

"Yet that intimacy," Timothy went on after a moment in a faltering voice and more reflective tone, "between God and his sons and daughters, is not easy to come by. Indeed, it is far easier to fall on one's knees in remorse for a life of evil, and pray a prayer of salvation for one's sins—this is far easier, I say, than to lay down what must be sacrificed in order to enter into intimacy with the Father.

"What is it that prevents this intimacy? What is this most difficult sacrifice I speak of?

"It is not primarily sin in the world, nor the wickedness of the ungodly. It is not poverty nor cruelty, not injustice nor inequality, not war nor killing nor greed. I speak rather of the sin which prevented me for most of my own life from entering into intimate relationship with my heavenly Father.

"I speak of the great invisible enemy of God's highest purposes—nothing more nor less than prideful independence of heart, that determination which says—*I am my own.* None other shall control me, none other shall dictate to me, none shall be over me.... I shall bow my knee to no one.

"This is the spirit that rules in the far country to which we modern respectable prodigals have given our citizenship.

"Do you hear me, men and women—simple *independence* ... that quality so admired by modern culture is in fact a mountain ten miles high and impossible to cross between that land where we have built our impoverished dwellings and the home of our Father.

"*Independence* is the great silent evil, not because its sin is so perfidious but because it keeps otherwise good and moral people ruled by their Selves. It keeps them eating spiritual swine husks rather than the meat of fellowship with Jesus and his Father. People like you, good listener ... and me."

The words rocked Amanda where she sat. Had she not known otherwise, she would have said of a certainty that the words of this sermon could not possibly be Timothy Diggorsfeld's, but must have been the words of Hope Guinarde herself.

So whose were these powerful words!

But today Amanda did not try to block her ears or keep from listening. No anger arose in her heart on this morning. The time for listening had come. Amanda sat calmly and allowed her heart at last to drink in the painful astringent of truth.

"The *Self*—that region of thought and deed, of motive and attitude—keeps *me* on the throne of life, and God off it. It keeps *you* on your own throne too, my friend. As long as you are on the throne where your *own* will rules supreme, God cannot exercise his true Fatherhood in your life because there can be only one Father and one child. Self-rule says—*I need no Father over me.* Self-rule is the god of the far country."

Amanda saw how right Sister Hope had been. How could she have known her so well!

Amanda had always ruled her own life. Her enemy was never her father, as she had supposed. The enemy had always been her *Self.* Her father had been but a mirror held up to her own willful determination to bow before no one but herself.

She had been her *own* enemy. Her father had done his best to help her overcome that *Self*.

Alas, she had rejected that help. He had only tried to help her win the battle against self-rule. Her father had tried to help her become a young woman of virtue. But she had angrily thrown that help back in his face.

"We are all prodigals together, my friends," said Timothy. "We have made self-rule our god. As a result we have become a prodigal humanity. Thus we do not know intimacy with our Creator and our Father.

"But we *can* know it. Jesus came to show us how. But we must return. We must leave the land where pride and self-rule reign as gods. We must be reconciled with our Father.

" 'How?' you ask.

"God will show you. But first we must say, as Jesus taught, 'I will leave this country. I will return to my Father's house.'

"That is something we can do in our own hearts. Now ... today. We can say to him, *'I am sorry for being a respectable worshiper of Self. I am sorry for thinking myself capable of living my life with no Father over me. No more do I want to rule my own life. I want a Father. I am ready to be a child. I am eager to become a true son, a true daughter. I ask you to be my Father.'*

"With such a prayer, we have indeed begun the journey home to our Father's house. Reconciliation is under way. Thus only can we enter into that intimacy for which we long and for which we were created."

As she listened, Amanda realized there was a double message in these words for her. She had been estranged from *two* fathers, to whom she must arise and go.

Yet with the realization again came the bitter truth that it was too late.

Even as she sat on the steps, at last Amanda began to weep great tears of remorse and overwhelming grief.

Suddenly she wanted her father!

She longed for him, longed for his arms around her, longed to be his little girl again, and yet—bitter truth—he was gone!

Again Timothy had stopped. Not a soul stirred from the small chapel where only some thirty or forty sat listening to the personal and penetrating message. Some remembered it from years before. Others, hearing it for the first time, recognized in it a different quality than their minister's normal mode of address.

"He is fashioning of us people of character and virtue," Timothy continued again. "He is building the fiber of mature spirituality within us. He desires to make us into men and women capable of carrying out his commands and walking in this world as individuals recognized as sons and daughters of God. He will help us. His Spirit will transform our self-reliant, self-motivated wills, if only we will turn those wills over to him, lay them down on the altar of chosen self-denial . . . and become children.

"This process of humble growth into sons and daughters begins by turning around and setting one's face toward home, toward the Father's house, where *he* rules. We must return to him and say, '*I choose for you to rule now, not me.*' It is a journey to be made in the heart. He is waiting along the roadside to welcome us . . . but we must go to him, we must return to our Father's house and say, '*I will be your child.*' "

A lengthy interlude of silence followed.

Amanda could tell the sermon was over. Some rustling followed, then the sounds of a piano beginning another hymn.

Quietly she rose, eyes blurry and blinking back the tears struggling to overpower her, and walked away from the church.

She walked for perhaps five minutes, when suddenly from out of the depths of her heart something cried out, "*Oh, God, what am I to do?*"

The answer which stole into her consciousness the next instant was simple. It was not a mandate to change the world as had brought her to London so many years ago, but rather concerned only one person in all the universe . . . Amanda herself.

It came in a gentle, quiet, yet definite command.

"*Obey me,*" was all the voice said. "*Then arise and go to your father.*"

105
A Meeting of Friends

*A*manda did not go far.

She walked away from the church for five, perhaps six or seven minutes. Gradually aloneness overwhelmed her. Her heart began to ache with almost physical pain for sheer despondency.

Suddenly it dawned on her that except for the sisters at the Chalet of Hope, who were beyond reach at this moment, she had no one to turn to. She had only one true friend in the city, as much as at one time she thought she had despised him . . . and it was the very man behind her in New Hope Chapel to whom she had been listening.

The next instant Amanda had turned and was half running along the sidewalk back toward the church.

No logic of her mind could have explained whatever impulse compelled her feet along the walk. Her heart was suddenly so very lonely she thought it would break. The grief of her father's death bore down upon her with a crushing weight of misery and desolation.

She did not think she could bear it another instant.

She needed a friend!

As Timothy Diggorsfeld stood at the door of New Hope Chapel shaking hands with the men and women of his congregation filing out in ones and twos, it was all he could do to maintain his composure. With near herculean effort he blinked back tears and did what he could to smile and mumble words of greeting. Officiating the service, then delivering the sermon his friend Charles had written had been an enormous personal ordeal.

But this was near agony! He was physically and emotionally spent.

If he could just get the last few minutes of the morning over, then he might seek the solitude of his study. There he could weep one more time for his friend.

The line was nearly done.

Wearily Timothy glanced up as he wished Mrs. Fretwell-Phipps a good day.

What was that figure down the block standing . . . watching him . . . just standing there in the middle of the sidewalk like a lost, forlorn human sheep!

Suddenly he was stumbling down the stairs, leaving the remaining six or seven in line where they stood in the foyer of the chapel. He bumped past Mrs. Fretwell-Phipps on the steps leaving the church.

He was running now . . . running as fast as he had run for years along Bloomsbury Way, presenting a sight such as those wide-eyed of his congregation could never have imagined, black Sunday robe flying out behind their normally sedate clergyman!

The lost sheep began running toward him.

Timothy slowed, tears of so many emotions he could not have counted them streaming down his cheeks. He opened his arms.

"Amanda!" he said tenderly.

She fell into his embrace, trembling and clinging to him like a frightened child who has found its mother. At last the gushing torrent of grief overflowed its dam, and she sobbed convulsively.

Back at the church, what remained of Timothy's parishioners continued to watch the strange display. Not one had any inkling that the young lady in their minister's arms was none other than the prodigal daughter of him whose words they had just been listening to.

"I didn't know where else to go," sobbed Amanda.

Timothy held her close for what may have been one minute, perhaps two.

"You cannot imagine how glad I am you came to me," now said Timothy, stepping back and smiling. "I cannot say it makes me happy, for I doubt anything at this moment is capable of that. My heart is grievously sore. But I am very glad you came."

Amanda wiped at her tears, then, to the extent she was able, returned his smile.

"Amanda . . . I am *so* sorry about your father and brother."

She nodded and began to cry again.

"Come . . . come inside with me," said Timothy. "We will have a talk."

He turned and led the way back toward the church. "We have both lost a friend," he said. "Now we shall have to be friends to one another."

They met the astonished lady as they passed yet again on the walkway. "All is well . . . all is well, Mrs. Fretwell-Phipps," said Timothy with a smile and a nod.

They walked up the steps. Timothy paused briefly to hurriedly shake the remaining hands, then led Amanda inside and to the adjoining parsonage.

106
An Honest Talk

*A*manda Rutherford and Timothy Diggorsfeld had been talking for more than an hour as they had never spoken with each other before.

Honest had been Amanda's confessions, frank Timothy's counsel. Nothing could be gained for either by pampering, hiding, or glossing over the truth. Too much had already been lost. The time to face serious spiritual reality had come.

Amanda told him about Vienna and Ramsay and the sisters at the chalet, including the counsel she had received and her reaction.

"I realize what a selfish girl I have been," Amanda was saying. "My father tried to tell me. Sister Hope tried to tell me. Probably God himself tried to tell me, too, through my circumstances. But I wouldn't listen. I was stubborn and selfish and independent, just like you said. I did nothing but what I wanted to do. And look what it got me. Into more and more trouble. I was not even a *respectable* prodigal, Mr. Diggorsfeld, as you said in your sermon."

Amanda began to cry.

"But I don't want to end up like Robinson Crusoe, Mr. Diggorsfeld," she went on, sniffling and wiping away her tears. "I don't want to spend another thirty years in misery. I've had enough misery to last a lifetime. I have been so selfish and foolish. I see it so clearly now. My father was not controlling. He was just trying to do his best to train me out of *my* rebellious attitude. I'm sure he saw it all along."

"He saw it, yes, and it concerned him," said Timothy. "He loved you, Amanda. That is why he was willing to risk even your rejection, even your despising him for a season, to try to help you learn to lay it down."

"And I never learned!" wailed Amanda. "I just blamed *him* for my own wrong attitudes. I can hardly bear it. What a great ordeal I must have put him through!"

Timothy said nothing for a moment.

"I talked with him, and prayed with him over you many times," he said at length.

"But . . . what am I to do now!" moaned Amanda. "It's too late to make it right with him!"

She broke down sobbing.

"You must do what we all must do, Amanda," said Timothy. "You must arise and go to your father. It is how all such stories must end."

"But it's too late, I tell you—he's dead!" she wailed.

"With God, it is never too late."

"But *how* can I go to him now?"

"You must go to your heavenly Father first," said Timothy. "Then he will show you how to go to your earthly father. But rest assured, reconciliation is *always* possible."

"But he is dead," repeated Amanda.

"Only to our sight. And that fact changes nothing about your responsibility. It still must be done," said Timothy. "It is not primarily for the father that straying young people must return with repentance in their hearts . . . but for *themselves*. It is something *you* must do. Though your father may be gone from the earth, in your heart his memory still lives no less today than when you were young and with him every day. I am confident God will show you how to make peace with that memory."

It was silent a moment.

"There is something I have not told you yet," Timothy went on after a moment, then paused.

Amanda waited.

"That sermon you heard this morning . . . they were not my words at all."

Amanda looked at him with an odd expression. "I wondered," she said. "They did seem . . . different somehow."

"Your father wrote those words, Amanda," he said. "I once asked him to preach at New Hope Chapel, many years ago. He wrote that sermon for the occasion. He called it his testimonial sermon."

Amanda took in the words soberly. Again her eyes filled with tears. A rush of deep emotion welled up within her. She realized she had actually been listening to her father's voice speaking to her, as from the other side of the grave.

"So you see, Amanda," said Timothy, "by responding as you have, and by taking his words to heart, you have already begun turning toward your father in a new way. The Lord has taken him from us. Yet in another way he remains with us through our memories of him, through his teaching, his character."

Amanda leaned forward and broke into sobs again. She sat in the chair with her face in her hands, her body shaking. The excruciating remorse was so deep she felt as if her very stomach would turn inside out.

Timothy waited with eyes closed. Even in the midst of his own grief, he knew it was impossible for him to fathom her guilt-stricken anguish at such a moment of loss.

When Amanda came to herself she knew a decision had been reached.

She had all her life been nothing but what *she* had wanted to be, done nothing but what *she* had wanted to do. Self-rule had dominated her character almost since the day she was born. She had resented any and all intrusion from her parents, from God . . . from anyone.

But how lonely had become such an existence. What kind of a life had she made for herself? She had squandered everything her father had given her—both his money and his training. Even hired maids back at the estate in Devonshire enjoyed a better life than hers.

As if reading her mind, at length Timothy spoke softly. "Have you seen your mother yet?" he said.

Amanda shook her head.

"You must," he said.

"I . . . I couldn't face her," said Amanda. "Not after what I have done . . . what I have been. I am so ashamed."

"You do not think she would receive you with open arms?"

"How could she?"

"She loves you more than you can imagine."

That Amanda knew Diggorsfeld's words were true only made the fact all the more heart wrenching that she had rejected that love, from both mother and father.

"I don't know if I can face her," she repeated softly. "It would be too humiliating."

What should have been the easiest thing to do in all the world—go home—she was afraid to do.

"So you think to add to the grief of the present by remaining estranged from her?" asked Timothy.

Amanda took in the words almost as if she had been slapped in the face. He was direct! Yet in some strange way she was glad. She did not want to be babied in wrong attitudes any longer.

"But how can I face her?" she wailed again in the most forlorn tone Timothy thought he had ever heard. "She must hate me!"

"You know that is not true."

Amanda sat without expression.

"You must arise and go to your father," he urged again, "even though it may be your *mother's* arms that will receive you."

PART V

◆◆◆

Heathersleigh Homecoming

1915

107
Heartache at Heathersleigh

$\mathcal{T}$he day at Heathersleigh Hall had been dreary and sad beyond comprehension.

Spring had begun to restore greenery and color to the landscape. A few species of trees were in tender leaf. Buds swelled everywhere with new life. The spring varietals in the heather garden—though not numerous—were bursting out in magnificent color.

But there was no springtime within the heart of any man or woman for miles.

A bleak pallor of grey dominated the internal landscape. The coldest winter of human desolation had descended upon the region.

Their beloved Sir Charles was gone, and George with him.

Charles Rutherford had brought such vibrancy to so many. Now life itself seemed to have departed. Sadness reigned over central Devon. Every eye at the service in Milverscombe was red on the Sunday following Saturday's tragic news. Some of the most stoic of the men wept the most freely. Never had there been a man, they said, like Sir Charles. Nor would there ever be again.

Jocelyn scarcely left her room in two days. She did not go out to attend the service. Catharine brought meals up, though they remained largely untouched. A few sympathizers from the village came and went. Most let their beloved Lady Jocelyn grieve in solitude.

A more pervasive quiet there had never been at Heathersleigh. The Hall became as a great stone tomb.

Silent . . . cold . . . empty.

Sarah ministered as she was able in spite of her own plentiful tears. She tiptoed about, trying to keep tea warm and food available should it be wanted, as if the very sounds of her steps echoing from floor to walls was an intrusion against the silence of mourning.

Sunday endured. Monday came.

The sun rose, but it brought no cheer.

When Margaret McFee awoke on the second day following news of Master Charles' and Master George's awful deaths, she detected strange stirrings in her heart.

If she hadn't felt so full of energy, she might have thought this was the day the Lord was preparing to take her home as well. But she doubted that was it. She knew dear Lady Jocelyn needed the companionship of her closest friends at this terrible time. As much as she longed to see her precious Bobby again, she was certain the Lord would not remove her from the earth just yet.

Then what were these peculiar flutterings within her? Something in the spirit realm was alive. She almost sensed the rustling of angels' wings.

"What is it, Lord?" she began to ask from the moment wakefulness overtook her.

Jocelyn ate some toast in bed and half a cup of tea, dozed fitfully, awoke and cried some more, then tried to sleep again. But it was no use. The raveled sleeve of her care was not so easily knit.

Sometime around noon, she decided to get up. Catharine helped her dress, for her mother was lightheaded from lack of activity and nourishment.

Together they went downstairs to the kitchen.

"Mother, you need to eat something," said Catharine. "I'll make some tea and we'll have a light lunch together."

Jocelyn nodded.

She wasn't hungry, but at least she felt she could eat. And probably should.

108
Unless a Seed Fall to the Ground...

As Amanda rode along in the train from London to Devon, she could feel the years tumbling away with each passing mile.

If ever one could progress backward in time, she felt such was now happening inside her. As she bounced along, all the dreams and self-centered motives that had driven her away from Heathersleigh to London eight years earlier now fell away.

How could she have been so enamored by such ambitions?

They were so false, so empty, and had proved so unsatisfying. How could her youthful spirit have been so consumed by what she now saw was meaningless?

A great metamorphosis had taken place over the course of those eight years, though it had required heartbreak and pain to bring it about. The change was simply this: She now wanted to *be* rather than to *do*.

At last she wanted to be a person of worth and character. Who she was *inside* finally mattered. It had never mattered before. Suddenly it became the only thing she cared about.

As earlier ambitions fell away like scales from her eyes, their absence allowed her to perceive many things anew—truths that had always been there but that she had never seen aright.

Chief among these was the realization that *character* had been the missing ingredient in her own life, a fact which had blinded her to the deep qualities of character that *were* present in her father and mother. It was a startling and humbling new revelation.

After Monday's lunch, Jocelyn wandered to the front door, then went out.

It was the first time she had crossed the threshold of the door in two days. The sun felt good on her face. She drew in a deep breath of air. It felt quietly and sadly invigorating to fill her lungs again.

She must go on with her life, she thought . . . for Catharine, for the household, for the villagers. Somehow . . . she must carry on.

She sauntered slowly away from the house. Before many minutes had gone by she found herself unconsciously approaching the heather garden. She would not have chosen to come here by herself, not now, not after what had happened. Yet as she began wandering its quiet and lonely paths, a strange sense of communion with Charles enveloped her.

Maggie had risen while the day was still early and had gone out.

The air was still. She felt a hush that was more than the mere absence of wind. It was the hush of expectancy.

The peculiar sensation remained with her throughout the morning. And now, as the sun rose high in the sky, and as she worked in her garden, sprouting and blooming gloriously to spring-life again, she glanced about every so often as if unconsciously expecting to look up and see a visitor approaching.

Indeed, Maggie's inner instincts were so finely tuned from years spent listening to the Master's still small voice that she now perceived the silent invisible awakening of a human-garden of which her own was but a passing earthly shadow.

She continued to pull a few weeds, cultivate the soft earth, and plant a few annuals . . . but her mind was elsewhere.

On Amanda's journey toward home, years continued to fall away, and image after image of her father came into her mind.

They were painful now to recall, but she did not resist their flow. Happy images of his exuberance, his compassion, his humor, his energy, his laughter, his wit, his intelligence, his constant attempt to teach her and George and Catharine and make them think, his persistent upward pull of their thoughts toward self-discovery and truth, and most of all his determination to walk as God's man whatever it might cost.

Every memory was suddenly happy and so full of life.

Where had these memories been for eight years!

How could she have forgotten what he was like? Suddenly everything seemed so plain.

Tears filled Jocelyn's eyes as she went slowly through the garden she and Charles had worked in and expanded together, and where they had spent so many hours praying. They were tears of the heartbreaking loss of a faithful companion, a true man, and all a woman could hope for in a friend.

Yet, too, they were now becoming tears of dawning readiness to face the tragedy and look forward again. As she went she began talking with Charles, as if he were still beside her, remembering many fond times they had spent here together.

"I miss you so much, Charles," she whispered, "but I will try to be strong and brave. I know that is what you would tell me . . . that God's love, and even yours, will outlive this present agony.

"I can almost hear you saying the words," she said, smiling thinly. "I can hardly bear it, knowing I will not see your face again . . . but I will try to smile and be thankful . . . for your sake. Oh, my dear, dear Charles . . . you were so good to me. I love you so much!"

Her heart fell silent.

There were too many words. There were no words.

Amanda's memories of Charles' happy, smiling face brought many tears, and an anguished renewal of the terrible grief of a daughter who has at last discovered her father but knows she will never see him again.

She let the tears flow. A catharsis was under way, and she knew she must yield to it.

She recalled incidents she hadn't thought of in years. Suddenly her father, in some strange and heartbreakingly wonderful way, was closer to her than he had ever been, closer than when they had sat side by side traveling along this very track to London when she was seven and her father was about to be knighted by Queen Victoria—closer because for the first time in her life he lived fondly in her heart.

At last she realized how deeply he had loved her. And for the first time his love became something to cherish.

Allowing that love mysteriously to wrap its arms around her brought a new flood of tears. Yet in a mysterious way they were cleansing and healing tears. For they also brought with them the realization that she now loved him too.

In the heather garden Jocelyn began to feel similar fluttering sensations that had all day been afflicting Maggie.

She heard the train coming. She paused to listen, glancing down the hill. She could see the smoke from its engine puffing up in white clouds through the trees. It crossed the bridge across the river, then continued on toward the village.

She turned along one of the winding pathways and left the garden, crossed the lawn, then felt herself drawn to the driveway coming up the hill to the house.

She wandered toward the drive, unconsciously peering down it. All was quiet again as the clacking sounds gradually died away in the distance.

Why was her heart beating so?

The train was now slowing. Amanda knew they were at last coming into the station at Milverscombe. She had forced herself not to look out as the train crossed the bridge. She was not quite ready to see the house yet.

She wanted to hold a moment longer the realization that she truly *loved* her father.

And with the transformation in her heart of recognizing that simple truth that had evaded her for so long, Amanda Rutherford was a prodigal no longer.

She was at last ready to love *both* her fathers, to accept their love unconditionally, to learn from them, and to become the daughter she had never been content to be.

"Daddy," she whispered, "I am *so* sorry!"

It was all she could say.

The train continued to slow.

"One day I will ask you to forgive me," she went on silently. "Until then I have to content myself knowing that you *always* forgave me, even when I thought I hated you. You always forgave, because your heart was so full of love. I am so sorry I could not see it. But I see it now."

And thus, as Timothy had foretold, Amanda had already begun to learn from the memory of her father's life. And so did the spirit of Charles Rutherford's character, through his death, begin to come to life within the heart of his daughter.

109

Heathersleigh Homecoming

From the drive, Jocelyn turned again toward the heather garden, though she now walked in a wide semicircle around it and down the gentle, grassy slope toward the road where it bent away from the river and continued toward Milverscombe. Through the thin trees she approached close to the road.

A sound came into her hearing. She peered down the hill through the wooded embankment toward the road. It was a carriage.

It was ... coming this way!

Why was her heart beating ... why was she afraid to look?

But she must look!

Jocelyn waited where she stood among the trees. The carriage came closer, now passing in front of her at a distance of about thirty yards.

A single horse ... a driver ... and sitting inside the enclosed passenger coach—

Had her eyes deceived her!

It couldn't ... but—

"Oh, Lord ... Lord ..."

Already Jocelyn had turned and was hurrying out of the trees and back up the hill to the house, forgetting her light-headedness, forgetting her grief, and forgetting her weariness altogether ... running as she hadn't run in forty years.

As the carriage rolled up the drive to the great Hall of her childhood, all was now changed for Amanda. She would turn twenty-five years old a few weeks from now. At long last, youth tumbled away behind her.

At last she was eager to be here. It was finally time to put away childish things.

She drew in a deep breath, of both courage and resolve, and looked out upon the familiar landscape that was at once unchanged, and yet

369

entirely transformed to her new-seeing eyes.

Standing at an upstairs window, Catharine Rutherford was staring absently down the road, wiping away a fresh set of tears, when first she glimpsed the distant approach of a carriage coming up the drive toward the house.

And there was her mother running almost frantically from somewhere out by the heather garden.

Catharine's heart skipped a beat.

Could it possibly—

She did not wait any longer to answer her own question than had her mother.

Already she was bolting for the stairs and bounding down them two at a time.

Before Amanda reached the Hall, she saw her mother running from beside the house and across the front courtyard. A great smile was spread over her face. Tears flowed down both cheeks in a glistening stream.

"Stop," cried Amanda to the driver.

She jumped out of the carriage before it had come to a stop and broke into a run toward the outstretched arms, crying like a baby.

Mother and daughter fell into each other's arms somewhere between carriage and house.

Amanda broke down and wept convulsively, her shoulders shaking in great heaving sobs. All former reticence was gone. She melted in Jocelyn's embrace and was at last content in her mother's love.

Catharine burst out the front door, then suddenly stopped.

The sight of mother and sister before her, standing in the middle of the courtyard tightly holding one another in their arms, each weeping on the other's shoulder, was too wondrous to intrude upon.

Catharine stood waiting in silence.

"Oh, God . . . God . . . thank you!" she said quietly through the smiling, weepy heaving of her heart.

She forced her eyes away. It was too holy an exchange even for a sister to gaze long upon, a moment reserved for mother and daughter alone.

Jocelyn could not prevent a new rush of grief from loss of husband

and son. But suddenly to have the daughter who was lost melt into her arms caused more emotions in her mother's soul than she could contain.

"Oh, Amanda," she whispered at length, "it is good to see you. I love you so much."

"I know, Mother . . . finally I really know. I love you too. I am *so* sorry!"

Jocelyn held her tight, comforting the daughter who again became as a little girl. She had not allowed herself to dream this moment would ever come. Now that it had, she thought she could stand holding her precious daughter forever.

How long they stood, whether minutes or seconds, neither knew.

After a long silence, Jocelyn tried to speak. "Oh, dear . . . dear Amanda . . . your father—"

Her voice broke in a choke.

"I know, Mother . . ." whispered Amanda, "I know."

Again it was quiet. Gradually they parted.

Catharine now ran to join them, and the embrace and tears were renewed. When such heights of joy intermingled with such depths of grief, there was nothing to do but weep.

Mother and daughters began walking toward the entry of the house.

The carriage had pulled in front of the door and the driver was now unloading Amanda's things. There were only two or three boxes besides two suitcases, containing the few things she had stored with the Pankhursts and at Cousin Martha's which Timothy had retrieved for her before putting her on the train that same morning. It was obviously more than a mere visit of a day or two would account for.

"But . . . but what are those boxes," said Jocelyn, "and what is that man about?"

"It's everything I have, Mother," replied Amanda. "I've come home this time to stay. That is . . . if I may."

"Oh, Amanda," exclaimed her mother, "Catharine and I are so glad to have you back. Now more than ever. This has always been your home."

"I know, Mother," replied Amanda. "I think at last I finally realize that this has been my home all along."

110

Glimmers

$\mathcal{I}$t was not until some time had passed, and they were having tea together, that the subject of Bobby arose. Now for the first time did Amanda become aware that there was yet a third beloved Heathersleigh man she would never see again. The realization stung her heart anew and deepened her grief that she had delayed her homecoming so long. In the midst of fresh tears, Amanda thought of Maggie, and knew she must see her without delay.

In less than thirty minutes the three Rutherford women were on their way to the cottage for a visit.

"I'm surprised you haven't widened this path to Maggie's so a car could make the drive," said Amanda as they rode along the well-worn carriage track.

"Actually," replied Jocelyn, "your father considered that very thing." She paused, and the quiet was broken only by the steady *clomp-clomp-clomp* of the single horse ahead of them. "But he decided it would take something away from the wood and the setting of the cottage by assaulting it with the disruptive sounds and smells of an automobile."

Having no idea they were on their way to see her, Maggie, meanwhile, was on her knees in the middle of her garden. As if stimulated yet the more by Amanda's homecoming, though she yet knew nothing of it, her earlier agitation had heightened as the day progressed. Her thoughts had come to gather about a time several months earlier when she had risen from a sound sleep with her Bobby's words about a hidden legacy in her brain, and now in her mind she relived the discovery she had made that night.

Whether Maggie had read every word in this Bible was doubtful. Some of the law and history books of the Old Testament had never infected her with particular interest. Theologians might find meaning in the lists of names and tassels and cords on the tabernacle, parbars westward or killings of bulls for the altar. Her interests had always been along more practical lines.

But of one thing she was sure—she *had* read every word of the New Testament. And the Gospels more times than she could count. She had pored over every word of them, especially the words from the mouth of the Savior himself. And now on this night she paused again here, as she had many times, in the eleventh chapter of Mark's Gospel to ponder the words underlined by her grandmother, in the Bible her own mother, Maggie's great-grandmother, had given her.

"To you is given to understand the mystery of the kingdom. . . ."

There were the words, faint now with the passing of years, added in the margin in her grandmother's own hand—words as familiar to her as this Bible itself. She had seen the brief note most of her life, thinking it merely a reference to the importance of the verse. She had tried to impress that importance on young Amanda one time long ago right here in this very cottage whose origins and history were now on her mind.

She read the words over again, then a third time, puzzling over the strange handwritten annotation.

There is a mystery, her grandmother had written in the margin, *and the key is closer than you think. The key . . . the key . . . find the key and unlock the mystery.*

Suddenly the words jumped out at Maggie with new meaning she had never seen.

Might this mean what she was now thinking! Was the late hour and silence of the night playing tricks on her brain!

A key!

How could she not have made the connection before now?

There was a small, old, peculiar key that had been kicking around her entire life in the drawer of the secretary. No one knew what it was for.

Could its purpose be connected to her grandmother's words!

Below the note had been added another reference, even tinier.

All it said was "Genesis 25:31–33."

Why had she not investigated it before? thought Maggie.

What did it matter—she would do so now!

Quickly she flipped back to the halfway point of the sacred volume's first book, scanned down the heavily underlined and annotated page, which also must have been among her grandmother's favorites, judging from the use the text had received. Her eyes stopped on the thirty-first verse.

"And Jacob said," she read, "Sell me this day thy birthright. And Esau said, Behold, I am at the point to die: and what profit shall this birthright do to me? And Jacob said, Swear to me this day; and he sware unto him: and he sold his birthright unto Jacob."

What could it mean? thought Maggie.

What birthright?

What had her grandmother been trying to convey? Were her marginal notes a cryptic message to someone in the future about this key . . . a mystery . . . a birthright?

Who were Jacob and Esau?

Again Maggie flipped back to the Gospel of Mark. There were the strange words again.

Find the key and unlock the mystery . . . Genesis 25:31–33

Suddenly her mind began racing feverishly.

Could what had just occurred to her really be possible?

The key . . . the mystery . . . the sale of the birthright.

The fantastic thought was so incredible that for a moment she sat reeling in disbelief.

Maggie rose, set her Bible aside, and walked to the ancient secretary, built, as her mother had told her, by her grandfather, Maggie's own great-grandfather. As she approached, she eyed it with eyes alive to sudden new possibilities.

With trembling hand she lowered the lid to the secretary portion. Above the desk was a small nine-inch-wide drawer. Carefully now she pulled it out. The drawer was small, only four or five inches deep. Inside her eyes now fell on the key she had seen resting there all her life.

"What is it for?" she remembered asking her own mother.

"Something about the secretary, I think, dear," Mrs. Crawford had replied. "My mother used to speak mysteriously about it, but

I never saw a lock anywhere about the cabinet, and never knew what it was for."

"But if Grandmother said—"

"She was old by then, Maggie dear. She may have been mistaken."

And there the key had lain all these years.

Maggie now removed it and turned it over slowly in her fingers. A tingle went through her. Something was here, she was sure of it.

Find the key and unlock the mystery. . . .

She was now convinced that the words her grandmother had written carried a meaning underlying that of the Scripture itself.

What mystery could this key be meant to unlock?

◆ ◆ ◆

Suddenly sounds interrupted Maggie's reminiscences. Her reflections were cut short as she glanced up to see a familiar carriage approaching along the lane through the wood.

111
Grandma Maggie's Embrace

◆◆◆

*T*he moment Maggie saw her visitors, she stood up in the midst of her garden. When she realized Amanda was with them, she began nodding to herself. *"I should have known it, Lord,"* she said quietly. *"Now I know what you were saying this morning. I don't know why it wasn't the first thing to come to my mind. I suppose I'm getting a bit thickheaded in my old age."*

She walked forward, tears already on their way. Again Amanda leapt from the carriage before it had stopped and ran forward. Amanda went straight to her arms and was swallowed in the grandmotherly embrace.

"I am so sorry about Bobby," said Amanda softly. "I only learned of it a short while ago."

"My season of heartbreak is past," said Maggie. "I am now able to rejoice that the dear man's in his new home. So don't be sad for me.—Oh," she said, now stepping back to arm's length as she held Amanda's shoulders and gazed upon her, "just look at you. It so gladdens my heart to see you, Amanda dear! I have prayed for you night and day all these years."

"I know you have, Maggie," said Amanda, "and for the first time in my life I can tell you how appreciative I am that you and dear Bobby didn't give up praying for me. I was very stubborn, but I am finally home. Thanks to the prayers of all of you who kept loving me."

Catharine and Jocelyn now came forward, and additional greetings and hugs, kisses and tears innumerable followed.

"Oh, but my heart is sore for the three of you," said Maggie, looking at each of her visitors with such depths of compassion. "My Bobby lived a full life and was ready to go, but poor Master Charles and Master George—"

Maggie's voice caught in her throat. The three gathered around her, the bereaved offering comfort to their friend. After a few tearful moments in a fourway embrace on the edge of Maggie's garden, they gradually moved apart. Then at last did a few smiles slowly begin to brighten the Heathersleigh landscape.

"Come in ... come in," said Maggie. "We'll have some tea. I want to hear all about my dear Amanda. I can hardly believe you are actually here, my dear! You have grown into a lovely woman indeed."

The smile on Amanda's face, and accompanying tears, was so different than any expression Maggie had seen on her countenance before. Amanda appeared years older, and, as much as might be said under these painful circumstances, more at peace with herself than Maggie had seen her.

Thirty minutes later, as Jocelyn sat watching Maggie, Amanda, and Catharine talking together around Maggie's kitchen table for the first time ever like grandmother and two grown-up granddaughters, she quietly took in the features of her two daughters.

Maggie was right, thought Jocelyn—Amanda was indeed a *woman* now. The eyes of her motherhood could hardly fathom it. Though Catharine was larger than all three of them, at twenty she still displayed the signs of youth. Her animated gestures and boisterous laugh and infectious energy curiously reminded Jocelyn of Amanda as a girl. How strange, yet how marvelous, Jocelyn thought, that in a way they had reversed personalities. Now it was Amanda quietly watching, listening, and absorbing, while Catharine chattered freely away. It was Amanda who sat with face slowly moving back and forth, smiling and responding, yet more reluctant to speak than before, taking it all in with the eyes and ears of mature adulthood.

Amanda's face had thinned, and both high cheekbones and jaw were more pronounced, lips, even in this difficult time, more inclined upward toward a smile than in past years, and evenly spaced white teeth not bashful to reveal themselves. The overall effect was of a woman's not a girl's face, and a pretty one, thought Jocelyn, thin and— strange as it was to think it—peaceful. Amanda's brown hair, lightly curled, was shorter than her mother remembered it, framing a full forehead, whose lines revealed thought and intelligence at last pointed in the right directions. She looked out upon the world from green eyes that seemed somehow larger than before, and more perceptive and awake, as if searching for meaning. They bore just the hint of a few lines at their edges, showing that youth was giving way to maturity, lines that may have come to her eyes four or five years ahead of their time, but whose pain would do its work and thus serve her character well. She walked slowly now, not always rushing ahead, even hanging a step or two behind Catharine, displaying a new reticence of nature that became her with grace.

Jocelyn could hardly prevent tears at the sight. She had never known whether to hope for such a day, and now here it was. Her reverie was interrupted by the sounds of Amanda's voice.

"As I see the two of you," said Amanda to Catharine and Maggie, "talking about so many things and such good friends, I realize how much I have missed out on by being away all these years. I only wish . . ."

Her voice faltered. She stopped and looked away.

"Don't fret, my dear," said Maggie, reaching out and placing a warm hand on top of Amanda's. "The Scriptures say that the Lord will return to us the years the locusts have eaten. I believe he will give those years back to you as well."

"But—"

"Yes, I know we've suffered our losses. And our earthly eyes cannot see how good can come of it or how those years can possibly be restored. But the Lord will see to all that too."

Dusk had begun to descend as Jocelyn and her two daughters rode back to the Hall several hours later. They had not been back for long when Timothy telephoned, saying he would be out to Devon the next day.

112

Mother and Daughter

◆ ◆ ◆

*T*hat evening, spirits at the Hall were subdued.

It had been a long day. Even the ride out to the cottage, in its own way, had wearied their hearts. Amanda especially had a myriad of new emotions to face. The realization that Bobby McFee was gone, and that she had not known it, added an extra weight to the burden she bore concerning father and brother. As the evening progressed, she grew especially quiet.

"How are you, my dear," said Jocelyn, "—tired?"

"I am, Mother. And very drained," replied Amanda with a thin smile. "This was a very hard day for me."

"I know," nodded Jocelyn. "I am tired too. We have all been through a great deal."

A peculiar look came over Amanda's face. She seemed to be trying to say something.

"I was ... I'm sorry ..." she faltered.

"What is it?" said Jocelyn.

"I'm so sorry—but I was afraid to come home. I ... didn't know if you would—"

She began to cry.

Jocelyn was on her feet, sat down next to Amanda on the couch, and had her in her arms in seconds.

"I know it must have been one of the most difficult things you have ever done," whispered her mother softly. "But I am so glad you did ... if ever we need to be together, it is now."

"And with Daddy—I feel so awful ... so guilty ... I don't know if I will ever be able—"

Amanda's voice broke.

Jocelyn held her, gently stroking her hair and patting her softly on back and shoulders. On the other side of the room, Catharine quietly rose and glided out, sensing again the need for the two of them to be alone.

It was for Jocelyn a moment of healing almost greater than anything the day had already contained. To hold her daughter again, and to have her at peace, able to receive her comforting embrace without twisting and squirming away, was a privilege she had not allowed herself to imagine she would ever experience. It lasted but a few seconds, but Jocelyn thought she had never felt such inner contentment as in those precious moments, such that she almost briefly forgot that Charles and George were gone.

For several long, precious moments Amanda allowed herself to weep in her mother's arms, more relaxed and at peace than she had ever been in Jocelyn's embrace. It felt so good to let her mother hold her.

Slowly Amanda sat back away, wiped her eyes, and smiled.

"Thank you, Mother. I am just very, very tired," she said. "I think maybe I need some time alone ... and then a good long sound night's sleep."

"You are home, Amanda dear. Your room is still as you left it. However you can be comfortable, whatever you want to do … I want you to feel that … I think you know what I am trying to say—this is your home too."

"I know, Mother—I realize it now … thank you."

"Good night, my dear. We'll have a good big breakfast together in the morning."

Amanda stood but hesitated a moment as she gazed into her mother's eyes.

"I love you, Mother."

Jocelyn's eyes filled.

"Thank you so much," Amanda went on, "for being the mother you have been to me … thank you for everything. I am so sorry I didn't see all you did for me, and all you have been for me sooner."

"We all have to grow, Amanda," replied Jocelyn tenderly. "I have had to grow myself. Perhaps now we can begin growing together. I love you, my dear."

Amanda smiled again, then turned and walked toward the stairs. Jocelyn watched her go, then turned back into the sitting room, found her chair again, sat down, and wept freely.

113

Going Home to the Father

*A*manda climbed the stairs to her former room.

How much the same it looked … yet how very different. How transformed did the eyes of adulthood make all the familiar sights of her childhood, at once smaller yet somehow larger, so poignantly and nostalgically imbued with new meaning.

As she went Amanda remembered her talk with Timothy about going home to her fathers. She had arisen and gone to one father's house, though as Timothy had said, it was her mother's arms that had received her. Going to her other Father would be equally difficult.

Amanda sat down on her bed. A telegram had come earlier in the day, informing them that the memorial for the men of the *Dauntless* had been scheduled for Thursday. The weight of what had happened suddenly came back upon her with renewed force. Tears again filled her eyes, and she wondered how there could be any left. It seemed by now the well would have run dry.

How long she sat motionless, numb, stricken with sorrowful contrition, Amanda didn't know. Gradually words from yesterday's sermon crept into her consciousness.

The crying need of our time . . . is intimacy with God, our Father . . .

All her life she had kept God at arm's length. If intimacy was the highest goal, thought Amanda, she had certainly failed to reach it. She had not let him get close, or anyone else for that matter. She had had a few friends, but none of particular significance or permanency. Where were they now? And in those most important relationships of all—with her father and mother and with God himself—she had done all she could to build up walls to *prevent* intimacy.

The great invisible enemy of God's highest purposes . . . prideful independence of heart . . . I am my own.

He might as well have been talking straight to her, thought Amanda. Being her own, being answerable to no one—all her life that very drive had been her sole creed. Now Sister Hope's words mingled with those she had heard from Timothy's mouth, which she now knew were her own father's.

Laying down the right of self-rule is the business of life—the only business of life. To learn this one lesson is what we are here for.

Had she ever even *thought* of such a thing—placing into *another's* hands the right to make a decision on her behalf? She knew the answer well enough. She had never consulted or considered anyone but herself, neither her father nor mother nor God. She had endured parental oversight as a teenager only so long as she absolutely had to. The moment an opportunity had presented itself to escape from it . . . she had turned her back on Heathersleigh.

Until today. Now here she was back home, in the room of her childhood. And what had all those years accomplished? They had robbed her of some of the most precious years she might have enjoyed with these people she loved.

Did she want to continue being her *own*? Could she look deeply into her heart? Did she finally have courage now to do what she could not do at the chalet?

Yes, Amanda said to herself.

She *would* probe, whatever she found, however it may hurt to be honest with herself. She was at last ready to admit what she had been.

Slowly Amanda got down on her knees. Beside her bed, on the very floor where she had once ranted and fussed with how she thought she hated life at Heathersleigh, she began to pray.

"Oh, God," she said softly, *"I am so sorry for seeking only my own will. I am sorry for not learning what my mother and father tried to teach me. All my life I did nothing but put myself first.*

"I am so sorry," Amanda repeated, weeping freely.

"I don't want to live that way any longer, Lord," she went on, praying softly through her repentant and healing tears. *"I want the intimacy Daddy spoke of in that sermon. I am sorry for thinking I could rule my own life. Forgive me. Show me how to be close to you. Help me ... I want to call you my Father."*

At the word, Amanda broke down and sobbed. It was some time before she could continue.

"Oh, God!" she struggled at length, *"forgive my blindness toward my father. Teach me to know both you as my heavenly Father and him as a father whom I now love. Please don't let it be too late in some way for me to be a good daughter.*

"At last I truly want a Father," Amanda continued. *"I am ready to become a child, the right kind now, if you will help me, if you will show me how. Teach me to become my daddy's little girl, and yours too. I think I am finally ready to be the person you want me to be."*

Amanda's prayers fell silent. Slowly she began to breathe more easily. When she continued, her voice was calm and deliberate.

"Take me, Lord," she said, *"—take me as I am. I want to give myself to you completely. Take away my independent spirit. If there is any good thing in me, anything you can make use of, please do so ... and make me your daughter."*

114
Plymouth Memorial

$\mathcal{T}$imothy arrived by train at Milverscombe on Tuesday morning. He had arranged for a supply minister, a student at Highbury Theological College, for the following Sunday. He was therefore able to remain with them through the weekend.

Early Thursday morning, he accompanied mother and daughters into Plymouth by train for the memorial for the men lost on the *Dauntless*.

"I cannot tell you how grateful I am to have you along, Timothy," said Jocelyn as they rode south through the Devon countryside to the coast. "I am not sure I could do this alone. I always depended on Charles, perhaps more than I realized, to protect me from the pressures and stresses of the outside world. With him gone, it is so good to have a dear brother with us."

"You will learn to be strong in your own right, Jocelyn," Timothy replied. "You are a strong woman. You have not perhaps till now had to rely on that strength. But believe me, speaking as one who has watched you through the years, you will rise to the task. You are much stronger than I think you have any idea. Charles contributed to that, no doubt. But I have the feeling you have gained more spiritual muscle through the years than you know."

"Timothy is right, Mother," said Catharine, "isn't he, Amanda? We can all see your strength. Daddy saw it too."

Jocelyn smiled. "You are both dears," she said. "But I cannot help being afraid, Timothy," she added, turning toward him again.

"Of what?" he asked.

"Of the future without Charles."

"You will be strong, Jocelyn. You have two fine daughters to help you. And you may call on me whenever you need me."

"As much as I cannot imagine the future without Charles, it would

383

be incomprehensibly worse without you. You have been a good friend to our family."

"As your family has been to me," replied Timothy. "You *are* my family . . . I think you know that."

Jocelyn smiled and nodded.

They arrived in Plymouth, were met at the station by an escort from the Royal Navy, and were taken by automobile to the naval parade grounds. There they went through the ceremony stoically, all dressed in black, the London minister now taking the place of an elder brother to the small clan of Rutherford women. Jocelyn stood somber and silent on Timothy's right and Amanda next to her, with Catharine on Timothy's left. Jocelyn's face was veiled. The two girls wore hats.

First Lord of the Admiralty Winston Churchill rose to speak. Partway through his remarks, he singled out Commander Charles Rutherford for special commendation. Though they remained steady, none of the three could prevent a flow of tears at hearing their husband and father honored in front of so many.

Immediately when the ceremony was concluded, many well-wishers made their way forward to shake hands and quietly express their sympathies. Jocelyn pulled back her veil, wiped her eyes, and did her best to make herself presentable to the public. With Charles gone, she knew duty required her to stand tall and proud in his place. She was far less conscious of her birthmark than she had probably ever been at a public gathering in her life.

Lieutenant Langham greeted Amanda and shook hands with Timothy.

"Lieutenant Langham," said Amanda, "I would like you to meet my mother, Lady Jocelyn Rutherford—"

"Lady Jocelyn," nodded Langham, holding his naval hat in his left hand and shaking hers with his right, "I am extremely sorry."

"Thank you, Lieutenant."

"—and my sister Catharine," Amanda went on, moving to Catharine.

"My pleasure, Miss Rutherford," he said, now shaking her hand.

"Thank you," replied Catharine. "I am happy to meet you, Lieutenant."

As the two spoke together briefly, Jocelyn noticed a man standing a few paces behind Lieutenant Langham in the background. He also wore the dress uniform of a naval officer, though with what appeared a large head bandage partially protruding beneath his hat. He appeared waiting for an opportunity to come forward and pay his respects. When Lieutenant Langham finally moved away, he came forward. Face and eyes were both red.

"Mrs. Rutherford," he said, clearly struggling to speak, "you do not know me, but I was acquainted with both your husband and your son. My name is Richard Forbes. Lieutenant Forbes to your son—I was his squadron leader."

He paused to take a deep breath, still not finding it easy to continue.

"Your son," he went on, "was the ablest and most dependable cadet in all my unit."

"Thank you, Lieutenant," smiled Jocelyn. "That is very kind of you."

"I am afraid I was occasionally a little hard on him at first. But he showed himself a man through it."

Again Forbes paused, this time more lengthily.

"I only know what I have to tell you now," he went on, "from others who saw it, because I was unconscious. I would have gone down with the ship . . . actually, I *should* have gone down. I was as good as dead. But apparently your son carried me from the torpedo room where I had fallen and injured my head—"

He gestured briefly toward the bandage.

"—he carried me on his shoulders up onto the deck and dumped me in one of the lifeboats. Your son saved my life, Mrs. Rutherford. I am sorrier than I can tell you for what happened. Both George and your husband were among the finest men I have ever known."

Amanda had been listening intently to the conversation. "Why didn't George get in the lifeboat too?" she asked.

"He turned and ran back to the middle of the ship," replied Forbes. "Even though it was obvious we were sinking, and every other man was running frantically *up* the stairs for the deck, George ran toward the stairs and flew straight *down*. One of the men told me he heard him call out as he disappeared, 'I'm going back for my father!'"

At the words, Jocelyn burst into a sob. But almost as quickly she recovered herself.

"I'm sorry, Lieutenant Forbes," she said, trying to smile. "For a moment . . . it was like hearing George himself again. That is exactly what he would have done. Thank you so much for telling us."

Lieutenant Forbes nodded to each of the three, then turned and left them.

By now Churchill himself had managed to work his way toward them from the front, where he and a few other dignitaries had been sitting.

"Lady Jocelyn," he intoned somberly, "let me again express my own deep personal condolences."

"Thank you very much, Mr. Churchill."

"Has your daughter told you that it is likely she will receive a commendation from the prime minister?" he asked, glancing toward Amanda.

"No, actually," replied Jocelyn, turning toward Amanda with surprise. "She hasn't said a word of it."

"Well then, I shall let her tell you about it."

The First Lord of the Admiralty then greeted both Timothy and Amanda with handshakes and a few words. Amanda introduced him to Catharine.

"I am afraid I have some unfortunate news for you," said Churchill, turning and speaking once again to Amanda. "We sent a Coast Guard ship down from Whitby to Hawsker. But by the time they arrived it seems our friends had disappeared without a trace. All that was left was the dinghy and an old Irishman making back for the lighthouse. But they could get nothing out of him. We're still trying to decide what to do with him. We don't know whether he was part of it all or not. We've shut down the operation at the lighthouse, of course. But I'm afraid the fellow Halifax as well as Barclay and the others are still at large."

Amanda shuddered at the thought.

"I wouldn't worry if I were you. I'm sure they made no landfall in England. There must have been a U-boat out there waiting for them. But under the circumstances, if you know what I mean, I felt you needed to be informed."

"Yes . . . yes, thank you for telling me."

As Churchill paid his final respects to Jocelyn and then ambled away to speak to some of the other bereaved families, Catharine whispered to her mother and sister, "Uh-oh, don't look now . . . brace yourselves!"

Shuffling toward them, somewhat nervously it seemed, were three figures attired in black from head to toe, a plump teary-eyed woman in billowy dress of ambiguous cut, flanked by two three-piece-suited businessmen of somber countenance. Seeing that they had been noticed, Martha Rutherford now flowed toward them in a gush of tears and chiffon and the smell of lilac and outstretched fleshy arms. She went straight to Jocelyn and surrounded her in an undulating embrace, while the two men of her entourage approached more stiffly behind her, then took up stoic positions at attention.

"Jocelyn . . . Jocelyn, my dear," said Martha in something like a tearful wail, "I am so sorry! You poor dear—what you must have been through. Oh, and Catharine . . . Amanda," she added, hugging each of them in turn. She gave Amanda an extra squeeze, then stepped back with a sad, and, Amanda thought, lonely smile. "It is so good to see you again, Amanda."

"And you, Cousin Martha," Amanda replied.

"I've missed you, dear."

"I know . . . I am sorry," began Amanda. "I left the country, as you know, with Mrs. Thorndike, and then—"

"No need to explain, my dear," said Martha kindly. "I understand that things have been difficult for you. We shall catch up together again one day."

"Yes . . . yes, I would like that, Cousin Martha."

"You shall all come into London and be my guests . . . when you're ready, of course," she added, glancing a bit nervously toward Jocelyn and Catharine, with whom she did not feel quite so intimate yet. Suddenly it dawned on her that perhaps she had overstepped propriety and been too forward with Jocelyn.

"Thank you, Martha," smiled Jocelyn. "That is most gracious of you. We shall, I promise."

At first opportunity, Gifford oiled forward and proceeded to greet the members of his late first cousin's family, cordially but with formality, mumbling a few somber condolences but obviously feeling awkward under the circumstances of the setting.

Geoffrey, meanwhile, had been standing expressionless behind his parents. At first sight of him, Amanda thought she detected a strange light in his face, as if he was trying to catch her eyes. Her first impulse was to look away, thinking he must still be harboring the kind of affections for her that had so repulsed her before. As she observed him, however, the more she realized the odd expression signified something else. She could not put her finger on what exactly. But there could be no doubt that his demeanor was much improved.

He now shuffled toward them as his father stepped back.

"Cousin Jocelyn," he said, "I really am sorry. I don't know what else to say."

"Thank you, Geoffrey. You are very kind."

He nodded with a nervous smile toward both Catharine and Amanda.

"Hello, Amanda . . . Catharine."

"Hello, Geoffrey," returned Amanda. Without further comment, he now slipped in close beside her, saying nothing but apparently listening with interest to the continuing conversation between their two mothers.

"I appreciate all you did for Amanda when she was in the city . . ." Amanda heard her mother say. She was too distracted, however, by Geoffrey's proximity to pay much attention.

Suddenly close at her side almost in the folds of her dress itself, she felt her cousin take her hand. Blood rushed to her head and for a moment, Amanda's old anger flared to the surface. She turned her face quickly toward him, though remained conscious of not making a scene.

"Geoffrey, what are you—" she exclaimed in a loud whisper.

His grip clamped tightly around her hand, almost crushing it into silence. Still he stared straight ahead, purposefully refusing to look in her direction. Amanda's eyes continued to stare at him in outrage.

The next instant Geoffrey's fingers began fidgeting oddly. Then she felt something else against the skin of her palm, something hard and metallic. Still Geoffrey made no sound, nor so much as hinted by his expression that he was aware of anything out of the ordinary.

Just as suddenly as he had taken it, he now released Amanda's hand and calmly moved away. Amanda clutched her own fingers around whatever it was he had just secretly given her. Geoffrey walked across the ground, taking his place again in the vicinity of his father.

The moment she could do so without calling attention to the fact, Amanda hurried a quick peek down beside her and opened her hand.

The keys! The very same keys he had taken from the tower of Heathersleigh Hall!

But why such stealth just to give them back?

Amanda glanced up again. One look at Cousin Gifford's face told her clearly enough. He obviously was not party to what Geoffrey had just done.

"If there is anything we can do," Cousin Martha was saying.

"Thank you, Martha," returned Jocelyn. "That is very kind."

But Amanda was hardly listening. Geoffrey was staring straight toward her.

She nodded her acknowledgment of the transaction with an imperceptible tilt of the head, though with bewildered expression. Geoffrey returned the nod so slightly that only she saw it, then followed it with the hint of a smile.

It was a smile, Amanda thought—perhaps the first such expression she had ever seen on his face—that seemed to contain no motive or guile. Maybe he too had changed in the year since she had seen him, she thought. Their eyes held each other's in a strange and rare moment of shared understanding. It reminded her of the drive they had taken together, which had been almost pleasant. Slowly Amanda returned his smile, then nodded slightly again.

Gradually the tide of well-wishers ebbed and flowed, and soon Geoffrey and his father were engaged in conversation with someone else.

"He gives me the creeps," whispered Catharine at Amanda's side while Martha and Jocelyn continued to talk.

"Who?" said Amanda.

"Cousin Geoffrey, who else?"

"He's not so bad," mused Amanda, whom the encounter had made curiously pensive.

"I hope they're not waiting for an invitation to come back to Heathersleigh," whispered Catharine again, this time directly into Amanda's ear. "I can see Mother thinking about it already."

The hint of a smile creased Amanda's lips.

"That's exactly what they're waiting for," Catharine went on softly. "Look at Cousin Gifford—can't you tell, glancing back over at Mother and Martha every so often. He's just waiting for a chance to snoop around without Daddy there."

"That's terrible, Catharine," whispered Amanda, though she could not help being amused. "You're so cynical."

"Don't do it, Mother," whispered Catharine, coaching her mum from afar.

"Catharine, stop it!" whispered Amanda in return. "You're going to make me start laughing. Besides, they'll hear you."

"But I can see her weakening. Look how she and Cousin Martha are chatting away. I can see it in Martha's face. She can almost taste Sarah's tea cakes.—M - o - t - h - e - r !" whispered Catharine in a loud exhale.

A brief snicker escaped Amanda's lips. She tried to recover herself, throwing Catharine a look of silent command, to which Catharine replied with an equally silent, *What did I do?*

"Oh-oh, here comes Geoffrey again. Run, Amanda."

"Catharine!" laughed Amanda, unable to help herself. "You are going to get us all in trouble. Look, he's just going over to talk to someone else."

Geoffrey was indeed sauntering away from the small family reunion. Amanda did not speak to him again that day.

As Martha eventually moved away in the direction of husband and son, Jocelyn's younger sister, Edlyn, and her husband, Hugh, approached. Feeling it their duty to attend, they came forward with an understandable awkwardness, for the interview was bound to be a difficult one.

Jocelyn's heart both sank and roused itself in indignation as she saw them approach. After the cruel letter Hugh had written about Charles, how could any word of sympathy about his death now carry much meaning?

As the Wildecott-Brownes approached she managed to catch Timothy's eye in silent plea. He knew her meaning in an instant and was at her side the next.

"Edlyn, hello," said Jocelyn as graciously as she was able. "How good of you to make the effort to come all this way."

The two sisters hugged without touching.

"We're very sorry, Jocelyn dear."

"Thank you.—Hugh," she said, nodding to her brother-in-law at Edlyn's side.

"Our sympathies, Jocelyn," he said.

Stiff handshakes passed between aunt and uncle and the youngest Rutherford daughter, who was less inclined even than her mother to extend forgiveness. Amanda, however, who knew nothing of the letter and had seen neither aunt nor uncle since the dinner at their home some two years earlier, greeted both warmly.

"Timothy," said Jocelyn, turning to her side, "I would like you to meet my sister and her husband—Hugh and Edlyn Wildecott-Browne.

Hugh and Edlyn, may I present Rev. Timothy Diggorsfeld."

Handshakes followed.

"Hugh, you may remember," Jocelyn went on to Timothy, "wrote me that very interesting letter two years ago—the one that Charles and I shared with you, and asked you to help us understand."

"What letter was this, Hugh?" said Edlyn, glancing toward her husband.

A series of nervous throat-clearings and a slight reddening of neck and cheeks accompanied the religious solicitor's attempt to explain the communication whose content he had never divulged to his wife.

"Yes, a very interesting letter indeed," said Timothy, moving purposefully in Hugh's direction. "It was a letter, if I may say, that I found very difficult to understand as well. I think it is time you and I had a serious talk, Mr. Wildecott-Browne."

Timothy led the man off across the grounds in such a way as to leave Hugh very little alternative but to accompany him. What passed between them neither man ever revealed to another soul. But its result was another letter to Jocelyn some months later, this time of very different tone, expressing contrite apology for what he had done earlier and for so completely misunderstanding the facts of the situation. By that time he and Timothy had begun meeting once a month for lunch.

Before the year was out, Mr. Wildecott-Browne had resigned his church deaconship so that he and his wife might become regular attendees of services at New Hope Chapel on Bloomsbury Way.

115

Healing and Looking Forward
◆ ◆ ◆

*T*he party of travelers arrived back at Heathersleigh Hall about five that afternoon. To Catharine's relief, the return trip was made *without* accompanying relatives from London.

"Catharine, you were positively terrible!" said Amanda on the train. "You almost made me laugh in front of Geoffrey."

"What was this, girls?" asked Jocelyn.

"Nothing, Mother," Catharine said. "I was just afraid you were going to invite our dear London relatives back to the Hall."

"Actually, I wondered if I ought to," Jocelyn replied. "But I simply didn't have the heart to face guests ... not now, not after the service. I wanted to be alone with my family. I hope they were not offended."

"If I know Cousin Gifford," said Catharine, "he was very offended, and is probably stewing about it right now."

"They're really not all so bad," said Amanda, though she could not help laughing a little to hear Catharine carry on. She never realized how funny her sister could be. "They were very kind to me in London, in their own way. Of course Geoffrey proposed to me, and *that* was beyond the bounds."

"Geoffrey proposed to you!" exclaimed Catharine. "Cousin Geoffrey ... that slimy weasel!"

Now even Jocelyn and Timothy could not help laughing.

"He had a horrid big diamond ring and everything. I'll admit, I wasn't particularly gracious in my response," said Amanda.

Suddenly she paused, and a sad smile of irony passed across her face.

"Although," she went on after a moment, "who knows how different my life might be if I *had* accepted? Even marriage to Geoffrey would have been better than the fix I got myself into in Vienna. And he did slip me these when his father wasn't looking."

She held up the brass ring with two keys dangling from it.

"What—you mean he gave them to you today?" Catharine said. "When?"

"When we were talking after the ceremony."

"What are they?" asked Jocelyn, puzzled.

"The keys from up in the old tower," Amanda replied. "I didn't know he had them until he showed them to me—it was probably three years ago. He took them from here—that time they were visiting at Heathersleigh, remember, when he and I went up to the tower when the rest of you were talking downstairs. I'm afraid I was rather mean to him, and I guess he thought he would get even by taking the keys."

"And he gave them back to you today—how peculiar," said Jocelyn. "What did he say?"

"Not a word, Mother. And I didn't ask. I have the feeling he did it behind his father's back."

"I bet Cousin Gifford put him up to taking them in the first place," said Catharine.

Maggie was at the Hall waiting for them when they returned. Along with Sarah, the two of them had prepared a sumptuous tea for the weary mother, daughters, and London minister.

As they sat with cups in hand later that evening talking casually, gradually the sense began to envelop all five, including Maggie, that a threshold had been crossed, that with the service behind them a new season of healing and regeneration had begun.

It was clear to all that a great change had come over Amanda. Each one saw it. The intrusive, importune personality they had been acquainted with since her childhood had remarkably begun to give way to a calm, even reticent, demeanor. More often now she waited for others to speak, listening, absorbing, thinking, reflecting on what was being said around her rather than blurting out whatever came into her mind. And as she listened, it was clear her ears were open to the flow of conversation, eager to learn, to hear what others thought . . . hungry to glean from them. Her mother and sister, who had not been with Amanda for eight years, occasionally glanced at each other. Though Amanda had now been home for four days, they still did not know what to make of this soft-spoken young lady in their midst.

That same evening, not to monopolize the conversation but realizing the importance of doing so, almost confessionally, Amanda began by degrees to fill in the details of her story since leaving Heathersleigh. She spoke softly and humbly, and the telling was not without many tears and interruptions. But she knew that for the healing of her homecoming to be complete, she must open her heart to mother and sister and pastor and allow them to be part both of her pain and her repentance. It nearly broke Jocelyn's heart to listen.

"Obviously it wasn't," said Amanda as she drew to a close after about an hour, "but sometimes I think the whole awful mess I made of the last eight years is almost worth it for the experience of being at the chalet. I didn't realize it at the time, but those dear sisters and their stories, their love for me and acceptance of me, and their complete honesty all played such a part in finally opening my eyes to see myself. Maybe their openness and transparency was, in a sense, a mirror held up to my own face. They were all so *real*. I hardly knew what was happening to me, even though I was right in the midst of it. One of the first things I need to do, once I catch my breath, is write them a very long letter, thanking them."

A quiet smile came over Amanda's face.

"You know, it's funny," she said after a moment. "I can almost feel the spirit of the sisters coming over me right now. I have the feeling they are praying for me. Suddenly it feels good. For so long the idea of being prayed for infuriated me. Why was that, Rev. Diggorsfeld?"

"No doubt it rubbed your rebellion a bit too raw for comfort, as it often does to people in such a frame of mind," replied Timothy. "When one is running from God, one of the things they hate most of all is the thought that another is praying for them."

"Well, I certainly did. All of a sudden I can scarcely believe I was the same person."

Amanda exhaled a long sigh.

"Another reason I need to write that letter," she said, "is to apologize to Sister Hope for some of the things I said.—Oh, how could I have been so mean to so many people!"

Again she began to cry.

"It is so hard not to feel an overwhelming sense of guilt," she moaned, "for everything! For what I said to the sisters, for how I treated Geoffrey . . . for horrid things I said and did to all of you—so many times I can't stand to think of it. I'm so sorry! And especially for Daddy and George. How can I not think that maybe if I had come home sooner, this wouldn't have happened and they might not have died?"

"You are not responsible for their deaths, Amanda," said Timothy.

"But how can I not feel guilty?"

"It is true that if you had come back sooner you might have had the chance to be reconciled in this life. However, I am certain good will come of it, and that God will use it somehow to help others. But as far as what actually happened with the ship, that is a burden you *cannot* carry."

"But I can hardly bear it."

"God is sovereign. This awful war which is consuming the world is certainly much larger than any of us."

"How can I know the difference between what I am supposed to feel, as you say, and not?"

"There are proper guilts we must face and shoulder to some degree all our lives. The Lord uses these to keep us humble and reliant on him. But there are false guilts as well which we are *not* meant to carry. Satan is always trying to mix up the two in our minds and make us carry what we shouldn't, and at the same time tempting us to make excuses for ourselves in those very areas where we are meant to be accountable. Learning to distinguish which is which is the challenge of dealing with guilt. But above all we must remember that nothing we do or do not do can thwart or alter God's ultimate plans or will. As I said, he is sovereign. He is sovereign even in the midst of our sin."

"But how do I live with myself, Rev. Diggorsfeld? How can I face the future? How is it possible for me to face myself?"

"For one thing, young lady," he replied with a smile, "I think you need to start calling me Timothy, like everyone else around here. I gave up the *Reverend* a long time ago under this roof."

Amanda smiled sheepishly.

"All right, I'll try . . . *Timothy.* Though it sounds funny coming from me."

"What would you say to her question, Maggie?" said Timothy. "You have had to face the death of your Bobby. How do you go on?"

"Life is not always a fairy tale," said Maggie. "In this life, the Christian often has to find victory in the midst of heartbreak."

"A good reply!" exclaimed Timothy. "What about you, Jocelyn—how would you say we go on?"

"Isn't that the lesson of the cross," said Jocelyn, "that our ultimate victory comes later?"

"Exactly," rejoined Timothy. "I couldn't have said it better myself. You can always depend on these ladies to give you good advice, Amanda. Let me try to respond to your question about facing the future by saying this," he went on. "This world will always bring suffering because we are sinners, but ultimately all will be reconciled. The cross is the symbol of suffering and death, just as it is the symbol of triumph and victory over the grave. You and your father *will* be restored to each other, Amanda, but in no fairy tale. Rather in the reality of eternity.

"Another lesson of the cross is that sin has consequences. You have to live with that, my dear, learning that portion of its lesson too. I do not like to say such a thing at this time. Yet if you want to know how to go on with your life, what good will it do you for me to speak empty words? So, yes, wrong choices have consequences. You have to face them. One of the consequences for you is that you will not see your father again."

Amanda began to weep. The realization was so bitter she could not stand it.

"But in the midst of those consequences," Timothy went on, "we may focus our eyes on the ultimate victory of eternity. That is the majestic triumph of the cross! We live in this world amid the consequences of sin, while looking toward that final triumphant reconciliation. It is what life as a Christian in this world is all about. And so at the same time as I say what I just did about consequences, I would also tell you that God's forgiveness is so tender that he wants only to wrap his arms of love about you, and hold you, and assure you that life will be good again. The challenge before you will be to somehow appropriate both the Lord's and your father's love and forgiveness.—You know that your father loves you right now, don't you?"

Amanda nodded.

"I know that you will learn to live in that knowledge, in the actual reality of knowing that he is still with you, but in a new way."

A long silence followed. Timothy looked around at the four women, and now addressed each of them.

"I would say the same thing to you all," he said, speaking as the elder statesman of the tiny congregation. "You have all lost your men. Maggie, you your dear Bobby. Jocelyn, Amanda, and Catharine, your dear Charles and George. In a sense you are alone now. God has plans and purposes that often go beyond our sight. The four of you must help each other to stand tall, encouraging and exhorting and leaning upon one another and giving one another strength.

"God has a purpose for each one of you, and for Heathersleigh— yes, both the Hall and the cottage—to fulfill. We cannot see what his purposes are, but I do not believe this is the end for you four, but rather a beginning. Something lies ahead, a new chapter in your lives."

"What kind of something?" asked Catharine.

"I don't know. But I do know that God has given to women a special courage and special strength for such times as these."

"Special strength?" repeated Catharine.

"Of course. In many ways women indeed are the stronger of the two halves of humanity. Not in brute physical strength, but in a host of inner ways where even greater strength is required. Some women never discover those reservoirs within themselves. But God has chosen that the four of you have no alternative. In a way, I am almost excited to see what might lie ahead, for this tragedy that has befallen us indicates in some way, I think, that God has some great thing in store, something he will reveal in time. Whatever it is will grow out of the ashes of your pain, and will flower as the result of the compassion perfected by your suffering."

Jocelyn began quietly to weep as Timothy spoke. Now slowly she rose, went to her room, and returned a minute or two later with the handwritten parchment Catharine had given her.

Timothy began reading. Before he was halfway to the end, his eyes were moist with tears. He continued to read it aloud.

For several long minutes it was quiet as they pondered the words Catharine had been given almost as if the Lord had spoken them himself.

"What you have written here, dear Catharine," Timothy said at length, "is prophetic. I truly believe it represents the Lord's word to the four of you. I believe you will discover that reservoir of the Master's nature together, and that God will use you to carry that discovery into the lives of many others."

He paused for a moment.

"I don't know why he has given you this road to walk," he added. "But as I said, there is a strength in womanhood that sometimes in life has to stand in the lonely places. I will be here to help you. I hope you know that. I will always be here for you. But you four women must join together in prayer and common vision, and discover what it is the Lord has for you now."

116
Milverscombe Remembers

♦ ♦ ♦

*O*n the following Sunday, the old stone church of Milverscombe parish was packed as it had not been except on two or three occasions during its long existence.

"We are going to cut short our regular service from the prayer book this morning," said Vicar Stuart Coleridge, "in order to spend some time remembering our dear friends Charles and George Rutherford.

"Last week, we were all so numb from shock of the news that I must admit I would almost rather have canceled services than go through them as we did, knowing our beloved Lady Jocelyn and her daughter Catharine were grieving and we felt so powerless to extend our love to them. Yet now a week has gone by, and we are pleased that Sir Charles and Lady Jocelyn's older daughter, Amanda, is now with us again. I hope, therefore, that the passage of this time will enable us to put these heartbreaking events into a perspective that will comfort our hearts and allow us to recall these cherished loved ones with joy, asking our Lord to bring a new dawn of hopefulness to our hearts.

"I have asked my good friend and yours, Rev. Timothy Diggorsfeld from London, to preside. Rev. Diggorsfeld needs no introduction, for he has been in our midst on many occasions throughout the years. As uncommon as it may be in other parts of Great Britain for Church of England vicars and dissenting Presbyterian ministers to exchange pulpits from time to time, I hope it will always be considered the norm here, where I and this man—whom I count among my closest spiritual friends and advisors—happen to believe in unity above doctrinal and denominational distinctions. That said, I will now turn the remainder of this morning's service over to Rev. Diggorsfeld."

Timothy came forward, shook hands with the vicar, then stood before the Milverscombe congregation. He remained silent for many long seconds. Finally he drew in a deep breath and began.

"Thank you, Vicar Coleridge," Timothy said. "The occasion that brings us together on this day is a grievous one to our hearts," he went on, "—grievous, I should add, as the world judges it. Though Vicar Coleridge is correct in saying the passage of this week has helped assuage the initial numbness and shock, I must tell you that I remain devastated by what has happened, and sad almost beyond my capacity to endure it. It should not be grievous to us, for *life* has come to these two men, father and son, whom we loved. But it *is* grievous. Who can deny it? We are weak humans, after all, and do not quite yet believe in eternity with all our hearts. We *believe* in it, of course. I do not say we doubt the truth of the resurrection. But we are not yet quite able to base our lives upon the full glory of that belief.

"What can we do, what can we say, to comfort one another? It is at such times that eternity intersects with our weakness, crashes cruelly in upon our earthly senses unbidden. And try as we might, even knowing that at such moments we may possibly catch glimpses of the faint glow of eternity from around the edges of the closed door of our fi-niteness . . . yet we mourn and cannot be comforted, because we are not yet given to see past that door."

Timothy paused, looked across the sea of faces, and tried to smile.

"I believe in eternity," he said at length. "I *do* believe, as I know each of you do. Yet I have wept this week, as have dear Lady Jocelyn and her two lovely daughters, and as I know have all of you. Something tells me I should not weep, that the faint shimmer from beyond the door ought to prevent it. But I did weep. I could not help it. For I am a man, a weak man. I cannot yet behold with clarity what lies beyond the veil we call death."

Again Timothy paused, this time for several long and thoughtful seconds.

"But Charles and George *do* behold it," he went on. "They are there. They are even at this moment bathed in the luminescence of that garden of light of which we are only able to discern hints and faint glows. That door has been opened to them. They have now been privileged to begin their eternal journey. And for that, however deep the aches in our own hearts . . . we ought to be able to rejoice.

"So I am going to ask whether we might this morning, for *their* sake, open the door if not in reality, at least in our imaginations, and rejoice . . . for *them* rather than grieve for ourselves.

"Can we do that, my friends?

"We shall weep together. I know I shall. My tears are not altogether dry. I miss my friends. But may we now weep with joy because eternity has visited us rather than weep for *our* loss?

"It will be difficult. But can we not try to do this together?

"Let us remember our friends as *alive*, as they surely are. Let us take courage to think of them among us and with us in the spirit now, at this very moment . . . smiling and laughing and spreading the goodness of life to those around them as they always did.

"They *are* here! Knowing that, I rejoice in the lives that Charles and George Rutherford lived when they were with us in the flesh. Rejoice with me, rather than mourn, that those lives were not as lengthy as we might have wished. Remember our Lord's words, *'No one who lives and believes in me will ever die.'*

"I think we must ask ourselves, *'Do* we believe the Lord?' He said they would *never* die! I challenge us to be strong to take our Lord's words into our hearts. Let us be strong to *rejoice* together for George and Charles Rutherford. As we do, let us find comfort in those truths about our heavenly Father that undergirded Charles' faith—his assurance that his God was trustworthy and good in all things. Charles believed, as I know George did as well, that God's goodness and trustworthiness extended beyond death.

"Therefore, we may trust God—yes, even trust that God is still good—in the midst of what appears a tragedy. What should be our response to this heartbreak? That God is good. Can we understand how it can be? No . . . but God is still good.

"Charles knew that, and based his life on it. For his sake, I challenge you—and I challenge myself—to take hold of that truth and refuse to let it go. Our hearts are sore . . . *but we know that God is good!*"

Timothy continued for another ten minutes, then opened the floor for brief remembrances of Charles and George from members of the community.

The instant his voice was still, a dozen hands rose into the air. Timothy hardly knew where to begin with the flood that seemed determined to unleash itself.

Never had the church seen such an outpouring of affection for one of its number. English reserve was cast aside for the opportunity to share about one they loved. The testimonials went on for forty minutes. And though tearful, they were remembrances of joy. The spirit of Charles' smiling face did indeed rise above the gathering and infect it with something of the same vibrancy as if he were personally among them.

Amanda sat as one stunned to hear of an aspect of her father's and George's lives to which she had been so oblivious. She almost wondered if they were talking about someone else. Yet through it all, the ring of familiarity was undeniable. She found image after image now coming back to her, as she faintly recalled many of the incidents spoken of, but realizing she had not taken note of their significance at the time.

At last they were dismissed. As Jocelyn and her daughters filed outside, it seemed the whole community clustered about them. Not a single person felt like leaving.

Amanda was introduced to some she did not know, and many she only faintly remembered.

"Amanda, you remember Gresham Mudgley . . ." said her mother. A simply clad man, with an unruly crop of grey hair coming out all around the edges of his cap, and with the faint odor of sheep's wool about him, drew near.

"Why, the girl is grown into a lovely lady," said Mudgley, with a tip of his hat and offering his hand.

"Hello, Mr. Mudgley. It is nice to see you again," replied Amanda with a pleasant smile, shaking the sheepherder's rough offered hand and remembering with a stab of conscience the comment she had once made to her father about him.

"Oh, and I want you to meet Sally Osborne—" said Jocelyn, turning away from Mudgley toward a beaming red-faced woman holding the hand of a chubby three-year-old at her side. "—and this little fellow is her son Hadwin."

"I am happy to meet you, Mrs. Osborne," said Amanda. She knelt down and smiled at the little boy. "Good morning, Hadwin."

As she stood, Amanda now noticed a man at Mrs. Osborne's side holding an exact replica of the same little boy. The look of astonishment on her face was plain to see.

"And this is Andrew Osborne and Gildan," said her mother.

"Hello," said Amanda, glancing back and forth between their two boys.

"—as you can see, Sally and Andrew are the proud parents of twin sons."

"Now I understand," laughed Amanda. "I thought I was seeing double!"

The press of the crowd and the constant greetings and handshakes and smiles almost reminded Amanda of being in London again. She had never been in the midst of such a gathering—so friendly and warm, like a huge family.

As she was turning back and forth between the twins, all at once in the background she saw two familiar figures approaching. But how changed they were!

"Agatha, good morning!" exclaimed Jocelyn.

"Oh, Jocelyn," said the other, hugging her emotionally, "I am so sorry!"

"Thank you, but this has been a good day. It is healing to hear how much Charles was loved.—Amanda, you remember Agatha Blakeley—"

"Yes. Good morning, Mrs. Blakeley."

Amanda swallowed hard as she glanced nervously to the man at her side.

"—and her husband, Rune."

"Hello, Mr. Blakeley," Amanda added, shaking Rune Blakeley's hand.

"Good day to you, Miss Amanda," he returned, then hesitated. He did not move away but shuffled for a few seconds back and forth on his feet. He obviously had something else he wanted to say.

"I don't know if you recollect the day, Miss Amanda," he said after an awkward moment, "when you and your mum was in the village and I'd been treating my Stirling a mite rough, and you ran up in a huff."

Amanda nodded with an embarrassed smile.

"I been wantin' to apologize to you for years for my rudeness that day," he said. "The drink did mighty bad things to me back in them days, and I got your own father and mother to thank for helping me get over it. Many a time your papa sat up most of the night with me. There was times I'd yell at him like I done you. I'm embarrassed to say that I tried to hit him once or twice too, I got so mad. But your papa was a shrewd one. I never could so much as lay a hand on him. I suspect he could have laid me out on the floor with one blow. He was a strong man, and nimble on his feet. But he was always gentle and forgiving, and never held any of that against me. He just kept being patient with me till I got over it. And now here I am, and I got him and your mum to thank. But I was terrible mean to you on that day, Miss Amanda, and it would do this heart of mine a heap of good if you'd say you forgive me for what I said that day."

Amanda's heart was stung by the man's simple apology. His spirit, in the midst of the acknowledgment of his sin, was like that of a child.

"Of course, Mr. Blakeley," Amanda said. "Of course I forgive you. But I should ask the same of you. I was just as insensitive myself, and I'm afraid I said some rather unkind things to my mother about you afterward. I too apologize."

"Think nothing more about it, miss. You were just a child. I was a grown man and should have known better."

"How is Stirling?"

"He's away at university, Miss Amanda—at Oxford," replied Mrs. Blakeley.

"That's wonderful," said Amanda. "I am so happy to hear of it. He must be a grown man by now."

"He still walks with his limp," his mother said, "but he's a good strong lad. He and your brother, George, were the best of friends."

"Your father was always real good to him too," added Rune.

"Tell Stirling hello for me next time you write him, will you please?" said Amanda.

"You could say the same to your sister," replied Agatha. "Stirling and Catharine have been writing since he left."

"Oh, I didn't know that. Just the same, I would appreciate your telling him too."

"We will indeed," Agatha said.

A jab in Amanda's ribs from Catharine turned Amanda again in another direction, where she was now as shocked as her sister to see Gwendolen Powell and her mother walking toward them. They had not seen them during the service.

"Hello, Amanda, Catharine," said Gwendolen, with a pleasant tone and far more gracious expression than Catharine in particular would have given her credit for being able to display. "I am so sorry about your father and George."

"Thank you," Catharine replied.

"I heard you were back, Amanda," Gwendolen said. "It has been a long time. I don't think I would have recognized you."

"Nor I you," Amanda smiled. "Are we both getting to that age where we start talking about the years flying by?"

"I hope not," Gwendolen replied with a laugh. "I do not want to relinquish my youth quite yet."

She paused as she looked momentarily at both girls with an unexpectedly shy expression.

"I . . . I would be happy to have you visit me," she said after a moment. "Anytime."

"Thank you, Gwendolen," said Amanda. "Perhaps we shall ride over this week."

"I would like that very much," rejoined Gwendolen.

"We are all very, very sorry," now said Mrs. Powell, shaking Jocelyn's hand. "Your husband was highly thought of in all of Devon."

"Thank you, Lady Holsworthy, that is very kind of you."

Mother and daughters turned to leave and were soon on their way home.

"What are you doing, Amanda?" said Catharine when they were alone a moment later. "I don't know that I am interested in going to visit Gwendolen Powell."

"Why not?"

"I don't know. I suppose I never cared that much for her. And what if Hubert is around?"

"I thought you told me he was married and getting fat."

"Maybe so, but the idea of visiting Holsworthy Castle is not one I find appealing."

"Can't you tell Gwendolen is lonely?"

"Lonely!" exclaimed Catharine in a loud whisper.

"It is written all over her face, Catharine. She's hungry for friendship—there's nothing so sinister in that. And I think I shall go visit her."

"Well, I'm not so sure."

"Suit yourself," said Amanda, "but I felt sorry for her."

117

A Mystery Revealed

*A*fter the service and greeting time finally broke up, Timothy boarded the train in Milverscombe to return to London. Jocelyn, the two girls, and Maggie climbed into Charles' Peugeot and drove back to Heathersleigh. The three Rutherford women then walked Maggie home to her cottage.

The sun shone warm and bright and they chatted freely as they went, feeling the beginning of a new day in their spirits. Laughter more easily escaped their lips, especially from the two sisters who, in reacquainting themselves as young adult women, were quickly becoming the best of friends. Though Jocelyn's smile remained tinged with sadness, for the first time since the tragedy she found it possible to breathe in deeply of the fresh warm air without reservation.

"This was an extraordinary day," Amanda said as they went. "After the service was over, no one wanted to leave. There was such a wonderful ... I don't know what to call it—such a feeling of oneness, like the whole community was one big family. Was it all because of Daddy and George and people wanting to talk about them?"

"There were a few more present than usual, I think," Jocelyn replied.

"But it is like that every Sunday," added Maggie. "Even when there's not so many."

"Do you mean people staying and visiting? Surely it isn't always like that."

"Oh, but it is," said Catharine. "It's the best part of the week."

"I've never known a church like that before," Amanda said. "Even Rev. Diggorsfeld's—I mean *Timothy's* church in London wasn't. He just got through with his sermon, then everyone shook his hand, filed out of the church, and left. But here everyone was so friendly—I thought it was going to go on all day."

"It was your father's idea," said Jocelyn.

"What was?"

"He's the one who started it. He decided one day that he wasn't going to leave, or let other people go home either, until he had greeted everyone. Before long everyone got into the spirit of it. It has been going on ever since."

They had just come into view of the clearing and the cottage. Suddenly Maggie burst into a labored, ambling run.

"Flora . . . Flora, you get out of there!" she cried, grabbing up a stick as she passed the barn and open gate into a small adjoining pasture. She arrived at her garden in front of the house, still yelling at the cow and proceeded to beat her on the hindquarters with all the vigor of Donal Grant taking his club to Hornie.

"Get out of the garden, Flora, you dumb beast. My flowers are not for your lunch. Get back into your field!"

The three others hurried after her. With the four making a slowly tightening semicircle, hands outstretched and blocking all directions but one, Flora soon began methodically wandering back toward her permitted grazing pasture, showing no inclination toward either hurry or concern.

"I'm too old for such foolishness!" panted Maggie. "It puts me in mind of the day Bobby had his fall, when suddenly I found Flora with me in my garden when she should have been with him."

Gradually Maggie turned pensive as they made their way toward the cottage.

"It reminds me too," she went on, "of what dear Timothy was saying just an hour or two ago in the church, about the glow of eternity."

"Yes, that was nice," added Catharine. "Very poetic, I thought."

"It seems to me that glow's getting a bit brighter for me lately,"

Maggie went on. "With Bobby's passing coming so sudden, and now George and Charles, one can never tell how or when the end might arrive."

"Don't talk that way, Maggie," said Jocelyn. "Don't you remember what Timothy told us—that we Heathersleigh women have to be strong and stick together. You can't leave us anytime soon. We need you."

Despite her comments, Jocelyn could sense Maggie's serious mood deepening.

"I'm no longer forty, my dear," said the older woman. "I'm climbing up to seventy-eight, and it won't be long."

"You're as strong as any of us, Maggie. You're not going to leave us for a good long time."

"Your Charles was as strong as most men," rejoined Maggie. "And look at your George—young and vigorous with his whole life ahead of him. But the Lord's got his own way of marking out our days, and even the strength of a bull doesn't carry much meaning with his schedule."

Maggie's words at last caused the others to grow pensive with her.

"And when a woman is my age," she continued, "it's time she spends some time thinking about that garden that lies *beyond* the door, like Timothy was telling us about, as well as the one in front of her house."

The other three now realized something serious was on Maggie's mind as they followed her into the cottage.

"I think it's time I had a talk with you three," Maggie said. She stoked the fire in her stove and put a kettle of water on for tea.

"What about?" Jocelyn asked.

"About Heathersleigh, and what's to become of my cottage here when I'm gone," answered Maggie.

She led them into her sitting room. They all sat down together.

"I know," she began, "that all this will come out eventually anyway. But I want you to hear it from my own lips. At first I kept it to myself. I didn't think the time was right to speak out. But with all that's happened this week, I think I oughtn't to remain silent any longer. Your being home, Amanda dear," she added, "may have something to do with it. You see, it was last October when the revelations came to me."

"Revelations?" repeated Amanda.

"I was praying for you, my dear," Maggie said. "I remember the night well. I woke from a sound sleep with my Bobby's words about a hidden legacy in my brain. I don't know if you remember, but it was something he said one time to you when you were visiting us."

"I remember," nodded Amanda with a smile.

"And I was telling you about the mystery of the kingdom and my grandmother's favorite passage."

Again Amanda nodded.

"As I said, I had awakened from a sound sleep. It was the middle of the night. I'd gone to bed, as I said, praying for you. When I awoke several hours later I was thinking about the past and the word 'legacy' from my Bobby's lips. And I wondered again how this cottage came into the hands of my family, a mystery that has perplexed folks around here for longer than most people can remember. And I found myself wondering what was to become of this place after I was gone.

"Many stories and rumors from my childhood began to come back to me—things my mother had said about the Hall and its people. And, of course, in the village everyone had their own opinion on the matter and were free with various speculations. Now they all began to rush back into my mind, things I hadn't thought of in years. It was as if I was suddenly alive to things I had heard sixty or seventy years before but had completely forgotten.

"My brain was so full by then that I got up and sat down right here, in this very chair, with my Bible in my lap. I found myself drawn to the passage I had told you about, Amanda, on that same day—the passage my grandmother liked so well. That was the night I made my discovery."

She got up and walked toward the kitchen.

"I think the water's ready," she said. "Let me make us some tea, and then I will tell you all about it."

♦ ♦ ♦

Find the key and unlock the mystery.

Maggie had read the words in her grandmother's hand in the margin beside the fourth chapter of Mark over and over. But what could the key she had just found in the secretary be meant to unlock?

She began snooping and looking about the old cabinet with enlivened interest. She pulled the small drawer above the desk all the way out and set it aside. Key still clutched in her left hand, with her right she sent her fingers probing into the opening. Her hand did not go far, for it was not a deep drawer. She now looked at the desk portion of the secretary. Neither was it of great depth.

In fact, Maggie thought, stepping back and examining the entire piece from the side angle, both desk and drawer only extended about halfway toward the back board of the cabinet. Why were they so shallow when the cabinet itself was at least twice as deep from front to back?

Again she probed into the empty drawer cavity, investigating every inch with the tips of her fingers.

What was this . . . the back panel felt loose?

She jiggled it, finally realizing it was meant to slide back and forth! Maggie jostled it vigorously and managed to slide it about half an inch to one side. She stuck a finger into the crack and the next instant had it sliding along grooves which were now suddenly visible. Behind it in the new opening her fingers felt a small metal apparatus.

Excited now, Maggie stooped and gazed into the cavity. A brass lock was built into the hidden recess of the cabinet, kept from view behind the panel of wood she had just slid away.

With fingers trembling, she took the key and inserted it. It slid into the mechanism as smoothly as if it had been oiled yesterday!

Maggie turned the key a quarter turn.

From somewhere inside she heard the faint metallic sound of a lock releasing.

Below the drawer, the back wall of the desk gave way and opened toward her. A secret panel, held vertical and secure by the lock directly above it, now swiveled smoothly down on embedded pivots somewhere in the cabinet, revealing a faceless shelf whose base was the opposite side of the back panel of the secretary.

Lying inside the newly revealed box-shelf lay a single folded sheet of heavy paper yellowed with age.

Heart beating, Maggie removed it, brought it out to the light, sat back down in her chair, and unfolded it.

Twenty minutes later Maggie still sat, shaking her head in disbelief. To think it had been here all along—the key, the lock, the hidden compartment—right in front of her eyes—and the answer to the mystery that had plagued the people of Milverscombe, and given rise to so many stories and rumors, for over half a century—how the cottage of the Heathersleigh estate had come into the hands of a poor local peasant family with hardly two shillings to rub together.

In her hands Maggie held the deed to Heathersleigh Cottage—this very cottage, sold, as was written on it, in the year 1849 from Henry Ruth-erford, Lord of the Manor of Heathersleigh, to one Arthur Crompton, Bishop.

HIDDEN LOCK BEHIND DRAWER

PANEL OPENS REVEALING SECRET STORAGE

What could its significance be but that to which her grandmother was referring as the sale of the birthright of the Genesis passage? Further doc-umentation seven years later, in the year 1856, apparently upon Crompton's death, recorded the transfer of the deed to Or-elia (Kyrkwode) Moylan, Maggie's own grandmother, to be passed to her heir after her death, or, in the absence of descen-dants, to the Church of England. The stamp of the solicitors' firm Crumholtz, Sutclyff, Stonehaugh, & Crumholtz attested to the le-gality of the 1856 transfer of ownership.

What were the circumstances behind this most peculiar trans-action? she wondered. Those circumstances were not illuminated by the deed. *Why* had Lord Henry sold the cottage to the bishop? And *why* had he in turn, apparently by a will, then given it to her grandmother?

She had discovered the legal origins to the long-concealed mystery . . . but not the *why*.

That she would have to fill in for herself.

As Maggie's reflections began to tumble back in time to her childhood, she tried to grab on to the ends of what mental threads her memory caught faint sight of.

There had always been rumors about old Lord Henry. Every-one knew them. As a girl growing up around Milverscombe, Mag-gie certainly had heard her share and trembled at them too. Chief among them was the rumor hinted at by old men with knowing glances and clicks of the tongue that Henry had done in his poor wife at the very moment she had given him an heir. No one actually used the word murder, but among the children of the village a certain singsong verse had always been sufficient to plunge fear into the hearts of timid little children whenever they played in the neighborhood:

Look where you go, watch what you do,
　　or Lord Henry will snatch and make you a stew.
He'll cut you in pieces, like he did that night
　　when his poor Eliza screamed out in such fright.
With his own hand he killed her, or so they say,
　　and began to go batty the very next day.
It will happen to you, no one will hear your call,
　　if you venture too close to Heathersleigh Hall.

No one actually thought he had cut her up, for the lady was buried with a proper funeral and lay even now under the ground behind the church. But according to a loose-tongued servant lad who lived at the Hall and had been sent that night for the vicar through the storm, there were indeed screams coming from the house.

But what did such rumors have to do with the sale of the cottage? wondered Maggie. And why would her grandmother have likened it to the sale of a birthright?

What did Bishop Crompton have to do with the affair?

Gradually sleep returned and Maggie extinguished her light and went back to bed.

The next day, at the earliest possible hour, she was bound for the parish church in the village.

"Hello, Vicar Coleridge," she said as the vicar greeted her.

"You are out early, Mrs. McFee."

"I am on an important errand, vicar. May I have a few minutes with the parish register?"

"Which book—births, deaths, or marriages?"

"Births and deaths."

The vicar produced the ancient journals. It did not take Maggie long to locate what she wanted. Not only were the entries in both books made in the same year, but on the very same day—February 11, 1829.

Henry's wife, Eliza, had indeed died on the very day she gave birth. Perhaps there was some truth to the old rumors after all! And both events were witnessed and recorded in the parish registry by none other than one A. Crompton, Vicar, Milverscombe!

There was the connection between the deed she had discovered and the fateful night of Eliza's death. Early in his career, the good bishop had been the presiding vicar of Milverscombe!

He had witnessed both events. Whatever had happened to cause Eliza's death, and if indeed old Lord Henry had snuffed out her life as the servant lad and abundant rumors maintained, the vicar must have known of it.

The sale of the cottage to Crompton years later after he became a bishop must have been a payoff for his silence!

Not only was Crompton there that fateful night, thought Maggie, if there was a birthing, then her grandmother, the only midwife in the region, would have been on hand too.

That was the connection between vicar and midwife! They shared the secret of that night.

Was it too much to conjecture that the bishop had paid off the midwife with the cottage in similar fashion as had Lord Henry paid him off several years before? It was certainly a credible explanation of the known facts.

But as Maggie thanked the vicar and left the church to make her way home, a feeling of unease began growing within her. She recoiled at the idea that the cottage that had been theirs all this time had come to her family by stealth and secrecy, and perhaps even to cover up a crime. They were not the rightful owners. Whatever manner of evil man Lord Henry might have been, the estate still belonged to the Rutherford family. They were the rightful heirs. It was their birthright, not her own or her family's.

And here she was nearing the end of her life, and she and Bobby hadn't a living relative on the face of the earth. If she didn't do something to set it right, the ill-gotten birthright would pass to the Church. She had nothing against the Church, but it seemed the cottage ought to belong to whom it rightfully had been intended.

She would consult Crumholtz, Sutclyff, Stonehaugh, & Crumholtz in Exeter. She could not undo what had been done years before. But she could at least put it back into the hands of the true heirs of the Heathersleigh birthright—if it lay in her power legally to do so.

She would go to Exeter, execute a will, and write a letter explaining what she had discovered.

"So though I've found the deed," Maggie concluded, "I can't say exactly why it all came about in the first place. But I've spent the past months thinking about it all and trying to figure it out, and that's how the thing appears to me."

"That old Lord Henry murdered Eliza?" said Amanda.

"He was more than just a little mad, as everyone knew," replied Maggie. "That much I know myself. Whether it is from the blood of murder on his hands as the verses say, who can tell? They say he desperately wanted a son to whom he could pass on his estate, but his wife Eliza did not give him one for many years. Although it wouldn't have mattered what kind of child she had, for the law governing Heathersleigh allowed that the estate would pass to the eldest whether it was a son *or* a daughter. I recall my mother saying it was openly talked about in the village when she was a girl. In any event, Eliza remained barren and Henry grew furious and more demented, like his namesake the old king of England of many wives, vowing to get rid of her and marry another. They say he came in time to despise the very sight of her, all the time becoming more worried, lest he grow too old or die himself. Should that have happened, Eliza's family would have inherited Heathersleigh, and Henry was said to hate a certain brother-in-law with a passion, Eliza's greedy brother, who would have done anything to possess the estate.

"Finally Eliza was discovered to be carrying a child. When the night of the birth came, she gave him his son, and not only a son, but twins, a boy and a girl. The second child sealed Eliza's fate. For now, even if something later happened to Ashby, the son which Henry had so longed for, at least he would have a daughter too. He had no further need of Eliza, for suddenly Lord Henry had *two* heirs. No matter what happened, his inheritance was secure, and Eliza and her brother would never get their hands on Heathersleigh.

"Lord Henry had his heir, and the next day Eliza was dead. The rumors began almost immediately that he had murdered her. I don't know how much they resulted from the servant lad—who himself, my mum said, met with an untimely end not many years later. But she said he told dreadful things about what he had seen and heard that night. And the fact was, Eliza was dead in the prime of her life."

Maggie now handed the deed to Jocelyn.

"The strange circumstances of this transfer of the cottage," she went on, "seem to substantiate the rumors. What else but such a crime would draw together the attending vicar and midwife into a secret transaction? Many children's rhymes are not so far off from the truth. Lord Henry must have sworn the two witnesses to secrecy, but later needed to pay off the bishop with the cottage to keep him quiet—the sale of birthright to cover the crime."

"But why would the bishop will the cottage to your grandmother several years later?" said Jocelyn, still puzzling over the dates on the document she was holding.

"The only thing I can imagine," replied Maggie, "is that the old bishop must have come to feel guilty over the affair, or maybe had pangs of conscience that he had prospered and my grandmother hadn't by their mutual complicity in the thing. So he gave the cottage to her when he died. Then it came to my mother, and then to me and my Bobby."

"That is logical, I suppose," remarked Catharine. "But I must admit, I am more than a little confused by everything you've said."

"But the reason I started to tell you all this," Maggie went on, "is because of the one other curious fact that came to light when I discovered the deed. That is the clause there—look, Jocelyn, in the fine print at the bottom. It says that should ever Orelia Moylan's heirs who are in possession of the cottage die without heirs themselves, the property would be transferred to the Church of England. I realized I was exactly such a one, and a woman getting on in years who had no will. That's when I went to Exeter myself to see those lawyers—you remember, Jocelyn, last October. I showed them the deed with that provision and asked if I could legally pass the cottage on to someone who was not related to Orelia Moylan by blood. They said they would look into the matter. But just to be sure, I made a will right then and left it at their office. Three weeks ago I received a letter back from Mr. Bradbury Crumholtz. He told me that the provision in the deed is somewhat ambiguous, but that my will was legal, and that it was doubtful it would be contested, especially by the Church."

"So what did you do?" asked Amanda.

"I wrote out a will leaving Heathersleigh Cottage to the two of you, Catharine and Amanda, and your brother, George," replied Maggie.

118

Mysteries Solved and Puzzles Remaining

*W*alking home as late afternoon began to give way to evening, Jocelyn, Amanda, and Catharine were all quiet, pondering the many things Maggie had shared with them and their implications. It was clear a change was coming to Heathersleigh. Jocelyn and Amanda were especially conscious of it, for the heartbreak of the accumulated years of their separation could not help in some ways but make the grief of these recent events keenest in their hearts.

"All Grandma Maggie's talk about the past," said Catharine as they approached the Hall from across the meadow, interrupting Jocelyn's and Amanda's thoughts, "makes me curious about the Hall's history all of a sudden too. Let's go walk through the secret passage again."

"Where does it go?" said Amanda.

"Just you wait—I'll take you through all sorts of twisting and turning narrow passages."

"I've been curious about the keys Geoffrey gave me to see where they might work. But let's hurry, before it gets too dark and spooky."

They walked inside and began climbing the stairs.

"Are you coming, Mother?" asked Catharine.

"Of course. You don't think I would miss out on such an adventure, do you?"

They made their way up, passing through the family portrait gallery. They paused before Lord Henry's portrait. Strange sensations came over them as they stared up at the subtle expression of mystery and recalled Maggie's story.

"A scary-looking old gent, if you ask me," said Catharine. "I'm not sure I altogether like the idea of being related to him!"

"Although the family resemblance is clear," remarked Jocelyn. "I think I can faintly see both your father and brother in his face."

"And look at those two, Amanda," said Catharine, moving a few steps farther down the corridor, "—see . . . the Bible is there in that one painting and gone in this."

Ten minutes later, with candles in hand, for there was no electricity in the secret passage, Catharine pulled back the swiveling bookcase in the library, and the three entered the dark chamber behind it.

"Do you remember when George discovered this?" asked Jocelyn. "Your father and I were sitting in the library reading, when all of a sudden one of the bookcases began to move, and out of the wall popped George. I don't know who was more incredulous, him or us!"

"I didn't pay much attention," replied Amanda. "I wasn't paying much attention to anything back then. I was never in here once."

"Well, then this will be even more of an adventure for you."

"I can't believe all this has been hidden behind these walls and I never knew it."

"I hope we don't stumble over any old bones from Lord Henry's stew."

"Catharine!"

"He might have cut up some of the local children, you know."

"That's not how the old rhyme went."

"Maybe not, Mother, but remember what Maggie said about the servant lad that was never seen again."

"That's not exactly what she said, Catharine," interjected Amanda. "You're exaggerating to scare us!"

"What better place to hide the bodies," Catharine persisted. "I'll bet that's why he had all these passages built. One of these days we are going to discover a secret door into a crypt full of bones."

"Catharine!" Jocelyn exclaimed a second time. "You are dreadful! How did you get so ghoulish?"

"Probably from George. He always teased me about ghosts in here," laughed Catharine. "I wish he was with us now. I miss him."

The reminder quieted the trio. They walked awhile in silence, with fearless Catharine leading the way.

"One of these days, Amanda, I must show you the chest George found up in the garret," Catharine said at length. "It's full of all sorts of old things about the Hall."

"What kind of things?"

"Records, journals, ledgers, architectural drawings, everything just thrown into a huge chest. I doubt if it had been looked at in fifty years until George opened it."

They arrived at what to all appearances was a dead end.

"Where does it go from here?" asked Amanda. "Did you take a wrong turn?"

Without saying anything further, Catharine reached out, turned a latch from somewhere not readily visible, then pulled and swung the end of the wall toward her. Amanda watched in astonishment as Catharine led them through the opening, and was even more shocked a moment later to find herself following her sister into the middle of the old tower at the northeast corner of Heathersleigh Hall.

"I can't believe it!" she exclaimed. "That is amazing. I had no idea we were going in this direction. And George discovered this?"

"He got into the labyrinth somewhere from the garret and first found his way to the library. Then eventually, after considerable more snooping and exploring, he found the handle I just used, turned it, and there he was in the tower."

"But it only opens from the inside," now added Jocelyn. "Look—"

She closed the door behind them.

"—once it's closed, it just looks like part of the wall."

"It's exactly as I remember it," said Amanda, looking around at the tower room. "I would never have known there was a door there."

"Except . . ." added Catharine, stepping toward it and sliding back a small panel in the door they had just come through that at first glance appeared immovable, "—for this."

"A lock!" Amanda exclaimed. "A hidden lock."

"*Without* any sign of a key," said her mother.

From her pocket Amanda immediately retrieved the keys Geoffrey had given her.

"Then let's try this," she said, and inserted the larger of the two into it.

"A perfect fit," she exclaimed. "I thought it might be for something in here!" She turned the key and again the door they had just closed swung open into the darkened passageway behind it.

"Ever since George discovered it," said Jocelyn, "we've only been able to open the door from the other side with the latch. I always wondered what happened to the key."

"Another mystery solved," said Catharine.

"Is everything about the old place suddenly coming to light?" added her mother.

"Not quite everything, Mother," replied Catharine. "Like where were these keys the day Geoffrey took them? And why hadn't we known about them before?"

As they talked Amanda was poking around the tower.

"I think the answer to *that* mystery is right here," she said, removing a loose stone in the adjacent wall. It revealed a small cavity with an empty iron key hook inside it. "As I told you before, the whole thing is my fault. I'm afraid I locked him in here from the main stairway over there. He was probably alone for three or four minutes. He must have found this loose stone and then seen the keys. And now that I recall the day, it seems I might have heard him fiddling about with something that might have been keys."

"Where were you?"

"Just outside the door there, on the landing of the stairs."

"I suppose that's it, then," said Jocelyn.

"But what could this small key be for?" said Amanda. "I don't see anything else in here."

"The tower's only got the two locks," said Catharine. "George and I explored every inch trying to find a key to the hidden door. There's nothing besides the main door where you say you locked Geoffrey in— and its key is still there outside in the lock as always—and the hidden door you just opened with the new key."

"Hmm . . . that is odd," said Jocelyn. "And it's such a small key."

Amanda set the ring on the iron hook.

"Well," Catharine said, "I suppose we ought to save some mysteries about the place for our children and the next generation."

They descended a few minutes later by the main tower stairs, leaving the two keys in what was apparently their original resting place. Catharine's comment had caused Amanda to grow quiet. Thoughts of marriage and children and future generations were confusing and painful right now.

With her younger sister's thoughts drawn into similar channels, and not realizing how painful her words would be, Catharine now blurted out as they went, "Amanda, let me get this straight . . . we haven't really talked about it other than a little the other evening, but I'm still confused. Now . . . you're actually *married*, right?"

Amanda nodded, though the reminder was like a knife plunging into her heart.

"How will that affect what Maggie told us? The future, I mean ... if you have, you know ... a husband?"

"I don't know, Catharine," said Amanda, shaking her head. "I'm afraid that is more than I can think about now."

"But then where ..."

Gradually Catharine began to realize the awkwardness of her inquiry.

"What will you do?" she added after a moment.

"I don't know, Catharine ... I just don't know."

It was silent as they reached the ground floor.

"What about you?" Amanda asked, trying to change the subject. "Are you really going to university?"

"I don't know," Catharine replied. "Like you, I'll have to wait and see. Everything is different now. But I think I would like to."

Indeed, more than any of them could realize, everything in their lives was bound to change now.

119

Heathersleigh's Women

The following morning, both Jocelyn and Amanda woke early.

Thoughts of the previous day filled mother and daughter, reminders of Charles and the church service in Milverscombe, and also Maggie's revelations and what they might mean to the three of them who remained.

But strangely with the waking came a sense of anticipation rather than heartache. Timothy's words of exhortation on Thursday evening, along with what Maggie had disclosed, combined somehow to infuse within them a sense that a new day was coming, and that the Lord may yet be able to make life at Heathersleigh a good thing.

Jocelyn rose and began to dress.

She glanced at herself in the mirror, paused, then smiled. In a strange way, she almost felt as if she were looking at her face—with the bright red birthmark over a third of it—as Charles might have seen it. She did not wince at the sight, but was reminded of his words of so long ago—*"It is his fingerprint upon your face, Jocie. When God made you, he touched you in a unique way . . . he left that mark to remind you that he loves you."*

Dear Charles . . . how could he always see such meaning and goodness in everything?

He had taught her so much. He had helped her to accept herself, gently guided her into an unconditional acceptance of God's love, and eventually to the capacity to love him in return.

Now her dear husband and friend was gone. It was she who must be strong now. Like it or not, from this day forward, she was head of the family.

Amanda too had risen early, not realizing her mother was also awake.

She got up and slowly dressed, then left her room on tiptoes, not wanting to wake anyone else as she crept down the hall. She had no particular destination in mind, but wanted to feel the quiet of the morning and what it might have to speak. Her feet unexpectedly took her toward her father's office. What drew her there she could not have said.

She entered, walked to the middle of the room, now so still and eerily silent, and stood gazing reflectively about her. There was the portrait of her grandfather . . . the old da Vinci sketch her father had loved . . . various devices and inventions on shelves and windowsills . . . cases full of a hundred or more bound volumes . . . the telephone he had installed . . . the favorite books on his desk, including several Bibles, sitting between the ivory bookends . . . the gold-plated telescope . . . objects familiar yet new to her adult eyes, and now suddenly all so poignantly reminiscent.

As she gazed and reflected on these objects that had, for one reason or another, been important to him in his life, Amanda realized she wanted to know her father, really *know* him deeply. Was it too late, as logic would suggest? In this one room he had left behind so many reminders pointing to the man he was, what he was interested in, what he thought about, what he valued, the books he read.

He was a remarkable man, Amanda thought. She had always considered his life after politics empty and drab and purposeless. Now she saw that perhaps his greatest accomplishments, especially in people's lives, had actually come later. Memories of his face in her mind would always bring pain, but perhaps she could learn from them too. She would not wallow in the pain, but would try to allow it to make her grow and become strong.

"It may be too late," she said, as if speaking to her father in the midst of this place which had been the heart and soul of Heathersleigh, "to listen to your voice and let you teach me in person. But I will look for what my memory of you can discover, and eventually I will be a daughter worthy to share your name and your heritage."

Jocelyn went out in the cool of the morning. A low mist hung over the countryside. She found herself walking the paths of the heather garden. Quietly she thought about Charles and their years together, reflecting on the many times they had walked here together.

It had been a little more than a week now since his passing. She would continue to grieve, to weep. But in the midst of it, she knew she must try to begin looking forward.

She thought about Heathersleigh and what it had always been to her. Charles had helped make it a retreat, an oasis, a place where she could just be herself and not have to think about anything or anyone.

But she would not be able to depend on Charles as she had for so long. He had protected her from the outside world in so many ways. Now, Jocelyn thought, that season of her life was past.

I have spent my whole married life, she thought, *having this as my private sanctuary. Maybe now it's time I no longer keep Heathersleigh to myself.*

She walked on as her inner conversation with herself continued.

In some ways, she thought, *I have been self-absorbed and self-conscious all these years, raising a family, learning who I am, and learning about life and God, about love and self-acceptance. Perhaps it is time I looked beyond that, looked beyond myself and began to ask what I can do for others. Perhaps it is time I followed Charles' example, and learned to be strong in my own right.*

"I *am* strong!" she said aloud. "It is time I let the strength Charles helped me have flow out into more lives than just my family and friends in the village. These years *have* given me strength. Timothy is right. Women can be strong in inner ways. It is time I passed on what I have, and did for others what Charles did for me."

She recalled Amanda's description of the chalet.

Might you have something like that you want to do here, Lord, something you want us to give out of the abundance you have provided us?

Amanda left her father's office full of many thoughts and questions.

Even if she was able to discover how to know her father more intimately, she still had to go on with her life. Heathersleigh had to go on too.

She realized she wanted to make up for what she had done. Not knowing it, her thoughts were progressing along similar lines as Jocelyn's. Mother and daughter were more alike than either realized, and would grow closer yet as the years passed.

"It is time I gave back," Amanda said to herself, "gave something into other lives."

The Chalet of Hope came into her mind too. As it did the question came with it—what would her father want them to do now with this estate . . . and what did *God* want them to do?

Catharine slept in longer than mother or sister. When she arose and sleepily walked to her window to see what sort of day it was, she saw her mother outside below walking slowly back toward the house from the heather garden. She knew it had been her father and mother's favorite place of prayer, and she more than half suspected that to be the purpose for which her mother had sought its solitude today.

"Lord," she said quietly, *"give Mother a new level of your strength now that Daddy is gone. Help her to be the woman you want her to be. And thank you for bringing Amanda home. But we need your help during this time. I need it too. We all need your help and guidance."*

The three went out together that Monday afternoon. They all sensed that a new dawn was about to rise over Heathersleigh. As they walked through the grounds, the heather garden, and slowly about the entire house, gradually they each began to share their thoughts.

"With the cottage and what Maggie shared with us," Jocelyn was saying, "who knows what significance it will have that the Heathersleigh estate is whole again, so to speak?"

"Or *will* be, don't you mean, Mother?" said Catharine with a questioning expression. "Grandma Maggie's will isn't in effect yet."

"You're right. That's what I mean—the effect it will have in future years."

"And its implications in our lives that we cannot yet see," added Amanda.

"Somehow God has something here that is bigger than us," Jocelyn went on, "perhaps bigger even than your father could have known or foreseen. I am convinced of it."

"And the fact that the long mystery of the cottage has come out now cannot be an accident," said Catharine.

"Could it really be true," Amanda asked, "like Maggie said, that the Lord will give back the years the locusts have eaten? I can't imagine how. It seems too good to be true."

"I don't understand that—what have the locusts eaten?" asked Catharine.

"The wasted years," replied Amanda. "For me it is these last eight years of my life. It breaks my heart to think of it. But if the Lord can restore that loss..."

She fell silent.

"Who can tell what God might have for us three women to do?" said Jocelyn. She paused. "You know, I was thinking this morning about the chalet where you were, Amanda," she went on after a moment, "and wondering, *Hmm ... Lord, might you have some similar thing in mind for Heathersleigh?*"

"So was I," rejoined Amanda. "I was thinking that very thing. Remember what I told you, how the Lord said to Sister Hope, if you pray they will come. We could do that!"

"Pray for who to come?" said her sister. "What would they come here for?"

"I don't know," replied Amanda. "Maybe we don't pray for people to *come* necessarily, but just for God to do whatever he wants to do with us and with Heathersleigh."

They were in the large meadow north of the house, and gradually turned to begin walking back. Rising up before them, the sun reflecting off its roof and corners from the southwest, rose the majestic grey walls of Heathersleigh Hall. They stood a moment, then both daughters flanked their mother, placed their arms through hers, and the three began making their way back toward the house.

"I wonder what the future will hold for this grand old place," said Amanda.

"Whatever is the future legacy of this family and Heathersleigh," said Jocelyn, "it is up to us. It is our legacy now. Our men are gone. It is no longer Henry's, or even Charles' or George's. That legacy has passed to us, Heathersleigh's three women. We have to be strong, for Charles' and George's sakes, to honor their memory."

"We can do it, Mother. We *will* do it . . . together. Remember what Timothy said about the strength of women."

"Thank you, Catharine. With you to help me, I'm sure I won't forget."

"Speaking for myself," Amanda added, "I certainly don't feel strong. But you two are. I see it in you both, just as Timothy described."

"Don't be too sure that strength isn't growing in you as well," said Catharine.

Amanda smiled. "I hope you are right, dear sister," she said. "For the present, I shall have to take your word for it."

They approached the Hall, walking around the east wing. An unfamiliar automobile sat in front, a touring car with top down.

"Who could that be?" said Jocelyn. "Why didn't we hear it drive up?"

"It's an expensive-looking car," said Amanda. "If I didn't know better I might think Hubert Powell had come calling on Catharine."

"Don't even think such a thing!" exclaimed Catharine. "Didn't you say Cousin Geoffrey had a touring car?"

"Yes, but that's not it."

They entered the front door and were met by Sarah Minsterly.

"There is a Lieutenant Langham calling," she said.

Amanda and Catharine glanced at each other.

"On business . . . something about Charles?" asked Jocelyn.

"I don't think so, Lady Jocelyn. He is not wearing a uniform. He asked if the young ladies were at home. He thought they might like to go for a ride."

Catharine and Amanda glanced at each other again, then Catharine began to smile.

"I don't know about you," she said, "but that sounds like an offer I do not feel inclined to refuse. Is it all right, Mother?"

"Of course. You're nearly a grown woman."

"What about you, Amanda?"

"That would be nice."

"Where is he, Sarah?"

"In the drawing room, Miss Catharine," replied Sarah.

120

What Do You Want Me to Do?

Summer came to Devon, and with it a new sense of peace to Heathersleigh.

Jocelyn was able to smile and laugh again. The Lord continued to infuse within the Heathersleigh women a sense of strength, though they did not know where it was leading or what that purpose might be. Anticipation for the future grew, though it remained as yet a book whose next pages they were not yet able to read. These pages would be turned in time by the Lord's hand and according to his schedule. In that knowledge they were content.

Life would never be the same without Charles. But Jocelyn had taken Timothy's words at the Milverscombe memorial to heart. She *did* believe the Lord, and was determined to fix her eye on the glow of eternity from around the edges of the doorway that faced beyond.

Amanda had by now been back in Devon long enough to feel comfortable and content. Heathersleigh seemed more home to her now than it had ever been in her life. She turned twenty-five without fanfare. She wanted only to quietly enjoy the day with mother and sister. They went out and brought Maggie back to the Hall for afternoon tea and cakes.

Lieutenant Langham visited Heathersleigh on several more occasions.

Stirling Blakeley returned to Milverscombe from Oxford. He and Catharine drew Amanda into their playful friendship, the three enjoying numerous rides about the countryside and many evenings reading together in the Heathersleigh library.

Amanda continued to be aware of changes taking place within her. Noise and bustle and activity, which had always been her very sustenance, grew foreign to her spirit. The thought of setting foot inside London again did not remotely enter her mind.

She became pensive, slow, given to early morning walks and reflective hours of contemplation, not anxious to make haste. She found herself especially drawn to the heather garden, though she did not know why. Jocelyn knew but said nothing. It was an answer to prayer she would share with Charles in the quietness of her own mother's heart.

As for the future, Amanda needed no plans. She did not fret to know what it held, for at last she was at peace with herself. Catharine's question about her marriage haunted her, but did not diminish her anticipation for what possibilities might lie in the future. She would wait for the Lord to guide her there too.

There remained deep sorrow in her heart. This could not be said to be a *happy* time, though she was at peace and eager to discover what the next chapter of life might hold. She accepted her sorrow as an intrinsic necessity of the slow transformation of her perspective, and thus allowed it to do its work in her heart. It was a well of sorrow, not a knife of sorrow, and therefore capable of being filled with the healing waters of selflessness, compassion, trust, and wisdom.

One warm afternoon in late June, Amanda found herself standing at the window of her childhood room gazing out upon the Devonshire countryside. She could not help but be reminded of the day at age seven when she had secretly followed her father to his prayer wood.

She would do so again. She would walk along the same path as before, to remind herself what she had been, and what now, perhaps as a result, she wanted to become.

As Amanda set out across the grassy fields and meadows on this day, how different were her thoughts and emotions from that day eighteen years earlier, and even from her visit a year ago before leaving for the Continent. The first had been filled with annoyance, the second with perplexity. Today, however, her heart was filled with quiet anticipation.

No less today was she following her father than that day long ago, though now she was following his footsteps for the right reasons, seeking her father's God, whom she had now made her own.

The walk took her nearly an hour. Amanda was in no hurry. As always during this quiet season of her soul, she was making peace with many things as she went. A sense of what was coming grew steadily upon her.

She arrived at the wood, paused briefly, then entered through the thick-growing surrounding stand of trees. A few moments later she stood inside the small grassy meadow. Yes, she thought, there was indeed a Presence here, just as she had felt a little over a year ago. At that time she had not been ready to apprehend its full meaning. It was not only the presence of her departed father she felt here in his tiny cathedral of trees.

The presence of God was here too. She knew that now.

Amanda walked about briefly, then sat down on one of the three large stones. So many thoughts and memories filled her heart. They deepened the sadness, yet were no less enriching, for they offered the spiritual nourishment of growth and maturity.

After several long quiet moments, slowly she eased to her knees in the grass, exactly as she had seen her father do, bent down her face, cradled it in her hands, and began to pray.

"*Lord and Father,*" she whispered, "*help me not be consumed by the guilt of what I was, for my selfish past. I cannot change it. And not even guilt will bring Daddy back. So I ask you to use it to make me the woman you want me to be.*

"*Show me truths that I blinded myself to for so long. I want to learn, Lord, and grow. I now see how Mother and Father grew so much after they gave their lives to you in ways I resented because I could not see properly. Now I realize those were difficult times for them. I see that it took courage to change as they did. And even if they made some mistakes along the way, they were doing the best they knew, and their motives were always to do right. Forgive my wrong attitudes during those times and for not respecting their courage.*

"*I wish Daddy were still here, because now I want to know him as I never allowed myself to before. But though he is now with you, show me what he was trying to teach me. Open my eyes to the truth of his life, even though he is no longer with me. Let me learn from his memory. In the same way the words of his sermon spoke what you knew I needed that day outside Timothy's church, perhaps other things about his life can help me grow in the same way. Give me new insight into his character and spiritual life, even though it must happen in the quietness of my own heart.*

"*And let me learn from my dear mother as well. I see what a woman of stature and dignity you have made of her. Daddy is gone, but I still have her, and I am so grateful for that. Thank you for bringing me home and that she has been so gracious and wonderful and loving toward me. Help her to know how much I love her. Help me to live that love toward her every day.*

"*And thank you, dear Father, for Catharine. What a joy to have a sister who is so fun, so full of life and energy, and such a good friend.*"

Amanda rose and walked about the small prayer wood breathing deeply, as if the very air itself contained some special life-giving quality, then sat down again and pulled out a small piece of paper. It was Catharine's Christmas gift to Jocelyn, which she had copied out again in her own hand at Amanda's request.

Before she had finished reading it again, as she had many times during the past few months, Amanda's eyes were full of tears.

"I want to be your woman too, Lord," she whispered. *"It seems I am so far behind both my mother and even my younger sister. But I will be patient for you to do your work. Let me do what Catharine's little story says, and follow the example you have given me."*

Again Amanda rose and now made her way slowly back through the passageway through the trees by which she had come.

"Give me strength to look forward," she prayed as she went. *"I ask you to somehow make good come of my past, though it is difficult for my eyes to look at myself and see anything but failure. I feel small for what I was and responsible for so much grief that has come to so many. Help me see which guilts I must accountably bear, and which I need to leave in your hands and not take up again. I know you can turn all things for good, so use my past for good . . . somehow . . . though at present I do not see how that is possible.*

"And use me, Father," she added, *"in the lives of others. If someday I might help turn one other person away from self-centeredness, so that he or she is prevented from bringing pain into their families, as well as into their own hearts, I cannot say that would make it all worth it, but I would at least feel that maybe my life had counted for something.*

"Turn my mistakes to good, Lord, and accomplish your will and purpose in my life."

121

Overdue Letter

⁂hat evening found Amanda in an even quieter and more reflective frame of mind than usual. The mood of the prayer wood had remained with her throughout the rest of the day.

"Is everything all right, my dear?" said Jocelyn as the three sat together after evening tea.

"Yes, Mother," Amanda replied with a smile. "I am just feeling quiet, you know. I think I'll go upstairs and read. There's a book I want to finish. Then maybe I'll finally start my letter to the sisters in Wengen." She rose and hugged Jocelyn. "Thank you, Mother."

"For what?" said Jocelyn, smiling up at her.

"For being you . . . for being my mother, for your patience and forgiveness. I love you."

"Thank you, dear. I love you too."

"I know, Mother," nodded Amanda. "I really do know it now."

Amanda walked over to where Catharine sat quietly writing a letter. Catharine glanced up, and Amanda bent down and embraced her.

"I love you, Catharine," she said. "I thank God so much for you. You're the best friend a sister could possibly have."

"Thank you, Amanda," smiled Catharine. "That is so sweet of you to say. You are a good friend too."

Amanda turned and walked up to her room.

The night had grown late, and both sister and mother were already in bed when Amanda sat down two hours later at her writing table. She took out a sizable stack of writing paper from its drawer, then set her pen to the top sheet, and began.

Dear Sisters Hope, Gretchen, Marjolaine, Regina, Luane, Agatha, Galiana, Clariss, Anika, and Kasmira, whom I hardly had the chance to know, if you are still at the chalet—

Greetings to you all from England.

This letter is long overdue. I have started it in my mind at least two dozen times, and on paper probably half that many. But somehow the time has never seemed right, and I have not been able to continue and say everything I need and want to.

But I think now that time has finally come. I am sorry it has taken me so long. Here I am at last, and I am determined to see it through this time, although it will probably be a very long letter. Someday, I hope in the not-too-distant future, I can visit you face-to-face and thank each of you for the very individual ways you were all used in helping me arrive where I am today in my personal journey. God used each one of you uniquely, though I could not see it as clearly then as I do now. Someday I will thank you and hug you each personally for loving me and opening yourselves to me as you did. Believe it or not, my mother and sister and I have actually talked about making a trip to Switerland whenever circumstances with the war permit. Until that time, however, I must content myself with the written mode of communication, although I doubt I shall be able to convey only a hundredth of what is in my heart.

There is so much to tell, and the story I have to share begins several years ago, with a visit a certain little girl made with her family to a city called London.

Just a few minutes ago I finished reading a book. Perhaps you have heard of it. The title is Robinson Crusoe. *As soon as I read the final page I knew the time had come for me to tell you this girl's story. She did not find herself marooned on a distant desert island, but was shipwrecked much closer to the land of her birth. Fortunately, it did not take her quite thirty-five years, as it did Crusoe, to find her own way back. I am pleased to be able to report to you that she is at last home, in her heart, I mean, though getting there was not without pain and loss.*

The girl's name is Amanda. . . .

Look for the fourth and final volume in
THE SECRETS OF HEATHERSLEIGH HALL, coming soon.

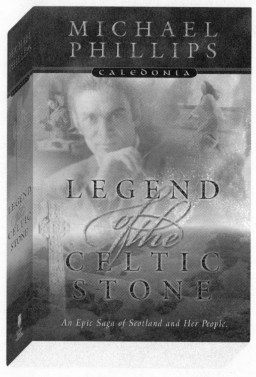

ALSO FROM MICHAEL PHILLIPS

The Garden at the Edge of Beyond

MICHAEL PHILLIPS

The Garden at the Edge of Beyond
Small Hardcover, ISBN 0-7642-2042-X

T he imaginative fantasies of C. S. Lewis and George MacDonald have charmed and delighted readers for decades with the message of the Gospel woven into stories that capture the hearts of old and young alike. Following in the tradition of these two great authors, Michael Phillips invites readers to enter *The Garden at the Edge of Beyond.*

In its other world setting, you will follow the fascinating inner journey of a man who "travels" to a world populated by many of the great Christian spiritual leaders of the past. These figures act as guides, enabling the traveler to use all his senses to explore the sights, sounds, and smells of the Garden. He is challenged to search within himself to answer the question, "After salvation, what can Christians do to prepare for heaven?"

Available from your local Christian bookstore (800) 991-7747
or from Bethany House Publishers.

BETHANY HOUSE PUBLISHERS
11400 Hampshire Ave. South
Minneapolis, MN 55438
(800) 328-6109
www.bethanyhouse.com